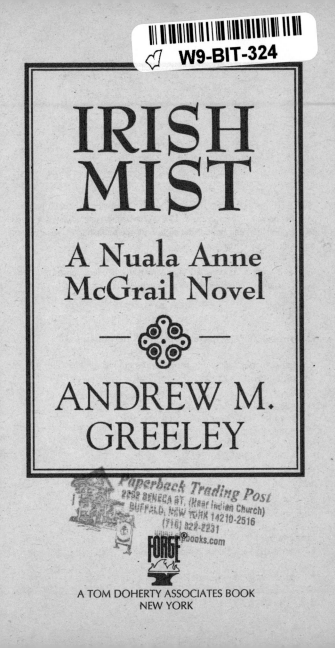

IRISH MIST

A Nuala Anne McGrail Novel

— ✥ —

ANDREW M. GREELEY

FORGE®

A TOM DOHERTY ASSOCIATES BOOK
NEW YORK

This is a work of fiction. All the characters and events portrayed in this novel are either fictitious or are used fictitiously.

IRISH MIST

Copyright © 1999 by Andrew M. Greeley Enterprises, Ltd.

A Forge Book
Published by Tom Doherty Associates, LLC
175 Fifth Avenue
New York, NY 10010

Forge® is a registered trademark of Tom Doherty Associates, LLC.

ISBN: 0-812-59023-6
Library of Congress Catalog Card Number: 98-47008

First edition: March 1999
First mass market edition: March 2000

Printed in the United States of America

0 9 8 7 6 5 4 3 2 1

Praise for Andrew M. Greeley

"In this deft addition to his shelf of novels, Greeley once again shows his knack for combining solid characterizations, folksy prose, a bantamweight sense of history, and understated Catholic morality to make highly entertaining fiction."
> —*Publishers Weekly* on *A Midwinter's Tale*

"Sentimentality and nostalgia for bygone days underlie this coming-of-age story from Greeley.... Fans will love it."
> —*Library Journal* on *A Midwinter's Tale*

"Fans of Greeley's trademarked light touch will enjoy yet another tale of the trials and turmoils of Chicago's own."
> —*The Irish American Post* on *A Midwinter's Tale*

"A witty and delightful inside-out Faust with angelic choirs, a variety of loving, and an ending with a special twist. Greeley has fashioned a novel about learning to love and doing it well."
> —*San Antonio Express-News* on *Contract with an Angel*

"Sit back and enjoy novel-writing Catholic priest Andrew M. Greeley's little fantasy about a wealthy and powerful businessman who turns his life around—none too soon—after a visit from a Seraph."
> —*Dallas Morning News* on *Contract with an Angel*

"Greeley's descriptions of each encounter are touching and, at times, poignant.... Greeley injects a bit of humor into the book [as well].... Like a good homily, the priest's message comes across quietly."
> —*St. Paul Pioneer Press* on *Contract with an Angel*

" 'Tis a charmin' tale that Andrew Greeley tells in his latest mystery novel, *Irish Whiskey*.... It's a lovely novel filled with Irish wit, interesting situations, and likable people."
> —*The Chattanooga Times*

Also by Andrew M. Greeley
from Tom Doherty Associates

All the characters in this story are creatures of my imagination. They exist only in my world and have no counterparts in God's world. In particular, none of the lawyers or judges or law-enforcement officers are based on real people.

For my Irish priest friends Conor Ward,
Eammon Casey, Christopher Dillon, Paddy Dowling,
Liam Lawton, Dermod MacCarthy,
Enda MacDonagh, Michael MacGriel,
John O'Donohue, and Liam Ryan.

I am the wind which breathes upon the sea,
I am the wave of the ocean,
I am the murmur of the billows,
I am the ox of the seven combats,
I am the vulture upon the rocks,
I am a beam of the sun,
I am the fairest of plants,
I am the wild boar in valour,
I am a salmon in the water,
I am a lake in the plain,
I am a word of knowledge,
I am the point of the lance of battle,
I am the God who created the fire in the head
                    —Amergin circa 500 B.C.E.

Our God is the God of all men, the God of heaven and earth, of sea and river, of sun and moon and stars, of the lofty mountains and the lowly valley, the God above heaven, the God in heaven, the God under heaven. He has his dwelling around heaven and earth and sea and all that in them is. He inspires all, he quickens all, he dominates all, he sustains all. He lights the light of the sun; he furnishes the light of light; he has put springs in the dry land and has set stars to minister to the greater lights.

                    —St. Patrick circa A.D. 450

Perhaps the only real definition of a Celt, now as in the past, is that a Celt is a person who believes him- or herself to be Celtic.

                    —Barry Cunliffe, *The Ancient Celts* (1997)

He, giver of the gifts we bring,
He who needs nothing
Has need of us, and
if you or I should cease to be
He would die of sadness.

—Paul Murray, O.P.

— 1 —

"WERE YOU the fella with whom I slept last night?"

The woman opened her eyes and peered at me.

"I was."

She closed her eyes again.

"How was I?"

"Memorable."

She snorted derisively, another hint that something was wrong in our relationship.

" 'Tis all a mistake," she sighed, curling up against me.

"Our sleeping together?"

"No . . . ourselves going to Ireland."

It was the first hint that she didn't think our trip was a frigging brilliant idea—to use her slightly cleaned up words.

"Why?"

"Bad things are happening," she said, cuddling even closer—as much as a first-class seat on an Aer Lingus Airbus 300 permitted.

"To us?"

"Won't we be involved?"

"The Irish media?"

"Them gobshites!"

My hand, always with a mind of its own where she was concerned, found its way under her loose Marquette University sweatshirt and took possession of a wondrous bare breast. Bras, she had insisted, were not acceptable on long overnight plane flights, a declaration I did not dispute.

She sighed contentedly.

"Anyway," she continued, "the woman didn't do it now, did she?"

"Didn't do what?"

"Didn't light the fire."

"Which woman didn't light what fire?"

"Och, Dermot Michael," she said somewhat impatiently as, under her blanket, she pushed my hand harder against her breast, "if I were knowing that, wouldn't I be telling you?"

Here we go again, I told myself.

We were at that stage of a transatlantic flight that is much like the old Catholic notion of Purgatory—the minutes seem like hours and the hours like days. The human organism revolts against all the indignities imposed on it in the last seven hours—dry mouth, wet sinuses, aching teeth, the guy across the aisle with a cough like a broaching whale. It will end eventually but only on the day of the final judgment.

My Nuala Anne is, among other things, fey, psychic, a dark one—call it whatever you want. She possesses, though only intermittently, an ability to see and hear things that happened decades ago or are happening now but at some great distance or haven't happened yet but will. Maybe. My brother George the Priest, the only other one in our family to know of my bride's "interludes," claims that her ability is a throwback to an earlier age of the evolutionary process when our hominoid ancestors, not possessing thoraxes suitable for our kind of speech, communicated mentally.

"There're a few genes like that around, Little Bro," he informed me, "but don't invest in any grain futures because of what she thinks she sees."

I had stopped investing in the commodities market several years ago, mostly because I wasn't very good at it.

"It's weird, George," I had argued.

"Part of the package," he said with a shrug.

Easy enough for him to say. He didn't have to live with her. Nor was he awakened in the middle of the night when she had one of her dreams.

She sat up straight in her seat, dislodging my predatory hand.

"They're going to shoot the poor man, Dermot Michael," she whispered, "and himself going to Mass!"

Fortunately, the man across the aisle hacked again, so violently that I thought the plane swayed. His explosion drowned Nuala's protest.

"Can we do anything?" I asked ineptly.

"Course not," she replied impatiently. "And ourselves up here in this friggin' airplane!"

We were getting into trouble again. Whenever my wife had one of her intense spells, it was a sign that we were stumbling towards another strange adventure. Like the time at Mount Carmel Cemetery when she saw that the grave next to my grandparents' plot was empty[1] or the incident on Lake Shore Drive when she heard Confederate prisoners crying out in pain in Camp Douglas at 31st and Cottage Grove—in 1864!

WON'T THE WOMAN BE THE DEATH OF YA? the Adversary whispered in my brain.

"Go 'way," I told him. "That's part of the package. Besides, your brogue is phony."

Nuala Anne is quite a package. She's the kind of

---

[1] *Irish Whiskey*

woman even women turn around to look at when she walks down the street. She looks like a mythological Irish goddess, though I've never seen one of those worthies. They travel in threes, I'm told. Nuala is all three of them.

Drawings of the Celtic women deities, however, hint that they have solemn, frozen, slightly dyspeptic faces, as if they are so displeased with mortals that they will not deign to notice our existence. Nuala's lovely face with its fine bones and deep blue eyes is in constant movement as emotions chase one another across it like greyhounds headed for the finish line—amusement, mischief, anger, sorrow, hauteur, devilment, fragility, sorrow. Each emotion represents one of the many different women in her complex personality: Nuala the detective, Nuala the woman leprechaun, Nuala the accountant, Nuala the athlete, Nuala the actress, Nuala the singer, Nuala the seducer, Nuala the vulnerable child.

I'm usually one step behind the most recent greyhound as I struggle to keep up with the rapid succession of personae. Her deep blue eyes can shift from tundra to Lake Michigan on the hottest day of the summer in the flick of a lash. And back. Heaven help me if I miss the flick.

She is tall and slender, with long and muscular legs and elegant breasts. Hers is a model's body, a model for athletic wear. She looks great in an evening gown with spaghetti straps but even more striking in tennis shirt and shorts. What she looks like with her clothes off is my business and no one else's—save that her beauty breaks my heart.

There is an ur-Nuala, I think. Her mask is that of the shy, quiet Irish-speaking country girl from Carraroe (An Cheathru Rua in her native Irish) in the Conne-

mara district of the County Galway. I love all the Nu-
alas, but I love that one the most.

However, I also love her hopelessly when she's busy
making trouble. Like the day when she showed for the
little bishop's Mass on the dunes at Grand Beach with
a red T-shirt that proclaimed in large black letters:
"Galway Hooker!"

The little bishop, George the Priest's boss, was un-
fazed.

"Have you ever crewed in one of the boat races, Nuala Anne?" he asked. "Am I not correct that the word
is based on the Dutch *houkah,* which means 'boat with
a long prow'?"

I had not seen that mischievous troublemaker for a
long time. Nuala Anne was upset that she was not pregnant. Moreover, for reasons that I could not fathom,
she was convinced that she was not a good wife. Un-
shakably convinced.

The pilot announced that we were an hour from
Dublin Airport.

"I suppose I should put on me bra," she sighed, stirring next to me.

"If you want to."

"If I don't, it will just give them friggin' bitches in
the friggin' media something to bitch about, won't it
now."

Nuala's first CD, *Nuala Anne,* had been a huge success, not bad for a young woman not yet twenty-one.
She has a lovely voice, trained first by her mother in
their tiny cottage in Galway, then by a teacher at Trinity College, where Nuala had studied accounting, and
finally by "Madam," a legendary voice coach in Chicago. The last named had told us that Nuala was a first-
rate talent for the pop world, though she would never
be an operatic singer. That was fine with both of us.

"Meself a friggin' diva!" she had exclaimed, as though it were a huge joke.

Her beauty, her charm, her acting ability, and her skill with an Irish harp contributed to her success. She had made the leap from Chicago pubs quickly, too quickly for the media in her native land. One Irish woman writer commented, "Don't we have too many pretty young Irish singers as it is without an American one trying to join the lot?"

This bit of envy ignored the fact that Nuala had lived in the United States for only a year when the first disk appeared.

The second disk was not supposed to be a hit. She insisted that she wanted to record hymns. The recording company grudgingly gave in. *Nuala Anne Goes to Church* was a combination of pre–Vatican Council hymns (like the May-crowning hymn "Bring Flowers of the Rarest"), spirituals such as "Swing Low, Sweet Chariot," a few Protestant hymns like "Simple Gifts" and "Amazing Grace," and some Irish-language religious music. There was nothing very new or very original on it, save for her voice and her devotion. The result was that the disk was a bigger hit than its predecessor, in both Ireland and the United States. The Irish critics were furious. How dare someone just out of Trinity become a celebrity so soon and so easily! Their envy, however, did not prevent Irish International Aid, an Irish social action agency, from inviting her to perform at a benefit concert at the Point Theater on the banks of the River Liffey (where Riverdance first appeared).

Naturally, Nuala did not hesitate. Nor did she show the slightest signs of backing off when the Irish papers attacked the concert as soon as it was announced. My Nuala never saw a fight she didn't like.

I thought the whole idea was crazy, but being a wise

husband (in some matters anyway), I kept my mouth shut.

I looked around the first-class cabin (my idea) as she walked towards the washroom. The two other people in first class were sound asleep, as were the cabin attendants. So I followed her.

"What would you be wanting?" she demanded, her face turned away demurely as I pushed in after her.

"To hook your bra, like I always do."

"All right," she sighed as she pulled the Marquette sweatshirt over her head.

I caught my breath, as I always did when I saw her naked to the waist. Making the process as long and leisurely as I could, I assisted her with her black lace bra. She sighed contentedly.

"Are you going to put your sweatshirt back on?" I asked when I had the last hook in place.

"Would it be fun if I walked into the cabin without it?"

"Be my guest!"

She snorted, tied her hair up, and donned again the maroon and gold of Marquette.

I had attended Marquette for two years after I was expelled—for academic reasons—from Notre Dame. However, I had not graduated from Marquette, or anywhere else.

"I thought you might try to fuck me in there, Dermot love," she said as we slipped back through the aisle to our seats.

"Would you have liked that?"

"Wouldn't it have been an interesting experience now?"

BLEW IT AGAIN, the Adversary crowed.

Suddenly Nuala stiffened in front of me and then collapsed into my arms.

"It's so hot, Dermot Michael. Call the fire battalion before we all perish with the heat."

Gently I guided her to our seats.

"Terrible, terrible hot. We're all burning up. Our lungs are filled with smoke."

Then she began to sob softly.

"Is your wife all right, Mr. Coyne?" a cabin attendant asked.

"Bad dream."

"It's not a dream," Nuala insisted when the young woman had returned to the small kitchen where she was preparing breakfast. "It's really happening."

"It's all right, Nuala Anne," I insisted. "It's all right."

Gradually her sobs subsided.

Shot on the way to Mass. Something like that had really happened in Irish history. Who was it? And when? Lord Edward FitzGerald?

I'd call George from Dublin. He knew everything.

"Haven't you married a crazy woman, Dermot?" she said with a sniffle.

"No," I said. "I married the finest wife in all the world."

She snorted again, as if to say, "Thanks for the compliment, but you and I know better."

Actually, I didn't know better. She was indeed a wonderful wife, fun to be with, glorious in bed, undemanding, eager to please me. Too eager. When I complained that she slammed doors and pounded through the apartment like a herd of horses and slammed doors like a security guard, she apologized and walked on tiptoes—making me feel like a heel. I had also protested when she turned her compulsive neatness loose on my desk. "I can't find a thing," I growled. Tears sprang to her eyes as she apologized.

It wasn't that big a deal.

Something was wrong, badly wrong, but I didn't know what it was.

YOU'RE A LOUSY HUSBAND AND A WORSE LOVER, the Adversary sneered.

I didn't answer because I was afraid he might be right.

Yet she certainly seemed satisfied with our lovemaking. She praised my skills in bed. I was the greatest lover in all the world, she insisted—which I knew I wasn't.

I tried to talk about what our problem might be, and she dismissed me brusquely: "How could anyone have a problem with such a wonderful lover as you, Dermot Michael?"

Yeah.

They served us our continental breakfast.

"Haven't I become so much a Yank," she said, "that I want a much bigger breakfast?"

"Are you a Yank or Mick when the media ask you?"

"Won't I have a good answer for them now?"

Which meant that she wanted to surprise me, too. Nuala played very few situations by ear. She doubtless had all the answers ready for the catechism that would greet her as soon as we walked out of customs.

"We are now crossing the coast of Ireland just above Galway," the pilot announced. "You can see Galway Bay through the clouds."

Her fey interlude forgotten, she climbed over me to look out the window.

"Och, sure, Dermot Michael, isn't it the most beautiful place in all the world? Isn't the green brilliant altogether?"

She arranged herself on my lap, a posture I was not about to protest.

"It comes from all the rain."

"Shush, Dermot love. It's me home, even if it is a

mite damp. . . . OH! Isn't that Carraroe down there?"

We had not visited Ireland on our honeymoon. "Haven't I seen everything there is to see?" she had said, waving her hand in a dismissive gesture that meant only an eejit would suggest such an absurd notion.

" 'Tis," I said even though I couldn't see.

"Isn't it the first time I've seen it from the air. . . . Oh, Dermot Michael, isn't it lovely?"

She wept again, this time at the joy of a brief glimpse of her little village from the air, the village that had been her world before she had left for Trinity College only a couple of years before.

"We should have come back here long ago!" she added.

Being, like I said, a sometimes-wise husband, I did not observe that I had proposed it as a honeymoon stop.

"I can hardly wait to see me ma and me da. . . . Och, Dermot, there's a great sadness on me!"

More tears. I put my arm around her, eased her back into her seat, and held her close.

"Well," she murmured, "at least I'm glad you're along to take care of me on this focking trip to this focking country."

A change of mind? Not at all, not among a people for whom the principle of contradiction does not apply.

"Haven't you been taking care of me," I replied, having learned the proper responses in seven months of marriage, "since we were married?"

"Go 'long wid ya!" she said, patting my arm in approval.

Mostly she had taken care of me. At least she organized everything, though she was always wary for the slightest sign that I might disapprove of her plans for anything from a movie to the furniture for our home across the street from St. Josaphat on Southport Avenue. She also decided that we'd be wise to keep our apartment at the John Hancock Center because it would always be a solid investment. Besides, she liked the swimming pool there better than the one at the East Bank Club.

"More privacy, if you take me meaning, Dermot Michael."

I did not disagree.

Her meaning was that we could return to the apartment and make love with less delay than if we had to drive from the East Bank back to DePaul (as our neighborhood, also known as Lincoln Park West, was called).

She also took charge of my investments. This meant that she talked to the broker and commodity trader who presided over my ill-gotten gains from the Mercantile Exchange and the profits from my novel—as well as, in a separate account naturally "so there won't be any confusion," the royalties from her recordings.

"Sure, aren't you a poet and meself just a focking accountant?"

Who was I to argue with that wisdom, especially when the trader whispered into my ear that I had one very shrewd wife.

Sure, hadn't I known that all along?

I am often referred to by the women in my family as "poor Dermot." That does not mean impoverished or suffering. Rather, it means that Dermot is a nice boy; isn't it too bad he doesn't have a clue?

About what?

About anything.

Or as one young woman not of the family had said at a black-tie dinner in the Chicago Hilton and Towers, "Yeah, he's a handsome hunk and kind of sweet in a dull way, but he's useless. He'll live off her for the rest of his life."

I was forced to constrain Nuala from tearing out the eyes of the aforementioned young woman.

"Sure, aren't you a great novelist and poet!" she had whispered fiercely before I pulled her into a corner of the massive lobby of that gargantuan hostelry.

"And a brilliant commodity trader, too!"

Her humor returned. "Well, I didn't say that exactly, did I now?"

The pilot announced that we were approaching Dublin Airport. Below us the bright green fields, a jeweler's display of emeralds, glowed in the soft light of the rising sun.

"It looks like God has swept away the Irish mists to celebrate your return," I said to my wife.

"Do you really think He has?" she said, clutching my arm more tightly.

"She," I corrected her.

" 'Tis true." She dabbed at her eyes with a tissue.

Another knock on me is that I'm lazy. It's true that I don't work very much, but the objection is aimed at the fact that I don't have a regular office or even a regular job. The youngest of a family of hot-shot professionals, I am viewed as a kind of spoiled baby who sits around and does very little. I get no points for having written a novel that was on the *Times* (New York, that is) best-seller list for fifteen weeks in hardbound (and was now on in its paperback manifestation). The occupational category of "writer," to say nothing of "poet," is not altogether acceptable in River Forest, Illinois. Moreover, to make matters worse, there is no visible evidence that when I start writing I work very hard at it.

I had done practically nothing since our marriage except scratch out a poem or two and develop (mentally) an outline for another novel for which I had a contract. Nuala had worked frantically on her voice lessons and her recordings while I had devoted myself mostly to enjoying her—a delightful full-time occupation. Moreover, I had engaged in this enterprise without putting on weight, as most young men of my generation do in the months after their marriage. Admittedly, Nuala Anne had shamed me into it by her good example.

Besides, running with her or swimming or working out together was part of the fun. She was fun in bed and fun in every other aspect of our life together, fun and funny, outrageous, contradictory, unpredictable, zany. Spouses, I have been told, often grow weary of each other. I could not imagine Nuala Anne ever boring me.

YOU'RE A SENSUALIST ON A SUSTAINED ORGY, the Adversary had informed me before he got on my case as a lousy lover.

"Yeah," I replied without the slightest feeling of guilt.

There were some problems in our marriage, clouds on the edge of paradise.

My wife was afraid of me. Though she played the role of organizer and administrator of our joint fun and fortune, it was always with a shadow of worry in her blue eyes, as if I were a drunken wife beater.

"I am not an ogre," I said to the little bishop.

I go to George the Priest when I want facts—such as who was the Irish leader shot on the way to Mass. I go to George's boss when I want advice.

"Indeed," that worthy had commented.

"Yet she's habitually afraid that she'll offend me."

"Adoration," he said with a loud sigh.

"I am not adorable."

"Arguably. . . . Yet she began to adore you on that

now legendary night you met at O'Neill's pub. Nothing that has transpired since has caused her to change her opinion."

"Will she get over it?"

"She will perhaps adjust to it."

That was bad enough. More recently I thought I detected an even darker cloud. Nuala had begun to suggest that she was half-convinced that she was not half good enough a wife.

"Does that make 25 percent?" I had asked the little bishop.

"More like 200 percent."

The Airbus touched lightly down on the green fields of Ireland. Nuala applauded enthusiastically, not because she doubted a safe landing but because she was on Irish soil again.

I had tried to discuss this strange notion with her, but she ruled me out of order.

"A lot you know, Dermot Michael Coyne, about what's a good wife."

Finally, she was worried about not being pregnant. Our plan—well, her plan—was that we'd have our children (arguably, as the bishop would say), three of them, before she was twenty-six, so our nest would be empty by the time she was in her earlier forties. The first would be a girl with red hair and green eyes who would be called Mary Anne (Nell after my grandmother, with whom Nuala has some sort of mildly scary psychic relationship).

Who was I to disagree?

However, the first pregnancy was not happening according to plan.

"On the average it takes seventy-five acts of intercourse to produce a conception," I observed, quoting, though hardly by name, George the Priest.

"Och, Dermot Michael, haven't we done it more often than that?" she said somberly.

Who's counting?

Nuala Anne, obviously.

I was sure she had consulted with my mother, who is a nurse, and that Mom had reassured her. Not that it had done any good.

So my Nuala had gradually become more pensive, more preoccupied, more obviously thoughtful, and less the exuberant organizer and imp than she had been only a month or two before our trip to Ireland. I had no idea what to do.

YOU'RE A FAILURE AS A LOVER AND A HUSBAND, the Adversary insisted.

"Shut up," I told him.

I was confident on neither subject. I remembered the South American novelist who said that after thirty years of marriage he knew his wife better than anyone else in the world and knew that he would never understand her. What did I know about the complex puzzles that stirred in the depths of my wife's soul? What did I know about a woman's orgasms? The woman from River Forest who had seduced me and then dropped me when I refused to go to work for her father had done a lot of screaming, but, looking back on it, I doubted that she had known any more about sexual abandon than I did. Nuala insisted that I was a wonderful lover and adamantly refused to proceed beyond that assertion.

I half-believed that she was half telling the truth.

The purser, in a brogue as thick as Nuala's, explained about immigration and customs as the plane taxied to the terminal.

"Well," said herself, "I'll have to get ready for them nine-fingered shite hawks, won't I now?"

"Won't you have to get ready to cream them?"

I had learned from a book that when the Irish answer a question by asking a question they are following in English a form adopted from the Irish language that adds emphasis to what has been said. Sometimes. Also, the word *self* added to a pronoun is a trace of the original melody in the language the English had stamped out—though every immigrant group before Cromwell had adopted Irish as their own tongue.

Nuala Anne sighed loudly.

The plane finally snuggled with relief against its jet bridge. Since we were in first class, there was less of the gang fight for the recovery of baggage from the compartments above our seats than there usually is. I was grateful for that. Once, on our honeymoon, a very pushy matron of uncertain nationality had shoved me aside to retrieve a large bag and then, having jerked it out of the compartment, bounced it off my head. I collapsed into a handy seat and thus cleared the way for Nuala Anne to charge after the woman, shake her fiercely, and threaten that if she ever dared to hit her husband again, she would kill her. The terrified perpetrator, not understanding a word but knowing she was in deep trouble, fled for her life. Two cabin attendants who had watched the contretemps in horror rushed to my aid. Having assured themselves that I would probably survive, they awarded us two bottles of champagne.

"Nuala," I had said as we left the plane, "that woman didn't understand a word you said."

"Ah," me, er, my beloved beamed, "didn't she get the point now?"

As we were leaving the plane in Dublin, one of the cabin attendants grasped Nuala's hand.

"Och, Nuala Anne, I love your songs. Have a grand concert over at the Point."

Point in Irish English is pronounced as if it were the

same thing from which one consumes a half-quart of
Guinness.

Nuala stuck out her hand in my direction. I reached
into the Aer Lingus flight bag I carried and produced
a CD. She signed it with a flourish and presented it to
the delighted cabin attendant.

Ah, you say, isn't Dermot Michael Coyne a nice
young man? Doesn't he carry around copies of his
wife's recordings so she can give them to people?

And doesn't he do it because the wife has asked him
to, very politely and timidly of course?

In the arrivals hall, a small girl child with red hair
rushed up and embraced Nuala's calf—a not infre-
quent reaction of children when they see her.

Herself lifted the delighted rug rat high into the air.
"Sure, don't I want one just like you," she said with an
enormous smile. "But I think I'll let your parents keep
you."

The parents knew who she was and smiled proudly.
I produced another CD and Nuala autographed it for
"Ciara with the bright green eyes!"

We recovered our vast pile of luggage—you can't go
on a concert tour without many changes of costumes,
even if it's only a one-concert tour. Nuala took charge
of her guitar and the small Celtic harp I had bought
her when she came to America. I piled the rest on a
cart.

"And meself coming to Dublin for the first time,"
she murmured disapprovingly, "with only one small
bag."

"Same wonderful young woman," I argued.

Again she snorted derisively.

"Nuala Anne," I said as we entered the green customs gate, "what's a nine-fingered shite hawk?"

"A journalist," she said grimly.

God help them.

"NUALA ANNE," demanded an angry young woman with a dishwater blond ponytail and hard eyes, "do you believe in God?"

We had stumbled out of the customs area to be greeted by a tall, skinny priest with a somber face and a jutting jaw, bald but young. He had tried to wave off the media, but they swept him away. There were eight of them, not counting three TV cameramen—five women and three men, all distinctly hostile.

"Sometimes," my beloved replied.

"How often do you go to church?"

"Wouldn't it be a shame not to go to Mass every morning and meself living right across the street and the man I sleep with going every morning?"

As though I were the leader in this devotional practice. Nuala was setting up the nine-fingered shite hawks.

"Why do you go to church if you're not sure there's a God?"

"Wasn't I after saying I believed sometimes?"

After is a trace of the Celtic pluperfect.

"Do you believe when you're at Mass?"

"Sometimes."

"And when you sing all those stupid old hymns?"

"All the time. . . ."

Based on my own experiences with journalists, I dislike them all. They were for the most part rude, envious, and dumb. The Irish variety were even worse. However, such comments as "stupid old hymns" did not bother me, because I knew that my poor spouse outnumbered them.

"And yourself not married to the man you live with?"

"Dermot Michael"—she turned to me as I stood there utterly useless—"you're the man I sleep with, aren't you?"

"I think so," I said with my best straight person smile.

"Did we ever get married?"

"I think so. . . ."

"So do I. . . . That's what the priest said."

"Wasn't it a bishop?"

"Wasn't it now?"

A crowd of people had begun to gather—American tourists, Irish families waiting for relatives, airport employees, the Guards.

"Are you her manager, Mr. McGrail?"

That question was from a very young male journalist, from the West by his accent.

"He is NOT! I'm me own manager. I'm an accountant with a degree from TCD! I manage him . . . and let me tell you that's a difficult task!"

" 'Tis," I said with a loud sigh.

She was turning the whole session with the shite hawks with one less finger than they should have into wild comedy.

"And what do you do, Mr. McGrail?" This from a gray-haired woman with a nasty sneer.

"Isn't he a poet?" Nuala Anne exploded. "And a sennachie and himself five months on the best-seller list!"

"Four months," I said modestly.

"Do you approve of your wife's career, Mr. McGrail?"

A man with a tape recorder in his hand shoved a mike at me.

"Are you married?" I asked.

"I am."

"To an Irish woman?"

"Of course."

"Then isn't that a silly question?"

The onlookers laughed. Score one for poor Dermot Michael.

"And isn't his name Coyne, 'son of the dark foreigner,' and himself a blonde?"

We were drifting into a Celtic wonderland. And I was the Mad Hatter.

"Are you a Yank or an Irish woman, Nuala Anne?"

"Isn't it part of the Irish genius to say both and?"

The crowd applauded. My wife had won them over.

Another young woman spoke up, this one with red hair and a pleasant smile.

"Nuala Anne, do you believe you have an immortal soul inside your body?"

"I do not!"

"You don't?"

"Certainly not! Isn't the body inside the soul?"

"What do you mean?" the woman said with a frown.

"Isn't me body limited to just one place? And can't me soul reach out far beyond me body when I think or love or sing or talk to other people? Isn't it me soul that's communicating with them? Isn't me body the base for me soul?"

Nuala Anne had donned her Celtic mystic persona. Soon we'd hear about the mountain behind the mountain.

"Are you glad to be home?" asked a young man with a friendly grin who had been scribbling away in a notebook, obviously not a hostile.

"Och, sure, 'tis wonderful to be back in the land of

Ireland and to feel under me the land beyond the land."

All right, this time it was the land and not the mountain. Maybe I was the only one who didn't get it. Many of the people in the growing crowd nodded in solemn agreement.

"Don't you think it isn't fair"—the woman with the blond ponytail again—"that you should be getting so much attention at the expense of other Irish women singers who are better than you are?"

There was a restless stirring among our audience. They didn't like this question at all, at all.

" 'Tis not me that's out here asking questions, is it now?"

The woman did not give up. "Did it not ever occur to you when you began to sing that there were already too many Irish women singers?"

Nuala opened her harp case and began to finger the strings. "How could there ever be too much of anything Irish, except maybe just a little too much talk?"

Applause.

"What do you think of the singing of Maeve Doyle?"

I didn't know who this Maeve Doyle was.

"Doesn't she have a brilliant voice?"

"Do you think that you have a better voice?"

"I don't like to make comparisons. Sure, hasn't God given us all different talents? I'm sure she doesn't like comparisons?"

"Wouldn't it be better if Maeve was singing at this concert and yourself getting all the free publicity?"

Nuala hesitated, as well she might. It was a nasty and loaded question.

"I came because I was invited to sing here for charity," she said simply.

"Doesn't it occur to you that you are depriving Irish women singers of the publicity you will be getting?"

"Couldn't they offer to sing at benefit concerts, too? Aren't there more good causes in Ireland than there are singers?"

Before anyone could ask another question, she began to sing "*O Sanctissima*," a hymn to the mother of Jesus from olden days. Most of the crowd joined in, including the journalist with the red hair, convent school no doubt.

Nuala sang the old hymn with gentle charm and deep devotion. Even I sang along, off key as always.

" '*O Sanctissima, O piissima,*
O Dulcis Virgo Maria!
Mater amata, intemerata, ora pro nobis.

" '*To solatum et refugium*
Virgo Mater Maria
Quid-quid optamus, per te sepramus
Ora pro nobis

" '*Tua gaudia et suspriria juvent nos, O Maria*
In te speramus, ad te clamamus
Ora pro nobis.' "

"Aren't you great singers now?" she said, continuing to strum on her harp. " 'Tis amazing, isn't it, how we remember the Latin, even though we didn't quite know what it meant? . . . I'll tell you one thing. Your Yanks never get beyond the first stanza. . . ."

Laughter at the expense of the poor Yanks.

"But I don't dast sing another one, because we don't want to keep all them media folks waiting, do we?"

Loud cries of, "More!"

"Well, just one more. Sure if I sing more than that won't Father Placid be mad at me for giving the whole concert away free?"

Everyone laughed except Father Placid Clarke, whose facial expression never changed through the press conference and the singing. I noted that he didn't sing.

"Well, there's one hymn that I think everyone in the English-speaking world can still sing, though the liturgical persons don't really like it much. I'll wager none of youse can sing the second and third stanza, like I can."

Youse is not bad grammar but merely an attempt to translate an Irish second person plural into English, much like *y'all*. English really needs a second person plural.

So she sang the hymn with great gusto, though unlike most slow and lugubrious renditions of it in church, Nuala's version was light and brisk:

" *'Holy God, we praise Thy name!*
Lord of all, we bow before Thee!
All on earth Thy scepter claim,
All in Heaven above adore Thee.
Infinite Thy vast domain,
Everlasting is Thy reign!
Infinite Thy vast domain,
Everlasting is Thy reign!

" *'Hark, the loud celestial hymn*
Angel choirs above are raising!
Cherubim and Seraphim,
In unceasing chorus praising,
Fill the heavens with sweet accord;
Holy, holy, holy Lord!
Fill the heavens with sweet accord;
Holy, holy, holy Lord!

" *'Holy Father, Holy Son! Holy Spirit,*
Three we name Thee,

While in essence only One,
Undivided God we 'claim Thee,
And adoring bend the knee,
While we own the mystery.
And adoring bend the knee,
While we own the mystery.' "

It seemed that everyone in the Dublin Airport joined in, just as if they were at Mass in their parish church. The TV cameras ground away. The news directors would certainly go with that as the lead in their coverage in the evening—"Nuala Anne gives an impromptu concert at Dublin Airport!"

Amid vigorous cheers, we worked our way through the crowd and towards the door.

"You can't bring the cart to the parking lot," the grim-faced priest warned us. "It's only a short walk to my car."

Not a word about the press conference or the songfest or the great free publicity my beloved had won for him. Nor did he offer to help us with our luggage. So I slung a couple of bags over my shoulders and lifted two heavy suitcases in my hands. Nuala took charge of two shoulder bags as well as her harp and guitar. We trailed after the priest, who did not slow down as he crossed the street and entered the parking lot.

"Dermot Michael," my wife said anxiously, "I'm sorry I made fun of you. I really don't manage you at all, at all. I really don't, and meself having such a big mouth."

See what I mean about being afraid of me?

"Woman, you do and I don't mind. Besides, I like being your straight man."

Mistake. Big mistake. I was the one with the big mouth.

"You're not me straight man," she said, close to tears.

ALL RIGHT, WISE GUY, the Adversary observed. LET'S
SEE YOU GET OUT OF THAT ONE.

"I thought we creamed that bunch of nine-fingered
shite hawks altogether. Good enough for them, says I."

She laughed happily. "Didn't we ever!"

We finally caught up with the priest, who was standing next to a small foreign car of dubious vintage and
provenance. Well, I was in a foreign country, wasn't I?

Nuala looked at our luggage.

"If we put all our bags in the car and get in ourselves,
Father Placid, sure, there won't be room for the half
of us."

Vintage Irish bull.

"It's not my fault," he said, "that you brought so
many things. Typical American consumerism."

Oh, oh, one of those—a Yank hater. There were very
few of them in Ireland, and they were mostly clergy
and academics.

"Typical American consumerists that we are, Father,"
I said calmly, "we'll take a taxi. Come on, Nuala."

"The taxi fare," he warned us, "will have to come out
of the proceeds of the concert. It will take food out of
the mouths of the suffering children of the world."

"We'll pay it ourselves," I said, voice tight. Nuala was
watching me anxiously.

"It would be better," the priest insisted, "if you saved
your money and gave it to the poor. But you Yanks are
so rich you never think of the poor."

"Look, Father," I said, my voice now deadly calm.
"I'll take care of my wife the way I want to. I don't
need any hypocritical piety from you. As for giving
money to the poor, perhaps we should have done that
with the money we paid for our airplane tickets and
not come at all."

My excuse for this outburst is that I was on jet lag.

I'll use the same excuse for one more totally unnecessary but very satisfying comment.

"Furthermore, you are a disgrace to the Irish tradition of generous hospitality. You should have had a limo here to greet Nuala Anne as a response to her generosity in coming over for your focking concert. Nor did you help us carry our luggage. Father Placid, you are a boor. Stay out of my way from now on!"

I turned on my heel and, despite my heavy load of luggage, strode briskly away.

"Och, Dermot love," says herself, a touch of awe in her voice, as she struggled to keep up with me, "weren't you grand! Didn't the gobshite deserve to be told off!"

"He did."

"And you're picking up all me bad habits."

"Such as?"

"Such as *focking* concert!"

We both laughed.

"Soon you'll be swearing like a native."

"I think we're going to run into others like him while we're here."

"They like to blame America for all the hungry people in the world . . . but sure I won't worry about them, not as long as I'm with you . . . and meself such a terrible wife."

— 3 —

I ROLLED over in my bed and reached for Nuala.

She wasn't there.

Where was she?

As a matter of fact, where was I?

I groped for my memory. It was jet-lagged, too. Jet lag? Ah, yes, I was in Jury's Hotel in Dublin. There was someone I had to phone. Who was it?

I remembered. George the Priest.

I dialed his number, got it wrong, told the young woman who answered that I didn't want to buy anything from Merrill Lynch, thank you very much, and tried again.

"Father Coyne."

"Yeah."

"Little Bro . . . you sound like you have a hangover."

"Jet lag . . . Who was the Irish politician who was shot on his way home from Mass?"

"When did this happen?"

"How should I know?" I said irritably.

"Ah, herself is seeing things again, is she now?"

"No comment."

"Like I tell you, Little Bro, it's part of the package. . . . Where in Ireland did this happen?"

"No information on that."

"Hmm . . . are you sure it wasn't going to Mass?"

"Maybe it was."

"Then it must have been Kevin O'Higgins. . . . He was the strongman who took over Ireland after Michael Collins was killed. Some folks say that if it were not for him, democracy would not have had a chance in Ireland because of anarchy out in the countryside. He was shot on the Booterstown road. Forgave his killers before he died. Daughter a Carmelite nun."

Sure enough, herself was on to something again.

"O'Higgins? Is that a real Irish name?"

"As I remember, he was born Higgins and added the '*O*' when he joined the Irish Volunteers."

"Was he involved in a house catching fire?"

George the Priest paused. "There was a lot of killing and burning out in the country at that time, Little Bro. First the Black and Tans, the English mercenaries, then the Irregulars during the Irish Civil War. People settling local scores or just for the pure fun of it. O'Higgins put an end to it. He was pretty ruthless. Signed the death warrant for the good friend who had been the best man at his wedding."

"Wow!"

"Yeah. And he got mixed up with Lady Lavery. That one was no better than she had to be. Born in Chicago."

"The one who chased Michael Collins?"

"The very one. The Big Fella got away from her, but Kevin O'Higgins didn't. The letters he wrote her were published only a couple of years ago."

"Sounds interesting."

And it also sounded like we shouldn't get mixed up with it, not that there was much choice.

"Well, good hunting. Give my love to herself. She'll be a big hit over there."

"She gave a miniconcert at the airport."

"What did she sing?"

" 'O Sanctissima' and 'Holy God, We Praise Thy Name.' "

"Figures."

I hung up the phone, sank back into my bed, and wondered what time it was. I rummaged around my nightstand and discovered my watch. Ten o'clock. At night? Then I noticed the alarm on the opposite night-stand. It said that it was 4:00. In the morning?

I struggled out of my bed and peered out the win-dow. The swimming pool area was dense with thick Irish mist. Yet there was enough light to suggest that somewhere the sun was still operating. I closed the drapes and crawled back to bed.

Damn Nuala.

Why?

Well, you have to understand that my bride has cer-tain very unattractive characteristics. Like endless en-ergy and boundless enthusiasm and total immunity to the negative effects of airplane travel. Here I was in our hotel room suffering like a lost soul and she was out cavorting around Dublin. It was not fair.

In the taxi we had first settled the matter of my tell-ing Father Placid that I would take care of my wife the way I wanted.

"I don't need me husband to take care of me, Der-mot Michael Coyne!"

"Well, I need my wife to take care of me," I had replied.

She had pondered that and giggled. "Fair play to you, Dermot love."

I then began to fade rapidly. She, on the other hand, picked up steam, just like it was really early morning— which it was. The Energizer wife. Since I was incapable of intelligent conversation, she turned to the taxi driver, who, like all of his ilk in Dublin, was gregarious and literate.

"The old city looks grand, doesn't it now?" she began.

"It will till the mists come back," I mumbled.

Neither of them paid any attention.

"Galway, is it now?"

" 'Tis," she sighed.

"Here to sing at the Point?"

Did everyone in the focking city know her on sight?

"I am," another sigh.

"We sold ninety thousand cars here in Dublin last year. Twice as many as four years ago. Pretty soon there'll be so many cars in the streets that we won't be able to drive them at all, at all."

Not quite Irish bull. Maybe just a statement of fact.

A third sigh, the loudest yet.

I opened one eye and peered out the window. We were on an expressway, new cars on all sides. In the distance mists hovered over the Irish Sea. I closed my eye.

They discussed golf and the Yanks who came over for golfing vacations. So many Yanks that it was hard for the locals, like the driver, to get on their own courses. He and his twelve-year-old son had played two Yanks the other day. Beat them. They were grand men, they were, the both of them.

A taxi driver had his own country club? Ah, the country must be prosperous indeed.

Nuala Anne admitted to playing golf even though she wasn't sure she'd ever be able to beat your man (me). Wasn't his handicap one and himself not working at it as hard as he should?

Actually, my handicap hovers between two and three. One is what Nuala thinks it ought to be if I practiced more.

The driver turned to the subject of Ireland's prosperity.

Wasn't Ireland being called the Celtic Tiger now because its growth rate was 10 percent a year, like the Asian Tigers before they collapsed? That wasn't going to happen here. And wasn't the Irish standard of living higher than them fellas over beyond across (Brits)? "And just think of how well we'd be doing if they hadn't kept us down for seven hundred years? Maybe better even than you Yanks."

Sighs from both of them.

Maybe the United States should have been a colony of Ireland and would never have wanted to rebel, I thought, but had more sense than to get swept up in a conversation in which I wasn't needed.

Lowest inflation rate in Europe, highest balance of payments, Dublin the best-educated city in Europe, Galway the fastest-growing city in Europe. Now we had to give money to the European Union instead of getting it from them. Still, fair was fair, wasn't it now?

Yeah, yeah. I just wanted to get to Jury's and collapse into bed.

I opened an eye again to consider Dublin. It looked good in the sunlight, as it always did—though the mists on the eastern horizon seemed thicker. Yet there was a sheen of prosperity in the city that had not been there when I first encountered herself in the pub outside Trinity College.

Why did it look more prosperous? I wondered, closing my eyes. In a few minutes I opened both of them to look out the window. The car was not moving. The driver's quasi bull had already come true. We'd never get to Jury's.

I observed that, as always, there were large crowds on the streets of downtown Dublin. The difference today was that they all seemed well dressed. Well, their

standard of living had a long way to go to catch up
with Yankland.

"We're here, Dermot love," she whispered to me as
though I were a small child.

"Sheffield Avenue?" I said, knowing full well that it
wasn't. The melodious voices had not really put me to
sleep. Not much.

"Jury's," she said as she paid off the driver, with a
ten-pound note as a tip.

I struggled to climb out of the car.

"Why are we in front and not at the Towers' entrance? We don't have to go through the lobby?"

"Don't we have to say hello to all our old friends?"

So I stumbled into the lobby. Our "old friends,"
from the general manager to the bellmen and the
women from the gift shop, swarmed around us as soon
as we came through the revolving door—as if they had
been waiting for our arrival.

Another one of Nuala Anne's objectionable traits is
that she never forgets a name. She remembered everyone who had worked in the hotel when she was acting
as my secretary, even in many cases the names of their
children.

There was much hugging and kissing and congratulating. My task in the situation was simple. I merely
had to smile my stupid smile and agree when I was
told repeatedly that I was a very lucky fella to have such
a wonderful wife.

I could hardly disagree, could I—even if I were in
such a rotten mood?

It was also my responsibility to supply herself with
CDs for her autograph.

Finally we made it to our room. Just as I was about
to collapse on the bed, herself displayed her most ob-
noxious trait—being right.

"Would you think now, Dermot love," she said hesitantly, "that it might not be a bad idea if we spent a little time in the pool to work the kinks out from the trip?"

"It's a terrible idea altogether," I said, doffing my jacket, "but as always, Nuala Anne, you're right."

"If you don't want to . . ."

"I don't want to at all, at all, but I think we should."

So we donned swimsuits and Jury's terry cloth robes and walked down to the swimming pool, an indoor-outdoor affair with the water temperature comfortably above eighty degrees Fahrenheit—a swimming pool for Yanks who, as Nuala had tartly observed when I was her employer rather than vice versa, had never swum in the Atlantic Ocean.

"I've seen that bikini before," I observed.

"Have you now?"

"I have."

"And where did you see it?"

The first time you went swimming in this place.

It was a modest dark blue ensemble, as if anything on Nuala Anne could be considered to be modest.

"I don't remember. A woman tried to seduce me in it, but I don't think she was successful."

She slapped my arm affectionately. "You're a desperate man altogether, Dermot Michael Coyne!"

"So I've been told."

We cuddled in the whirlpool, a concession, it was implied, to my weakness. She had undressed in our room and was now lying compliantly in my arms as the waters bubbled around us. Both were pleasant aesthetic experiences, but my hormones were on a temporary hiatus due to circadian dysrhythmia. I promised myself I'd make up for it later.

YOU'RE PRETTY YOUNG TO BE TURNING IMPOTENT, the Adversary informed me.

"Don't be ridiculous."

We then swam for a half hour. The exercise did not improve either my physical condition or my mental disposition.

"I'll never make it to our room," I complained.

"Poor Dermot love," she said. "Your nap will be a lot healthier now."

"I don't want health; I want sleep."

"Poor dear man."

Just like I was her boy child—which might be what I was.

I collapsed into bed and watched her dress in light gray slacks, matching sweater, and a blue blazer.

"Where would you be going, Nuala Anne?" I asked.

"Out to look around Dublin's fair city to see how it's changed in a year and a half." She bent over me and kissed me lovingly. "I'll visit a lot of the places where we courted."

"We didn't court here."

"You didn't, but I did," she said defiantly as she flounced out the door.

Then I had fallen into the deepest pit of sleep and woke much later in the day to call George the Priest and learn from him about Kevin O'Higgins.

Booterstown road, was it? Well, I wouldn't tell her. Serve her right. We'd forget the whole subject.

I groped for the phone again and phoned Fred Hanna's, my Dublin bookstore.

"Dermot Coyne here," I said. "I have an account with you."

"Just a minute, Mr. Coyne, while I look it up."

Right. You gotta be sure I'm not lying.

"On Sheffield Avenue in Chicago, is it now?"

" 'Tis."

"Welcome to Dublin, Mr. Coyne. . . . We're all waiting eagerly to hear herself sing."

Sure they knew who I was. Nuala Anne's husband.

"You can see a preview on the telly this evening. . . .
I wonder if you could help me with a couple of books."

"I'd be delighted to, Mr. Coyne."

"Would you have a biography of Kevin O'Higgins?"

"By DeVere White? I'm sure we do somewhere, perhaps only secondhand. Would that be all right?"

"It would. . . . Then there's a book about that woman
he might have been involved with?"

"Lady Hazel Lavery? Yes, I'm quite certain we have
that in stock . . . That one was no better than she had
to be, Mr. Coyne."

"And herself from Chicago at that. . . . Would it be
all right if I stopped by tomorrow morning to pick
them up?"

"Certainly, Mr. Coyne. We'll be looking forward to
seeing you again. Perhaps you could sign some copies
of your novel for us."

"I did write a novel, didn't I?"

"We could arrange a cup of tea for you."

"And scones?"

"Of course."

"Done."

So I was a novelist after all. Nuala Anne's husband,
who happened to write novels.

I closed my eyes, merely to rest them. However,
when herself bounced in the door I was sound asleep.

"Still sleeping, Dermot love? Ah, but don't you look
a lot better now, and meself feeling guilty that I was so
wide awake."

She didn't mean a word of it.

"Did you visit all our old haunts?"

"Didn't I go to O'Neill's and Trinity and Bewley's
and Irishtown and meet a lot of me old friends. They
were so glad to see me, not a touch of envy. It was
brilliant, Dermot love, dead brilliant. They all wondered where yourself was."

She doffed her jacket.

And her sweater.

I made no comment.

"And you told them?"

"That you were resting up from the plane flight and would be as fit as a fiddle tomorrow morning. . . . And didn't I make a dinner reservation for us at the Commons at half seven. I'll pay."

The Commons was in the basement of Newman House on the south side of the green, the house where Newman had given the lectures that became *The Idea of a University*, where Gerard Manley Hopkins died, and where your man with the dirty mind went to college. When I took her there for the first time, she thought the menu was too dear altogether. Now she wanted to pay for dinner.

"I'm hungry now."

"Well, can't we ring for tea in a little while."

"And how's Dublin?"

"Och, Dermot, isn't it scary how much money there is in this city? I'm afraid all the Irish are becoming materialists."

"Better than living on the edge of starvation."

" 'Tis true . . . ," she sighed. "I found a bunch of secondary school girls playing Camogie. They let me have a run or two on the pitch."

Camogie is the woman's version of hurling, a dangerous, if exciting, sport in which a couple of dozen Irish folk were equipped with clubs.

"In your good clothes!"

"I took off me shoes."

"How did you do?"

"I'm afraid," she said, making a motion of swinging her club, "that I astonished the poor children. . . . What did His Rivirince say?"

She sat down on the bed next to me.

"Which reverence?"

"Your brother George, what other rivirince?"

She kicked off her shoes and slipped out of her slacks. George was always treated with great respect, a wise and holy man. I was still poor Dermot.

"Why would I be calling George the Priest?"

"About the man who was killed walking to Mass."

Of course she knew that I would call George. Why would I think she wouldn't know that?

"Oh, that. . . . Does the name Kevin O'Higgins mean anything to you?"

She frowned. "Wasn't he one of the gobshites that killed Michael Collins?"

"No, he was on Collins's side. Apparently he became the backbone of the new Free State Government. He cracked down on the violence in the country and made a lot of enemies. He was killed on the way to Mass down on the Booterstown road."

She nodded.

"Apparently he became involved with my fellow Chicagoan, Lady Hazel Lavery."

"THAT one!"

"Unlike the Big Fella, who seems to have evaded her, O'Higgins left a trail of letters that are in a new book."

"Hm . . ."

"I called our bookstore over by the Railings, and I'll pick up a biography of O'Higgins and the book about Lady Hazel."

Hanna's was across the street from the wrought-iron railings of Trinity College.

"Och, Dermot, aren't you a grand husband to put up with my craziness."

"Actively promote it."

"You do indeed. . . . We've got to prove that the woman didn't start the fire; don't you see that?"

"If you say so. . . . What woman and which fire?"

"If I knew that, would I not have told you?"

"So we have to find out?"

"We have to find out."

I'd been there before.

"Nuala Anne, WHAT are you doing?"

"Taking off your shorts."

"Why?"

"Because you are so beautiful with all your clothes off."

With one hand she caressed my chest and with the other unhooked her bra. Then she brushed her lips against mine.

"I love you, Dermot Michael; I love you something terrible."

My hormones seemed to be working again.

— 4 —

I'M a terrible woman, terrible, terrible. And it's all Your fault. Why did You make me such a focking good actress? Poor Dermot, he's such a dear sweet man. He deserves a good wife, one who doesn't pretend all the time.

I did mean it when I said his naked body is beautiful, so trim and strong and solid. I like to feel him inside me. I like it when he kisses and caresses me and holds me in his arms.

But I have to fake that I'm having real sexual pleasure. I'm a terrible good fake. Or at least good enough to fool him. I don't think that woman he made love with could have been all that passionate either.

I AM passionate, but maybe not enough. I don't know. I don't know anything. But I don't think I enjoy what some other women enjoy. A lot of them say they fake it often, too.

All the time?

I started faking the first night because I wanted him to feel like he was a great lover. According to what I read in the books he does all the things a good lover should do. It's not his fault that I'm such an iceberg. He's kind and sweet and gentle and thoughtful—and clever, too. He knows what buttons to push, but my buttons just don't seem to be working.

I kept thinking that I'd catch on soon, but I didn't. Then I got so much into the habit of faking I couldn't change. I start out with the feeling that I have to fake it.

The books say that I should talk it over with him. But how can I tell him that I've been acting all these months? It would humiliate him altogether, and it isn't his fault.

He tries to make me discuss orgasm, but I won't do it because I'm so ashamed of faking. He'll find out eventually and then he'll blame me. He won't love me anymore and I'll lose him. All because I'm living a lie.

Will I really lose him?

Maybe not, but I might. He'll be disgusted with me.

Why did You let me do this?

It won't do any good to deny Your responsibility. You made me a faker.

I'm sorry. I don't mean that. It's not Your fault. I know that You love me and want me and me husband to be happy. I know that You're always present to me, no matter where I go. But what am I supposed to do? Won't I lose him no matter what I do now . . . and meself lying to him all these months?

Am I not pregnant because You are punishing me for me lies? That's what the nuns would say. Maybe they'd be right.

I know You wouldn't do that.

Would You?

Am I a frigid Irish cow? Do a thousand years of inhibitions make me afraid to abandon meself to him, like that feminist woman wrote in the Irish Times *this morning?*

Or should I just wait and see what happens?

That's what me ma says. I suppose You got a good laugh out of two Irish women talking around THAT subject! Still, we did all right. She says I should stop worrying and trust You and that it will all work out just fine.

You know I'm not the kind to do that, don't You?

But maybe Ma is right.

Please help me.

I love him so much.

— 5 —

THE NEXT morning I picked my way through the mists to Fred Hanna's, drank my cup of tea, demolished my pile of scones, and autographed a couple of dozen of my novels. They must have bought out the local wholesaler.

"Won't the poster be saying," I asked the very pretty young woman who had answered the phone the day before, " 'autographed novels by Nuala Anne's husband'?"

The young woman blushed. "Not if you don't want them to."

" 'Tis all right," I sighed. "Now I know what Michael Jordan's wife feels like. . . . Sure, couldn't we get her to stop by and autograph them, too!"

"We'd never do that!" She sounded angry at the very suggestion, but her eyes glittered.

"She wouldn't mind," I said, well aware that my wife might go through the ceiling at any suggestion that I was a subsidiary character. On the other hand, she might think it great fun. With THAT one you could never tell.

"And wasn't she grand on the telly last night? Didn't she destroy them focking gobshites!"

"Didn't she now!"

"You must be terrible proud of her!"

"I am that."

"Wasn't that Maeve Doyle person terrible, and herself saying that a Yank shouldn't be singing at the Point?"

That Maeve Doyle person, a tall woman with a sweet face, had appeared on the telly after the clips from our press conference and denounced Nuala. Nuala had fled to the bathroom when the clips of her singing had started. So she hadn't heard the woman with the saccharine passive aggressive martyr's tone say sadly that everyone knew that my wife was an untrained amateur. Wasn't it most unfortunate that one so young could become a tool of an American effort to take over Irish art? Wasn't it inconceivable that an Irish singer would dare sing such trashy hymns in public? Didn't most Irish women think that Nuala should go home to America where she belonged?

It was all done with so many sighs that you almost didn't realize how much she resented Nuala.

"Would you donate your services for Irish International Aid, Maeve?" the interviewer had asked.

"I think that it's a shame that the church in this country is unwilling to pay Irish performers the decent wages to which they're entitled. I'm sure that poor little Nuala Anne doesn't realize that she's taking money away from us. I would certainly cut my fee for a charitable performance. I only wish the clergy would realize that not everyone is as wealthy as they are."

Not a nice lady.

"Doesn't the woman have green eyes?" I replied to the young woman at Hanna's.

"Isn't she mad because she's not as pretty as your wife? And isn't there no vitality in her singing at all, at all?"

This exchange of questions could have gone on all

morning. I sighed, escaped from Nuala's adoring fan, and took a cab over to the Point on the banks of the Liffey to watch the rehearsal. Herself, in jeans and her "Galway Hooker!" T-shirt, was having the time of her life. She had charmed all the other performers, the dancers and chorus, and the warpipe players and the bodhran drummers. In fact, when I came in she was pounding on a drum and singing some kind of Gaelic battle hymn. Or maybe it was a love song. It's hard to tell the difference.

"Now I want all of the rest of youse to be quiet except the drummers and the pipers. I'm going to sing the '*Pange Lingua*,' and I will want the drummers and the pipers to accompany me, but very solemn and gentle like, because this is a procession in church and it has to be very respectful, doesn't it now?"

The crowd of them became quiet instantly, and Nuala sang the hymn, which was allegedly written by Thomas Aquinas. I had heard it often on Holy Thursday, but it had never been quite so solemn, so reverent, so moving.

Ah, the woman knew her stuff.

My Nuala Anne, I thought lovingly, remembering our romps before and after supper. The "latter ride," as the Irish called it, was especially spectacular. I seemed to float between earth and sky, between clay and Heaven. She said it was grand altogether. I wondered whether it was.

As she sang I imagined her clothes dropping away. I ordered my fantasy to be still.

You're besotted with her, the Adversary told me.

"I'm not denying it."

My life had concentrated itself for many months on making love to my wife. Nothing else really mattered.

And herself not enjoying it, the Adversary continued.

"She said she did."

He snorted at me, as if I were a fool to believe her.

Fascinated by the painting of Lady Hazel Lavery on the cover of Sinead McCoole's book, I began to read about the early years of her life in Chicago. It was soap opera but tragic soap opera. She was the elder daughter of a vice president of Armour Meat-packing, a close friend of Philip Armour himself. Her first home was at 514 North Avenue. While she was still young her family moved to Astor Street in the heart of the Gold Coast. She was tutored at home and at a couple of "finishing" schools, one in New York. Her father died suddenly when she was seventeen, leaving a modest inheritance, which her mother squandered. Philip Armour contributed to the support of the family. At nineteen, already a much-admired member of the Gold Coast elite, Hazel made her debut. She was a modestly talented artist, and her early exhibitions won praise from the art critic of the *Chicago Tribune*. She spent several summers in France with her mother and sister. At an artists' colony in Brittany she met and fell in love with John Lavery, a widowed Irish painter twice her age with a daughter her own age. Lavery loved her in return. Her mother opposed the relationship and forced her into a marriage to Ned Trudeau, a suitor from her finishing school days in New York. Dr. Trudeau died within six months of the marriage, leaving her pregnant with her only child. At twenty-four the former Hazel Martyn was a beautiful and talented widow with a daughter and a mother who bitterly opposed a marriage to John Lavery until her own death five years later. She was engaged to a man who disappeared just before the wedding. Only when her mother was dead did Hazel, at the age of twenty-nine, marry John Lavery, who had been her first love. Shortly after Hazel and John were married, her sister Dorothy died from anorexia (as we would call it). Before she was thirty, Hazel had lost her parents, her first husband, and her sister. She bade farewell to Chicago with obvious relief and never returned.

In London, the wife of a now famous and successful painter, the young Chicago socialite became the dazzling center of one of London's most famous salons. While flirtations were expected in that culture and love affairs frequent, it is hard to tell whether Hazel was unfaithful during her early years in London. Ms. McCoole seemed to think not. When the Irish revolutionaries came to London to negotiate a peace treaty and some kind of independent Ireland, Hazel (whose father's family was from Galway) became deeply involved in the process. Her salon was a center and a refuge for the Irish delegates and also a locale for informal meetings among some of the members of both delegations. Her husband said that she came alive with enthusiasm for the Irish cause. Both sides later claimed that she was instrumental in the development of the treaty. At the time, she was forty years old and still radiantly lovely. She claimed to be thirty-three, virtually the same age as the young Irish delegates Michael Collins and later Kevin O'Higgins.

She'd come a long way from North Avenue. Though she seemed both flighty and flaky, her personal achievement was, in its own way, impressive.

I felt sorry for her.

Nuala was singing songs in Irish up on the stage of the Point. I had no idea what they were about, but I noted once again that she was her most beautiful when singing in her first language.

I turned to DeVere White's account of the death of Kevin O'Higgins. The story began with a dinner the night before his death:

When the visitors arrived the conversation turned to other topics: he remonstrated with one of his colleagues who suggested that the Party should refuse to form a government when the Dáil reassembled but should leave the task to a coalition of the opposing parties. To do this, so long as they were the largest Party, was a breach of faith with the electorate, O'Higgins contended. Then he left his friends and went up to bed. He came back to the room after some time, half undressed, looking, he explained, for the toy gramophone which he promised to leave beside Maeve's [O'Higgins's daughter's] bed and which he had hidden in the piano to protect himself from Hogan [his aide-de-camp]. Before going out of the room, he turned to McGilligan and said, in the mock Irish way in which he habitually talked when at home: "It is when I am undressing that I do be thinking over things and I have been turning over in my mind what we were discussing tonight. You know enough about natural history to understand how the coral insects make their beautiful little islands. I do be thinking that the part some of us may have to play is to leave our bones like the coral insects behind us for others to build upon."

After his friends left, he went downstairs to look in his shelves for a book containing a poem, "The Song of Defeat," by Stephen Gwynn. It was a favorite of his, and when he could not find the book he refused to go to bed until he had searched the house and discovered it eventually in the guest room. Then he sat on his bed and read it aloud before going to sleep; read of:

the women of Eire keening
For Brian slain at his tent—

and on through those heroic verses which tell
of Ireland in the ancient, kingly days—

of a land, where to fail is more than to triumph, and victory less than defeat.

In the morning, he was up before breakfast
to have his usual swim at Blackrock. It was one
of those fine summer days when it seems that
nature is entirely genial, that life must be
pleasant, and that evil, if it exists, has been
shamed into hiding below the ground.

Before breakfast O'Higgins played with the
children and inspected all the toys which
Maeve laid out for him. Hogan had obtained
possession of the gramophone again and was
making a nuisance of himself. Everyone felt
happy and O'Higgins had completely cast off
the mood in which he had gone to bed. Hogan
always drew out the best from him and their
conversation was very lively this morning, the
first they had spent together since O'Higgins
had gone to Geneva. There is no diversion so
pleasant as the verbal dueling of two friends
who have wit and who are mentally in tune
with one another. Wit is a dangerous weapon
for any man to carry about in the world, it
sometimes goes off at inappropriate moments,
its mere presence is assumed by the timid to
carry a threat to themselves. It can only be produced with safety when the combatants are
well matched and trust one another.

A meal seldom passed without a discussion
of politics, and when they had laughed enough,
O'Higgins put out his idea that there should be

some form of honor which the State could
award to those who served her without any
public recognition. "There are so many fine fellows," he said, "who do such fine things so quietly."

The household had gone to church earlier in
the morning, and O'Higgins went off by himself
to twelve o'clock Mass at Booterstown. At the
corner, where Cross Avenue meets Booterstown Avenue, there was a seat, and Mrs.
O'Higgins, on her way home from an earlier
Mass, noticed, without attaching any signifi-
cance to the fact, that men were sitting there.
When O'Higgins left Dunamase to go to the
church he did not bother to call his personal
guard, who had accompanied him on the swimming excursion earlier in the morning. His wife
was in the hall arranging flowers; he kissed her,
and went to see his daughter, Maeve, who was
playing with her toys. The child had first to be
kissed, then the dolls in turn, and finally Una,
the baby of the family, asleep in her pram. A
policeman stood on duty at the side gate of the
garden through which O'Higgins passed. A few
minutes later a burst of revolver fire was heard
coming from the road. Hogan, who was waiting
for a friend to take him to play golf, ran from
the house, revolver in hand, in the direction of
the shooting.

Dunamase is only a few hundred yards from
the corner where Booterstown Avenue joins
Cross Avenue, and, as O'Higgins approached
the turn in the road, a boy on a bicycle gave a
signal to a motor-car which was parked on the
side of the road. A man came out and fired at

point-blank range. O'Higgins turned and tried
to run for cover to the gate of Sans Souci, a
house on the other side of the road. His at-
tacker followed, firing as he ran; O'Higgins had
only strength enough to cross the road. On the
other side he fell upon the path, whereupon two
other men rushed out from behind the car and
fired at him as he lay upon the ground. One
stood across the body, pouring the contents of
his revolver into it. The murder party then
drove away, and the first person to arrive on
the scene was an old colleague, Eoin MacNeill.

O'Higgins was alive, but in dreadful agony.
One bullet had entered the head behind the ear.
Six were in his body. But he had not lost consciousness, and when MacNeill bent over him,
he murmured: "I forgive my murderers," and
then, after a pause while he collected strength
to speak, he said: "Tell my wife I love her eter-
nally." The discipline with which he had habitually controlled his mind did not leave him
now, and lying weltering in his blood on the
dusty road in the torrid midday sun, he dictated a will. A priest came and administered
the Last Sacraments, a doctor was summoned
and attended him there on the side of the road
until an ambulance arrived.

"I couldn't help it," he said to his wife when
they carried him into his house and laid him on
an improvised bed on the dining room floor. "I
did my best."

He lay pale but fully conscious, speaking
slowly and clearly. That he was going to die he
was quite certain, but he was gay in the face of
death. Of himself, or his pain, he never spoke,
but he asked for each of his family in turn, and

sent messages to those who were away. Again and again he affirmed that he forgave his murderers. To his wife he said: "You must have no bitterness in your heart for them." Then remembering the problem with which the Government would be faced, he exclaimed: "My colleagues! My poor colleagues!" His friend, Surgeon Barniville, who had been summoned from a distance, arrived early, and noticing his pain, lay down to support him with his arm. "Barney hasn't had his lunch," said O'Higgins, looking up at his wife: to each of those who tended him he had a word of thanks and apology for the trouble he was giving. A doctor offered brandy. He refused it. "Every man ought to drink his quota," he said; "I have drunk mine in my day." His strength must have been abnormal: he lived for five hours, his life oozing gradually away, his mind clear to the last, although, as he neared the end, he had to be told who they were that came to say good-bye. Sometimes he spoke of the affairs that had filled his last years, and, like other dying statesmen, sighed for the future of his country. Of De Valera, he said: "Tell my colleagues that they must beware of him in public life; he will play down to the weaknesses of the people." He spoke of death. His wife said: "You will be with your father and Michael Collins and your little son." He smiled and pictured himself sitting on a damp cloud with a harp, arguing about politics with "Mick." A blood transfusion was given to him; he knew there was no prospect of life, but he agreed to have it. "I'll fight, child," he said. "They are so good to me, but they know I was always a bit of a diehard." "Do you

mind dying, Kevin?" his wife asked. A smile
came over his face. "Mind dying? Why should
I? My hour has come. My job is done." When
his friend, Patrick Hogan, knelt beside him, he
said: "I loved you, Hogan. Good-bye, Boss. We
never had a row." Hogan whispered: "You can
die happy, Kevin." The words had a magical
effect, and from that moment he became quite
tranquil, praying the simple prayers of child-
hood. Shortly before the end, he murmured:
"God help the poor devils," and then he prayed
again. Since early in afternoon the room had
been full of people. Some stood against the
walls, others knelt in prayer. A crucifix had
been placed in his right hand, from which a
knuckle had been shot away, so that his wife
had to keep her hand pressed against the cross
to hold it there.

There was silence in the room, save for the
whisper of prayers and the quiet summer mur-
murings that came through the window from
the garden. With undefeated fortitude he had
looked up at his murderers that morning, as he
lay on the side of the road; and his serenity did
not desert him as the hours passed and his
strength ebbed away; it lighted his face when,
a few minutes before five o'clock, a doctor, taking his pulse, found that he was dead.

I closed the book, tears smarting at my eyes, my
hands clenched, my throat dry.

Could Kevin O'Higgins and the tormented, as I
thought of her, socialite from Chicago really have been
lovers? It didn't seem possible.

On the stage, Nuala was singing:

> *"O Mary, we crown thee with blossoms today,*
> *Queen of the Angels, Queen of the May!*
> *O Mary, we crown thee with blossoms today,*
> *Queen of the Angels, Queen of the May!"*

How incredibly Irish! How unbearably Irish! You die with a wisecrack, a smile, and forgiveness.

Murdered on his way to Mass! How many great men had to die so that Ireland could become the Celtic Tiger and pass England in its standard of living. Generation after generation had to die. Those that the English did not kill the Irish killed themselves.

"Mick" and O'Higgins arguing politics in Heaven—not a bad metaphor, at all, at all.

Why was the ghost of Kevin O'Higgins haunting my Nuala? And who was the woman in the fire?

Was it Lady Lavery? I hoped not. I wanted no part of THAT one, even if I did feel sorry for her. Besides, even if she were a Chicagoan, her family was probably Republican. Nor did I want to read about her love affair with O'Higgins.

That afternoon we'd go out to Booterstown at herself's insistence. I wouldn't give her the DeVere White book or tell her what I'd read. We'd see if she could really reconstruct that terrible Sunday morning. Not for a moment did I doubt that she could and would.

I shivered slightly. As George the Priest said, the fey dimension of her personality was part of the whole package.

I looked up. The whole package was descending upon me, a happy grin on her face.

"Isn't it going to be grand, Dermot Michael? Aren't these brilliant people? Won't the audience love it?"

"They will indeed."

"Did you see them eejits in the papers this morning?

Won't they help us get a crowd? Won't people come
to see if I'm as awful as they say I am?"

So much for my wife's sensitivity to twisted and envious media coverage. They spelled her name right,
and that was enough.

"Wouldn't it be nice to have lunch at Bewley's on
Grafton Street before we take the DART out to Booterstown?"

She slipped into a white windbreaker with the logo
of the Chicago Yacht Club on it.

"It would . . . and supper?"

"I thought maybe at the Shelbourne, if it's all right
with you, Dermot Michael?"

"Won't it be grand to turn nostalgic again and drink
a bottle of wine. I like you, Nuala Anne, when you have
a half-bottle of wine in you."

She blushed modestly.

"Go 'long with you, Dermot Michael Coyne!"

Before we entered the bustling café on Grafton
Street, we slipped into the Clarendon Street Carmelite
Church, which is just across a narrow alley from Bewley's. Nuala prayed with more than her usual fervor—
and usually she is very intense at prayer.

What is she praying for? I asked the Deity.

Well, whatever it is, she's my wife, so I second the
motion.

I had the impression that Herself (or Himself if you
wish) replied that She was well aware that she was my
wife and I was a very lucky fella and I should accept
the whole package.

—6—

NUALA BECAME silent and solemn on the short ride on the Dublin Area Rapid Transit (DART for short) from the Landsdowne station to Booterstown. We went through the "suburban" towns that huddle up against the Irish Sea—Sandymount the most famous, the one from which your man with the dirty mind walked into eternity. The Booterstown station, roughly even with the new campus of University College a mile or so inland, is right above the strand (beach to Americans). One has to walk across Rock Road to get into the town proper. The sun had won its daily battle with the Irish mist. Indeed, the clouds had retreated so far out on the Irish Sea that they were out of sight. They'd be back.

Nuala doffed her Chicago Yacht Club jacket and tied it around her waist.

Behind us in the bright, cloudless sky loomed the electricity works and beyond them Houth Head at the top of Dublin Bay (as in Houth Head and Environs [HCE] in the last novel by your man with the dirty mind). In front of us were the piers of Dun Laoghaire and farther south the other end of the bay, Bray Head.

"When the sun is out and the sky is clear," I said, "couldn't this be Naples?"

She was startled out of her reverie.

"Water's a bit too cold." She took my hand in hers and clung to it. "We'd better walk down to Blackrock Strand. That's where he went swimming the day he died."

Me surprised?

I was indeed, though I half-knew (as she would say) that it was coming.

Lunch at Bewley's had been great fun. Crowded, busy, chaotic, it's the best people-watching place in Dublin. The best people to watch are kids and their parents. Ireland is the greatest place in the world to be a kid. The Irish not only love their kids; they love to play with them. Three small rug rats had accosted Nuala Anne and demanded that she tell them a story, PLEASE! She told them a story about a little leprechaun that didn't like to play tricks on people and how hard he had to work to persuade kids to trust him. He finally succeeded because of the efforts of a bossy little tyke named Nessa who sounded like a younger version of herself.

A young mother had thanked Nuala Anne for the story, "Sure, 'tis wonderful to take time with these brats and yourself preparing for the concert, day after tomorrow."

Of course the woman knew who she was. Didn't everyone?

"They're more fun than the whole crowd in the Point," my wife had replied. "I wish we could fill it with kids. Maybe next time."

"Weren't you grand last night on the telly? Don't let them awful women who write the articles in the papers get to you. Aren't they just envious gobshites?"

"Ah, the poor things. Don't they need to find the corner in their souls where neither time nor flesh gets in the way?"

The young matron nodded in solemn agreement, as if she knew all about that corner.

"Who said that?" I had asked as we emerged on Grafton Street.

"Wasn't it Meister Eckhart?" she said as if everyone knew that.

Eckhart's wisdom did not seem to help much as we walked down Rock Road to Blackrock Park and the adjoining strand.

Her hand clutching mine, her voice soft, Nuala began to describe the events of Kevin O'Higgins's death:

"He woke up early in the morning—there had been a party the night before and a bit too much of the drink had been taken—and he came down here for a swim to clear his head."

"Ah," I said, as if I understood.

"It was a blazing hot day, much hotter than today. He came out of the water feeling grand. He'd been to a meeting of the Commonwealth countries in November and a session in Geneva about warships. He was optimistic for the future of Ireland. He thought the Irish were the brightest people at both meetings."

"Naturally."

"Would you ever put your arm around me, Dermot Michael? I'm perishing with the cold, and it being a warm day."

I did.

Out on the bay white cruisers, sailboats with multi-colored jibs, and sailboards crisscrossed the blue water, a peaceful, quiet spring festival on the waves.

"Not much of a beach there anymore," I observed. "No one using it."

"Everyone has cars. They can drive to other strands."

I frivolously wondered whether she thought of our place in Grand Beach as Grand Strand. Not likely; she made the shift from one version of English to the other without much difficulty. But what did I know about what went on in her head?

"All right," she continued, "we'll walk back to Booterstown Avenue now."

She huddled against me, as though I could keep the horror away from her.

After a quarter-mile or so, we took a left turn down a street with lovely late Victorian villas on either side, shaded by comfortable old trees. Except for an occasional mother pushing a stroller, the street was deserted. I tried to feel some sense of terror or horror, but all I sensed was a pleasant spring afternoon.

"He lived at the lower end of the street," she said, "twenty minutes' walk. Do you ever mind walking that far, Dermot Michael?"

"Not with you," I replied.

She smiled faintly.

We passed a school and a small marketplace with a few prosperous-looking shops. The first cross street we came to was appropriately called Cross Avenue.

"The church is down to your left," Nuala informed me. "On the right is a villa called Sans Souci Park."

We stopped.

"His wife went to an early Mass while he was swimming. She was pregnant, you know. . . . See this bench here?" She pointed at a worn stone bench at the corner.

"Yes."

"When his wife came home from Mass, she noticed a couple of men sitting on it."

"Indeed. . . . Do we go down to the church now?" I asked, nodding in the direction of a church steeple a block down on our left.

"No. . . . We'll go to his house. It's farther along Booterstown Avenue. It was called Dunamase."

In a few minutes we stopped.

"This is the house," she said simply.

The villa was on the left-hand side of the street, now almost hidden by the trees that had had seventy years to add height and foliage since the Minister of Justice and External Affairs left it for the last time in the summer of 1927.

"By the time he got here, some of his optimism had faded. His party had won the last election but not by much. There wasn't much flair in his colleagues. He feared that De Valera would eventually take over the country and it would stagnate."

"Which it did."

"He also had an idea to bring unity to Ireland of which he was quite proud. . . . The King of England would come to Dublin and be crowned King of Ireland. He'd spend six weeks here every year. They would replace the tricolor with a flag of St. Patrick's blue with a harp on it."

"Dual monarchy?"

She glanced at me. "I suppose you'd call it that. . . . Would it have worked, Dermot Michael?"

"I doubt it. Maybe it was worth trying, however."

She nodded. "He ate a big breakfast and played with his daughters for a while."

"You can see all this, Nuala?"

"Not exactly, Dermot love. . . . I feel it. I feel what's inside of him. . . . Sometimes he thinks that he is not going to live long. . . . No, he knows it. But he doesn't think that this will be the day. He also feels guilty. There's another woman. . . . He's obsessed by her. Wants to break away. Is trying. Prays that he can do it."

"Hazel."

"I suppose so. . . . She drives him out of his mind."

"Some women do that."

"He loves his wife, too. He kisses her very tenderly as he leaves the house. She is arranging flowers. They had made love the night before. She is the center of his life, he tells himself. He comes out of the house. There's a Guard standing outside. He exchanges a joke with the Guard and walks out the gate. He thinks that perhaps he should bring along his personal bodyguard and then dismisses the idea. He didn't need him to go to the strand this morning. He certainly won't need him to walk to Mass."

We turned and walked slowly down Booterstown Avenue. I thought to myself that all she was telling me was in the closing four pages of DeVere White's book. Was it not possible that she was merely reading my mind?

"As he walks along the street he prays to God that he can forget the other woman."

We approached the fatal crossroad.

"The car is parked over there—just around the corner where that Audi is now. As he comes to the corner, a boy on a bicycle gives a signal to the three men in the car. One of them rushes out and . . ."

Nuala screamed as if the first bullet had pierced her body. She began to sob.

"He runs across the street, trying to escape into Sans Souci. But he doesn't make it. . . . Oh, Dermot Michael, 'tis terrible! Terrible!"

She leaned against me. I extended both my arms around her and held her close.

"He falls on the pathway across the street," she went on, not looking at the spot where his helpless body had lain. "Two more men jump out of the car. They stand over him, pumping shells into his body. They stop because they know he'll die. . . ."

She was sobbing now. The story came in gasps.

"Then he talks to them. He recognizes them. He says he understands why they would want to kill him and forgives them. They're frightened by his forgiveness.

Now they feel guilty for shooting a man on his way to Mass. They turn and run to the car, and it drives away. The boy on the bicycle is weeping. He goes down to the church to get the priest. The poor man is bleeding terribly."

None of that was in the book. She was really there on that summer day in July of 1927.

"The priest comes," she continued, controlling her sobs. "The doctor, the ambulance. They bring him back to the house. He's very brave. He jokes; he warns his wife to forgive those who killed him just as he has; he talks to his friends and colleagues . . . tells them to be careful of Dev. . . . Do I have to go on, Dermot Michael?"

"I don't think so, Nuala. Let's get the hell out of here."

Limp and spent, she held me fast, shivering like she was in the middle of a Chicago winter. Her T-shirt was soaked through to the skin. I helped her put on the windbreaker.

"He was such a brave man."

"He was indeed."

"We can leave now," she said, reaching for a tissue in her shoulder purse. "It's over."

It had been over seventy years before.

Hand in hand, in silence, we walked back to the DART station. I decided that I wanted never to return to Booterstown.

"What did it all mean?" I asked her as we waited for the green train.

"I don't know, Dermot Michael. I don't know at all, at all. I know I had to be there."

"Who were the men who shot him?"

She seemed surprised by the question.

"Weren't they the men from the burning house?"

"Oh. . . . Did you hear their names?"

"Not exactly. . . . I'd remember them if I heard them, I think."

"The book says they were Archie Doyle, Tim Gannon, and Bill Murphy."

"No," she said firmly. "Those weren't the names. They were . . . Liam, Paddy, and Tommy."

Maybe we were supposed to find out who the killers really were. But why?

"It doesn't make any sense, Nuala," I said as the DART train rushed towards us.

"I know it doesn't, Dermot Michael. But we have to find out more."

On the train as we pulled away from the Booterstown station, she leaned against me and said, "While I'm rehearsing for the concert, would you write one of your nice little reports for me?"

"I will."

After the concert, perhaps I could talk her into canceling the visit to the Benedictines out in County Tip and going home to the United States, where beaches are beaches, not strands.

— 7 —

 IF IT is all the same to You, I don't want to do this anymore. Can't You get some other fat Irish cow to solve mysteries from the past? I don't want to be fey. I don't want to be a detective. I want to be a good wife and mother and sing songs occasionally.

And beat poor dear Dermot at golf.

Didn't I know as soon as we got on the train to ride back to Landsdowne Road and Jury's that I would make love with me poor husband as soon as we got into our room? Even if there're no skyrockets, I says to meself, it's nice and I need to be loved.

So there were no skyrockets, but poor Dermot was pleased with me and himself thinking that it helped me to get over that horror in Booterstown. I don't have to tell it takes days for one of those things to wear off. Sure, I'm good at faking that, too.

Good at faking everything.

What are we supposed to do now?

Why don't we make a deal? Why don't I solve whatever mystery You want me to solve and You make me a good wife and a good mother?

Isn't that fair?

I know that You don't make deals, but, sure, couldn't You do it just this once?

No comment, huh?
I didn't think so.
You insist that You love me?
Don't I know that?

— 8 —

I SUPPOSE it was my fault that they thought they could kidnap Nuala.

Everyone thinks I'm a pushover. I'm a big blond lug with a pleasant disposition and a sweet smile. Not too bright, they say, and not very ambitious and certainly not a fighter. Didn't he quit the football team in high school and refuse to go out for the Fighting Irish? One solid punch and he's flat on his back. You unleash a big tough on him and he's dead meat. Right?

I admit that the image is generally accurate. Like the Adversary says, DERMOT, YOU DON'T HAVE THE HORMONES TO BE AN ALLEY FIGHTER, SO YOU SHOULDN'T TRY IT.

He forgets, like I often do, that, in addition to an Adversary, there's also a Daemon inside me. The Daemon is very dangerous.

Naturally, we made love when we got back to our room, mostly because Nuala seemed to want it, even need it. Love exorcised the scene down in Booterstown. She slept peacefully. Then we had a swim and a turn in the whirlpool and another swim. She seemed to have left behind the death of Kevin O'Higgins and become once again Nuala Anne the World Traveler.

This was a persona who appeared often on our honeymoon—a gorgeous, flawlessly dressed, sophisticated woman of the world, polite, reserved, gracious, and infinitely superior. This lovely Irish contessa could walk across the lobby of, let us say, the Hassler hotel in Rome like she had stayed there twenty times before. All the time, her shrewd eyes would be taking in every detail of the place so she could be even more superior when she rode down on the elevator to cross the lobby again.

You'd think she was nobility of some sort or at least a world-class celebrity. In fact, she was nothing more than a shy peasant child from the Gaeltacht in Connemara in whose home there were no "conveniences" for most of her life. Mind you, the World Traveler was not a fraud. It was simply one of the people my wife could become when she made up her mind to do so.

I never did figure out whether she dressed to fit the persona or her clothes created the persona.

That night the dress oozed sophistication—a summer-weight black minidress with a thin gold belt and a low scoop in back and front. For jewelry she wore diamond studs, her engagement and wedding rings, and a gold salmon pendant, a sign of wisdom in Celtic mythology. The ensemble (and the accompanying perfume) said that she was someone so sophisticated that she didn't need to pretend to be sophisticated.

Got it?

The young women at the desk in the Towers gasped audibly as Nuala Anne sailed by them, myself in tow.

"You look wonderful, Nuala Anne!"

"What a beautiful dress, Nuala Anne!"

Mind you, the first name tainted the image a little. Better that they called her milady.

She did not object to their familiarity. "Sure, haven't youse both swallowed the focking Blarney Stone."

We could have gone out the door of the Towers and found a taxi on Landsdowne Road. Instead she led the way to the main lobby of the hotel, without consulting her poor spear carrier. Hence the sensation she created in the main lobby of Jury's was self-conscious and deliberate, just as was the awe she caused the first time she had done that on what was technically our first date. There was not an eye in the lobby that was not following her progress out the door in the early evening sunlight.

"Nice exit, Nuala Anne."

"Sure, don't the poor things have nothing else to talk about?"

She created the same sensation in the lobby and the dining room at the Shelbourne.

Was this the same woman who, T-shirt soaking wet, had cowered in my arms only a couple of hours before?

That was not just a rhetorical question.

Supper was a delight. She imitated all the people who were involved in the rehearsals for the concert, especially poor Father Placid and the "media bitches" who had tried to harass her.

She was still the World Traveler but now the World Traveler as Comedienne, a frequent companion at our honeymoon suppers. I often wondered whether the show was entirely for my entertainment, to keep poor Dermot happy after another hard day of travel. Now I presume it was certainly that, but not only that.

We decided to walk back to Jury's in the long spring twilight, down Baggot Street, across the bridge over the Grand Canal, and then on Pembroke Road to the hotel. The evening was perfect, a light breeze, a touch of delicate warmth in the air, glowing Dublin light, strolling couples, many of them with arms around one another just like us.

We were crossing the bridge with its low red-brick parapet. I had said something about the Brendan Kennelly whose statue now sat on a bench on which he himself had reflected every day for many years. She reminded me that I was to write her a report the next day while she was at her rehearsal.

Everything happened very quickly, as it does in such a situation. Out of the corner of my eye I saw a black Humbler pull up next to us and three big guys with stocking masks pour out of it. A bright light went on across the street—someone with a TV minicam. One of the guys grabbed me from behind and pinned me against the brick wall of the bridge. The other two dragged Nuala towards the car. Women were screaming.

That's when the Daemon took over. I became a mixture of Finn MacCool, Conan the Barbarian, and Dick Butkus.

The guy who had pushed me to the wall had a choke hold around my neck and was trying to crush my ribs with his other arm. Big, I thought, and not really very tough. Beer on his breath. Stupid and half-drunk. With a single quick movement, I pushed both arms away, spun him around towards the street, and hurled him into the path of a car. A screech of brakes and more screams. The car hit him. He rolled over on the hood and then fell on the street.

My poor wife, her dress torn, was giving a good account of herself, as she always does in a street fight. She poked with her elbows, jabbed with her knees, and kicked with her feet. Her assailants screamed with pain after every blow.

What was the name of Conan's woman?

"Hold still, you focking bitch," one of the guys ordered, "or we'll cut off your tits."

I had yet to see the flash of metal, but I wasn't about to wait for that.

I grabbed the bigger of the two, pulled him off her, chopped at his neck, lifted him up in both hands, and threw him over the bridge into the Grand Canal.

He landed with an angry shout and a loud splash.

The man with the TV camera had closed in on the scene. He stood only a few feet away from me. The light temporarily blinded me. I'd take care of him later.

In the brief moment that I blinked, the remaining thug had produced a knife and was threatening Nuala's face with it. She kneed him in his private regions. He yelled and raised the knife to strike. She tore away. I reached out, grabbed his arm, twisted it so he dropped the knife, and then broke his arm. He screamed again, more loudly. I seized him, spun him through the air, and tossed him into the Grand Canal.

The cameraman continued to grind away, more interested in his story than in helping people under assault. I yanked the camera away from him and sent it after the two thugs.

"That's my camera, ya focking Yank bastard!" he shouted. "I'll sue you."

"Not before I sue you!" I pulled him towards the parapet.

"Don't hurt me!" he pleaded.

I became aware that there were people screaming all around me.

A guy was in my face shouting that I had ruined his car. Nuala Anne was howling in Irish. A woman assistant of the cameraman was yelling that I had ruined their scoop.

The crowd was bellowing conflicting advice:

"Throw the focker into the canal!"

"Don't hurt the poor man!"

"Kick him in the balls!"

"You're a murdering focker!"

I lifted the cameraman to the edge of the wall. "You set us up!"

"I'm not your focking bodyguard."

He was a little guy with a red face and a high-pitched voice. I held him over the water.

"Dermot Michael," my wife ordered, switching to English, presumably for my benefit, "put the poor focker down."

Naturally, I did what I was told.

Then a guy began to pound on my chest. "You ruined my car, you focking Yank. I'm going to sue you."

"You want to go over the wall, too?"

He scurried away.

Nuala returned to her first language to denounce the crowd. My World Traveler had become Grace O'Malley, the Warrior Witch. They cowered and became silent as she told them in no uncertain terms that they were cowards. At least I assumed that was what she was doing, though I caught only a few Anglo-Saxon words. Such as "focking gobshites!"

I glanced down at the canal. Two of our attackers had pulled themselves out of the murk and were hobbling away. The third man was still lying on the street, moaning softly. Well, he wasn't dead, though he deserved to be.

I became aware that I was breathing heavily, that my fists were clenched, that I was glowering at the crowd, and that I was desperately looking for someone else to throw into the canal.

As if in response to that wish the Guards arrived, their blue patrol car wailing like a wounded rabbit. It ground to a halt only a couple of feet from the injured thug. A pint size and imperious officer bustled out of the car, waved his transceiver at the crowd, and announced intelligently, "Here now, what's going on?"

A woman cop in her thirties emerged after him and took in the situation with a worried frown.

Traffic had piled up on both sides of the bridge. Oblivious of our little drama, motorists were leaning on their horns.

"Those men"—I gestured towards the canal—"tried to kidnap me and my wife. Arrest them before they get away."

"The Garda Siochana," he informed me, "will make its own decisions about taking people into custody."

"He ruined my car!" the outraged motorist bellowed.

"Threw this focker into our way!" his wife, a frizzy blonde, screamed.

"The kidnappers are getting away!"

"He threw my camera into the canal!"

"They're focking Yanks."

"Seamus," the woman Guard whispered, "I think this is the woman who sings. . . ."

"I know what I'm doing, woman."

"They pulled a knife on me and my wife," I pleaded, now trying to sound sensible and reasonable.

A low, guttural noise came from the direction of Nuala Anne. She was, I gathered, getting *really* angry. Galway was not all that far from the Stone Age.

I extended my arm around her. She was as still as a bronze statue.

"The fockers might have hurt you, Dermot Michael. Are you all right?"

"I'm fine! The trouble now is that we have a very dumb cop on our hands."

"I think you'd better come to the station and make a statement, sir," he informed me pompously. "We cannot have conditions like this on a busy street in Dublin."

"Seamus, ya oughta call an ambulance!"

"Why?"

We *would* draw a truly dumb cop.

"That poor focker lying there on the street!"

"He doesn't look badly injured!"

"That's not the point, you eejit. You know the rules."

"You call them." He thrust the transceiver at her.

"Now then, sir"—he grabbed my arm—"you and your woman will have to come along with me to the Garda station and make statements."

I brushed him off like an annoying insect. "Take your hands off me, you nine-fingered shite hawk."

"I'm placing you under arrest."

"How do I know that you're not part of the kidnapping plot?"

He frowned for a moment, puzzled by the suggestion that there might have been an attempted kidnapping.

"We'll discuss any alleged plot at the station."

He didn't mention "alleged" perpetrators or "alleged subjects" like American cops do on television.

"You too, ma'am." He seized Nuala's arm, from which hung the tatters of her elegant dress.

That was it. As my teenage nieces would put it, I went postal.

I lifted him off the ground and held him high in the air. "Can you swim, focker?"

I had slipped into the vernacular.

"NO!"

"Grand!"

Into the drink he went.

The woman cop tried to make a call. I pulled the transceiver out of her hands and tossed it after her colleague.

"Good on you, Dermot Michael!" my wife shouted exultantly.

"You're all a disgrace to the Irish race!" I yelled at the crowd, having learned long ago from Ma (as I called my grandmother) that this was the insult to end all insults. "You stand here and gawk while a man and his wife are assaulted in broad daylight by knife-wielding barbarians! With a TV camera there to take it all down. Then this focking asshole of a cop arrives and focks things up worse and you stand there grinning like the pissant gobshites you are! I'm leaving this country and never coming back. I'll tell everyone in America that the Irish are shite-faced savages!"

That was not bad for an American anyway. Yet I was a long way from a character in a Roddy Doyle novel.

The growl that been lurking in Nuala's throat exploded into an ear-piercing roar, a wild Gaelic war cry rising from the Irish soil of antiquity. Or perhaps it was only, as she would explain later, the shout of a hurling player running down the pitch.

The onlookers, properly terrified though my good wife held neither a pike nor a hurling stick, quickly faded away, save for the camera crew, the motorist and his wife, and one very frightened woman Guard.

And one masked thug who was still lying on the street groaning. Traffic was now crossing the bridge again. None of the drivers seemed to notice the injured man. The shades of night were rushing down the street.

Nuala bent to take his pulse.

"My name," I informed the terrified Guard as I shoved my business card at her, "is Dermot Michael Coyne. I am a poet. My wife is Nuala Anne McGrail. She sings. You can reach us at the American embassy, where we are taking sanctuary until such time as the Guard and the Irish government apologize for this incident and guarantee us that it is safe to walk the streets of this savage city at twilight."

The Irish take poets very seriously. Indeed, they are just a little afraid of them. Long ago, when there was no law enforcement in the country, a king who fancied he was injured would hire a poet to denounce his enemy. You had to be careful with your poets.

"You shouldn't have thrown poor Seamus over the bridge." She took the card and stepped away from me. "That wasn't right."

"I don't like people pushing my wife around."

I was still breathing heavily. Indeed, I was still looking for someone to toss into the canal.

Poor Seamus was clinging to the bank, crying pathetically for help.

"I think the shite hawk will live," Nuala announced as she stood up. "Maybe the Garda will finally get an ambulance to take him away. . . . You"—she turned contemptuously to the woman Guard—"had better go down there and help the focking amadon out of the canal. We wouldn't want him to drown before we get him into the courtroom."

Ah, it was a country of litigators.

She rearranged her torn dress, accepted my jacket as a wrap, linked my arm in hers, and led me down Pembroke Road.

"Weren't we something else altogether, Dermot Michael Coyne?"

"We were that, woman," I agreed.

A postberserk reaction was creeping into my body. I wasn't sure that I could walk the couple of blocks to Jury's. My wife, now the warrior queen returning from battle, seemed serenely confident.

"What was that all about?" I asked as I slipped into a daze.

"Och, that's for you to figure out, Dermot love. Aren't you the great detective?"

She signaled for a taxi and ushered me into the car. "Sure, Dermot Michael, you aren't the man you used to be after these street fights. Too much sexual intercourse, probably. It saps one's strength."

YOU'RE A REAL ASSHOLE, the Adversary informed me.

"We had to defend ourselves."

WHAT WAS THE POINT OF THROWING THEM INTO THE CANAL?

"Immobilize them."

EVEN THE GUARD?

"He pushed Nuala."

SHE CAN TAKE CARE OF HERSELF.

"What was going on back there?" she asked the driver.

"Didn't some drunk throw a couple of fellas into the Grand Canal?"

"Did he now?"

"Even threw in a Garda."

"Good on him!"

"Me very words," the driver admitted with a laugh. "They could throw the whole focking force into the canal and it wouldn't bother me."

An interesting position.

Maybe throwing the pompous punk in had been a bit much. Still, if it came to a court action I would plead that I couldn't believe he was a police officer because he refused to apprehend the alleged perpetrators and therefore I thought he was part of the plot.

My sister Cindi, the lawyer in the family, would like that defense.

At the door of the Towers, Nuala took charge. I was a nice little boy who had worn himself out in a street fight with some other unruly boys.

Actually, I was Conan the Barbarian, wasn't I?

Or Finn MacCool?

Or Mike Singletary?

"You'd better get your security people in to block the door," she told the startled young woman at the desk. "Them media gobshites will show up. We don't want to see them. Turn off our phones. We'll use me portable. If the Gardai show up, tell them we're at the American embassy."

Then, without waiting for a response, she stalked to the elevator, guided me into it, and pushed the button.

"We'll have you in bed in just a minute, Dermot love."

She called room service and told them to bring up a double Bushmill's Green Label.

Not on the rocks, of course. That would be sacrilege.

She hung up her tattered dress and muttered, "Someone is going to pay for that."

"The Guards."

"Maybe . . . Now let's get you into bed, Dermot love; you need a nice long nap."

Even though she was now wearing only negligible bits of transparent black lace, I was in no condition to frolic with her.

My drink arrived and I was instructed to drink every drop of it.

"Sure isn't it better than that Prozac thing?" she said as she kissed me good night.

As I fell off to sleep, I heard her making phone calls on the portable phone that I had not seen before. It seemed that she was talking to the American Ambassador, the President of Ireland, my sister Cindi, her own mother, and Mike Casey, a former Superintendent of Chicago police and now the head of a group called Reliable Security.

I collapsed into the land of nod thinking that I had nothing to worry about. Sherlock Holmes was on the case.

I remembered just as I went into the pleasant black pit that we had no idea who had tried to kidnap my wife.

— 9 —

IF YOU don't mind, I think I'll keep this poor man as me husband. Wasn't he wonderful out there on the bridge? What terrible things might have happened to me if he weren't so strong and so quick?

Isn't he quick, though? In a few seconds them fellas were routed and I was safe in his arms. They never thought he was so quick, did they? The next time they try to kidnap me, they'd better send three fellas to hold him down, and won't that not be enough?

He really doesn't like fighting, though he's terrible good at it, isn't he? When we got rid of all them gobshites—pardon me language, but that's what they were—I thought he was going to collapse on me. He's fine now, but he'll ache all over tomorrow morning, and himself having to write that report for me.

I love him so much. I really do. Lying here in bed with him in me arms and meself all naked, I know I'm the happiest woman in all the world.

And just maybe the best protected, too.

I won't ever let go of him. Never. Do You hear that?

Well, as long as it's all right that I hang on to him. If You want to take one of us home first, I'll go—though You'll have to find someone to take care of him. Someone to order those double shots when he needs them.

Without the ice.

If only I were the kind of wife he deserves.

Maybe me ma is right. Maybe that will all work itself out. Maybe I'm too obsessive. Maybe I want to control everything, even the things you can't control.

We Irish women have that temptation, don't we now?

"Mary Fionnuala Anne," me ma says to me, "you think you have to control everything. But you can't. Aren't you dealing now with things you can't control?"

I don't like that, but I suppose You don't like it when I try to budget Your time for You.

Anyway, he's mine and I won't let him go.

Unless You insist.

And I don't think You will.

— 10 —

"WAKE UP, Dermot Michael! Aren't we on the telly!"

My body a single solid ache, I rolled over and peered out at a hostile world through narrow eyes. My wife was standing next to our bed, a towel wrapped around her loins.

With that view, the world seemed much less hostile.

Yielding their possession of her reluctantly, my eyes focused on the television monitor.

Sure enough, we were on the telly.

I was amazed at how quick the action was, twenty seconds at the most. The three thugs piled out of the car; two of them grabbed herself; one of them pinned me to the parapet of the bridge. I threw him out into the street. Nuala was engaged in a fierce tugging match with the other two. With what looked like a single motion I pulled one of them away and threw him into the canal. Then, in the tiniest fraction of a second, I twisted the other man's hand so he dropped the knife, broke his arm with a single quick twist, and sent him into the river. The camera was in my face. I glowed with a wild cheerful smile. Then the camera twirled in a circle and caught a brief moment of the Grand Canal rushing up towards it.

The woman anchorperson, in a soft Dublin accent,

announced that the cameraman intended to sue for the destruction of his property.

"Not too badly destroyed if he could rescue his film," herself snorted.

"The Gardai reported that there was apparently an attempted kidnapping of Nuala Anne McGrail, the singer," the woman continued with a faint smile, "and that they were investigating the matter further. They also reported that one of their officers had also been thrown into the canal. Perhaps"—her smile broadened—"he got too close to Ms. McGrail's husband, a young man who is clearly to be reckoned with."

"Isn't he ever!" my wife chortled, clapping her hands and bounding around the room. "A man to be reckoned with!"

"That one, at least, is on our side," I said.

"Won't they all be on our side! Sure, Dermot Michael, and wasn't it a good thing the tape wasn't ruined!"

"They're still invading our privacy!"

"Be nice to them now, Dermot Michael. Don't they all think you're a man to be reckoned with!" She clapped her hands.

"Pretty quick," I admitted. "Not really quick enough to be a great linebacker, but still pretty quick."

"Dermot Michael Coyne! Stop looking at me that way! You'll be giving me dirty thoughts and meself with a rehearsal in an hour. . . . Come on, put your clothes on; don't we have to go down to the lounge and eat our breakfast?"

"Yes, ma'am."

"Wasn't it a good thing," she observed as she discarded the towel and drew an almost nonexistent pantie over her loins, "that the water destroyed the sound? Sure, didn't we use terrible language altogether? And wouldn't me poor ma have been shocked?"

I didn't think that her poor ma would be shocked by anything at all, at all. Nonetheless, we had to keep up the pretense that Nuala's vocabulary had not been ruined by her time in Dublin. Not to say Chicago.

"It was really a quick fight," I said, rolling out of bed. "Scary quick."

"Into the shower with you," she insisted, swatting my rear end. "Don't we have a busy day ahead of us, and yourself going to write that report for me!"

In the elevator riding down to the Tower's lounge, she kissed me solidly. "I love you something awful, Dermot love. Won't it be grand for me to have dirty thoughts when I come back from the rehearsal?"

"If I finish my report."

She was genuinely shocked—and perhaps a little hurt. "I wouldn't do that to you, Dermot. Not at all, at all."

"Woman"—I hugged her—"don't I know that?"

The elevator door opened before we could continue, but she was beaming happily.

Outside, the Irish mist had turned to Irish rain, a soft rain—that is, one that drizzles all day or even all week. Rain would not keep us out of the pool. Herself did not approve of permitting rain to interfere with exercise.

We attracted no attention when we came into the lounge, a nice young couple—maybe on their honeymoon—in jeans and sweatshirts, herself in a white one (tight) with "Galway" in thick green letters and myself in dark blue (loose) with a white outline of the Chicago skyline. If you don't know what it is, don't ask. None of the American tourists or European businesspeople in the room could possibly imagine us as the two berserkers who had been on the telly that morning.

The Towers serves a complimentary continental

breakfast in its lounge every morning—rolls, scones, fruit juice, and coffee and tea. It was hardly my idea of what a breakfast ought to be, but, as herself argued, it was both quick and free.

She conducted me as though I were an invalid to one of the comfortable couches in the corner and assisted me to sit down.

"Are you all right now, Dermot?"

"Grand!" I sighed contentedly as she dashed away to collect our food.

Actually, every muscle in my body ached, but her tender smile was a remarkable cure.

SHE'S MOTHERING YOU AGAIN, the Adversary murmured.

"Who's complaining?"

Nuala flounced back with a teapot and cups. She sped away again and returned with grapefruit juice for herself and scones and three glasses of grapefruit juice for me.

"You're spoiling me rotten, woman," I protested.

"I don't spoil you enough, Dermot love."

I figure that a husband has no right to be mothered (except when he's sick—maybe), but that when such tender loving care is proffered he should accept it gratefully.

"You don't have to, Nuala Anne."

"I WANT to."

That settled that.

"Ah, woman, if you keep working on it, won't you become a grand wife!"

For a brief moment her eyes flashed dangerously and I was afraid that I had gone too far. Then she grinned and said, "Och, Dermot, aren't you having me on?"

"A substitute for having you."

She flushed dark red. "Hush, Dermot Michael

Coyne. Aren't you embarrassing me something awful with such suggestive talk?"

Nonetheless, she was pleased by it.

The assistant manager on duty managed to smuggle me a plate of ten small raisin rolls, which I devoured with great relish.

"Weren't the two of you grand on the telly," she said to us. "Didn't it serve them gobshites right?"

"Didn't it ever?" Nuala agreed as she poured my tea.

"And the focking Garda, too," the young woman added.

"They don't dare mess around with me man," Nuala said as she buttered one of the rolls and popped it into my mouth. "And himself so sweet and nice most of the time."

"More jelly on the next one please, Nuala Anne, or I might lose my temper again."

Both women giggled, confident that Nuala Anne had tamed me, though my wife knew I was born tame.

I was halfway through my plate of rolls when a tall, handsome man with wavy gray-tinged hair, twinkling blue eyes, and an easy smile appeared and glanced around the room.

"Cop," I said.

"And a very important cop," my wife added.

He saw us and grinned. Even though his gray suit could have used a pressing and the knot in his tie wasn't quite right, it was clear that this man was in charge.

"Before I risk a swim in the Grand Canal," he said easily, "perhaps I should claim that I'm a good friend of Mike Casey and I spoke with him last night and again this morning."

"Well," said Nuala Anne judiciously, "that might keep you dry for a few more moments."

Two blarney artists.

"My name's Gene Keenan and I'm with the Gardai," he said apologetically.

"Deputy Commissioner, if I read the Irish papers right," I said as I stood up and shook hands with him. "Sit down and have a cup of tea."

"If you're good," Nuala added, "Dermot might even give you one of his rolls."

"No thanks, I've had me breakfast, but I could stand a small drop of tea—with milk, if you don't mind."

Nuala, who had acquired the American habit of drinking tea the way God made it, borrowed a pitcher from the empty table next to us.

"Well, I suppose I should begin my apologizing for the failure of the Garda last night. Patently he should have concentrated on arresting the criminals."

"He wasn't armed," I said, almost by way of excuse.

"We aren't armed because a great man named Kevin O'Higgins insisted on an unarmed Gardai. However, he could have summoned help easily and we would have tracked them down quickly. As it is, we have only the man you threw into the street, Mr. Coyne. And himself having a case of amnesia this morning."

"Dermot," I said.

"Gene . . . Well," he went on, rubbing his chin, "that officer will have a considerable time to reflect on proper police tactics at his new assignment in Donegal . . . We have also arrested the independent television crew as accessories to the attempted kidnapping. I don't think they'll go to jail, but they won't do any TV work for a long time . . . and neither of you with serious ill effects?"

"My neck hurts," I said.

For a moment our new friend looked anxious; then he realized I was kidding and smiled.

"Pay me man no heed, Commissioner," herself explained. "He's having you on . . . He's a solid mass of ache and pain, poor dear man, but we're not going to sue the Gardai."

"I had a call from one of the best solicitors in Ireland last night and again this morning. You must have made a lot of phone calls last night, Ms. McGrail."

"Sure, doesn't everyone call me Nuala Anne?"

"Actually"—he shifted uneasily on his chair and sipped from his tea—"I think we should have been more concerned about your security. To tell the truth, we thought the worst you had to fear were the Irish media. Now they're on your side and blaming us for not taking care of you."

"Gobshites," said herself fervently.

"Better to have them on your side, however, than on the other side . . . In any event, we want to correct our previous mistake. With your permission, we will put our most discreet security people on you. More, Commissioner Casey wants to assign the best personnel from Reliable, Dublin."

"I hope there's a comma between those last two words."

"Sometimes there is and sometimes there isn't," Keenan laughed. "You didn't realize that Michael is worldwide?"

No one ever calls him Michael, not even his lovely wife.

"Didn't we take it for granted?" Nuala replied. "And isn't he a brilliant man?"

Brilliant is the superlative adjective, for which *super* is the comparative and *grand* the base. One can even used *dead friggin' brill* if one wants to emphasize excellence.

"He is that . . . and if you wouldn't mind, we'd like to take you over to the Point in one of our cars this morning, a detective car of course, and bring you back here after the rehearsal."

"Super!" Nuala announced. "It's all super!"

YOU DON'T GET TO VOTE, the Adversary observed.

"Naturally not."

"Who were the assailants last night?" I asked, changing the subject.

"Amateurs," the cop said, frowning. "One always thinks of the lads when one encounters a kidnapping in broad daylight. But the lads have been quiet lately as the peace negotiations grind on, and their snatches would be a lot more professional. Moreover, our Special Branch people keep a close tab on them. We would have known that something was going down if any of the various Sinn Fein groups were involved. . . . Do you have any ideas who it might be?"

I felt my gut tighten. If the local police had to ask us, then they didn't have a clue.

"Not really," I replied. "Nuala and I have had some scrapes in the last couple of years, but there's no one out there who might try to kidnap her. Maybe it was a couple of local crooks who wanted to pick up some extra punts."

A punt is an Irish pound. It is sometimes written IR£.

The Deputy Commissioner nodded thoughtfully. "That's our line of thought, too. The Canal House bridge is not the best place for a snatch. We will pursue our leads and keep a tight but unobtrusive security ring around you."

"Fair enough," I agreed.

"See," I told the Adversary, "I did get a chance to vote!"

"Och, Dermot Michael, I'll be late for me rehearsal! I'll run upstairs and get me slicker."

"I'm married to one like that," Gene Keenan observed as Nuala Anne galloped away towards the elevators.

"Lucky man!"

"Sure, don't I know it! And if I should forget it, I'm promptly reminded."

We sighed together.

The Irish sigh, you must realize, is a sudden intake of breath, almost a gasp. If you're not familiar with it, you might think it is the beginning of a serious asthma attack. Sometimes it stands by itself. Sometimes it precedes a statement. On other occasions it ends a statement.

I have no idea what it means to them, but I have learned when to use it.

Nuala returned almost at once, wearing a red transparent rain cape and hood.

"All ready, Commissioner," she announced.

"We're going to take you out the back door, Nuala Anne. So the media can't climb all over you with their sympathy and support. . . . Dermot, why don't you go out there and make some sort of statement to them."

"He'll love that," my wife commented.

"I'd like to talk to you afterward, Gene," I said.

"Certainly."

Two husky Guards, Rory and Aisling, met us at the door—with an umbrella for herself. She kissed me and dashed for the unmarked car. The soft day was turning hard.

I went to the main entrance of the Towers, where a ring of Guards in rain slickers kept what must have been half the journalists in Ireland at bay. One of the Guards rushed up to protect me with an umbrella. I noted that Gene Keenan was lurking discreetly in the background.

Smart cop. No wonder he and Mike Casey were friends.

I was greeted with loud applause.

"Sure, aren't youse all so wet that there'd be no point in throwing any of you into the Grand Canal."

Laughter, somewhat uneasy.

"Are you and herself going home?"

"To America? Certainly. On schedule."

"You're not going to cancel the concert?"

"Why, woman, would we ever do that?"

"Because of the security risks!"

I glanced around at the ring of Guards. "Sure, don't I feel perfectly secure now?"

"You're talking like an Irishman, Dermot!"

"Doesn't it get contagious?"

Herself was right. I love sparring with the media.

"Are you going to sue the Gardai?"

"Wasn't I after telling Commissioner Keenan that I had this terrible pain in the back of me neck?"

Laughter from everyone.

"How's herself?"

"Hasn't she gone off in a Gardai car for her rehearsal? She's fine. Meself, I ache all over, but you're not interested in how I feel, are you now?"

"Did you see it on the telly this morning, Dermot?"

"We did!"

"And what did you think about it?"

"I was convinced that I really am Finn McCool! Or maybe Conan the Barbarian. And me woman is clearly Karela the Red Hawk."

"You talk like you do such things every day!"

"Usually only on weekends!"

"Were you scared, Dermot?"

"While the fight was going on I was too angry to be afraid. Afterward, wasn't I scared shiteless!"

"Do you think the battle of Canal House will help sales for herself's concert?"

"Isn't it sold out long since? . . . Now I have to get back to work. See you at the concert."

Everyone departed the scene in high good humor.

"Fair play to you," said Gene Keenan.

"They didn't even ask who the kidnappers might have been."

"They'll save that for us."

I thanked the protective ring of Guards, especially the woman who had held the umbrella.

Back in the lounge I filled up the teapot again and accepted a new plate of raisin rolls.

"Mind if I take one of those?" the Deputy Commissioner asked.

"Only one!"

In Nuala's absence I had to smear on the butter and the raspberry preserves myself.

Keenan poured the tea, having half-filled his cup with milk.

Filthy habit.

"Well," I said, exhaling expansively as an Irishman is supposed to do when beginning a serious conversation with another Irishman, "I want to talk about Kevin O'Higgins."

That blunt announcement was not the approved way for an Irishman to begin a discussion. It was so blunt that Gene Keenan was physically startled.

"What about him?"

"I've been reading DeVere White's book about him."

"Have you now?"

"It's a good book."

" 'Tis all of that."

We were circling around again in the approved Irish way.

"Who killed him?" I said, turning blunt.

"Not the men that DeVere White names in his afterword."

Now we were getting down to business. I figured I could trust him.

"Do you believe in the dark ones, Gene?"

"The dark ones?"

"Those who may have a touch of the fey about them?"

"Aye"—he rubbed his chin again—"not to say *believe* exactly. But I know there are such people. They frighten me."

"Isn't she one of them?" I said, nodding in the general direction of the Point Theater.

He shivered slightly. "One would never suspect it."

"Part of the package," I said briskly with a mental nod to George the Priest. "I like the package."

"Understandably."

We both sighed, as Irishmen are supposed to do.

"Can I tell you a confidential story or two?"

"Certainly. . . . Does it have implications for the attempt last night?"

"I don't know . . . probably not . . . but it might."

I told him first about the Camp Douglas conspiracy affair[1] with which we had dealt while we were courting. (I didn't mention that herself was the only one of us who knew we were courting.)

"And you're living in the lacemaker woman's house?" he asked me in astonishment.

"We are."

"Any, uh, manifestations?"

"I don't think so, though with Nuala Anne you can never be really sure. Letitia Walsh Murray would be a benign presence in any case."

"Aye," he said, not at all convinced.

Then I told him about the incident on the Aer Lingus Airbus coming over (though I left out the burning house), about my reading DeVere White's book, and about our trip to Booterstown the day before.

"You had quite a day," he said grimly.

"Now that you mention it."

[1] *Irish Lace*

"She said that O'Higgins talked to the men who shot him? That isn't in the book, is it?"

"No."

"I see. . . . And she knew that the killers were not the ones DeVere White names."

"Yes."

He was silent for a moment. "You understand, Dermot, that it was a long time ago?"

"Seventy years."

"No good purpose could be served by bringing it up again."

"I presume so."

"Irish politics are finally leaving the divisions of that terrible era behind."

"We have long memories."

He nodded grimly. "There's no obvious connection with what happened last night."

"None that I can imagine," I replied.

He rubbed his chin again. "Still it is strange, Dermot. Strange and scary."

"And there is the matter of the book about my fellow Chicagoan."

"Hazel . . . sad woman."

First time I'd ever heard that adjective used about Lady Lavery.

He shook his head as if trying to clear away a lot of unrelated facts, indeed facts that could not possibly be related. Could they?

"A long time ago," he continued, speaking slowly and softly, "Kevin's daughter, a Carmelite contemplative, began the custom of having a Mass on July 10 for the repose of her father's soul. She included all those who died during the War of Independence and the Civil War and subsequent terrorism. She invited the killers themselves and their families."

"Did she really!"

"I know you're thinking that could happen only in Ireland. You're right. . . . At first they didn't come. Mind you, they could have been arrested, though there wasn't any proof and their side was in power by then. But the O'Higgins family was not interested in revenge. Only forgiveness. Eventually some of the family members came. Then the next year the man who actually killed him. When they were very old, the other two came. Kevin's wife, who had remarried, embraced them both. . . . Forgive us our trespasses, Dermot, as we forgive those who trespass against us."

I sighed, very loudly.

"The masses continue. The only one still alive from the drama, besides the nun, is the boy who gave the signal and then ran for the priest, as your woman correctly reported. He's about eighty now. But the children and grandchildren on both sides show up every year. They say they'll never let the custom die.

"A lot of people know about it, including some journalists. But it's too sacred an event to violate. My wife and I represented the Gardai last year."

My throat felt very dry.

"As you can imagine, the Lady Lavery revelations were a great shock to everyone."

"Nuala Anne says that his wife was the only woman he ever really loved."

"I believe that, though many thought the letters were damning. . . . Still and all, we humans are weak, are we not?"

We both were silent. I filled his teacup again.

"Thank you," he muttered absently.

"They were with the Irregulars?"

"The killers? Oh, yes. A few years later Dev's party took over the country, but by then he had compromised with both the oath to the King and the division of Ireland."

"If he had done that earlier, there would not have been a Civil War and Collins and O'Higgins would have probably lived long lives."

Keenan nodded. "What might have been. . . . Dev had to face the same problem that Collins and O'Higgins faced: the IRA intransigents. There's always a new IRA, Dermot. There probably will be one after the present peace process wraps up. Dev outlawed them and repressed them as vigorously as had the Big Fella and Kevin. Between the early nineteen-thirties and the early nineteen-seventies there were frequent outbursts, not very important perhaps, but still people died. Then the Brits made their usual mistakes, and it's been going on up north for more than a quarter-century."

"So," I said, "you don't really want a replay of the O'Higgins murder?"

"Not if we can avoid it, not now anyway. Still, it's not a matter of overwhelming importance like it once might have been."

"Why these three killers?"

"Och, Dermot, that's an even more twisted story. But since you and I are playing sennachie this morning let me tell you the story of Major General Sir Hugh Tudor."

"Who was he?"

"He was sent to Ireland in 1920 to take over the Royal Irish Constabulary. The RIC had fallen apart. An Auxiliary Constabulary had replaced them, the Auxies, demobilized enlisted men from the army. Churchill told him to restore order, no matter what he had to do. He was also the commander of the Cadets, as they were called, unemployed officers who also had been demobbed. Many of them were war heroes, some of them with Victoria Crosses."

"You mean . . . ?"

"Yes, Dermot. Because of the uniforms of the Auxies, they were called the Black and Tans. You might want to glance over this history some of our lads put together."

"I will."

"Now," he said firmly, as though he were not convinced that I was fully literate.

— 11 —

LATER THAT day, after I had finished my conversation with the Commissioner, I scanned his historical record into my computer (with Paperport) and wrote an introductory note:

The first part of this report is easy, Nuala. I didn't have to write a word. It's a document compiled by historians of the Irish Guards that your man the Commissioner gave me. I've edited some of it out so as not to bore you, which heaven forbid.

Hugh Tudor was the youngest man ever to become a major general in the British Army till that time. He had fought in India during the war and then in France. His division held the line during Passchendaele and thus prevented an even worse bloodbath. The name, by the way, was authentic. In fact, he was christened Henry Hugh Tudor as if he were King Henry IX. He was a descendent of the winning family in the War of the Roses. Probably he had a better claim on the English throne than the bourgeois Germans who have occupied it the last couple of centuries. It doesn't seem that he cared much for that distinction.

He was the last Inspector General of the Royal Irish Constabulary. The son of a sub-dean of Exeter Cathedral, Henry Hugh Tudor was born at Newton Abbey, Devonshire, England, in 1870. On July 25, 1893, he became a lieutenant in the Royal Artillery. When the Boer War started in 1899 he was serving with M Battery Royal Field Artillery at Woolwich. He was involved in the advance on Kimberley and was wounded at Magersfontein. While recovering in hospital, he received a message in December 1899 from Winston Spencer Churchill (who was then a war correspondent) wishing him a quick recovery and "all the luck of war." Churchill later sent him autographed first edition copies of each book that he wrote. Tudor spent the remainder of the War serving on the Staff and by the end of the War he had reached the rank of Captain.

He married his wife, Eve Edwards, in 1908. She was eighteen years old at the time, an exquisitely lovely young woman to judge by her pictures, and twenty years younger than Tudor. Like him she was the child of an impecunious Anglican clergyman. They had three children in the next twelve years, two daughters and a son.

It's hard to get a fix on what kind of a man he was. He seems to have been a typical British officer, spit and polish, ramrod stiff, devilishly handsome. He must have been more than that, however. He was brave but not foolishly so and very bright. Moreover, he made many friends, even among his own troops, and when he fled into exile it was to the land of one regiment of his division. On the basis of his service in Ireland, he was not overly troubled by conscience. Perhaps like many men who had fought in the trenches, the Great War twisted him.

During that war, he served in both Egypt and India, but it was as commanding officer of the Ninth Scottish Division in France that he became renowned as a fine military leader. Tudor developed the creeping barrage and the box barrage to isolate fields of battle. The box barrage was smoke and heavy artillery bombardment on both sides and in front of the attacking area to isolate, thus preventing enfilade fire and reinforcements. The creeping and box barrages were used everywhere in the later stages of the war. He also became renowned in the British War Office for his use of smoke screens to cloak his troop movements, and in the process saved the lives of thousands of his men. In March of 1917 when there were massive Allied retreats throughout the western front, Tudor's men stood fast. Churchill said that "Tudor was like an iron peg in the frozen ground."

Following the executions of the leaders of the 1916 Easter Rising and the 1918 threat of conscription there was widespread civil unrest and resistance (both armed and passive) to British rule in Ireland. The Sinn Fein MPs refused to go to Westminster and set up their own parliament and government. The Irish Volunteers were waging an intensive guerrilla war against the British establishment which many claim was sparked off by the ambush of two RIC officers at Soloheadbeg, Co. Tipperary, on January 21, 1919.

The Royal Irish Constabulary, which had earned the title of "Royal" from Queen Victoria for their part in quashing the Fenian Rising of 1867, were unable to contain the latest insurrection. Policemen (many of whom were Irish-born Catholics) were being killed and injured either in their barracks or while on patrol. One source reports that by the end of May 1920, 351 evacuated barracks were destroyed, 105 damaged, 15 occupied barracks were destroyed and 25 damaged, 19 Coastguard stations and lighthouses were raided for explosives and signaling equipment, 66 policemen and 5 soldiers were killed with 79 policemen and 2 soldiers wounded.

De Valera and other members of the Sinn Fein government urged the shunning of the RIC and their families by their neighbors and friends and that the RIC should be treated as agents of a foreign power. As a result of the violence and shunning there were widespread resignations from the RIC.

Lloyd George's Westminster Government created a temporary police force to supplement and assist the RIC in their duties in the alarming situation which was developing in Ireland. The members of the new force were appointed as temporary constables. The Auxiliaries, as they were later called, were recruited from England, Scotland and Wales, with possibly a third of the new recruits from Ireland. They were rank and file World War One enlisted veterans who were then unemployed. They were employed on a contract basis and arrived in Ireland in March 1920.

It was due to a shortage of the dark bottle green RIC uniforms that the "Auxies" were fitted out in a uniform which was half black (the dark bottle green police) and half khaki (army). Hence the name "Black and Tans."

A second temporary police force was created on July 27, 1920. This time the recruits were unemployed World War One veterans who had been officers during the war. They were given the rank of Cadets. They wore either the RIC uniform or army officers' uniforms with dark Glengarry caps. Together these new forces became known as "Tudor's Toughs" after their commanding officer. Sometimes he was called "Bloody Tudor."

In May 1920, at the recommendation of Churchill, who admired him enormously, the government appointed Tudor as the Inspector General of Ireland, the police advisor to the Viceroy and commanding officer of both the Royal Irish Constabulary (RIC) and the Dublin Metropolitan Police (DMP). It was widely believed that he was ordered to bring order back to Ireland by whatever means necessary, no matter how ruthless.

Like the German soldiers of World War One who in-

vaded Belgium, Tudor's troops were not trained in guerrilla warfare. Every civilian was a potential sniper and
reprisals were widespread.

The IRA's Flying Columns were active in nearly every
part of the country. Perhaps it was due to the frustration
that they encountered in trying to capture and fight the
hidden enemy that they ended up as looters, arsonists and
murderers. Both sides engaged in bloody reprisals, the
most notable was perhaps "Bloody Sunday," November
1920. After 11 English intelligence agents were assassi-
nated, the Black and Tans fired upon unarmed spectators
and players who were playing Gaelic football.

Many towns and villages were burned and looted by
Tudor's men. Two famous incidents which later involved
Tudor occurred on February 9, 1921. On that date a
contingent of Auxiliaries went on the rampage in Trim,
County Meath, while in County Dublin near Drumcondra
two young Irish prisoners were shot dead in a field by an
Auxiliary commander named King. General Crozier went
to investigate the Trim incident and dismissed 21 Auxiliary cadets and held 5 more to be tried for their part in
the raid (two of whom later broke out and robbed a publican). He returned to investigate the Drumcondra shoot-
ings but later claimed the evidence was rigged. His
power to dismiss Auxiliaries was taken away by Tudor in
November 1920. Five of the Trim Cadets were later con-
victed and nineteen reinstated. Crozier resigned on February 25, 1921, and the London press filled with accounts
of Tudor's treatment of him and Black and Tans atrocities.
Later, Mrs. Asquith, wife of the former British Prime Minister, commented to Crozier: "They tell me that you are
as much a murderer as any of them, only you like things
done in an orderly manner, and at Trim they were dis-
orderly."

Peace eventually came with the Truce of July 1921 and
Tudor's Royal Irish Constabulary was disbanded follow-

ing the Anglo-Irish Treaty in 1922 and a new police force, ("The Civic Guard" later renamed the "Garda Siochana"), was created by the Irish Government. Many of the barracks once occupied by the RIC were handed over to the new police force. Dublin Castle was formerly handed over on August 17, 1922, when Commissioner Michael Staines led his new police force through the castle gates. The Dublin Metropolitan Police (the last of Tudor's police forces) was finally amalgamated into the Garda Siochana in 1925.

In 1922, Tudor like many other British veterans of the Anglo-Irish War (and the remnants of the Black and Tans) went to Palestine, where he was appointed General Officer Commanding and Inspector General of Police and Prisons. Three years later, at the age of 55, Tudor, who had been the youngest Major General to ever attain that rank in the British Army, retired. He emigrated to Newfoundland and began working for Ryan & Company, a fish merchant in Bonavista. He later moved to St. John's and worked for George M. Barr's fishing industry and resided with Barr's family.

His name rarely appears in any Irish history of those troubled times. He was completely forgotten in Ireland, but clearly remembered in England. In 1938, Tudor was invited to a royal reception held in honour of King George VI's visit to Newfoundland. According to Paul O'Neill in his book, Tudor attended, hoping that his Irish service would be unknown to the monarch, but when his name was announced, the King looked up and said in a loud voice, "Are you the man who commanded in Ireland?"

There is no information available which would explain why the Irish forgot him and the English did not.

He grew to love his adopted homeland and her people and became renowned for his equestrian skill. Illness and failing sight forced him to live his final years as a recluse.

Tudor's wife remained in London and was in Newfoundland only briefly. So he remained in his self-imposed exile without his wife, two daughters and son until his death in the Veterans Pavilion of the General Hospital, St. John's, on September 25, 1965, at the age of 95.

He was given a full military funeral with the Royal Newfoundland Regiment (which was a component of the Ninth Scottish Division that he'd commanded during World War One) acting as his pall-bearers. His wife, two daughters, and son did not attend the funeral, but instead were represented at the funeral by J. D. O'Driscoll, one of his friends and former army colleagues.

After I had glanced over the first part of the document I looked up at Keenan.

"Interesting," I said cautiously

"You wonder why the Deputy Commissioner of the Gardai would know so much about Tudor?"

"I figure you're a history buff."

"That I am, but there's more to it. . . . You've noticed, I trust, that many English officers, the English newspapers, and some members of the English upper class like Lady Asquith disapproved of the tactics of Tudor's toughs?"

"More sensitive than I would have expected."

"Perhaps . . . but he also gained a reputation as a monster who was an embarrassment to England. Given their past history in this country, that must have meant that he was a pretty horrible person, did it not?"

"I suppose so."

"Moreover, by the time he retired in Palestine the IRA was no longer settling scores against English officers. So why go into exile in such an inhospitable place as Newfoundland—which, by the way, was independent of Canada till 1949? Also, why was he never promoted to Lieutenant General? Certainly his distinguished service merited such a rank, and a little brutality in Ireland never prevented promotion of a decorated British officer. Why was he so eager to keep his service in Ireland a secret? Why was he so upset by King George's unfortunate comment? What did King George know besides the story of the Black and Tans? Why did his wife and family refuse to join him in Newfoundland? Why didn't they come for his funeral? Granted that Eve was in her seventies in 1965, the children were certainly young enough to travel across the Atlantic and there was an international airport at St. John's."

"Good questions. . . . Maybe the family didn't like the Newfoundland weather."

"Not enough to break up a family in that social class at that time."

In the absence of herself, I was Holmes again, not Watson.

"Probably he was in disgrace, pretty serious disgrace at that, if it affected even his family. He chose Newfoundland because there were men who had served under him during the war and liked and respected him. So his disgrace had to come in Ireland. Something happened there, something more than just shooting a couple of rebels, which separated the first half of his life from the second half. In Newfoundland he was able to block out what had happened in Ireland."

"Bravo!" The Commissioner poured me another cup of tea and helped himself to one of the two remaining raisin rolls. "For many years he had a discreet and apparently affectionate liason with a woman there, a widow of an officer in the Royal Newfoundland Constabulary, most of whose members had been members of the RIC and perhaps protected him from possible IRA gunmen."

"And his wife?"

"She apparently formed a relationship with a retired officer whose own wife was hopelessly insane."

I paused to consider the data, again wishing that my wife, Ms. Holmes, were present.

"Well," I began, "I would have to assume that he became involved with a woman in Ireland and that involvement somehow ended tragically in some way because of the Tans."

He pondered me with half-closed eyelids. "Should you ever want a job with the Gardai, Dermot, me lad, I think we could get you on board as a Chief Superintendent."

"I'm a fiction writer, not a detective, though it may come to the same thing. . . . So I have to assume that the woman was someone very important, a member of the British elite? Hazel?"

He smiled grimly. "No, not Hazel. Her tastes ran to Irish revolutionaries and English politicians. Someone much more important."

"And this is somehow linked to the death of Kevin O'Higgins?"

"Yes indeed. Indirectly perhaps but ineluctably. Otherwise I wouldn't be bothering you with this obscure corner of early twentieth-century Irish history."

"And with the attempted kidnapping last night?"

He rubbed his jaw again. "Candidly, I don't see how it could, but I'm not ruling out any possibility. . . . May I show you another document?"

"Please do," I said, quite unnecessarily.

"It was written by another man as a confidential memo for me—one of the brightest and most literate men in the force. I wouldn't be surprised that someday he ended up in your trade, Dermot."

"I don't have a trade," I said. "I'm a retired commodity broker."

"I meant sennachie."

"Oh," I said as I began to read the second Garda's analysis.

Later I scanned that document into my computer and added it to my first report to herself.

Tudor was present in Listowel when the whole barracks of RIC men refused to take orders from their Inspector General. The confrontation ended peacefully enough. Tudor did not play a major role in the mutiny, at least according to the story which appeared in the papers. He always seemed to be able to lurk in the background. His name became generally known only when his colleague General Crozier denounced him in London. Moreover, he shook hands with the police who had mutinied. He had arrived in Ireland only a couple of weeks before. This was the first hint of what he might be fighting. The police force he was commanding was falling apart. He needed new police, first the Tans and then the Cadets, who were worse even than the Tans. The country, he must have perceived, was on the edge of anarchy. He did not learn the obvious lesson of the encounter at Listowel: if the IRA was strong enough to cause the police in that town to mutiny, they would not be suppressed by counter-terror—or anything else.

The events at Listowel and Tudor's restrained reaction are on the public record if not well known. What follows is not public knowledge and is based in part on stories that still circulate in the rural country west of Limerick Town. The author of this document urges that the attempt to reconstruct the story be read with caution.

Apparently two nights later something happened that changed Tudor's mind completely and turned him into a killer. It also sent him down the path which would make him a lonely horseman riding the stony hills of Newfoundland.

He motored north from Listowel towards the Shannon Estuary. His plan was to visit Lady Augusta Downs, the widow of Colonel Sir Arthur Downs V.C., a young officer on his staff who had died when the Ninth had held the line at Cambrai. Maybe he had come to Listowel as a pretext to visit her. More likely, he felt he had to face down the mutineers. When he discovered that Castle Garry was only twenty miles away from Listowel, he decided that it would be appropriate to make a call on her even though it was late and a fierce storm was blowing in off the Atlantic. He had greatly admired Down's courage and recommended him for his Victoria Cross. It does not appear that he had ever met Lady Augusta, though probably he had seen her picture. Since he was an upright British officer and Lady Augusta was nobility, he probably had more or less honorable intentions. Or told himself that.

Lady Downs was a McGarry, the last of a great Munster landowning family which had converted to the Church of Ireland during penal times, as many others had, so as not to lose their land. Their Big House, Castle Garry, a late-eighteenth-century manor, was out on the Shannon Estuary south of Limerick. The family, which by intermarriage and education had become more Anglo-Irish than Irish, was nonetheless popular with their tenants who did not hold a religious change two hundred years old against them. Sir Arthur was petty English nobility from Cornwall, a likeable young man, by all accounts, who endeared himself to the local Irish by learning how to play Irish football. When they brought his body home from Flanders, the Catholics in the area mourned as much as the few Protestants. The parish priest, rather in violation of the Church's rules at the time, said a Mass for the repose of his soul. Naturally, Lady Downs attended in the front row. All in all, the situation in the McGarry lands was quiet, peaceful. The lads were not active that far out in West Limerick. There was no animosity between the Land Lady and her people. Castle Garry was a long way off everyone's beaten path.

One can imagine what was on the mind of Major General Henry Hugh Tudor as his car, followed by a lorry of soldiers, picked its way down a muddy country road in the rain and the fading light of a long spring day.

It is fair to assume that he did not want to be in Ireland. At that time no English general in his right mind would want to risk his career in that sinkhole. Even less did he want to fight a guerrilla war for which he had no experience. Why had he accepted the assignment? Perhaps because his good friend Winston asked him to. Perhaps because, like many officers who had fought in the trenches, war was the only reality in which he felt comfortable. Perhaps because he wanted to get away from a marriage that had turned unhappy. That his wife did not stand by him later suggests that relationship was probably in trouble even in 1920, as were so many of the other marriages of men returning from the war.

Remember that he had shaken hands with each of the mutinous constables back in Listowel, a very soldierly thing to do by British standards. He was still at that moment a decent man who could respect his enemies.

When his little convoy turned east at Trabert—where the car ferry across the Shannon is now—he had the Estuary on his left as they plowed down the dirt road. They left the rain behind for a few moments and saw the waves seething on the Estuary in the lightning which cut across the sky. I know that because I looked up the Limerick weather for that night.

When they finally turned up the road through the park to Castle Garry, he saw a scene which would change his life forever. The outbuildings around the manor house were on fire. The fire had spread to one wing of the castle itself. The sea was roaring behind the castle, its huge waves illumined by the flames. A mob was smashing windows and throwing furniture out of the house. Several men, servants presumably, were lying dead on the ground. Lady Augusta, in her nightdress, was tied to a tree. Women were pelting her with mud.

Something must have snapped inside of General Tudor. He could have subdued the rabble, led by a handful of rag-tag Irish volunteers—mostly local thugs—by a few shots over their heads. However, the young woman was the wife of an English officer, a hero, and a friend of Tudor's. The men and women who were destroying her home and threatening her life were less than human. He ordered his men to fire into the crowd.

Six men died, three of the rebels, who were from below in Kerry, and three local youths, all of whom it would later develop had far too much of the creature taken. The rest of the crowd fled into the night and the oncoming rain storm. His soldiers rounded up five prisoners, all of them men. Tudor gave the order for their summary execution.

It is not unreasonable to assume that Tudor and Lady Augusta became lovers that night as the storm which had put out the fires raged above them in the battered manor house. Surely they were lovers soon after.

Garrytown, the local village, was a long way from Dublin and a long psychological distance from Limerick. A report was issued that the British Army had won a major pitched battle in West Limerick, a victory which would mark the beginning of the end for the IRA. A British Army patrol had come upon an IRA mob assaulting Castle Garry. The soldiers had driven off the mob and saved the castle. Three servants at the castle had been killed, as had ten armed IRA men. None of the local people disputed this account, not very loudly at any rate. The McGarrys were, as I have said, a popular family, indeed one which had for many years been sympathetic to Irish freedom. The Garrytown version was that a group of criminals from

Kerry had stirred up trouble in a local pub, accusing the local men of being cowards.

"Good enough for the lot of them," Garrytown said with something like relief. Arson and murder, assassination and reprisals, were now commonplace in the Irish countryside. Later on, everyone had good reason to want to forget the horror.

Somehow a story developed about his love affair with Lady Augusta in which he was depicted as a rapist. The events at the end are obscure. Just before Dev and Lloyd George agreed on a cease-fire in the autumn of 1921, an IRA flying squad from Kerry returned to Garrytown looking for revenge. They encountered a detachment of Cadets at Castle Garry, protecting Tudor's whore as they claimed.

We will probably never know what happened that night. According to the folk story, which may not be accurate in all its details, the castle was set afire again, the Cadets, who knew that the lads were coming, had no trouble routing them. Somehow, during the battle Lady Augusta was shot and killed, perhaps by accident, perhaps not. Her charred body was found in the ruins several days later, the very day, in fact, that the truce was announced. According to legend, Hugh Tudor had ordered her death. There never was any proof, but by that time the English were willing to believe anything about him.

It was two Kerrymen who tried to kill him in Palestine in 1925. Depending on who you believe, the British government informed him that they could no longer guarantee his safety. So he left the army and went to Newfoundland, where some of his old mates from the Royal Irish Constabulary would protect him. It's hard to believe that the British Army really forced him out, whatever his reputation. Churchill was out of power and would remain out of power till the next War, but he certainly had enough influence to protect Tudor. Perhaps he wanted to escape to a place where he could forget and be forgotten. The attempt on his life in Palestine may not have been an official IRA hit but a personal grudge. Anyway, for forty years he was a forgotten man—by everyone, family, old friends, and old enemies. Clearly he liked it that way.

—12—

"QUITE A story," I said as I gave the document to the Commissioner. "Your man indeed has the skills of a storyteller, though I suspect that he is a woman."

Commissioner Keenan sighed. "We can't hide much from you, can we, Dermot? . . . Keep the document. Show it to herself if you want."

"As if I had any choice."

He laughed and then waved his hand as if the whole story were a bit of a bore.

"A little mystery from the backwater of Irish history, hardly worth repeating, eh, Dermot? But tragedies like that have been part of Irish life for centuries. That they are so numerous does not mean that they were not painful and often deadly for the poor people who were involved."

I sighed.

"Maybe there won't be any more of them," he continued. "Maybe we won't need a Special Branch in the new Ireland."

"How does Kevin O'Higgins fit into this story?"

"The Kerry Brigade of the Irregulars, as the Free State called the IRA, wasn't much good at fighting. They concentrated on burning down houses and shooting people in the back. The Free State Army swept them away without so much as a single pitched battle. They were for the most part a group of young louts who used the ideals of the republic, one and indivisible, as a pretext for criminal burning, killing, blackmail, and loud pub talk. When Kevin took over after Collins's death, he knew that he had to stamp out such groups all over Ireland if anarchy wasn't to prevent Ireland from becoming a democracy. Stamp them out he did. In a sense he succeeded where Tudor had failed. He argued that Ireland would be a better place without the Kerry Brigade. The Free State soldiers swept up the lot of them, and then there was no more Kerry Brigade, except for the three men who shot Kevin. That was the end of it for them, too. Kevin's forgiveness overwhelmed them."

"They forgot about Hugh Tudor?"

"Or figured he wasn't worth hunting down. Perhaps if he had returned to England they might have gone after him."

"Not much of a connection between Tudor and O'Higgins."

"Except that the executions of the remnant Kerry Brigade, five men, by the Free State Army were in front of the ruins of Castle Garry. Like someone was sending a message."

"And the message was?" I asked.

"That's what we don't know . . . though if Hugh Tudor had not ambushed the ambushers that night in 1921 the Kerry Brigade might have simply faded away. It was kept alive by its own need for revenge."

Back in our room after I had scanned the two police documents into my HP Omnibook, I wondered if I had learned anything that was pertinent to Nuala's waking dreams. I didn't know what to make of the story of Hugh Tudor, Augusta Downs, and Kevin O'Higgins. I didn't see how there could be any connection between the first two and the third. Tudor was gone from Ireland and Augusta was dead by the time Higgins replaced Michael Collins as the strongman of the Free State Government. Both Tudor and O'Higgins were targets of Kerry revenge. That was the only link between them, and it seemed thin. How could it have anything to do with Nuala's experiences on the plane or at Booterstown? Or with the attempted kidnapping yesterday?

It made no sense, not at all, at all.

Why would the Deputy Commissioner of the Garda Siochana waste much of his morning telling me that tale, other than for the sheer love of spinning a yarn? Indeed, a couple of mostly unrelated yarns?

Perhaps because he didn't like the obscurities in his story and thought that we might be able to clarify a few of them.

And maybe find a connection between them and the clumsy attempt to kidnap us?

Maybe.

It struck me that none of it was any of our business. After the concert we should fly out to Galway to see Nuala's parents, cancel our visit to Glenstal Abbey till another day, and catch the first plane from Shannon to Chicago.

Except who was the girl that, in Nuala's interlude on the airplane, did not start the fire?

I glanced at my watch. She should be home from her rehearsal soon.

Then the Adversary intruded into my life again.

ISN'T IT ABOUT TIME, BOYO, THAT YOU ADMIT THAT YOU'RE NOT THE GREAT BIG MACHO LOVER THAT YOU PRETEND YOU ARE?

"What do you mean by that?"

WHEN IT COMES TO PASSION, YOU'RE ABOUT AS DYNAMIC AS A FIRECRACKER.

"You gotta be kidding!"

ALL RIGHT, YOU SCREW THE GIRL WHENEVER YOU WANT AND SHE DOESN'T SEEM TO MIND. . . .

"I make love with her."

CALL IT WHAT YOU WANT . . . YOU FIGURE THAT BE-CAUSE YOU'VE READ THE BOOKS ABOUT WHAT TURNS WOMEN ON AND BECAUSE YOU'RE GENTLE AND CONSIDER-ATE WITH HER YOU ARE THEREFORE A SKILLED LOVER. THAT'S A LOT OF BULLSHIT AND YOU KNOW IT.

"I know no such thing!"

THEN HOW COME I KNOW IT? I'M A PART OF YOU, EVEN IF YOU LIKE TO PRETEND THAT I'M AN OUTSIDE VOICE.

"I never claimed to be an experienced lover!"

DAMN GOOD THING!

"Go away! Don't bother me!"

He ignored my orders.

LOOK, YOU EXPERIENCE SEXUAL RELEASE WITH HER AND SHE'S PLEASED ABOUT THAT BECAUSE SHE ADORES YOU. BUT YOU CONTROL THE WHOLE EXERCISE. IT'S A NICE, NEAT LITTLE EXCHANGE WITHOUT ANY RISK AND WITHOUT MUCH PASSION.

"I don't agree!"

LOVE IS ABOUT ABANDONMENT, he went on implaca-bly. *REAL PASSION THROWS ASIDE NOT ONLY CLOTHES BUT INHIBITIONS. NO WAY DO YOU DO THAT. YOU PRETEND THAT YOU'RE UNINHIBITED, BUT YOU'RE NOTHING BUT A BLAND COCKTAIL OF INHIBITIONS.*

"You want me to be violent."

I WANT YOU TO BE PASSIONATE.

"What's that mean?"

WELL, LET'S TRY, FOR STARTERS, OUT OF YOUR MIND WITH DESIRE.

"I don't want to hurt her!"

NO WAY YOU'RE GOING TO DO THAT!

"I don't believe in violent lovemaking!"

THE WAY GOD DESIGNED YOU HUMANS, IS THERE ANY

OTHER KIND? ANYWAY, LET'S NOT ARGUE ABOUT WORDS. CALL IT VEHEMENT, IF YOU WANT. THE POINT IS, DERMOT MICHAEL COYNE, THAT YOU ARE AN INNATELY CAUTIOUS MAN. YOU DON'T LIKE TAKING CHANCES. YOU DON'T WANT TO TAKE CHANCES WITH THAT ONE. YOU ARE AFRAID OF THE ENERGIES YOU MIGHT UNLEASH IN HER. MAYBE SHE'LL BE TOO MUCH FOR YOU, HUH?

"No way! Besides, I wasn't cautious last night, was I?"

PROVES MY POINT. ONLY WHEN SOME OUTSIDE FORCE TURNS YOU ON DO YOU BECOME PASSIONATE. WHY DON'T YOU GIVE THE GIRL A CHANCE?

"You want me to act like a wild man?"

PARDON ME FOR LAUGHING! DERMOT COYNE A WILDLY PASSIONATE LOVER? YOU GOTTA BE KIDDING!

"I could be if I wanted to."

YOU'RE AFRAID TO TRY, AFRAID THAT SHE MIGHT REACT THE SAME WAY.

"I'm not afraid of her!"

THE HELL YOU'RE NOT!

I turned him off.

But he had scared me. Usually the Adversary appealed to my dark side. He had just done that again. But maybe he was right. Maybe . . .

I tried to stop thinking about it.

Still the fantasy of a wild "ride" with herself in which we both abandoned our inhibitions was not without appeal.

And what would she really be like if I unleashed all her womanly passions?

The possibilities were delightful.

And scary?

Yeah, well, I'd concede that to the Adversary.

With considerable effort, I turned my attention back to the story of Henry Hugh Tudor.

Where had I heard about McGarry before?

Recently.

Was that one of the places we were supposed to stay? Perhaps when we visited Glenstal Abbey?

Where had the woman put our reservations? I was not to be trusted with them because I might lose them—a not completely unreasonable assumption.

I rummaged around the room hunting for them. Drat! Why did she have to be so neat!

Then reason took over. She would put them in the small shoulder bag she carried. Where was it?

Undoubtedly hanging in the closet!

Brilliant, Holmes!

I opened the bag and there, sure enough, on the very top were our tickets and reservations.

We were scheduled to stay three nights at a certain Castlegarry, Garrytown, County Limerick!

Yikes!

I reordered the reservations, put them back in the bag, zipped it up, and hung it on the closet hook.

This was not a good idea at all, at all. If I told her about Commissioner Keenan's story, she would insist that we had to stay there. If I didn't tell her, she would want to know why I wanted to cancel—and be greatly displeased that I had hidden evidence. Watson had to tell the truth to Holmes.

I remembered a book about Irish castles converted to hotels I had seen in the gift shop of the hotel. I raced down to the lobby, searched for the book, and finally found it behind an Irish financial news magazine. There was indeed an entry for Castlegarry (sic).

Castlegarry, Garrytown, County Limerick

This spacious and comfortable late-eighteenth-century manor house is one of the finest castle hotels in the west of Ireland. Located on a cliff over the Shannon Estuary and complete with an

eighteen-hole golf course, Castlegarry is a warm, friendly house with eight expansive guest suites and one honeymoon suite directly facing the estuary. The chef is reputed to be the best in the west of Ireland and Tonia and Paddy MacGarry, the hosts, are delightful conversationalists. No one will regret resting a few days in this lovely and historic setting.

Historic setting indeed. At least two firefights and a dozen or so murders. Perhaps lots of ghosts—Irregulars, Black and Tans, Anglo-Irish gentry, maybe even Henry IX. Haunted castles were popular with tourists. Why weren't such assets listed for Castlegarry? Perhaps Tonia and Paddy wanted to stress the warmth and the cooking and the golf course. Perhaps the ghosts were a little too scary.

I was willing to bet that the proprietors were from the Catholic side of the clan, recusants of one sort or another. Hence *Mac* had replaced *Mc*. Time does sort things out, doesn't it?

I walked slowly back to our room. The mist outside the windows was "soft" again. The only thing I could do was level with Nuala Anne about the castle. We would doubtless stay in the honeymoon suite, which was probably the master bedroom where Hugh Tudor and Augusta Downs consummated their illicit love.

Great fun.

Maybe we could spend a lot of time on the golf course. If it didn't rain.

What did they call it? Black and Tan Links?

In our room I plugged in our portable Brother printer and began the slow process of printing out the first chapter of my report.

Then the door flew open and a jean-clad comet

burst into the room, leaving behind a comet trail of energy.

"Och, Dermot Michael, isn't it grand altogether?" she shouted as she embraced me and spun me around with exuberant delight.

" 'Tis!" I said weakly.

"Sure, didn't I forget that you were all banged up from last night! . . . I'm terrible sorry, Dermot love. Aren't I the most selfish woman in all the world?"

She backed off, contrite and humiliated.

"Woman, you are not! Don't your arms around me cure all me ills?"

She giggled. "Aren't you beginning to talk like me . . . but, Dermot, don't I have wonderful news!"

The thundering herd returned.

"And what is the wonderful news?"

"The RTE is going to broadcast the whole concert live! Me ma and me da will be able to see the whole thing!"

They'd be in the front row at the Point, but that was still a secret.

"Brilliant."

"And look what Brown and Williamson sent me to make up for the dress which was ruined last night!"

She pulled a black-on-gold garment out of a B and W bag that was distinguished, it seemed to me, by the limited amount of fabric invested in it.

She held it front of her for my inspection.

"Isn't it wonderful altogether!"

"A nightgown?"

She stamped a foot impatiently. " 'Tis not. Isn't it a slip dress!"

I knew that. "You mean you wear it outside the bed-room!"

She knew I was kidding, but she couldn't resist the argument. "OF COURSE, I do. Isn't it lined? I don't have to wear anything under it but a pantie!"

"You're not going to wear that at the concert, are you?"

"Och, Dermot, you're a desperate man! You know I'm going to wear me modest white suit and a green scarf, just like a respectable upper-middle-class Dublin housewife would wear to Mass on Sunday. This is for tonight."

"I can hardly wait."

She kissed me again, being careful not to touch my bruises and aches.

"And didn't everyone at the rehearsal say that you were a terrible fierce man the way you protected me? They all wondered if you'd been badly hurt? And didn't I tell them that you were in perfect physical condition and there was no need to worry about you?"

"And they told you what a lucky woman you were to have such a stalwart husband?"

"Och, that wasn't their exact words, but I won't tell you, because it will go to your head."

She kissed me again.

GO AFTER HER, the Adversary suggested.

I ignored him.

"I've been working on my report," I said, pointing at the pages grinding out of the printer.

She looked at it uneasily. "Maybe I shouldn't look at it till after the concert?"

"I agree. I have a lot more work to do."

"Grand! Shouldn't we have a swim and a bite of lunch now?" She began to cast her clothes aside.

"A big bite for me."

"Naturally."

Now quite naked, she reached for her swimsuit.

GO FOR IT!

I removed the suit from her hands and crushed her

in my arms. Thereupon followed the most passionate embrace I have ever attempted.

"Och, Dermot," she moaned weakly, terrified by the ferocity of my assault.

"You object?" I said, pausing in my attack for a moment.

"You scare me."

"That upsets you."

"No," she said. "Not really."

"Good!" I said, reassuming my assault. The Daemon began to emerge, confident, competent, determined.

Was it part of passion that you scare your lover with the ferocity of your desire?

I decided that it was but then lost my nerve.

"Swim, then lunch, then love," I suggested.

"Fine." She sagged against me.

ASSHOLE, sneered the Adversary.

— 13 —

WASN'T I petrified altogether? I don't know what got into me man. It was like last night when he threw them eejits into the Grand Canal. Is that what a man is like when he's really passionate, like he wants to absorb everything you are? I felt like he had stripped off all me clothes—though I had done that meself—and all me fears and all me defenses and all me inhibitions and that all that was left was meself. He adored me, every inch of me. He wanted me with ferocious hunger, all of me; he couldn't do without me; he HAD to have me.

He's never been that way before.

It was frightening, but wonderful. I wouldn't resist, couldn't resist, didn't want to resist. I didn't know what would have happened, but I wanted to find out.

Then he stopped. Why?

Because he knew that I would be no good at that sort of thing?

I would like to have had a chance to see if I could respond to such fierce need.

Is that wrong to think? Would I have been only a sex object?

I don't know. I don't think so, but I don't know.

Anyway, after we swam and ate lunch and came back here to the room, we did make love. Very gentle, very nice, very *reassuring. But it was nothing like what had been about to happen when he stopped.*

Maybe I should have responded with the same hunger. I almost did. He didn't give me quite enough time. If he does it again, won't I claw at his clothes and be just as fierce as he was?

Will I?

Maybe.

Wouldn't that be wrong?

I know if You talked back at me You would tell me that it is a ridiculous question.

The next time I talk to me ma, I'll have to ask her whether men really act that way sometimes and what a woman should do. Maybe I'll even ask her whether a woman can initiate such assaults.

That would be, I think, kind of fun.

I can just imagine the circumlocutions of talking to Ma about such matters.

Will there be a next time like this morning?

I hope so.

— 14 —

 "THE THING is," my wife informed me, "that you gotta see the bridge behind the bridge, the real bridge that's not hidden by your Irish mists."

"Ah," I replied. She pronounced *thing* as though it had no *h,* as was the local custom.

In fact, the mists had disappeared. It was another pleasant spring evening, with the delicate touch of a breeze, a faint sniff of sea air mixed with my woman's alluring perfume, and soft sounds of night in the distance, a romantic evening for young lovers, if that is what we were—I personally felt very old.

We were eating supper at an outdoor table in front of the Dropping Well restaurant beneath the Miltown Bridge over the Dodder River. Other couples nodded and smiled as they passed our table but did not harass us. Many of the Irish are delicate about respecting privacy. They would even leave Michael Jordan alone if he were eating supper on a warm evening in Dublin.

The Dodder wanders aimlessly through the south and east sides of Dublin before finding the Liffey at Ring's End, shortly before Anna Livia, following your man's injunction to "river run," plunges into the Irish Sea. It is the first of the seven rivers that your man (same man, different book) crosses during these twenty-four hours in 1902.

The bridge was illumined by floodlights and somehow represented much of Dublin history, a lovely relic to a troubled past. Both the Bellefield campus of University College Dublin (or the National University of Ireland, Dublin, as it now must be called) and the National College of Industrial Relations (Jesuit in origin, but, as Prester George says, there's nothing necessarily wrong with that) were but a few hundred yards away. However, the restaurant was an old building that had been a morgue during the famine times.

"Didn't the bodies float down the river?" my wife had informed me. "They pulled them out and gave them a decent burial. Nothing more they could do, was there?"

This was my fey bride, one of the dark ones who could sense a psychic vibration a mile away, calmly and with considerable gusto, devouring a large helping of Scallops Mornay and a bottle of white Rhône, as she talked about the famine years in the country just outside Dublin. I, on the other hand, did not feel much like eating.

"No memories lingering here, Nuala Anne?"

She had frowned as through that were a ridiculous question. "Why should there be, Dermot Michael? Aren't all those poor folks safe in Heaven?"

So too were the Confederate soldiers whose bodies had once been buried in Lincoln Park in Chicago, some of whom had been washed out into Lake Michigan. But Nuala had been aware of them.[1]

I thought it best not to raise the issue.

We had paused at the slender, elegant memorial on the bank of the river to the Choctaw Indians who had sent food to Ireland during the famine.

[1] *Irish Lace*

"We Irish never forget our friends," she had said. "Didn't them poor Indians do more for us than the bloody Brits?"

"Or your enemies?"

"Och, sure, aren't we nice to all the English people who come here to visit us?"

"You are indeed."

"And ourselves now living better than they do!" she had said with a superior grin. "Though not as good as us Yanks."

The net of security that both the Guards and Mike Casey had spun around us was invisible. However, I thought I saw at the far side of the little outdoor plaza in front of the restaurant the tall, elegant figure of Gene Keenan. He seemed to be with a blond woman who at a distance was equally tall and elegant.

My wife then had explained to me that England didn't cause the potato famine directly. The Brits were not responsible for the blight that had destroyed the potato crops. However, they were indirectly responsible because they had reduced Ireland to such poverty through hundreds of years of oppression that millions of people were dependent for their survival on marginal subsistence farming.

Nuala Anne the Economist.

I would have to learn about this extraordinary woman.

Then we began to discuss bridges.

"You see, Dermot Michael," she said, "the bridge up there is real enough. We Celts are not your Platonists."

"I'm glad to hear that."

"The bridge is really up there. In fact, it's really there even when Irish mists hide it, isn't it now?"

"I take your word for it."

"No!" She pounded (gently) on the table. "You know 'tis there because you've seen it."

She was, by the way, wearing the slip dress she had threatened to wear, with only the minimum beneath it as she had threatened. Maybe a little less than the minimum.

"Right."

"So it is with the bridge behind the bridge. Just because it's hidden in mists now doesn't mean that it's not there—if you take me meaning."

"Uh-huh . . . but what is the bridge?"

"Sure, haven't I been after telling you! 'Tis the bridge between Heaven and earth!"

She hadn't just told me that at all.

"Which is?"

She waved her hand as if to dismiss my pathetic ignorance.

"The rainbow of Noah, the baby in Bethlehem, the Cross of Jesus. Doesn't everyone know that?"

"Is there a lover behind the lover?"

"Why wouldn't there be? When you love me passionately, doesn't that stand for God loving me?"

SEE, ASSHOLE, said the Adversary.

When I had held her naked and scared in my arms earlier in the day was that a hint of what God was like? I wasn't sure that I liked that kind of God, a voraciously hungry deity turned on by His creatures.

"I see," I said to her.

Still maybe that was a pretty cool God, one head over heels with desire. Maybe I wanted Him on my side.

"Both of you put up with me, even though I'm not a very good wife."

"Woman," I said irritably. "I want to hear no more of that shite; do you understand?"

"Yes, Dermot," she said meekly.

"Is there a person behind the person?" I asked.

"Ah, sure there is; doesn't there have to be? This is the person we really are beneath all other persons we pretend to be. The trick of it, if you take me meaning, is to figure out who you really are. Then being the other people you are but not really is no problem at all, at all."

"Ah."

"So you're wondering if I know who I really am behind all the different people I'm pretending to be most of the time?"

"The thought did occur to me, Nuala Anne."

She considered the issue. "Well, I kind of half-know . . . I'm not sure I like her."

"Who is she?"

"Och, don't you know that without me telling you?"

"I want to hear it anyhow."

"Well," she said, pouring more wine into my glass, "isn't she the shy slip of a girl from the Gaeltacht in Connemara who is afraid of her own shadow and probably shouldn't have gone any farther than Galway City? She is also very good at pretending to be someone else, but isn't she afraid to be found out?"

She finished her scallops, wiping the plate clean, like all we Irish (and Irish Americans) are taught to do when we're kids.

"Of course she is found out," I picked up the theme, "because she wants to be, just to make sure that people don't hate her."

"Well, I still don't really like her, Dermot love."

"Everyone else does, myself included. She's the woman I married."

She waved that topic away.

"I suppose, Dermot Michael Coyne, that you think you're transparent and that there are no mysteries about you at all, at all."

The best defense is a good offense, huh?

"Well . . ."

"Aren't you the most mysterious fella I've ever met.

You pretend to be the sweet, even-tempered kid who wouldn't play football and couldn't succeed at the Board of Trade. But you love competition and enjoy a good fight, especially a verbal one, and like to fend off the media and put nerds like me older brother in their place.[2] And you write passionate stories and erotic love poetry. Ah, no, you're impenetrable altogether."

"I'm not," I said bluntly.

"You are, too." She touched my hand with her fingers. "Mind you, I like me men that way."

"Are you suggesting, young woman, that I change my personas as quickly as you change yours?"

"Not at all, at all!" Her fingers drummed on my hand. "I'm an actress and I can be someone else in a couple of seconds, but, sure, you change so slowly that I almost don't realize that there's another man who wants a ride with me."

"Another man altogether?"

"Just about, but doesn't that make it interesting?"

SEE, AMADON! SHE'S ALLUDING DISCREETLY TO YOUR LOST OPPORTUNITY.

She then ordered our dessert—apple crunch with heavy cream and a "small" sip of Baileys.

"You won't be needing any Bushmill's tonight," she explained to me.

"Are you afraid of some of the people I become?" I asked, realizing I was skating out on thin ice.

"Terrified altogether, but isn't it a nice kind of terror?"

An invitation to explore more deeply our sexual responses, about which neither of us knew very much?

"Where are we staying in the west?" I asked, deliberately changing the subject.

"Let's see, in Galway we'll be with me ma and me da

[2]Irish Whiskey

at their new bungalow, of course, and then we'll go
down to Limerick. We'll visit the monks at Glenstal and
do the recording at the University of Limerick. We'll
be staying for a couple of nights out on the Shannon
at a place called Castlegarry, one of them great country
houses which have been turned into hotels. They have
a fine golf course, and we'll play a few rounds to make
up for all the time you've missed at Long Beach Country Club. Then we'll go home to Chicago."

She squeezed my hand. Chicago was home now. And
forever.

"What's this Castlegarry place like?" I asked slyly. I
wanted to see what she knew about it. Had she perhaps
deliberately signed us up at a place where we would
find out about arson and death?

"Sure, I haven't been there. But wasn't I after saying
that it had a golf course? Do we need to know anything
else about it?"

"Is it haunted?"

"Most places in Ireland are not haunted, Dermot Michael Coyne. 'Tis only you Yanks that want haunts
everywhere."

If I conceded that Nuala's fey interludes were authentic—and on the basis of the evidence how could
I deny their authenticity?—then the question was
whether these instincts had been activated by her decision we would stay in Castlegarry or the instincts had
dictated our choice of hotels in the west of Ireland.
Practically, it didn't matter much. If I told her the
truth, which I had better do, there was no way we
would find another hotel, much less fly home after our
stop in Galway.

Over the apple crunch, which was too large by half,
and tea, we discussed the plans for the morrow. Herself
would go over to the theater at half ten, rehearse a bit

more, and then make sure everything was the way it should be, especially with RTE.

You must understand that the *R* is pronounced as though it were *oar*.

This arrangement was fine with me. I could pick up her parents at the Heuston Street station and smuggle them into the hotel. Their appearance at the concert would be a total surprise.

"You figure that if you aren't at the Point worrying, something will surely go wrong?"

"If you're Irish," she said, in her Yank accent, "you know that God will punish you if you don't worry enough."

"What God?"

"Not the one I'll be singing to. Isn't He a real sweetheart?"

"Well, since I won't be seeing you tomorrow, I suppose I should be giving you this preconcert present now."

"What have you done now, Dermot Michael?" she said suspiciously as she considered the small box I had placed on the table.

"Open it, woman, and find out."

Gingerly she untied the ribbon and peeled away the tissue and peeked into the box.

"Och! Dermot!" she cried out as she flipped it open. "Aren't they the most beautiful diamond studs in all the world! Sure, they must have cost too much altogether! Dermot Michael, you shouldn't have done it!"

"Woman! You're breaking all the rules!"

Her shoulders slumped. "I am now. I'm such a terrible woman."

"Another rule down the drain!"

"Right!"

She gathered herself together, struggling to remember the rules.

"Dermot love, they're wonderful presents! I'm very grateful," she recited the prescribed response from memory. "It's very generous of you to give them to me. I'll always remember the night I received them . . . fair play?" She grinned like a street hoyden.

"Fair play indeed."

She leaned across the table and kissed me. Then, very carefully, she took off the earrings she was wearing and put on the new ones. They glittered like dancing moonbeams in the soft light.

"They'll fit perfectly with me white suit tomorrow night, won't they now?"

"That was the general idea."

Actually, studs of that size were hardly what an upper-middle-class Dublin matron would wear to Mass on Sunday, but that really didn't matter.

"Aren't they beautiful, Dermot Michael?"

Her smile was far more radiant than the diamonds. I was overwhelmed with love for her.

SURE, DON'T YOU WANT TO REACH ACROSS THE TABLE AND TOUCH HER BREASTS AND THEN PULL OFF THAT SILLY DRESS AND MAKE FRANTIC LOVE WITH HER?

"Not here," I told the Adversary.

SOON.

I knew that I wouldn't. Not tonight. After all, didn't she have a concert tomorrow?

The Commissioner and his wife strolled over to our table. She was indeed a tall, blond, Viking princess type with a solemn face and pale, mischievous blue eyes.

Nuala Anne constrained them to sit down and enjoy a glass of Baileys with us. They both complimented her on her new studs and her new dress.

"Didn't me man think it was a nightgown?"

"But nightgowns are not lined, are they!" Orla Keenan protested, dismayed by my seeming ignorance in the matter.

"A good thing," her husband added with a chuckle.

They both wished herself every success at the event the next night, for which they had tickets.

I took the Commissioner aside as we drifted towards our cars.

"Any leads on the kidnapers?"

"They seem to have vanished from the face of the earth. The survivor says he didn't know them, thought they were Brits . . ."

He hesitated.

"There has been another development, I'm afraid. . . . We are screening your incoming messages and phone calls, just to make sure. I hope you don't mind. . . ."

"Not in the least."

"There was a crude note this afternoon from a group calling itself the Real IRA."

"Oh?"

"They want fifty thousand dollars or they will kidnap your wife and this time kill you if you try to stop them. It seems that as a rich American you are bound in conscience to make restitution to the republic, one and indivisible."

"Only fifty thousand?" I said, as my throat turned dry.

"It did seem a bit modest. . . . We don't think that the men who are negotiating up beyond above would settle for such a trivial sum. Nor would they tolerate such threats in such a sensitive phase of the negotiations. These lads are either a disgruntled offshoot or not real IRA at all, at all."

"Amateur night?"

"In a manner of speaking."

"Which doesn't make them any less dangerous."

"We'll get them, Dermot; never fear."

"I'll take your word for it," I said with more confidence than I felt. "I have something to tell you, Gene. Something that makes me shiver even to think about it. Before we left America, didn't herself make reservations for three nights at a hotel on the Shannon Estuary called Castlegarry?"

He closed his eyes and rubbed his chin. "What the hell . . . !"

"My very thought."

"Why would she choose it?"

"Mostly, I think, because it has a golf course. She is determined to beat me at golf, which I don't think she'll ever do."

"Strange indeed . . . but then someone might know that you're going out there."

"Lots of people. The travel agents and the hotel staff for starters."

He nodded thoughtfully.

"Of course. . . . We will keep our network around you until you return to America."

"I'd appreciate that."

"She really is a dark one, isn't she?"

"Tell me about it."

— 15 —

AFTER NUALA had left for the last day of rehearsal at the Point, I walked through the mists (a nice evening in Ireland does not predict a nice morning the next day) over to the Trinity College Library, where I had obtained a little clout, courtesy of George the Priest and his boss, the little bishop.

Herself had been tense and uncommunicative as she dressed for her "worry session" before the concert itself. When she was in her worry modality, I was wise enough to keep my own big mouth shut.

Nonetheless, her good-bye kiss was as affectionate as ever.

"Dermot Michael," she said, turning towards me (still in bed) from the door. "I learned a new poem yesterday. It's by Father Paddy Daly. Would you ever like to listen to it?"

"I would."

" 'All day long
She has been arranging our welcome:

" 'Scouring down the house,
Sweeping under beds,
Pulling out the old crocheted counterpanes,

Shining glasses and tableware,
Dusting sideboards and picture frames.

" 'Now she sits in a deep chair
Till we come crunching under the beeches
To the door.' "

"It's lovely," I had said. "Sounds like your mother getting ready for our visit."

"Doesn't it now? . . . I was thinking of reciting it tonight."

"Sounds like a good idea. . . . What's the title?"

"God," she said as she went out the door and closed it as my Nuala Anne always closes the door—with a loud slam.

God?

The woman was reading too much Irish mysticism altogether. Still the poem would be a grand success at the concert. It would make everyone stop and think, which is why the clever witch (good witch of the West) would read it.

At the TCD library I found to my surprise two listings under "Downs, Lady Augusta, 1888–1922."

The first had been published in 1917. It was titled simply *Poems*. The description on the computer page said: "Poems written by a woman whose husband was serving in Flanders."

The second was *The Life of Colonel the Lord Arthur Downs, V.C., K.C.B.* Publication date was 1922. Perhaps it was a posthumously published book.

I shivered slightly as I looked at the computer screen. I was not sure that I wanted to get into the tragedy of those young lives. Nor did I want my good wife to read about either of them.

Well, there was no helping that, was there now?

The two books were delivered to me. I walked to a

table in the reading room, as far away as I could get from the *Book of Kells,* by which passed a steady stream of American tourists. Both of the books were thin and poorly bound. Some of the pages of the biography had detached themselves from the spine, and the others barely clung to it. I turned the pages slowly, and carefully.

Augusta Downs's poems were light and lovely, not deep, not great, but filled with affection and hope. She was serenely confident that just as spring had returned to Ireland, so, too, would the man who is "the spring-time of my life."

Her religious faith permeated all of the poems. She was not attempting to teach the reader faith, much less demand it, but neither did she hide the radiance of her belief "we will always be together no matter what may intervene."

I wept for her. Why did some generations of young people have to suffer so terribly?

Reluctantly, I turned to her memoir.

The frontispiece was a picture of "Lord Arthur Thomas John Michael Downs, V.C., K.C.B. 1884–1918." He was dressed in the British military uniform, dark jacket, light trousers, Sam Browne belt, but was not wearing a cap. He did not look like a striking figure. His hair was too thin, his face too narrow, his neck too long, his smile too weak. His eyes, however, were different. Eighty years after the picture had been taken, the eyes seemed to leap off the page at me—intelligent, humorous, determined.

For a minute or two I stared at the picture, unable to escape those eyes. This is not, I thought, your typical British military officer trained on the playing fields of Eton. This was a man without illusion, a man who would do his duty but not kid himself about the folly of war.

Again I wanted to weep for him and Lady Augusta. Yet they had happy years together. They had married in 1907, when she was nineteen and he twenty-three, not all that much different from Nuala Anne and myself. Eleven years together, the last four interrupted by war. Not long enough; it is never long enough.

I pictured them walking hand in hand along the estuary in that glorious summer of 1914, the most beautiful weather in a half a century according to those who lived through it. Gerald would predict, as did most English officers at the time, that the war would be a short one. It would be a good thing; it would stiffen the back of the nation and teach the Kaiser a lesson he needed.

Perhaps Lady Augusta—would he have called her Gus?—told him how hard she was praying that there would not be a war and that he would not have to leave Castle Garry.

Neither could have possibly imagined the horror of the Great War, the destruction of an entire generation in the mud and blood of northern France. Nor would they have believed that the optimism of the Victorian and Edwardian Ages would disappear, never to return.

No children. A great loss for both of them.

What would have happened if he had lived? Those eyes suggested that he was the kind of man that neither Ireland nor England could afford to lose. Would he and Lady Augusta have moved to England to escape the chaos? Or would they have stayed on? Might he eventually have come to serve in the Free State Government?

Foolish questions!

His wife's memoir was restrained. Her grief was palpable, but it did not overwhelm her. She told the story simply and cleanly. Nonetheless, the man with the vibrant eyes leaped out of the pages.

I knew I would love him before we ever met. I was at a dull ball at Lord Mayo's home in Dublin. I heard a man's laugh in the next room. I told myself that was a laugh with which I could fall in love. I peeked around the corner and saw this handsome young man with a wonderful smile. He didn't seem to have a young woman in attendance. He looked at me and smiled even more wonderfully. I smiled back. We both knew that instant that we were one another's destiny, even though we didn't yet know each other's names.

Like herself and myself in O'Neill's pub on College Green.[1]

As I look back on our fleeting years together, I realize that he made me laugh. I was a very serious young woman, deeply committed to the good of my people and my country—Ireland, not England, though I thought of myself as both English and Irish. I started to laugh at him that night and never stopped.

Arthur was pro-Irish and a strong supporter of Home Rule. There was Irish in his background, though his family lived out on the edge of Cornwall—"a place so desolate that it makes the Shannon Estuary look like the Bay of Naples." The people of Garrytown were skeptical of an English lord, but he won them over by his first visits to the local pubs and by his athletic enthusiasm.

He rode passably well, not as well as I did, he would always say. He liked fishing but abhorred hunting. However, he excelled in soccer and became quite good at both Gaelic football and hurl-

[1] *Irish Gold*

ing. There was some opposition to him
participating in either sport because English men
were theoretically banned from them. However,
Canon Muldoon, the darling P.P. who was also
president of the local G.A.A., accepted his word
about his Irish ancestors. Everyone in Garrytown
celebrated the decision, some of them I fear a little too vigorously.

He and the priest became close friends.

I always thought that the Canon, a strong Republican, distrusted me because my family had become Protestant a couple of centuries ago. But he
loved Arthur and eventually came to like and even
admire me. He is a great consolation to me in
these days of my widowhood.

Separated by war, the two young lovers missed each
other deeply. Yet "his letters were wonderful, full of
fun and joy and laughter, just like the rest of his life.
I felt he was in the room with me when, with trembling
fingers, I would open a letter. He said the same thing:
When he read a letter from me, it was almost as though
I were standing in the trench with him."
Wow!
He made no attempt to hide the horror of the
trenches from her.

He grieved at the good men under his command
who had died. He described the mud and the danger of the trenches. He often feared that the war
would go on forever. In some of the letters he
seemed very discouraged and even spoke of the
possibility of his own death. Yet his laughing spirit

could not be suppressed. He found cause for laughter even in the most terrible circumstances.

She quoted many of his letters, cutting, I suspected, the most intimate love passages. Arthur Downs was as shrewd as he was witty.

We took some German prisoners yesterday, a patrol which had advanced too far into our lines. We trapped them so they could not retreat. They fought till their ammunition ran out and then climbed out of their dugout, hands in the air. They were frightened that we would shoot them. Some of my men wanted to kill them as reprisal for the murder of our troops by the Germans who had taken them as prisoners. Such things happen on both sides when nervous and exhausted men take out their rage on the defenseless. I forbade any executions. Even in the trenches we must strive to remain decent and moral human beings. Most of my men seemed glad that I had intervened.

The poor wretches, none of them over twenty, were shaking with fear. Change the uniforms and they would have been the same as us. Brave young men doing their duty in a foolish war into which old men have led us and do not know how to end. They have parents and wives or sweethearts at home praying for them, just as our fellows do. I tell you, Gussie, Haig and French and men like them on the other side have a lot to answer for. They saluted me and thanked me as they were marched off to prisoner stockades. The war is over for them. If they don't come down with some terrible disease, they'll go home eventually to those who are praying for them. They're the lucky ones.

Do I sound cynical, Gussie my love? I suppose
I am. I don't believe in this war anymore. We are
led by fools and incompetents. I hide my cynicism
from my men. I wonder if they see through my
enthusiasms.

I wondered how many British officers had felt that
way in 1916. How many would have dared to have been
so blunt in letters home?

And how many had wives who could absorb such
sedition? Augusta included none of her own letters in
the book. It was supposed to be about him, not about
her. Yet she revealed a lot of herself in which segments
of his letters she chose to put in the book.

Finally, General Tudor entered the picture. In a letter after a brief leave in Garrytown, Lord Downs wrote:

Still can't get over how wonderful it was to be back
in county Limerick with you. It seemed like the
waking world and the trenches over here are nothing more than a bad dream. The Ninth Scottish
has a new officer commanding. Man named Hugh
Tudor, of all things. Everyone is afraid to ask him
if he is a descendent. From India. Very much the
pukka sahib. Stiff, aloof, doesn't smile. Artillery
bloke. He can't be any worse than the fool he replaced.

A couple of weeks later, Gerry sent a much more
favorable report on the new commander of the division:

Hugh Tudor is a military genius. He has developed a technique for laying down what he calls a
"box barrage," a combination of artillery shells
and smoke which clears a segment of no-man's-

land before an attack. It works remarkably well. The people on the other side don't know what to make of it and don't like it one bit. They pull back very quickly when we start one of these things because they don't relish us showing up in their trenches without warning. Marshal Haig was here the other day to watch a demostration. He seemed impressed, though mostly he is impressed only by himself. The man is a pompous, foppish fool. The blood of tens of thousands of Tommies is all over his effeminate little hands and he doesn't even know it.

Still later he told his wife:

The General wants to make me his Chief of Staff. Colonel Downs, does that have a nice ring to it? He told me that I was one of the few intelligent officers in the division. I know that we both agree with that, but it was still a bit odd to hear it from one's Officer Commanding. He's not a bad bloke at all. Kind of man I could get to like. I told him that I didn't much believe in the war. He was silent for a minute and then said softly, "Neither do I, Art, but we've got to end it somehow so we can send the men home—those who are still alive."

So I accepted his offer. At least I'll be out of the trenches and in much safer circumstances.

Later he added a brief P.S.:

Hugh Tudor's first name is Henry and he does seem to be some descendent of the Royal Tudors, though, as he says with a laugh, on the wrong side of the sheet. He is a first-rate soldier and a first-rate human being. He cares about all of his men.

He does everything he can to keep casualties down. His artillery tactics have been so successful that the generals above him leave him pretty much alone. He writes a letter every night to his wife back in Exeter, with whom he is almost as much in love as I am with you.

The last letter she received from him, in the spring of 1918, revealed no premonitions about death but only a renewed hope:

The other side seems to be getting ready for another big offensive, perhaps their last one. Russia is out of the war, but the United States, with its huge population and resources and its grim Protestant determination, is in it. For the Germans, it is a matter of winning now or giving up. There is nothing subtle about their plans. They intend to drive on Paris, just as they did in 1870 and 1914. They also intend to break our line, drive a wedge between us and the French, and then head for the sea to encircle us. If they lose, I think it will be their last offensive and they may pack it in. If they win their gamble, I think the French will pack it in. What we will do, I don't know. British people— to say nothing of us Irish—can be very stubborn about surrendering. Every battle but the last sort of thing. I believe that we will hold them and then counterattack at the end of summer. No matter how stupid our generals, that should finally defeat the Germans. If that happens and with any luck I'll be back with you in Garrytown by Christmas. And won't we have a wonderful time celebrating!

Arthur Downs was correct in his analysis. The last desperate German offensive failed, though it was, as the Iron Duke said of Waterloo, a damn close thing. The final Allied offensive sent the German Army reeling. A new German government sued for peace. Arthur Downs's body was home for Christmas.

Gussie contented herself with the printing from the citation for his Victoria Cross:

Colonel The Lord Arthur Thomas John Michael Downs. In action at Cambrai on 15 April 1918 this officer, chief of staff of the Ninth Scottish Division, carried a message from his Officer Commanding to the Third Battalion of that division, with which communication had been lost. Arriving at the position of this unit, he discovered that the enemy had overrun the battalion, that its senior officers were dead or wounded, and that German soliders were occupying its trenches. Realizing that the position had to be held if the flank of his division were not to be turned, Colonel The Lord Downs assumed temporary command of the battalion on his own initiative, rallied the troops, and drove the enemy from its trenches. Though wounded three times he continued to lead the counterattack until our position was completely restored. He died from his wounds at the very end of the action. However, his initiative and courage undoubtedly saved his entire division from destruction.

Gussie added Hugh Tudor's letter:

I was fond of your husband, one of the finest men I have ever known. I miss him greatly. I can only begin to comprehend how much you miss him. His bravery was both exemplary and typical. He did save the day for us. Our line held that day and

perhaps changed the course of this terrible war. Gerry was the man responsible. I do not know how much consolation it will bring you, but most of us would have been dead at the end of the day if he had not acted far above and beyond the call of duty. I shall never forget his smile, his laugh, his good spirits, his courage. Never.

> H. H. Tudor
> General Officer Commanding
> Ninth Scottish Division

Typical of the kind of letter an officer had to write many times during war. Yet also unique and special.

Gussie cited the sermons of both the Anglican vicar and Canon Muldoon. The latter, she tells us, broke into tears during his eulogy.

Naturally he spoke the highest Irish praise: "We'll not see his like again."

Her own final words were brief: "I have loved my husband since I first met him at Lord Mayo's. I miss him. I will always love him. Often I feel him very close to me. I'm sure he is. I know I will be with him someday in a better world than this. Until then I must honor his memory by not feeling sorry for myself and not abandoning my responsibilities."

At the end there is a drawing of a simple tombstone on the grounds of Castle Garry and of his Victoria Cross.

"Damn!" I muttered to myself.

A librarian at Trinity College was happy to make me a photocopy of the little book.

"Worth reading?" she asked.

"Yes indeed."

"Victoria Cross? Brave man. English or Irish?"

"Both, I think."

"Must have been hard in those days."

"Not for him."

Would I show the book to Nuala Anne?

Maybe. But she'd probably figure it all out anyway.

— 16 —

NUALA'S PARENTS were peasants. They earned their living by raising a few head of cattle on poor land way out on the far end of the Connemara Peninsula. They also served tea and scones to tourists who roared up to their neatly painted (blue) little house in the charming town of Carraroe—strips of land between lake and ocean crossed by gravel roads and whitewashed stone fences. Some of the tourists were impressed by the austere beauty of Connemara, and others made no effort to hide their opinion that it was a savage place inhabited by savage people—Europe's last Stone Age race, in the words of an English poet.

The German tourists were the worst. When I had been permitted to help Nuala serve tea to a busload of them during our courtship (as she defined it) she warned me sternly not to get into any fights with them.

"Their culture is different from ours," she said primly.

I held my temper under control, though just barely.

"Our is better," I said after their bus left.

"Yank or Irish?" she said, her nose firmly pointed in the air.

"Is there a difference? We deserve credit for being

hospitable. You don't because it is programmed into your genes."

She sniffed disdainfully.

Annie and Gerry McGrail, however, did not look or act like peasants. A handsome couple in their middle fifties, they passed with ease as upper-middle-class professionals when they dressed up in their best clothes, which Nuala and I had discreetly purchased for them. At our wedding reception they had fit in perfectly with the doctors and lawyers and professors and clergy who filled the place. Nuala had come by her ability to fit into every situation naturally enough. They were also very intelligent people, readers of the Scripture and Shakespeare and the Bible and Irish poetry, though they had at the most six years of education.

They also adored their youngest child, who revered them and treated them with the greatest respect, a difficult task for most adult children. She never argued with them, but then they never argued with her.

As far as they were concerned, I was wonderful, indeed well nigh perfect. This conviction seemed to be based on the assumption that their Nuala Anne would never choose a man who was not well nigh perfect.

It didn't hurt that I put a telephone in their cottage so that Nuala Anne could call them when she went to America. "Just like she's right around the corner," Annie had said happily.

"It is practically just around the corner," I suggested.

Now they had a computer and E-mail, toys in which they reveled.

So they embraced me warmly when I greeted them as they got off the Galway train at Heuston station behind St. James Brewery on the banks of Anna Livia.

You could not possibly tell that they had never been to Dublin in their lives. They took in everything but did not give the slightest hint that they were staring.

"Well," said himself, " 'tis not attractive as Chicago."

"A lot more history."

"Aye," he said skeptically.

"How's herself doing?" Annie demanded. "Worrying, I suppose?"

"If you're Irish you have to worry lest God punish you for not worrying!"

"Doesn't she save God a lot of time?" her father said as we entered the limo I had brought over from the station to take them to the Towers at Jury's.

"Ever since she was a little girl, hasn't she been saving God a lot of time?"

Their laughter at Nuala Anne was good-hearted. She could do no wrong in their eyes.

"Wasn't that quite a TV show you two put on the other night?" Gerry observed.

"They'll think a long time before they try that again, won't they?" Annie added.

"I hope so," I said fervently, not being sure who "they" were or why "they'd" done it. Or why "they'd" wanted it on television.

And were they the same people who had sent a note in the name of the Real IRA and had made two phone threats already today? Or were there two separate groups, one exploiting the publicity gained by the other?

"She'll be just as good tonight as she was out at Dublin Airport," Annie observed.

"Even better," I said confidently.

I understood my wife well enough to know that she was now a nervous wreck and that anyone, especially her husband, who came near her would be in serious danger for limb and life. I also knew that when the show began she would be radiantly charming. I was not about to derail her with the information that "Ma" and "Da" were in Dublin. On the other hand, if I failed to show up a half hour before show time, I would be in the most serious trouble since I first met her on that foggy night a half a lifetime ago (actually less than a year and a half ago).

As we inched away through the traffic jam on Steven's Lane and towards Thomas Street, I noted a car pull out of the hospital parking lot on the right of the lane. Gene Keenan's men, I presumed, though a little more obvious than usual.

It was patent in the backseat of the car how much the couple loved each other. They held each other's hands unobtrusively, as though they were on their second date. Annie McGrail was a striking woman, the model from which their daughter had been designed. It would be hard not to love her. Good sign for your future, Dermot Michael.

EXCEPT THAT YOU'RE NOT HALF THE MAN HER FATHER IS, the Adversary announced.

Finally, after inching our way forward slowly and painfully, we reached the stoplight on Thomas Street and turned left into it when the light became green.

Suddenly the car from the hospital parking lot spun into the opposite lane, raced through the stoplight, and cut us off.

"Focking gobshites!" our driver exploded as he slammed on his brakes and skidded into the sidewalk.

Here we go again, I thought.

The car, a big English Rover, stopped in front of us, the door opened, and two men emerged, big guys with the required ski masks.

Not big enough, I told myself, fingering the cosh I was carrying in my leather Chicago Bulls jacket pocket.

Then blue lights exploded in every direction as the Guards rode over the hills like the Seventh Cavalry. The men in the Rover hurried back into the car, slammed the doors, and in reverse rushed by us towards Basin Lane.

Madman that I am, I jumped out of our Benz and chased them.

In the course of this berserk pursuit I wondered what I'd do if I caught up with them.

Then I did catch up with them, momentarily.

I smashed the window on the passenger's side and then smashed the thug. I had aimed for his head but succeeded only in hitting his collarbone as the car pulled away from me. I heard the passenger screaming in agony.

Good enough for him.

"You're out of your focking mind," said the Guard who had caught up to me.

"You're supposed to protect us from them gobshites!" I shouted, turning on him.

He backed away from me. "We just did," he said mildly.

"You did that," I said ruefully, returning my weapon to my Chicago Bulls jacket (on the back of which there was the magic number 31). "Thank you."

"You're quite welcome," he said with a smile. "Sure you almost stopped them for us. Never fear; we'll get them this time."

Three squads careened down Basin Lane and around the corner into Rainsford Street.

"I certainly hope so. . . . Incidentally, the one in the passenger seat probably has a broken collarbone."

"Fair play to you."

"Ask the Commissioner to ring me at Jury's."

"Sure you can count on him doing that."

I returned to our car. "I was just saying to herself that it was not such a long time after all before they'd tried again."

"Our Nuala will never lack for protection," Annie

agreed, "will she now?" As calm and as philosophical as though I had left the car to chase a herd of recalcitrant sheep out of our right-of-way.

"Are you all right?" I asked the driver.

"Fine, sir. Weren't your man and I thinking about the tire irons in the boot when the Gardai arrived?"

"You work for Mike Casey?"

"Isn't he the best cop in the world?"

As we picked our way through the crowded streets of Dublin, I pondered this latest folly.

It was an act of sheer madness. How could they have hoped to get at us in broad daylight on the streets of Dublin with such crude tactics? Didn't they know that the Dublin Guards would be hanging around? They were amateurs, minor leaguers, tough guys who were not wise guys, would-be gangsters with not quite enough brawn and very little brain. The "boys" out on the West Side of Chicago would laugh at them.

Yet what was the point? Why were they trying to harass us? Could it be that it was all an act? Did they want to frighten us out of Ireland? Might they have dropped Nuala off a half an hour after they had lifted her?

If it was a form of psychological warfare, it was a risky business.

We checked the McGrails into the Towers. I showed them up to their room. They acted like they had stayed in hotels like this and, indeed, better ones all around the world. Anyone seeing them walking down the corridor from the elevator would have assumed that they belonged here.

Which, in fact, they did.

" 'Tis a nice room," Annie said judiciously.

"It'll do," himself agreed.

Then they both laughed, as though the three of us knew it was a grand joke.

"Would you ever like a bite to eat?"

"Well," he said, "after the long train ride and the long night ahead of us, wouldn't it be better if we had a bit of a nap first?"

"And then a little dip in the pool that Nuala tells us about? Sure I can't believe it is as warm as she says. Won't we perish with the heat?"

" 'Tis a bit warmer than the Gulf Stream out in Carraroe," I admitted. "Suppose I meet you in the lobby for a cup of tea and some scones and maybe a sandwich or two and a sip of sherry at half five? Then we can go over to the Point. The woman will want an annulment if I don't stick my head in her dressing room a half hour or so before she starts."

They agreed.

They'd do more than take a nap, I thought to myself and shut off the Adversary before he could make any obscene comments.

I began to work on my report. I'd write up the story of Kevin O'Higgins first and then turn to the mystery of Castle Garry or Castlegarry, as it was now called. I had no way of knowing which order herself would like, though I was pretty sure that whatever I chose would be the wrong choice.

The phone rang as I opened my Omnibook 800CS.

"Dermot Coyne," I announced.

"Keenan, here."

"Indeed!"

"I'm sorry about this afternoon."

"I should hope so."

"You weren't in any danger, you know, not until you jumped out of the car. My people arrived in plenty of time."

"And you found the bad guys?"

"Ah, no."

"Why not?"

"They abandoned their car, stolen, as you might have expected, and, ah, disappeared."

"Almost like they'd planned it?"

"Uh, just so."

"So they're both stupid to try such an attack in daylight with half the Dublin police lurking around and yet smart to have an escape hatch?"

"You might say that, Dermot."

"I did say it."

Silence.

"You still carrying that cosh?"

"I am."

"Is that altogether necessary?"

" 'Tis."

Silence.

"You might want to try a shillelagh."

"I don't happen to háve one."

"I'll get you one."

"Grand. . . . Now what about tonight?"

"We'll be using metal detectors at every door. There'll be hundreds of our people in the audience, most of whom are delighted to be able to attend. We will monitor every corner, every corridor, every possible place for the bad guys, as you call them, to hide. I believe it will be quite safe. . . . The only way to make it perfectly safe of course would be to cancel the concert. That is your decision."

"No, it isn't, as you well know."

"I suppose not."

"The sun could cancel its rising tomorrow morning before herself cancels the concert."

"You could not talk some sense into her on the matter?"

"You gotta be kidding!"

"I suppose so."

We were both silent for a moment.

"Do these attacks make any sense to you, Gene?" I asked, backing off from the hostility of my earlier remarks.

"Candidly, Dermot, they do not. . . . Our friends have frightened you. But they have inflicted no physical harm on you. Quite the contrary, you have inflicted considerable physical harm on them. . . . I shudder to think what you might do to them with a cosh AND a shillelagh."

"Do you think they want to stop the concert?"

"Possibly . . . but for what purpose? I can't think of any. Can you?"

"No. Only the poor will benefit from it."

"Actually," he said, "our fraud people have taken a look at it, just to be sure. It seems perfectly legitimate."

"The Garrytown factor?"

"I have considered that since you told me that you were going out there. The present proprietors, distant cousins and Catholics you may be interested to know, are decent folk who do a fine job. There's no trace of anything questionable in their past or their present."

"Hmm . . ."

"We'll be watching closely, Dermot. You can count on that. You may find some consolation in the fact that we were there this afternoon."

"You're not really going to give me that Celtic club, are you?"

"If you leave your cosh behind."

"All right."

I had not, however, quite made up my mind to that.

"Good! I might add that we have added a very Celtic secret weapon that you will encounter when you go over to the Point. It is very effective."

"I can hardly wait."

Celtic secret weapon indeed! I was in the land of the

fairies and the leprechauns and the pookas.

And the dark ones.

I was not yet ready to take the cosh out of my jacket pocket.

SHILLELAGH IN hand, I approached herself's dressing room with considerable caution. I had better not be either too early or too late. It was in one of the back corridors of the Point Theater on the banks of Anna Livia, a vast and not totally unattractive barn. I had anticipated some problem with the security people, even though at the moment I was only slightly less well-known on this misty island than was my wife.

In fact, there had not been any mist all day.

I had settled my in-laws in our seats, halfway back so as not to distract Nuala Anne. I noted when I left them that in one hand herself was holding her husband's big paw—he would have been quite good with the tire irons—and in the other her rosary.

Yep, it was still Ireland.

I had, incidentally, left my cosh behind, though with considerable misgivings.

The security precautions were almost a security blanket. At every step of the way, grim-eyed Celtic warriors checked my passport, my driver's license, and the ID card that the Reliable, Dublin, driver (a certain Paddy) had passed on to me from Commissioner Keenan. At certain key points I was carefully examined to make sure I wasn't carrying any concealed weapons. With the utmost reluctance—and without a trace of Celtic wit and laugher—they let me through.

There were four of these unsmiling Fenians at the door to my wife's dressing room.

"I'm her husband," I said, displaying my assorted credentials.

Each mark of my identity as Dermot Michael Coyne was carefully considered seriatim by the quartet.

They nodded slightly as if they were just barely willing to admit that I might be telling the truth.

"Might I knock on the door?"

They considered the question carefully and glanced at one another.

"All right," said the woman who seemed to be in charge, "but, mind, not too loudly!"

"Yes, ma'am."

"And you'd better let me have that cane of yours. You'll scare the poor woman half to death with it."

"Yes, ma'am," I said, though I doubted that it would scare Nuala much.

I knocked very gently, more in fear of herself than of the four Fenians.

"Come in," said a very unhappy voice that might have belonged to my Nuala Anne.

I opened the door and was greeted by a very large and very suspicious Irish wolfhound, no doubt a product of pre-Christian antiquity.

"Dermot Michael Coyne, where the fock have you been! You're late!"

"No, ma'am," I said meekly. "I am precisely on time. However, I'm afraid I can't come in unless you call off this fearsome creature who seems ready to chew off my head."

"Och, Dermot, that's only Fiona. She knows that you love me, don't you, Fiona girl?"

The Celtic secret weapon responded with what

sounded like a low growl, then licked my hand with approval and offered her oversize head for affection.

"Nice, Fiona," I said tentatively as I petted her.

"Isn't she a darlin' girl!"

"She sure is!"

To show her approval, the darlin' stood on her hind paws and slobbered on my face.

"See; I told you she'd like you. . . . Down, Fiona. Me fella is a touch fastidious."

The pre-Christian creature did as she was told.

The dressing room was fit for an Academy Award winner. But the only person in it was the shy lass from Carraroe, indeed a shy and woebegone lass from Carraroe, wearing an elegant dressing gown (apparently provided by the house) and holding a brush in her hand.

"Dermot, me love," she said, collapsing into my arms. "I'm sorry I shouted at you. . . . I shouldn't be doing this. . . . I'm the most terrible eejit in all the world. . . . I'm a disgrace. . . . I'll humiliate you and me ma and me da and everyone I know. . . ."

"You'll probably humiliate Fiona, too."

That canine, who had curled up at our feet, heard her name, lifted an ear, and then decided that the two humans in each other's arms did not need her attention.

"I will not, Dermot Michael; won't she stay out there on the stage with me, no matter how bad I am?"

"Arguably, as the little bishop would say."

We both giggled.

So the secret weapon of the fairies would be onstage. Nice touch. I wouldn't need my cosh.

Not at all, at all.

"I suppose the final run-through was terrible," I said, taking the hairbrush out of her hand.

"No, it was perfect," she said in despair. "That's why

I know the performance will be awful altogether . . .
and meself letting down all the wonderful people
here . . ."

"To say nothing of myself and your ma and your da!"

She giggled again but clung to me for dear life.
"Who do I think I am, carrying on like an amadon and
meself not even two years out of TCD."

"Only just a year."

"Och, Dermot," she wailed.

"You will, of course, love every minute," I said, "just
like you did that day I saw you lament that you'd lost
the last playboy of the Western world."[1]

Laughter this time.

"I found the last playboy of the Western world,
didn't I? . . . Dermot Michael, did you bring roses for
me tonight like you did that time?"[2]

"Woman, I did not!"

In fact, I had left them with the stage manager.

"You did, too! I know you did!"

We held each other in silence for a moment.

"Well"—she sighed the loudest west of Ireland sigh
I had ever heard—"I suppose I must do my makeup
again, and yourself making me cry."

Which meant, Dermot Michael, get the hell out of
here.

I left, content that I had done my duty. Good-dog
Fiona barked her approval.

"All we need now is your boss," I said to the Fenians
as I emerged from the dressing room.

"Boss?" one of them said softly.

"The REALLY big guy with the REALLY big club."

"Finn himself, is it?"

"Who else?"

[1] *Irish Gold*
[2] *Irish Gold*

I walked away from them satisfied that I was one up.

Father Placid was lurking backstage, looking even more dyspeptic than he had at Dublin Airport.

"Cheer up, Father," I urged him. "You'll make a bundle tonight."

"These things are expensive," he said in his usual dismal baritone. "A lot of money is wasted."

Right.

"She's a terrible wreck, isn't she now?" Annie Mc-Grail asked as I sat down next to her.

"Totally out of control. . . . I wouldn't let go of that rosary, if I were you."

All three of us laughed.

"Didn't she always love the limelight?" her da observed.

"Didn't she ever?" her ma agreed.

The lights went down in the house and up on the stage. The background hinted at stained glass and round towers and beehive huts and old Irish monasteries. The audience waited expectantly.

However, before herself could appear, didn't Father Placid show up?

The lights went up.

"I want to say a word," he informed us in the tone of a man who had many words to say. "You've all come here tonight to be entertained by listening to songs you used to sing in church. I wonder how many of you went to church last Sunday. Ireland is a post-Catholic country now. We have to bring you to a theater to persuade you to give money to the poor and starving of the world. You all have nice jobs and nice homes and nice clothes and nice motorcars and nice food. You forget what it was like not so long ago in this country to be hungry and cold. You don't bother to thank God for your money and your success. You don't realize how transient such things are. You don't realize how

transient your selfish, consumerist lives are. They are
even worse than the lives of the stupid Americans because you ought to know better. Soon you'll stand before God's judgment seat and have to render an
account for your silly, shallow, materialist lives. God
have mercy on all of you. Keep those truths in mind
while you listen to the music tonight. If the songs don't
make you feel guilty, then you'll probably spend all
eternity listening not to the angelic hymns but the tormented screams of the damned."

The audience was silent, resentful perhaps, but also
troubled. Father Placid might easily have ruined the
evening. He certainly had tried to do so.

"Let's hear it for the stupid Americans," I whispered
to the McGrails.

They both chuckled.

"Shush, Dermot," my mother-in-law murmured in
the tone of voice that meant "fair play to you."

The lights went down again.

Suddenly my wife, radiant in her white suit and
green scarf, harp in hand, appeared, accompanied by
the faithful Fiona, who curled up at the foot of the
harp.

Thunderous applause trailed off into silence as,
seated at her harp, she waited to begin.

Then suddenly:

" 'Hail, Holy Queen, enthroned above, O Maria!
Hail, Queen of mercy, Queen of love, O Maria!

" 'Triumph all, ye Cherubin!
Sing with us, ye Seraphim!
Heaven and earth resound the hymn,
Salve, Salve Regina!

" 'Our life, our sweetness here below, O Maria!
Our hope in sorrow and in woe, O Maria!' "

The audience cheered and then joined in on the chorus.

There is probably not a Catholic in the English-speaking world who hasn't sung that hymn, usually at the top of her voice. But no one ever heard it sung with the delicacy, the reverence, and the ethereal joy with which my Nuala sang it.

"Softly now," she said, as we went into the second refrain, "so we won't wake up the sleeping Christ child!"

> " 'Triumph all, ye Cherubin!
> Sing with us, ye Seraphim!
> Heaven and earth resound the hymn,
> Salve, Salve Regina!' "

Suddenly, we were in church and Sister Superior was warning us not to forget that God was present.

Next to me Annie McGrail was crying happily.

"Well, now," me wife said, standing up and revealing her long, slender figure and her modest knee-length skirt, "isn't that a lovely song when we sing it right. We're not in church, of course, so there won't be a collection or a sermon . . ."

Laughter.

She was wearing her Dublin persona. Hence her accent was strictly West Brit.

"But still we're singing prayer songs, so we should remember that we're praying. . . . Most of the hymns I'll sing tonight are songs we grew up with. Some of them are quite lovely, and others, well, they're still part of our heritage and we have to respect them. Even if we're glad we don't sing them anymore!"

More laughter.

"I'll sing a song or two in Irish, because that's me real language. And I'll sing a couple of new songs, too,

because in Ireland and in Catholicism there is room
for the present as well as the past."

She strummed the harp a couple of times.

"I want to dedicate this night to Mary the mother of
Jesus, who gave me the courage to come out here tonight even though I felt like a total eejit . . . and to me
ma and me da, who are watching out in Carraroe. They
told me all the wonderful Catholic stories when I was
a very little one and have lived those stories as an example to me every day since. . . ."

She switched to Irish for a sentence or two. Her ma
grabbed in her purse for a new tissue.

Sure, the Irish will cry at almost anything, won't they
now?

"Now," herself went on, "I'm going to sing the
'Lourdes Hymn,' which I think is just wonderful. Sure,
isn't it written for a pilgrimage, but isn't our life a pilgrimage? I'll sing it in French first. You French people
here will have to excuse me terrible French accent.
Then I'll sing it in Irish and you Dubliners will have to
excuse me terrible Galway accent. Finally I'll sing it in
English, and I'll make no apology at all at all for my
west of Ireland brogue."

The folks with the pipes and the bodhran drums
slipped onto the stage and provided soft marching music. We were on our way to Lourdes and a rendezvous
with wonder. Many of the congregation, as I was now
thinking of them, seemed to know the hymn in all
three languages. The brief stanzas rolled on. Yank that
I was, I could remember only a couple of them—the
first two and the last!

> " 'Immaculate Mary, your praises we sing.
> You reign now in splendor with Jesus our King.
> Ave, Ave, Ave Maria! Ave, Ave, Maria!

" *In heaven the blessed your glory proclaim,*
On earth we your children invoke your sweet name.
Ave, Ave, Ave Maria! Ave, Ave Maria!

" *We pray for the Church, our true Mother on earth,*
And beg you to watch o'er the land of our birth.
Ave, Ave, Ave Maria! Ave, Ave Maria! "

"Well now," my friend went on, " 'tis time we come back from Lourdes to Ireland, isn't it? Next I'm going to sing a more modern hymn. The melody is from 'Simple Gifts,' a Shaker hymn, poor dear folks. And I'm going to sing their version first. Then I'll sing it as 'Lord of the Dance,' a poem Sidney Carter wrote. I first heard it sung on a record by Mary O'Hara. It was a dark, dark night out in the Gaeltach [her accent now was pure Connemara]—and it gets pretty dark out there. I was sitting by the fire. As I heard Mary sing it, I imagined a lot of little Irish feet dancing around the room in front of the fire. So I danced meself with me big Irish feet. I see the small ones dancing whenever I hear it. So I thought we'd have them dance with us and for God tonight."

A group of little Irish dancers flounced out on the stage—the oldest girl child was certainly no more than eight. As Nuala sang they danced. The fairie folk had returned, only now to dance with Jesus.

And didn't herself join the small lasses in the final whirl of their dance, herself a small one again?

Through all of this, good-dog Fiona, curled up near the harp, didn't move. Indeed, she almost seemed to be sound asleep. Her ears twitched a little at the dance music. However, her eyes, alert and intelligent, watched the audience intently. She glanced quickly at the dancing colleens, as if she would like to join them. However, she stuck to her job.

"Now," Fiona's charge announced, "I'm going to do a couple of hymns that will give your fiddle players and your choir a chance to join us for the evening. Youse know them well, but I want to sing them a little different tonight, so you'll kind of hear them for the first time."

Dutifully the strings and the choristers appeared behind her.

"Panis Angelicus" on Nuala's lips was not a doleful signal that a wedding mass was winding down but a light, mystical hymn of celebration in which the soaring voice of the soprano was less important than the joy of the lyrics. Herself was relying on her own Irish-language spirituality in which God was not merely and not even mainly in His Heaven but lurked in the lanes and the hedges and the little lakes and the stone fences, always close and always eager to have a quiet word with us.

"That's the way we'd sing it in Connemara," she informed us. "Now I want to read a paragraph from a book by a man from Connemara who writes about the spiritual life in the Celtic world. Since I really can't preach a homily in the church—well, not yet anyway—I thought a quote from John O'Donohue would be just right. It's for all of us who are afraid of something tonight, including especially meself."

" 'No one but you can sense the eternity and depth concealed in your solitude. This is one of the lonely things about individuality. You arrive at a sense of the eternal in you only through confronting and outpacing your fears. The truly lonely element in loneliness is fear. No one else has access to the world you carry around within yourself—you are its custodian and entrance. No one else can see the world the way you see it. No one else can feel your life the way you feel it. Thus it is impossible to ever compare two people because each stands on such different ground. When you compare yourself to others, you are inviting envy into your consciousness; it can be a dangerous and destructive guest. This is always one of the great tensions in an awakened or spiritual life, namely, to find the rhythm of its unique language, perception, and belonging. To remain faithful to your life requires commitment and vision that must be constantly renewed.' "

Then we did Schubert's "Ave Maria" in the Galwegian mode. It began to dawn on me that Nuala Anne had reached not only into her own creative imagination for her approach to the concert but also and perhaps not altogether consciously into the spiritual memories of Irish Catholic antiquity. She had done such a fine job of it that the minutes of the concert slipped away like snowflakes melting on the ground.

I noticed a young man, neatly dressed in sweater and jeans, sitting at the far end of a row two ahead of ours. He was moderately good-looking, too well-groomed to be a student. Perhaps a young man from the countryside come to Dublin to work as a clerk at an accounting firm. He squirmed nervously in his seat, twisting and turning like a golfer eager to escape from church. There was something just a little unnerving about him. I resolved to keep my eye on him.

"You know what?" she asked us. "I think I've forgotten about the Holy Spirit altogether, haven't I now? Sure, I don't want to hurt Her feelings at all, at all, and Herself taking such good care of me all me life. So let's sing a song to Her. It's not the greatest hymn ever written, but youse all know the words, and we'll sing them quiet like they're going to float away on a gentle spring breeze and catch up with God's gentle spring breeze, which Jesus told us blows wither She will."

So we did the old clunker "Come, Holy Ghost," though I don't think any of us had ever sung it Nuala Anne's way before.

" 'Come, Holy Ghost, Creator blessed
And in our hearts take up Thy rest
Come with Thy grace and heav'nly aid
To fill the hearts which Thou hast made.
To fill the hearts which Thou hast made.

" 'O Comforter, to Thee we cry,
The heavenly gift of God most high.
The font of life and fire of love,
And sweet anointing from above.
And sweet anointing from above.

" 'To ev'ry sense Your light impart
And shed Your love in ev'ry heart.
To our weak flesh Your strength supply:
Unfailing courage from on high.
Unfailing courage from on high.' "

Who is this astonishing young woman? I asked myself. I consume her with my kisses. I sleep with her every night. I hold her naked in my arms. I bathe her in the shower. I nibble her breasts. I lick the smooth skin of her belly. I taste the sweetness of her loins. I intrude my body into hers. I know a little bit, not much, about her moods and her fears and her passion for neatness. But I really don't know her at all. At all. She is pure mystery. A mystical genius. She has turned this night at the Point into a spiritual experience for all the people here and for everyone who is watching on this soggy, mystical island. Pure mystery and pure genius. I don't deserve her. Worse yet, I have no idea about how I should properly cherish her.

HAVEN'T I BEEN TELLING YOU THAT ALL ALONG, ASS-HOLE?

"Shut up and listen to the music."

"Now, aren't we going to sing a song I hate? We've stolen it from poor old Ludwig V and we're not paying him any royalties for it. I think the lyrics are all tarted up. Why are we singing it tonight? For the same reason we sing it, maybe too often, at Mass. Great music!"

So we did poor old Ludwig V's "Ode to Joy" in its contemporary Catholic "tarted-up" form. Nuala didn't have to do anything, however, to save the glory of the music. The whole company swarmed out to join her.

" *Joyful, joyful we adore Thee,*
God of glory, Lord of love.
Hearts unfold like flow'rs before Thee,
Praising Thee, their Sun above.
Melt the clouds of sin and sadness,
Drive the dark of doubt away.
Giver of immortal gladness,
Fill us with the light of day.

" *'All Thy works with joy surround Thee,*
Earth and Heav'n reflect Thy rays.
Stars and angels sing around Thee,
Center of unbroken praise.
Field and forest, vale and mountain,
Blooming meadow, flashing sea.
Chanting bird and flowing fountain,
Call us to rejoice in Thee.' "

"Sure don't I hope when I meet your man in Heaven He doesn't hold that song against me. We didn't do all that badly by Him, did we now? . . . Well, in a couple of days, aren't me man and I going out to Galway to visit me ma and me da? And I can just imagine herself working all day long to clean up the house for us— though it's always neat and spotless. So I thought maybe I'd read a poem from Father Paddy Daly about that."

She read with her thickest Galway brogue:

> " 'All day long
> She has been arranging our welcome:
>
> " 'Scouring down the house,
> Sweeping under beds,
> Pulling out the old crocheted counterpanes,
> Shining glasses and tableware,
> Dusting sideboards and picture frames.
>
> " 'Now she sits in a deep chair
> Till we come crunching under the beeches
> To the door.' "

"Och, didn't I forget to tell you the title? What would you think the title is? I'll tell you: Doesn't Father Paddy call his poem 'God'?"

The singing went on. She rehabilitated the old war-horses—"Bring Flowers of the Rarest," *"Pange Lingua,"* "Lead, Kindly Light," "Lord, I Am Not Worthy." She sang some old Irish-language hymns, which like all Irish songs sounded sad. ("Och, Dermot Michael, are all the happy songs about lovemaking?") Good-dog Fiona continued to glare at the audience.

"Would youse ever let me read another one of Father Paddy's poems? It's called 'Journey's End':

> " 'After the tempests
> And the lightening at sea,
> I am ashore in a sunlit place.

" 'I lift myself to climb the shingle
But my feet give way
And I crawl to the marram on my elbows.

" 'I wait now,
Watching the white perfection of the gulls,
Until He welcomes me.' "

"And," she went on, "doesn't he use the capital *haitch*
for *He?*"

She let that sink in for a moment. The anxious
young man half stood from his seat and then slouched
back into it. I hope that one of Gene Keenan's swarms
of Guards had seen him, too.

"Well," she went on, "isn't it time for some brand-
new songs?" They're written by me good friend Father
Liam Lawton down below in Carlow, and I like to think
that this is the way Irish sacred music will develop in
the years ahead? Didn't your man write it for the fifteen hundredth anniversary of Colm of Iona? It's
called 'Sail the Soul,' and can't you hear the boat rac-
ing over the waves between Ireland and Iona?

" *'Lord of the pilgrim and Lord of the way,*
Guide every footstep, every journey I make,
Lord of the seeker and Lord of all truth,
Clear be the vision wherever I look.
Be Lord of my longing, be Lord of my life,
Lord of the pilgrim and Lord of the way,
May safe in our shadow be our rest each day.

" *'Sail the waves, may God safely guide us,*
Through all the days, may Heaven inspire us,
Comforting winds in glory will sing,

Soft falling rain God's healing will bring,
Sail the shore and find Heaven's shelter,
Sail the soul in waters so gentle remain.

" 'Lord of the story and Lord of the song,
May all of our voices unite now as one.
Lord of the symbol and Lord of the sign,
Gathered together we share bread and wine.
And when the land is parched and dry,
Be Lord of all wellsprings and Lord of all life,
Lord of the story and Lord of the song,
Be our companion till life's work is done.

" 'Sail the waves, may God safely guide us,
Through all the days, may Heaven inspire us,
Comforting winds in glory will sing,
Soft falling rain God's healing will bring,
Sail the shore and find Heaven's shelter,
Sail the soul in waters so gentle remain.' "

"Lord of the story, lord of the song," Nuala Anne
observed, "isn't that just the right God for us Irish? . . .
Your man's other song that I want to sing is called 'The
Cloud's Veil.' "

" 'Bright the stars at night
That mirror Heaven's way to you
Bright the stars in light
Where dwell the saints in love and truth

" 'Even thought the rain hides the stars,
Even when the mist swirls the hills,
Even when dark clouds veil the sky,
God is by my side,
God is by my side.

Even when the sun shall fall in sleep,
Even when at dawn the sky shall weep,
Even in the night when storms shall rise,
God is by my side,
God is by my side.

" *'Blest are they who sing*
The fellowship of saints in light
Blest is Heaven's king
All saints adore the Lord Most High

" *'Even thought the rain hides the stars,*
Even when the mist swirls the hills,
Even when dark clouds veil the sky,
God is by my side,
God is by my side.
Even when the sun shall fall in sleep,
Even when at dawn the sky shall weep,
Even in the night when storms shall rise,
God is by my side,
God is by my side.' "

The suspicious-looking young man seemed to have settled down. I relaxed. Still I'd be happy when we got out of the Point and back to the private dining room at Jury's where I had arranged for a dinner party for herself and her parents and the young men and women who had helped put on the concert. Ah, the creature would flow all night long!

"Well," she said with a monumental Galway sigh, "isn't our concert almost over? Aren't concerts just like life? They slip through our fingers and before we know it, it's almost over? Doesn't the priest from out our way have something important to say about that? In Connemara, you know, the ocean is everywhere. You only have to walk a little way and there it is. Och, isn't a walk by the ocean just the thing for it when you're discouraged and feeling old and tired?

"The ocean is one of the delights for the human eye. The seashore is a theater of fluency. When the mind is entangled, it is soothing to walk by the seashore, to let the rhythm of the ocean inside you. The ocean disentangles the netted mind. Everything loosens and comes back to itself. The false divisions are relieved, released, and healed. Yet the ocean never actually sees itself. Even light, which enables us to see everything, cannot see itself—light is blind. In Haydn's *Creation* it is the vocation of man and woman to celebrate and complete creation.

"Isn't that grand now? . . . Well, I hope I've helped you just a little bit tonight to push down that world towards complete creation? I'm going to sing one more song now. It's not religious exactly, though in a way it's about life being stronger than death. It's about a Dublin lass who wasn't as fortunate as we are today. She died very young, but, like I say, as long as there are Irish anywhere in the world, they'll sing about her. I sang it the first time I met me poor man who has to put up with a temperamental singer for a wife. I knew as soon as I sang it for him that he'd be me man, though, sure I wasn't after telling him that then!"

Annie's gentle elbow pressed against my ribs.

Dead silence in the house. They did not know what was coming. I knew since I'd heard her sing the song once or twice before—melancholy at the beginning, triumphant at the end.

> " *In Dublin's fair city.*
> *Where the girls are so pretty*
> *I first set my eyes*
> *On sweet Molly Malone*
> *She wheeled her wheelbarrow*

Through streets broad and narrow,
Crying cockles and mussels
Alive, alive oh!

" *'Alive, alive oh!*
Alive, alive oh!
Crying cockles and mussels
Alive, alive oh!

" *'She was a fishmonger,*
But sure 'twas no wonder,
For so were her father and mother before
And they both wheeled their barrow
Through streets broad and narrow
Crying cockles and mussels
Alive, alive oh!

" *'Alive, alive oh!*
Alive, alive oh!
Crying cockles and mussels
Alive, alive oh!

" *'She died of a fever*
And no one could relieve her,
And that was the end of sweet Molly Malone,
But her ghost wheels her barrow
Through streets broad and narrow,
Crying cockles and mussels
Alive, alive oh!

" *'Alive, alive oh!*
Alive, alive oh!
Crying cockles and mussels
Alive, alive oh!' "

After tumultuous applause, Nuala and the company
did a couple of encores. In response to their cries, she

also did "Molly" again. Then the company bowed and bid the happy crowd good evening. But we weren't ready for the party at Jury's yet. Not by a long shot.

Father Placid walked out on the stage, his portable mike in hand.

"Sit down, all of ye," he ordered. "You're not going home quite yet."

— 18 —

"I WANT to thank everyone who helped me," the somber cleric began. "A lot of people let me down, but you have to expect that's going to happen when you serve the poor and the hungry. I don't have to name the people who let me down. It should be obvious to everyone."

The audience did not know quite what to do. Most of them did sit down, partly out of politeness and partly, I suspect, out of curiosity.

"Everyone thinks that there are no expenses," he continued, "in running a concert like this. You hear that the singer isn't taking any money, so you figure it's all free. Well, let me tell you that no celebrity is ever free. They want all kinds of things and people to flatter themselves, and that costs money, money that could just as well have gone to the poor. They're spoiled folk and you have to pay a lot to keep them happy, let me tell you. We take all the risk, and they get all the free publicity."

Next to me Annie McGrail went stiff. Her husband's fists were clenched, as were mine. I wanted to poke the bastard in his twisted, hateful mouth. The audience was immobile. The stupid fool was killing himself and his organization. The Irish do not take kindly to men who violate the rules of hospitality.

He ranted on, attacking abortion, divorce, premarital sex, television, the media, American consumerism. He predicted the ruination of the Irish people because of selfish American materialism. He didn't miss many bases.

People began to drift out, quietly and sullenly. They were angry that a wonderful evening had turned bitter. He had destroyed the spiritual impact that Nuala had worked so hard to create.

Would he ever stop?

Good-dog Fiona watched him grimly. He was, the wolfhound realized, a bad man.

The members of the company stirred uneasily, not quite sure what to do. Their final curtain call had been aborted. Should they walk out? Should they try to silence this terrible man?

He returned to Nuala. He said he would pray that as she grew up she would learn the meaning of poverty and suffering.

Would he ever stop?

Fool that I was, I figured I had to stop him.

Me woman beat me to it.

Accompanied by Fiona, she strode up to the raving priest and snatched the microphone from him. He tried to pull it back but retreated from Fiona's growl.

" 'Hail, Holy Queen, enthroned above, O Maria!
Hail Queen of mercy, Queen of love, O Maria!

" 'Triumph all, ye Cherubim!
Sing with us, ye Seraphim!
Heaven and earth resound the hymn,
Salve, Salve Regina!' "

The remnants of the crowd caught on. They joined with the Cherubim and the Seraphim.

" 'Our life, our sweetness here below, O Maria!
Our hope in sorrow and in woe, O Maria!

" 'Triumph all, ye Cherubin!
Sing with us, ye Seraphim!
Heaven and earth resound the hymn,
Salve, Salve Regina!' "

With the air of a man who expected to be martyred,
Father Placid slithered away. I relaxed.

In response to cries from the crowd, Nuala sang
"Molly" again.

As she sang, the nervous young man leaped out of
his seat, produced a Swiss army pocketknife, and raced
for the stage. Berkserker that I was, I charged after
him, knocking aside a couple of kids who were cheer-
ing enthusiastically for my wife.

Naturally I forgot my shillelagh—Sir Lancelot without his lance.

No one noticed the man with the knife. He glided
through the crowd like a slippery ghost.

The stage manager arrived with my two dozen roses
and presented them to Nuala. She accepted them with
a bow and a hoyden smile, a little girl who had received
a reward for at last doing something presentable.

In the confusion of the departing crowd and the celebration on the stage no one had seen the man with
the knife. He vaulted onto the stage, much too big a
jump for a man as slight as he was.

I jumped up onto the stage after him. It didn't look
like I would catch up to him.

Suddenly a fierce howl filled the Point, a howl from
the forests and the bogs of the Ireland of long ago, a
howl from the days of Finn McCool, a howl from a
descendant of Finn's faithful Bran, the howl of an angry wolfhound.

I didn't need to catch up to the man with the knife.

With a single bound Fiona sank her huge teeth into his shoulder. He screamed in pain and dropped the knife. He tried to break free from her implacable grip. He kicked and jabbed and twisted. Fiona hurled him to the floor, released his arm, and gripped his throat with her vast mouth. The young man was crazy enough to try to fight her off. Perhaps the Gardai had taught her not to kill unless there was no choice. Her teeth were poised to sink into his throat, she was holding him down with her massive weight, but she had not yet torn the throat out of his body.

The young man groped for his knife.

Fortunately for him, I got there first.

"All right, Fiona, girl!" a young woman Guard shouted. "Good dog, good dog! You can let him go now!"

Fiona was not about to let him go.

The young man yelled and pushed and begged, but the wolfhound clung to him like a cat playing with a captive bird.

"This seems to have got through your metal detectors," I said to Gene Keenan, who had materialized next to me, as I gave him the Swiss army knife.

I turned to see my wife standing next to me, her harp held in the air like a weapon.

"Nice, Fiona," said the Guard. "Good dog. It's all right now."

Fiona did not seem so sure about that.

A phalanx of Guards swarmed around us on the stage. Everyone seemed to be screaming.

Except my wife, who was ready for battle.

Gently I took the harp out of her hands and replaced it with the roses she had dropped to the floor.

"Isn't she a cute little thing?" she said.

"Who?" I asked foolishly.

"Poor little Fiona."

I didn't argue that Fiona seemed just fine.

"Let him go, Fiona," she said firmly.

The wolfhound did as she was told. She eased off the terrified young man and barked at him, as if warning him never to try such foolishness again. He sobbed hysterically as the Guards pulled him to his feet and slapped handcuffs on him.

He was a little guy, at least eight inches shorter than me and two inches shorter than herself.

"He had opened the nail file," Commissioner Keenan murmured.

I extended my arms around Nuala Anne, who rested her head against my chest.

"This is a nightmare, isn't it, Dermot Michael? I'm going to wake up in a few minutes and know it's all a dream, won't I now?"

Of course my Nuala Anne wouldn't turn hysterical.

She probably didn't need me or Fiona, who was now pacing around nervously, edgy after her triumph. If the would-be assassin had reached Nuala Anne, she would have smashed his head with her harp, my harp, the harp I had given her the first day she came to Chicago.

I felt a solid nudge against my thigh. It was Fiona, demanding attention.

"Fiona, leave the poor man alone," said the Guard who was tugging on the wolfhound's leash.

I bent over and embraced our canine heroine.

"Fiona, you are the absolute greatest."

She barked contentedly and wagged her huge tail.

"The poor little girl just wants some attention." Nuala knelt next to me and rested her face on the dog's huge head. "Don't you, doggy?"

Fiona showed her agreement by trying to lick both our faces at the same time.

"Hasn't she bonded with the both of youse?" said her handler.

"Aren't we going to have to take her home with us?" Nuala Anne pleaded with me, as if I would have any say about such a decision.

I was aware that flashbulbs were popping all around us. Great shot for the morning papers—wolfhound and friend.

"Dermot Michael," the friend said to me. " 'Tis, too, a dream. Poor little Fiona is just a dog in a dream."

"It's not a dream, love. Both Father Placid and this punk are real."

I continued to pat the dog, who seemed especially fond of me.

"Me poor ma and da out beyond; won't they see it all on the telly?" She continued to lean against me.

I looked around. Annie and Gerry were waiting patiently beyond the line of Guards.

"That good-looking couple over there," I said to the Commissioner, who was still standing next to us, "the woman looks like Nuala. They're her parents."

"Right!" he said and waved at the Guards who were keeping them off the stage.

"Me ma and da!" herself shouted and ran towards them, leaving me and the wolfhound to fend for ourselves.

She began to sob only when she held both of them in her arms.

"Ms. McGrail is fine." The Commissioner had found a microphone somewhere. "The Gardai have taken the young man who created the disturbance into custody. It's all right to go home now."

The crowd left reluctantly, perhaps wondering what we would do next.

Later at the party in Jury's—at which vast quantities of Guinness were being consumed (though not by Nu-

ala and her parents)—Maeve Doyle showed up with
her huge black-bearded scowling husband. No one had
invited them, but they were there anyway. She was
dressed in a black skin-tight dress with an enormous
gold belt that was not adequate as a corset. Before I
could intercept her, she went straight to Nuala, a bulg-
ing Celtic Valkyrie bent on revenge.

"I just want to congratulate you, child," she said, oozing passive-aggressive sweetness. "You were really wonderful. You deserve all the praise you'll receive."

"Thank you," my wife said, taken aback by this weird
apparition.

"You shouldn't forget that they'll turn against you
eventually. They always do. I'm sure you'll have the
courage to stand up to them."

Pure poison.

"That will be as may be," I said, cutting in front of
her. "Nuala Anne, you owe me a dance."

We danced away from Maeve, who glared at me like
an angry banshee.

" 'Tis yourself that's quick, Dermot Michael," herself
sighed into my chest. "Another second and I might
have clawed her eyes out."

Maeve whispered into her huge husband's ear. He
nodded and began moving towards us.

I hoped he'd keep coming. I was in the mood to
flatten someone.

Gene Keenan slipped up easily on the advancing giant and said something with a casual smile. The giant
and his outsize wife departed quickly.

"Och, Dermot, didn't your man just save that fella's
life."

"I wouldn't have killed him, Nuala Anne."

"Ah, no, but wouldn't you have put him in the hospital."

"Just thrown him into the swimming pool."

MACHO ASSHOLE, the Adversary reprimanded me.

Gene Keenan winked. Later, when herself was dancing with one of the drummers, the Commissioner reported to me.

"The kid with the knife is a nutcase, Dermot. They just let him out of a home. He thinks he's St. Patrick and has a mission to purify Ireland. Your man's little diatribe up beyond set him off."

"You should put Father Placid in a home, too."

"I don't think they'd take him. . . . Seriously, he couldn't have done too much damage with a blunt nail file, not with our secret weapon and your wife's harp."

"It looks like we're stuck with the secret weapon."

Fiona was curled up in the corner of the party, sleeping the sleep of the just.

"You're welcome to her, God knows. . . . Still, Dermot . . ."

"You don't think the kid . . ."

"Sean MacCarthy. . . ."

"Is involved with the other characters."

"I shouldn't think so."

I nodded agreement. "Not very likely."

"We managed to keep your little escapade in Thomas Street out of the media. No word from the allegedly 'Real' IRA about it, so it looks like they were tagalongs."

"That's nice. . . . Do me a favor and get them anyway."

"We'll try. . . . I noticed, by the way, you didn't have your shillelagh with you on the stage tonight."

"No time to pick it up off the floor," I said lamely.

His wife appeared with diet Cokes for the two of us and slipped away. She had apparently been told that her husband needed a word or two with me.

"You have a tough decision ahead of you, Dermot Michael."

"Do I now?" I said, sipping at the Coke.

"Your wife is a beautiful and incredibly gifted young woman."

"Funny that you should mention it, but I noticed the same thing."

"Her performance tonight was a *tour de force* if I've ever seen one. She knows what Catholic Ireland really is because it's all there in her Celtic soul. Your man over at Drumcondra ought to hire her to teach religion on RTE every night of the week."

He was referring to Dublin's hand-wringing archbishop.

"He won't be that smart."

"Probably not. . . . Incidentally, if you haven't heard already, RTE cut off your man just as he started to talk. He has a bit of reputation, you know."

"I didn't know."

"But my point is . . ."

He said "pint" of course.

"Yes?"

"I'm not making excuses for our failures so far. Still, the point is that she is so spectacular that she is bound to stir up resentment not only here but back in America, too. I don't think she understands that or ever will."

"I very much doubt that she could imagine such twisted perceptions."

"You saw how the witches from the media treated her at the airport. They hated her because she was beautiful and brilliant and happy and had a wonderful husband."

"Yeah?"

Wonderful, indeed!

"They had to lay off because she put them down and because she won everybody's sympathy with that show over above at the Grand Canal. The reviews will be good tomorrow because if anyone attacks her just now they'll be laughed off this island. But once she's back in Chicago they'll start in again."

"Sick!" I exploded.

" 'Tis all of that," he sighed. "Envy is a great sickness."

"Where does my decision come in?"

"Whether she goes on with her career. If she does, there will be a lot of sick people who will want to hurt her."

That was true enough.

We both glanced across the room. Riding the crest of a wave of triumph, Nuala was dancing with her da.

"You think I can stop her?"

He shook his head sadly. "Of course not."

"THE FOCKING bitch is right." Herself waved the *Irish Times* at me. "I'm a focking hypocrite."

"She didn't say that," I replied mildly, knowing that my comment would do no good at all.

"And meself up there in front of the whole of Ireland acting like I was Rosin Dubh herself."

She hurled the paper across the room.

"I thought you were just being Nuala Anne."

"Fock Nuala focking Anne!" she shouted.

My woman, as is probably obvious, was in a vile mood, as vile a mood as I had observed since I had first met her in O'Neill's pub.

She was curled up in a chair in our room, almost in a fetal position, huddling in a terry cloth robe. She wanted no part of the world and no part of me.

The Irish mists had returned, this time as dense fog. The swimming pool below was invisible. So were the lower floors of the hotel. The fog fit her dark mood.

No, she did not want to swim.

No, she did not want to run in the park with Fiona (who was waiting for us in the kennel in the bowels of the hotel, which was reserved for dogs prominent enough to stay at Jury's).

No, she didn't want to talk to me.

No, she didn't want me to go down to the lobby and work on my report.

No, she didn't want me to stay in the room with her.

No, she didn't want any breakfast.

No, she didn't want to take a shower.

No, she didn't want anything.

Moreover, she wasn't hungover. She had consumed only one pint of Guinness at the party. However, she had not even bothered to get into bed but had spent the whole night sulking in the chair like a little girl who had been grounded for a bad attitude. I had the good sense not to argue with her.

The reviews in the morning papers had been wonderful. There was no mention of either Father Placid or Sean MacCarthy but pictures of Nuala and Fiona kissing each other. Somehow I didn't make it into the pictures. Good enough for me. A columnist in the *Times* had been a bit grudging:

Ms. McGrail has a pretty young voice which may eventually mature into something much better, though it obviously will never be quite as good as that of Ireland's most beloved woman singer, Maeve Doyle. However, she is gorgeous and has more stage presence than all of the Riverdance troupe put together. She is, above all else, an actress, a skilled and instinctive performer who wins over even the most critical instantly. In a startling display of courage, she chose to re-create in an hour and a half the whole history of Celtic spirituality. Astonishingly, she almost carried it off. For those who admire the absolute purity of Ms. Doyle's highly artistic performances, Ms. McGrail's west of Ireland exuberance may well seem offensive, even a bit too American. However, within the obvious limitations of her talents, she

**is a compelling presence. We will hear more of
her and from her in the future.**

I thought that wasn't half-bad, not for an *Irish Times*
columnist who was clearly a friend of Maeve Doyle. Nuala Anne chose to interpret it as a charge of hypocrisy,
doubtless because it confirmed her feeling that she was
a focking fraud and a focking phony.

We were to have a late lunch at the Commons with
her parents, who were determined to return to Galway
on the six o'clock train. I thought it inappropriate to
remind her.

"Well," I said with a sigh that was a fair imitation of
hers, "if you want to know what I think . . ."

"I don't," she snapped, "not at all, at all."

"Nonetheless, you're going to hear it. . . . You're
astonished at how well you did and at how much the
people liked you. You're afraid of success, because
you're convinced that you're a worthless little gobshite
from the Gaeltacht who has no business singing about
God and Mary and the Baby Jesus and talking about
the Celtic soul. You think it was all an act to cover up
that your voice has room to improve."

No response.

"I think that's a ton of horseshite. I think you know
it is. I think you'd better face up to who and what you
really are. And, since I've bought his book, now I can
quote your man from the Gaeltacht, too:

" 'We are so privileged to still have time. We have
but one life, and it is a shame to limit it by fear and
false barriers. Irenaeus, a wonderful philosopher and
theologian in the second century, said, "The glory of
God is the human person fully alive." It is lovely to
imagine that real divinity is the presence in which all
beauty, unity, creativity, darkness, and negativity are
harmonized. The divine has such passionate creativity

and instinct for the fully inhabited life. If you allow yourself to be the person that you are, then everything will come into rhythm. If you live the life you love, you will receive shelter and blessings. Sometimes the great famine of blessing in and around us derives from the fact that we are not living the life we love, rather we are living the life that is expected of us. We have fallen out of rhythm with the secret signature and light of our own nature.' "

I put the book down on the armrest of her chair, very gently. She wouldn't look at me.

"Now I'm going down to the lounge and work on my report. Someone in this family has to get things organized."

I picked up my Omnibook 800CS and walked to the door. I turned as I was about to leave. She was glaring at me, her eyes pools of sapphire fire.

"Oh yeah, I know what your next CD will be: *Nuala Anne Celebrates Christmas.* Maybe we'll call it *Friggin' Nuala Anne Friggin' Celebrates Friggin' Christmas.*"

I think she giggled as I shut the door. I didn't stop to find out.

Och, your man Dermot Michael is a tough one, isn't he?

I asked the starry-eyed young woman in charge of the Towers whether she would ever be able to get a big breakfast delivered to me in the lounge.

"Wasn't herself brilliant last night?" she demanded. "Didn't she show up that terrible Maeve Doyle woman?"

"Sure," I replied, using the interrogative of emphasis, "wasn't she dazzling altogether?"

"And isn't that poor little doggy a darlin' girl altogether?"

"Hasn't she taken over me whole family?"

Then the young woman deigned to order me, er, my breakfast.

I settled down at a table, plugged in my Omnibook, pulled together my notes, and began to work. While I earn my living these days by writing stories, such as they are, I found the story of Kevin O'Higgins a difficult one to tell. I was also astonished that there had been only one biography of a man who played a critical role in turning Ireland into a peaceful and democratic country almost immediately after two bitter wars, one with the English and one among the Irish themselves. He was a little too forbidding a man to like, yet clearly those who knew him did like him. There was also the mystery of his romance with Lady Lavery, so contrary to his adamant Catholic principles. I almost wrote "poor Lady Lavery" because she, too, was a tragic figure.

When my breakfast came, I ate it as I wrote. Real writers can eat and work on a computer at the same time. Right?

As I was finishing up around noon, I heard a loud slobbering noise. I looked up and there was Fiona, vast paws on the table, delicately finishing off the remains of my scrambled egg.

A woman began to sing:

> *"We three kings of Orient are,*
> *Bearing gifts we traverse afar*
> *Field and fountain, moor and mountain,*
> *Following yonder star.*
>
> *"O star of wonder, star of night,*
> *Star with royal beauty bright,*
> *Westward leading, still proceeding,*
> *Guide us to thy perfect light"*

"Not bad," I observed, "for a still-immature voice."

I looked up. Her hair was tied in a prim knot, and she was wearing white shorts and her beloved Marquette sweatshirt, thus hedging against the Irish weather. The "soft" mist had soaked her clothes and pasted them against her body. Her face was covered with a mix of rain and sweat. I smelled all kinds of wonderful womanly aromas.

"Sure, isn't that fine, because I'm still an immature person."

I looked her up and down approvingly. "Not in every respect."

She blushed. "Aren't you the one with the dirty mind, Dermot Michael Coyne?"

Fiona, having cleaned my plates, turned to licking my face. Her fur was wet from the rain. I hugged her.

"Good dog," I told her.

"That's enough, girl," my wife informed the new member in our family. "I have kissing rights on that face. . . . I'll put her back in the basement. Then will I be after seeing you up in our room?"

"There's just a chance of that, woman."

A few minutes later, she charged through the door, pulling off her sweatshirt as she did.

I almost, almost, became a wildly abandoned lover.

But I didn't.

ASSHOLE.

This time I didn't argue with him.

— 20 —

THAT WAS not bad. It wasn't what I wanted. But it was an improvement. What did I want? I wanted ecstasy. I wanted something to heal my reaction to last night. I wanted to lose control. Well, I almost did. I was so close, but then the focking actress in me took over and I was playing games again. They were nice games. I'm grateful to You for them. But I wanted more. I think he did, too. But he never tells me what he wants. Fair play to him! I never tell him what I want either. I don't know what I want.

We were so close.

And the gobshite has the nerve to read to me from me own spiritual book! Isn't he wonderful!

I love him so much.

I had a talk with me ma last night. (Why am I telling You this? You know it already!) Typical Irish woman talk about such matters—round about, indirect, lots of silence, and sighs and winks and nods of the head. Well, me ma doesn't wink, but it's the same thing. And we're talking in Irish, which must be the most indirect language in the world.

Me: Aren't there some women now who don't like sex at all, at all?

Ma: They say that there're some so prim and proper that they never lose control.

Me: Control, is it?

Ma: (sigh).

Me: 'Tis all right for the men to lose control, but not for the women?

Ma: Sure, aren't the men often just as much afraid as women?

Me: (sigh).

Ma and Me: (silence).

Ma: Och, there isn't much point in it, is there, unless both of them lose control?

Me: Isn't the thing about ecstasy?

Ma: Isn't it, now?

Me: You can't control ecstasy, can you?

Me and Ma: (sigh).

Me: Sure, it doesn't happen all the time, does it?

Ma: It doesn't have to . . . but the more the better.

Me and Ma: (silence after that uncharacteristically candid comment).

Ma (sigh): 'Tis fear.

Me (sigh): 'Tis.

Ma: Of the body.

Me: And the things it makes you want, too.

Ma: Aye, you have the right of it . . . a little bit of fear every time you start.

Me (like I know what I'm talking about): Sweet fear.

Ma: Aye. Delicious terror.

Me: (sigh).

Ma (after long pause): Some say that women want it more than men.

Me: And why shouldn't they?

Me and Ma: (quiet laugh, just a little suggestive).

Ma: Well, there are those who say it's all about the fire inside, if you take me meaning.

Me: Aye, 'tis the fire.

Ma: They say that the fire inside the woman burns something fierce.

Me: Do they now?

Ma: 'Tis said that when the fire burns bright inside a woman it glows in her eyes.

Me: Some would want to hide it.

Ma (sigh): How else can their man tell it's there?

Me: How else?

Ma: I wouldn't know about them things, but isn't it the fire they're afraid of?

Me (to meself): The hell you don't know about it.

Me: Aren't they afraid if they let go there'll be nothing left of them at all, at all?

Ma: 'Tis them prim and proper ones who feel they have to hide so they can control their man, as if that was what love was all about.

Me (to meself): That was pretty direct for her.

Me (taking the risk of being equally direct): Aren't they the ones who figure that if they take off their clothes that's enough?

Ma: And in the dark, too.

Me and Ma: (Silence).

Ma: Them as wants ecstasy has to take off more than their clothes, don't they now?

Me: Sure, you have the right of it, woman.

And that was that.

When she and me da were going up to their room (and didn't I know what they are going to up there? Wasn't the fire in her eyes?), she hugged me and said, "Things work out, Maire Fionnuala, when we give them a little time, don't they?"

Delicious terror? I've never felt that way! But I want to!

The fire has been burning inside me since I saw him consume me with his eyes that foggy night in O'Neill's. I want to let it out.

Please help me.

21

IT'S TIME, Nuala Anne, that I begin to write my report, first of all about Kevin O'Higgins and then about Lady Augusta Downs. I'm not sure how they're connected or even whether they have to be, except that they lived at the same time, a bad time for Ireland.

I'm going to provide some background before you read the two stories the Gardai have put together and which I have scanned into my computer with Paperport.

When you were growing up, my love, Ireland was one of the most peaceful countries in the world. It still is. The crime rate here is the lowest in Europe. Even Northern Ireland, despite, the political violence, has the lowest crime rate in, you should excuse the expression, the United Kingdom.

The Irish people are peaceful folk if left to themselves. Unfortunately, they have not been left to themselves for half a dozen centuries or so. Since Cromwell and the Penal Times after him, there have always been revolutionary movements in the country, the United Irishmen in 1798 and the Fenians in 1848, for example. In addition to these organized rebels, there have also been waves of rural terrorists who fought the landlords, sometimes for freedom and justice, sometimes for their own profit. Such groups, often with names like the Ribbon Men and the White Boys, terrified the English and scared the Irish peasants. The modern IRA is not all that different from its predecessors. It was hard to tell who was a patriot and who was a thief. Most of them were both perhaps, because that is the way things are in an occupied and oppressed country, where starvation lurks at the next bend in the road.

Still most Irish people were too hungry and also too peaceful to be rebels or terrorists. The United Irishmen in '98 and the Fenians in '48 were intellectuals, not peasants. After the Land League battles at the end of the last century and the distribution of land to the peasants, Ireland became a peaceful country again, especially since everyone believed that the English would keep their promise to grant Home Rule. Indeed, if they had not used the beginning of the Great War in 1914 as an excuse to postpone Home Rule, it is pretty likely that all the "Troubles" since then would never have happened.

Even then Ireland was peaceful during the early years of the Great War. Thirty thousand Protestant Volunteers marched in the North to make it clear they wanted no part of Home Rule. The Irish Republican Brotherhood, a secret society (of which your man the Big Fella was the head by the way), was plotting revolution. Their own Irish Volunteers were also marching, often with makeshift uniforms and wooden guns. Most Irish folk considered them to be eejits. No one took either set of volunteers all that seriously. The Irish, as I say, have always been a peaceful law-abiding people—when others leave them alone and give them a chance to be peaceful.

Then on Easter Monday 1916, your man Willy Yeats's "Terrible Beauty" was born. At the last minute a split occurred in the leadership of the Volunteers. There

was no rising at all in the west, and the rising in Dublin
drew little support. The men who proclaimed the Republic of Ireland at the General Post Office knew they
would lose, but they firmly believed that their sacrifice
would launch the beginning of the end of English rule
in Ireland.

They were right, but only because the English, as
usual, did exactly the wrong thing. Most people in
Dublin and around the countryside thought that the
Volunteers in their funny dark green uniforms were a
pack of amadons. If the Brits had simply put them in
jail, no one would have given them another thought.

However, to the English mind, they were rebels in
the time of war, rebels who might even be allied with
Germany. So they shot the lot of them. The whole
country was shocked. Public opinion indicated the people were now ready for revolt. In the election of autumn 1918, Sinn Fein swept most of the Irish districts.
Its elected representatives refused to take their seats in
the English parliament. Instead they gathered in Dublin and proclaimed themselves the Dáil Éireann, the
duly elected parliament of the Irish Republic.

Then public order began to collapse. Young men
swarmed into the Volunteers (who soon were calling
themselves the Irish Republican Army, a name that
may never go away), many just home from the war and
many others with nothing else to do.

It is difficult now and it was even more difficult in
those days to distinguish between revolutionary action
and terrorism, pure and simple. Most IRA men did
nothing at all. The Cork Brigade, for example, was well
organized, properly drilled, and influential at the
meetings of the army. But it didn't do any fighting.
When the ragtag Free State Army (the Big Fella's
crowd) landed at Cork in August of 1921, they swept
the Cork Brigade away without any trouble—and

didn't even interfere with the annual Cork Regatta.
Other units were much more active. They ambushed
army patrols, burned down RIC barracks, executed col-
laborators, and set fire to the homes of the English and
killed some of them.

General McCready, the commander of the British
Army in Ireland, advised London that he did not have
the men to put down the now-open revolt. The English
had one more chance. If they had offered to negotiate
then, they probably would have got a better deal and
the violence, which had not yet become a way of life,
would have diminished. In fact, they did just the opposite, as the two reports from the Gardai describe.

The burning and killing went on, some of it aimed
at the English army, some at settling old grudges.

Then came the cease-fire and the treaty and the
breakup of the Irish Republican Army. After the death
of Michael Collins, there was no hope of a peaceful
solution. The Free State Army had little trouble winning the few pitched battles that actually happened.
The "Irregulars," as they called the IRA, turned to terrorism. The anarchy in the countryside was now worse
than ever.

The leaders of the Free State Government were convinced that they had to show the world that the Irish
knew how to govern. Indeed, they had launched the
Civil War by shelling the Irregulars in the Four Courts
on the banks of the Liffey under English pressure—
especially from our old friend Winston S. Churchill.
He warned Collins that unless the Free State took action against the Irregulars, the British Army would
have to intervene and restore order.

He was talking through his hat. The British Army
had not been able to restore order before and could
not do it now. General McCready dreaded the results
of an English attack on the Four Courts. Nonetheless,

the Irish leaders felt that the whole world was watching them to see if the Irish were really capable of self-government.

That must seem a strange idea to you now. Ireland is a successfully functioning democracy that has built one of the most prosperous economies in Europe. But in those days Ireland was a very new nation. It never before had a national government of its own. A lot of people, influenced by English propaganda, expected that the Irish would prove too immature to govern themselves.

Moreover, democracy itself was in doubt. The people of Ireland had voted in favor of the treaty. The Irregular army felt that it represented the republic and the people who had voted for peace did not. Therefore, its decisions cancelled out the election. This, by the way, is the same logic the IRA uses today.

The challenge, then, for the Free State was to restore peace and validate democracy. That meant it had to repress the anarchy in the countryside. There was no gentle way to do that. Therefore, harsh measures were required. After Collins's death, Kevin O'Higgins was the man who had to impose order on the country. He did that and paid for it with his life. Collins died because he had created a free Ireland, O'Higgins because he had created a peaceful and democratic Ireland. Both men were geniuses.

Later, when De Valera came to power, he was equally ruthless in dealing with the rump IRA that had broken with him when he accepted the Free State. There was a nice irony in that the man who had set loose the furies eventually had to fight them himself.

That, then, is the background to understand the times in which Kevin O'Higgins lived and died. He lacked the charm and the imposing physical stature of Collins. He was just as smart and just as determined.

Moreover, while he was certainly troubled by the need to approve the execution of men who had been his friends, it probably bothered him less than it would have bothered the Big Fella if he were still alive.

Unlike the Big Fella, however, O'Higgins apparently did not successfully resist the allurements of Lady Hazel Lavery, the temptress from Chicago who seemed to take special delight in seducing Irish revolutionaries. I'd just as soon leave her out of this story. But she may be involved in the puzzle we are wrestling with. Besides, if I try to leave anything out, you'll know and I'll be in trouble.

There was little in the early life of Kevin Higgins (as he was known when he was growing up) that would suggest he was the man to restore order to Ireland— and, by the way, to decide that the Irish police, like the English, would be unarmed. He was the fourth of sixteen children (that's right, SIXTEEN). His father was a doctor, his mother the daughter of a lawyer who was also Lord Mayor of Dublin. Thus, unlike Collins, whose father was a farmer, O'Higgins was a member of the solid Catholic upper-middle class. He was obviously intelligent but did not like to study. He drifted from school to school and spent some time in seminaries, both Maynooth and Carlow, and was thrown out of both of them for smoking.

He joined the Irish Volunteers but was not involved in the rising. While at law school in Cork, he was arrested for "unlawful assembly" and spent three months in jail. After his release he ran for parliament and came to Dublin to serve as a member of the underground Dáil. While there, he passed the bar examination with highest honors. William Cosgrave, the Minister for Local Government in the secret government, needed an assistant. Impressed with O'Higgins's intelligence and determination, Cosgrave chose him for the job.

The Black and Tans burned down his family home and arrested and imprisoned his father. By this time his father, at first opposed to the revolutionary movement, was a strong supporter.

O'Higgins was only a year younger than Collins at the time. The latter was a major figure in the strange shadow government that operated successfully in the half-light of Dublin, despite English efforts to snuff it out. O'Higgins was only a minor player, though a tough and resourceful one. He would not be in a minor role for long.

He was already winning for himself a reputation. He describes himself in a letter to Brigid Cole, the young woman he was to marry, ironically an English teacher at the seminary he attended in Carlow: "Whenever there's an abusive letter to be written, Cosgrave says, 'Here, Higgins, you're a cross-grained divil; you'd better deal with this fellow—and for God's sake work off some of your spleen on him instead of on me.' "

Apparently, this was supposed to impress her. Apparently it did, because they would be married during the cease-fire and go to London on their honeymoon while Collins was negotiating with Lloyd George and Churchill. His young assistant Rory O'Connor, of whom he was deeply fond, was the best man at the wedding.

Those were great days for O'Higgins. He was an increasingly important leader in an underground government working for the freedom of his country. He was on the run constantly from the English. He was in love with a beautiful young woman, and she with him. One wonders how all of this could be going on at the same time.

DeVere White offers an explanation:

If this seems incongruous, in the dark setting of those days, to a reader who did not know them, it

will not surprise anyone familiar with the times. For they were very incongruous times; people continued to live normal, even cheerful, lives in Dublin, while lorries, fenced with wire, in which hostages sat, surrounded by their captors in black berets with rifles cocked, dashed through the streets. Very few people were taking part in the struggle which was being carried on in their midst. Races, dances, theatres flourished, but violence was intermittent, sporadic, like death which occurs every day everywhere, but of which we are hardly conscious until it turns its eye on someone near us.

When Collins came back with his compromise treaty, the best he could get without going back to a war for which he did not have either the weapons or the support of a war-weary Irish people, O'Higgins had no problem supporting the treaty—as did a majority of the Dáil. He wished as they all did that the terms were better, but it was all they could have and it was a beginning. Moreover, he did not trust De Valera, and he did not like the men around Dev, whom he considered to be thugs. Moreover, he worshiped Collins. When De Valera and his minority resigned from the Dáil, O'Higgins became one of the strongest advocates of the treaty. His intense belief in democracy did not permit him to think that the IRA had the authority to overrule the majority of the Dáil and the wishes of the majority of the people of Ireland.

The die was cast.

His friend Rory O'Connor had gone over to the antitreaty forces. When challenged that his argument that the army's rule was supreme was an invitation to dictatorship, O'Connor did not disagree.

O'Higgins became a member of the new "Provisional Government," which, as he said, was "eight young men in city hall standing amidst the ruins of one administration with the foundations of another one not yet laid and with wild men screaming through the keyhole." His job was to supervise the transfer of the financial structure of the English government in Ireland to Irish control. He went at it with his usual vigor and determination. He also accompanied Collins to London for further negotiations. Like previous Irish delegates, he enjoyed visits at the house of the painter Sir John Lavery and his American wife, Hazel (born in Chicago, Nuala Anne, at 415 North Avenue, just down the street, more or less, from our house).

Looking back at it, Nuala my love, it's hard to see why the Irish hung around Sir John's home. Lady Hazel was then in her early forties—ten years older than Collins and O'Higgins—and was, if one is to judge by photographs of her, something less than a raving beauty even when she was much younger. Her salon, however, must have been charming and gracious. It provided access to English political society, a place where one could chat with Winston Churchill in relaxed and even jovial circumstances. With a long record of liaisons with English political leaders (possibly including Churchill), she was surely accomplished in the arts of seduction. An incorrigible romantic, she had made the cause of Ireland her own, something useful in a life that had been mostly dull and unhappy. Judging by the letters to and about her, she smothered men with a kind of reassuring and motherly affection. Even Michael Collins, who, it would seem, stayed out of her bed, considered her an important and affectionate friend. O'Higgins, if we are to judge by his letters to her, fell hopelessly in love with her and remained that way for the six years of life that remained to him. In the pictures of him with her and

Sir John (who apparently did not mind his wife's sexual flings) he is an intense young man with a receding hairline and dangerous eyes.

Perhaps her ingenious sexual allure was overwhelming to these dedicated young men, who had never met a woman quite like her. She overwhelmed O'Higgins, a stern and upright Catholic and a married man. He wrote to her the year before his death: "I am so unhappy and I want you, want you, and it is so miserable to have to pretend that I haven't a wish in the world except to win the elections, which is absurd and suggests a convict clamoring for heavier balls of lead around his ankles."

Later, in January of the year he died and a few days after the birth of his second daughter, who is now a Carmelite nun, he wrote: "I am lost and broken. You are my life and my breath my sun and air and wind. Having absorbed everything, having become all life holds for me."

There can be no doubt, Nuala, that he wrote those letters. Nor can there be any doubt that she passed them around, practically guaranteeing that they would be discovered someday. It's none of our business, nor is it our right to judge either of them, any of them, anyone.

She died in 1935 in her early fifties. Her last fling was with Evelyn Waugh, who dedicated his first novel to her. Waugh was twenty-three years younger than her, yet he was one more victim of her powers of enchantment. At the end, she murmured over and over again, "My house is built with straw. My house is built with sticks."

The Brompton Oratory, founded by Cardinal Newman, was the site of her funeral mass. Oh, yes, she was a Catholic, like everyone else in this strange story. May she rest in peace, like all the rest of them.

Meanwhile the Civil War continued in Ireland. Beaten in the field, the Irregulars turned to terror, burning, ambushing, murdering. Their targets this time were members of the the Free State Government. At first squeamish about killing men who had been their allies and friends, the Free State leaders concluded that violence must be met with violence. Their ruthless policy was successful because the Irish people, who had supported the rebellion against the English, were fed up with the Irregulars.

Erskine Childers, an English-born leader in the War of Independence, was captured and shot because he carried a gun at the time of his capture. His son later became President of Ireland (and the son of Cosgrave, who had ordered his death served as his Prime Minister). In December of 1922, two members of the Dáil were shot as they were leaving their hotel. In reprisal the Free State Army demanded the execution of four captured leaders of the Irregulars, including O'Higgins's old friend and wedding best man, Rory O'Connor. Reluctantly O'Higgins accepted the decision and defended it before the Dáil. Since then he has been known to many in Ireland as the man who ordered the execution of his best friend.

After the execution of the four Irregular leaders, there was another election in which the killing was a major issue. O'Higgins's party won in a landslide. The ordinary people of Ireland did not like the executions, but they liked even less the violence, which had now continued for eight years.

The executions, which he had defended as a necessary deterrent, had their effect. Terrorism against the government ceased. By 1925, when De Valera ordered a cease-fire and the "caching" of weapons (which was bluster, because there were few weapons left to cache), the Irregular movement ceased to exist, save for a few die-hards. O'Higgins had successfully ended anarchy in Ireland. In a very short time Ireland would become a stable democratic society. It was an extraordinary accomplishment, one at which political scientists today marvel.

He spent his remaining years establishing a working governmental structure at home, including the unarmed Garda Siochana, and representing Ireland as "Minister for External Affairs" abroad. He thought that a dual monarchy, in which the King of England would also be the King of Ireland (crowned in St. Patrick's Cathedral after he was crowned at Westminster Abbey), would solve the Northern Ireland problem.

It was probably too late for that. Ten years before, it might have done the trick.

What kind of a man was he, Nuala love?

To tell you the truth, I don't know. He was stern, upright, just. Grimmer and tougher than his hero, the Big Fella. An utterly dedicated Catholic, as DeVere White describes him:

A man who fasts for half a year before he marries, as a preparation for the ceremony, is not an ordinary man, according to the ideas of this age, in which ascetical practices are immediately suspect. There was a time when it would have seemed not an abnormal practice for a Christian on the eve of a sacrament. It fits the idealized conception of a dedicated knight. O'Higgins was not a psychopath; he was a Catholic who took his religion seriously, who lived in the light of his religion. It is impossible to interpret his character on any basis other than that of a man to whom religion was the inspiration of life. With his remorselessly clear and logical mind, he found it impossible to make the usual compromise between the claims of this world and the next. It would, however, be quite misleading to leave the impression that O'Higgins made any demonstration of unusual piety. Of his moral strength all were aware, but, just as his family were surprised when he declared his intention of becoming a priest, so were his friends unaware of any unusual religious fervor. He had no pomp, nor did he smear his speech with the oil of sanctity.

Yet there was always his infatuation with Lady Hazel Lavery. How does one reconcile that with the stern Catholicism that drove his public life?

One doesn't. Nor, since we are not media journalists, whose job it is to render judgment on men and women of the past, do we.

We do know that if Collins is the "man who made Ireland," Kevin O'Higgins is the man who made Ireland a peaceful democracy.

I don't know much help this, my report, in combination with the two stories from the Gardai, will be, Nuala love. It is not as clear or as clean as some of the other reports I have made in my Dr. Watson role. I don't see how Kevin and Birdie O'Higgins and Hazel Lavery (from 415 Ninth Avenue) fit into our lives. Nor do I understand how they relate to what happened at Castle Garry, which also seems to fit into our lives.

To tell you the truth, the whole business frightens me.

22

"LET ME read your report about Kevin O'Higgins again, Dermot love?"

Arguing that she wanted to approach the data in the same order I had, Nuala had studied Gene Keenan's two memos before she read my account of Ireland during its Civil War. Then she had returned to Keenan's memos.

I gave her my report about Kevin O'Higgins. She handed me back my notes about Garrytown and the photocopy of Augusta Downs's book.

We were sitting on a bench in Merrion Square, enjoying the delightful spring warmth that had won its most recent confrontation with the Irish mist. Fiona was curled up at our feet, panting contentedly. Nuala was wearing white jeans and a purple knit shirt. She was sufficiently lovely that everyone who passed us by had to have a second look. Man with a beautiful woman and a beautiful dog. Lucky guy.

The beautiful woman was all business this morning, no time for lollygagging.

Somewhere near cops were lurking, but I didn't see any of them.

"So much suffering," Nuala said, giving me back the report, which I put in my briefcase with our other files.

"There is certainly plenty of that."

"Look at all the marriages that were destroyed—Brigid O'Higgins, Augusta Downs, Eve Tudor, maybe even Hazel Lavery. If that ever were a marriage."

"He certainly loved her."

"That doesn't make a marriage, Dermot Michael."

" 'Tis true."

"Don't think that's going to happen to our marriage," she warned. "I'm not about to let you get away."

"I wasn't planning on it."

"You'd better not," she said, patting my knee. "We're not going to let him get away, are we, Fiona girl?"

The wolfhound wagged her tail and slobbered.

"Do you think Birdie O'Higgins knew about Hazel?" I asked.

"Sure she did. . . . Did she write a letter to Hazel after Kevin's death?"

"I think so," I said, taking Sinead McCoole's book out of my briefcase. "Yeah, here it is."

" 'I want to thank you and Sir John Lavery for your loving messages on the death of our dauntless hero, my beloved Kevin. You were his dear, dear friends—he loved you *both* and he will be with you in and by your sides when death comes. His own death was an inspiration—quiet—great, beautiful! ! ! ! ! Sometime I want to tell you about it! I'm sorry you were not here to say adieu to his noble spirit, for "Nothing in his life/ Became him like the leaving it." It was magnificent. He conquered death as he conquered life. He was serene. But oh! for those who are left . . . it is unthinkable—and yet with dying breath he charged us all "to be brave and to carry on" and "orders is orders." ' "

"She knew all right," Nuala said. "And she is telling Hazel that he died as her husband. I bet Hazel didn't like the letter at all."

"She showed it around to people and remarked on how strange it was. . . . Hazel had a lot of lovers in her life. Men who were captivated by her, wrote poetry about her, risked everything for her. Churchill, Ramsey MacDonald, who was the first Labour Prime Minister, Lord Londonderry, Lord Brinkenhead. None of them, however, gave up their wives and family for her."

"Poor woman," Nuala said with a shake of her head. "She was a pet like Fiona here. Her life depended on men showing her attention. Unlike Fiona, she served no other useful function in life. She wasn't a great watchdog, was she, adorable little girl. . . ." She bent over and petted the dog's huge head. Fiona responded by slobbering.

"She thought the cause of a free Ireland gave purpose to her life for a while."

"Did Sir John marry her so he would have a model to paint?"

"Probably," I replied. "He even painted her on her deathbed."

Nuala shivered. "It gives me the creeps, Dermot Michael. . . . No children, I suppose?"

"Actually, she had a daughter and a stepdaughter. Her first husband, a New York society M.D., died six months after they were married of a pulmonary embolism—in her presence. Her daughter, Alice, was born six months later. Sir John had a daughter who was Hazel's age. He was twenty-five years older than Hazel."

"You're wrong, Dermot, to say she wasn't attractive." Nuala took the book away from me and glanced at the pictures. "Not the kind which would attract you, thanks be to God, but still enchanting."

"I guess she had to be to have had so many lovers."

Nuala handed the book back to me. "If she really did, poor woman. . . . Did Birdie O'Higgins remarry?"

"She did."

Nuala nodded her approval. "If I die before you do,

Dermot Michael, I want you to marry again."

"You'll outlive me. According to Prester George, you have ten more years of life expectancy."

She snorted, dismissing that possibility. "Anyway, Lady Hazel," she continued, "is probably only a distraction. She's not part of our problem."

"And what is our problem?"

She turned to face me. "Dermot love, I haven't the foggiest. I don't know why we should be interested in Kevin O'Higgins or Birdie O'Higgins or Arthur Downs or Gussie Downs or Sir Henry Hugh Tudor. I don't know what connection they have with our lives. I don't see how they can be connected with them focking eejits who tried to kidnap me or who make those crazy phone calls. All I know is that I felt Kevin's death and I felt the fire."

"And knew that the girl didn't start it. . . . What girl?"

She shrugged. "They're not video replays, Dermot Michael."

"I understand."

Two young men were walking towards us on our side of the park. They looked tough and dangerous, but that was the way even the most innocent of students from Trinity College was supposed to look these days.

Fiona, however, did not approve of them. She stood up, then sat on her haunches and glared at them, her tail wagging dubiously. Me shillelagh cane rested next to me on the bench.

"It seems to me that we usually encounter these phenomena when we become involved with something from the past that causes you to feel vibrations. Like visiting Pa and Ma's and at Mount Carmel[1] or living in Lettitia Walsh's home.[2] Do you think that making a

---

[1] *Irish Whiskey*
[2] *Irish Lace*

reservation at Castlegarry is what started it this time?"

The young men were coming closer. They were grim and unsmiling. Fiona uttered a low, ominous growl.

"Maybe, Dermot," Nuala said with a sigh. "It's a reasonable idea, but this dark talent of mine—if it's a talent at all—isn't exactly reasonable."

The received wisdom, promulgated by George the Priest, is that Nuala's psychic sensitivity to "vibrations" from the past is a trait inherited by a few of us modern humans from a proto-hominoid ancestor, *Homo antecessor,* or *Homo habilis,* or even *Homo erectus*— not from the Neanderthals, which, according to the priest, are not now thought to be our ancestors. At one time, before language evolved as fully as it has in us, this ability was useful for survival. Now it carries with it no evolutionary advantage.

The little bishop had listened skeptically to that explanation. "Maybe," was all he'd said.

"Dermot Michael," Nuala had said with a big smile, "is His Rivirince suggesting that I ought to be living in a tree?"

"More likely a savannah in Kenya."

Then we had to explain to her Kenya and that a savannah was not merely a newly popular woman's name or a city in Georgia.

"Well," she had said, "I'd never call a daughter of mine Savannah."

Later I had asked her what she'd thought of George the Priest's analysis.

"Och, isn't His Rivirince a grand man, and himself being so smart. But then sometimes he's really full of cow shite, isn't he?"

I tentatively subscribe to the priest's theory, but mainly because I need some kind of explanation.

There's no doubt, however, about her "sensitivity"— if that's the right name for it. She knew that my sister-in-law was pregnant with her first child before the. young woman herself did. She also knew the sex of the child.

There are, of course, purely rational explanations for these individual phenomena. As far as that goes, there's surely a purely rational explanation for all of it. Only it's still spooky.

And scary.

"Anyway," she said, continuing our conversation in Merrion Square, "the answer to it all is out there in Limerick. So we have to go there after Galway."

"I'm not so sure. . . ."

Fiona growled again, more loudly.

"Shush, darlin'," Nuala whispered. "They only want me to sing a song for them."

The two lads stopped a few feet away from us. Fiona apparently accepted Nuala's reassurance. She remained on her haunches, however.

"Good morning, ma'am," one of them said shyly.

Herself replied in Irish. I knew the sound well enough to know that she said, "Jesus and Mary and Patrick be with you all this day."

" 'Tis a lovely dog you have there," said the other.

" 'Tis me darlin' Fiona."

I was out of the loop, apparently where I belonged.

"Could we pet her?"

"Fiona, these nice young men from TCD want to pet you."

The lads, who were surely no older than eighteen, didn't seem to think it strange that she knew where they went to school.

I, however, thought that it was strange beyond belief that my gorgeous woman knew these kids were harmless before the Guard's wolfhound did.

Where was that tree?

They approached the good dog gingerly. Fiona put

her paw out to greet them, a new trick. Both lads solemnly shook hands with her and then patted her massive head. She responded by slobbering all over them, much to their delight.

"I went to Trinity meself."

"We know, ma'am."

"We saw you on the telly."

"This is me husband, Dermot."

"You played American football, didn't you, sir?" one of them said as we shook hands.

"A little," I said.

I was not being modest. I had played only a little and had quit after my junior year because I disliked the brutality.

"Would you ever sing a song for us, Ms. McGrail?"

"Ms. McGrail is me ma. I'm Nuala Anne. . . . I bet you want to hear 'The Cloud's Veil.' "

They nodded their heads solemnly.

She sang only the refrain, which was what they wanted to hear from "The Cloud's Veil."

They asked herself for an autograph in each of their notebooks, shook hands with the three of us, and departed.

"They didn't ask for my autograph," I said.

"Washed up linebacker! . . . Anyway, as I was saying, Dermot Michael, we have to go out to Limerick; that's all there is to it. I must sing those hymns with the monks!"

"We don't have to stay at Castlegarry."

"Yes, we do; that's what the mystery is all about."

"The place is haunted."

"All castles in Ireland are haunted, Dermot. You know that. 'Tis only the cottages which can't afford ghosts."

There was no point in arguing. Still, for the record, I had to make my point.

"It might be dangerous out there on the Shannon Estuary."

"No more dangerous than on the Grand Canal here or in Carraroe. Sure, might we not have a tidal wave wipe us out in Connemara?"

"The Gulf Stream doesn't do tsunamis."

"Besides, won't me darlin' lass here take good care of us? And won't the Gardai be everywhere?"

"They're not around this morning."

"Are you daft, Dermot Michael? Aren't their two men over beyond behind those trees? And the woman who's pushing the empty baby buggy down below? And the red car up beyond us on Fitzwilliam Place? Are you blind altogether?"

"And won't you see the tsunami coming at us in Connemara?"

"Is that what they call tidal waves?"

" 'Tis."

"Then it's all settled, isn't it now?"

IF YOU HAD ANY SENSE AT ALL, AT ALL, the Adversary informed me, *YOU'D LAY DOWN THE LAW NOW. SAY THAT YOU'RE GOING HOME TO AMERICA AND THAT WILL BE THAT.*

He might be right about sex, but he was wrong about how to deal with Nuala Anne. We had to take our chances.

"If you say so. I just want to go on the record . . ."

"So, if something goes wrong, you can say, 'I told you so.' Well, Dermot Michael, nothing's going wrong. And anyway, you wouldn't dare say, 'I told you so.' "

" 'Tis true," I said with a sigh.

"I promise nothing will go wrong."

"You know that for sure?"

"I do. . . . Now what is your man not telling us?"

"Which man?"

"Your fancy Gardai Commissioner."

"He's not telling us things?"

"Certainly not!" she said with the forced patience of a mother with a dense little boy. "Isn't he telling us more than he wants to tell us because they can't find the kidnappers? Still he doesn't want us to find out anything more about the murder of Kevin O'Higgins, does he now?"

"It was seventy years ago, Nuala!"

"That's only yesterday in this country, Dermot love. His job is to keep peace in Ireland. That means keeping secrets that would stir up trouble today. So he tells us that the people that everyone thinks killed O'Higgins really didn't, but we know that already, don't we? He tells us about General Hugh Tudor, and ourselves not knowing about that one. But he figures that we're going to find out. Then he tells us that there is a connection between the death of Lady Augusta Downs and the death of Kevin O'Higgins. . . . Don't you see the problem, Dermot?"

I thought I'd better see it or I'd be written off as a terrible eejit altogether.

"He told me," I said slowly, "that O'Higgins was responsible for the execution of the men who burned Castle Garry. Then the men who killed him were seeking revenge. But he didn't mention the names of the killers."

She patted me approvingly on my thigh. "The connection is very obscure, isn't it now? And why was General Tudor in such disgrace? Because he had an affair with Lady Downs? Would he be the first English officer to have an affair with the wife of a dead comrade? Why was he afraid to live in England? What really happened the night they burned Castle Garry to the ground? He didn't tell us that, and I'm sure he won't."

"Maybe he doesn't know?"

She removed her head from the place it had found

on my shoulder and sat up straight, like she had been startled.

"Maybe he doesn't! But then what's he afraid of?"

"What could have happened seventy-five years ago at Castle Garry that might trouble this prosperous country today?"

I extended my arm around her waist and rested my hand on her belly, brushing against a luscious breast in the process. She leaned comfortably against me.

"If it wasn't for your man, it might not be prosperous."

"And if it wasn't for De Valera it might have been prosperous long ago . . . but where does that get us?"

"The mystery, Dermot Michael, is not down below in Booterstown. It's out on the Shannon!"

"Out in the real Ireland!"

She leaned closer to me. "You've got the right of it, man, haven't you now!"

"I have a hunch that Hugh Tudor is the key to it all."

"Weren't he and Kevin O'Higgins doing the same thing?"

I let that sink in.

"You mean they both were trying to end the violence by using violence?"

She nodded.

"And weren't they both committing adultery with enchanting women?"

My fingers touched the breast for which they had yearned.

"Dermot Michael, you're feeling me up!"

"I am!"

"Why?"

"Because you're my wife!"

"With all them coppers watching us?"

"I forgot about them."

"I didn't say stop, did I? Just be a little less obvious, if you take me meaning."

We both giggled. I became a little less obvious.

"And," she went on, "weren't they both heroes whom history has written off as villains?"

"Fair play to you, Nuala Anne," I admitted.

"One died young and one died very old, but wasn't Hugh Tudor half-dead when he went off to Newfoundland a disgrace?"

"So much a disgrace that he was humiliated when the King of England remembered who he was a decade and a half later."

We were silent for a moment.

"Can't you just see the headlines, Dermot Michael? 'Reveal Link Between Death of O'Higgins and Disgrace of British War Hero!' Wouldn't that stir up the pot now, and with all the negotiations going on up above in Storemont? And wouldn't your man rather not have that pot bubble over and himself on the Gardai bridge, especially since it's all been covered up?"

"We are running far ahead of ourselves, Nuala Anne."

She sighed. "We're not. I am. . . . Come on, darlin' girl; let's go home."

Fiona, still slobbering, bounced to her feet, ready for anything and everything.

Nuala decided to walk back to Jury's "the long way around," which meant Mount Street and Northumberland Road. If there was any immediate change in deployment of the "coppers," I didn't notice it.

"You want to read the book about Hazel?" I asked. "It's interesting in a way. Chicago beauty keeps most interesting literary and political salon in Europe. Sleeps with rich and famous. Dies unhappy."

"Should I?"

"I think so. . . . There's one interesting difference

between her account of O'Higgins's death and that of DeVere White."

"And what would that be, Dermot Michael? Be careful! The cars come from opposite directions here!

She pulled me back on the curb. Fiona nudged me as if I were a focking eejit.

"Thanks."

"The difference between the two accounts?" she persisted impatiently.

Watson must concentrate on the subject when he's talking to Holmes, even if he looks the wrong way for cars.

"According to White, the killers had been lying in wait for him all morning. According to McCoole, it was a chance meeting. They happened to be driving through Booterstown and saw him coming down the street."

"Hmm . . . so there are different stories still floating around. Just like about who killed Mick."

"What do you think?"

She shrugged her shoulders as we crossed the Grand Canal. "I don't know, Dermot. . . . The boy was local, I know that. He knew the priest and went to get him. He might not have known what the gunmen were up to . . . Dermot!"

This time the near-accident was not my fault. The light at the corner of Haddington Road and Northumberland Road had changed to green. I stepped into the street. A large blue sports car ran the light and bore down on me. I jumped back. He missed me by inches.

Fiona went wild. Straining at the leash in Nuala's hand, she barked furiously at the escaping car. She turned to us and barked angrily because we wouldn't let her go. Then she tried to break lose again.

"Easy, me darlin', easy now. Himself is all right! You are all right, aren't you, Dermot love?"

She clung to me with the arm that was not engaged with enraged Fiona.

"It wasn't my fault," I replied, for the moment dazed and disoriented.

"Och, it wasn't your fault at all, at all! You had the right of it, didn't you?"

A man in a dark double-breasted suit with a vest, commodity trader I thought, stepped up to us.

"Are you all right, sir?"

"They missed," I said in an utterly phony display of nonchalance.

"I got the license number, sir."

Copper.

"What do you want to bet that it's stolen?"

"Yes, sir."

"Tell my friend the Commissioner that this is a very dangerous city."

"Yes, sir . . . a fragile city, too, isn't it?"

"I've read O'Seadhil, too, Officer."

"Yes, sir," he said, impressed.

Poetry-reading cop. Unarmed, too, thanks to Kevin O'Higgins.

"Are you all right, Dermot?" My wife now clung to me with both arms. Fiona's leash had somehow tangled itself around both of us. The wolfhound alternately barked in the direction of the sports car and nudged me to make sure I was still alive.

"We linebackers move pretty quickly for big men," I said with a laugh.

Linebackers don't scare, do they? Not real linebackers!

"That's quite a dog, ma'am," the Guard said, now speaking to the obvious head of the family.

"Copper dog," I remarked.

We assured him that we would be able to walk back to Jury's. I noted that some of the other watch persons whom herself had spotted were lurking in the background. There was definitely no baby in the stroller.

"Maybe we should go home right away." Nuala took my arm as we crossed Haddington Road.

"No way," I said firmly. "Now it's personal."

JERK, said the Adversary. *BIG MACHO AMADON.*

23

"THAT ONE'S real, Dermot Michael," Nuala Anne informed me as our Mercedes limousine crossed the Shannon River at the Athlone Bridge and entered the "real" Ireland.

I opened my eyes, which I had been resting on the drive under gray and gloomy skies across the trim waist of Ireland from Dublin to Galway. This time we had a limo and a driver and a chase car. Our driver was almost certainly a Guard.

"Sorry I woke you up," Nuala murmured, not at all sorry.

"I wasn't asleep."

"You were so, ever since we left Maynooth."

"Was I now?"

"You were . . . Anyway, we're in the *real* Ireland now. You should be awake."

There wasn't much left of the *real* Ireland. As Ireland changed from an agricultural society to a modern society, the best and the brightest of the young people had gone off to the cities—Dublin, Cork, Galway. While Galway was in the west, it had changed rapidly and indeed was now the fastest-growing city in Europe. There were still farms, mostly cattle and dairy farms, and the farmhouses were often new and comfortable bungalows like the ones that the elder McGrails had built with help from the government, the European Union, and Nuala and meself. Myself. The old stone houses with the thatched roofs (perhaps replaced by corrugated iron) and the newer gray stucco places survived, but many of them were empty.

I was willing to bet, though I had not asked, that Gerry and Annie had kept their stone hut near, if not attached to, their new place. It would have been "bad luck" to tear it down. Perhaps they used it as a historical curiosity for the tourists—mostly German—who stopped by their place for "tea."

There was plenty of room in the limo, so Fiona was curled up at our feet, sleeping soundly. Somehow, custody, if not outright ownership, had been transferred to us.

"Och," said the young Guard who had been her trainer. "Hasn't the poor thing worked hard enough? Isn't she entitled to have a family, and meself not ready to start one quite yet?"

I was sure that Nuala had made the arrangements for this transfer without bothering to burden me with the details. Not that I minded, because I kind of liked the large, slobbering pooch meself. Myself, damn it.

"I agree that Augusta Downs is real," I said as if to show that I was, too, awake. "Are the cops still following us?"

"They are and when we stop at the pub in Ballinasloe for a pint and a sandwich we should invite them to join us. I don't think anyone will try to harm us out here, not in the *real* Ireland!"

My wife was exuberant. She was returning, however temporarily, to her roots, the holy ground from which her character and her talent had sprung. What we had all seen the other night at the Point was a product of that slowly dying "real" Ireland.

If the slow death of rural Ireland meant her parents could move out of the stone hut in which Nuala's ancestors had lived for centuries, that was a great improvement. But would it mean the end of the creativity that flowed out of my beautiful wife?

I was sounding like a local with that worry. You don't have to be impoverished to be creative. What about our children? Could they be both Irish and American?

How could they not be, given their mother? Still we ought to keep them in touch with Ireland by bringing them over here often.

"Not till we get to Garrytown anyway," I said.

"Maybe you should go back to sleep," she said.

"Not now that I'm wide awake."

I nudged the wolfhound with the toe of my shoe. She opened one eye, dismissed me, and closed her eye. The two of them had bonded against me.

"Well, do you agree with me about herself?"

I stretched and shifted my position in the car. "I think that the book is honest and authentic. I don't know about her getting mixed up with Hugh Tudor."

"At the most," my wife informed me, "once or twice. Until she found out he was married."

"People do strange things in wartime, Nuala Anne," I said. "Please God we can avoid that."

"And our children."

"And our children."

Silence while she worried about the absence of children.

"I would imagine," I went on, "she's buried next to her husband on the grounds of the castle."

"And that there's a great focking picture of her in the drawing room."

If Nuala Anne thought so, it would certainly be there.

"Maybe we'll get something out of the relatives who own it now."

"Not if they can help it, Dermot Michael. They have a legend, I'm sure, which they don't want to sully."

"But they'll know something, won't they?"

"People in the west of Ireland have long memories. There'll be plenty of stories floating around. We'll have to figure out what ones to believe."

"You mean you can't believe all the stories they tell out here in the *real* Ireland, Nuala Anne?"

"Sure, Dermot, you know very well that they're not told to be believed."

We had a grand time at the pub in Ballinasloe. Six "coppers" plus the two of us and our driver. And naturally Fiona, who made friends with everyone in the pub and cleaned up every bit of sandwich that had been left on our plates. No more than one pint a person, because two pints brought too close to a violation of the stern new Irish laws about driving under the influence of alcohol. Several of the Guards were Irish speakers and the rest of them understood the language, so there was a lot of babble from which I was excluded. I didn't mind because I was still half-asleep. I had the impression, as I often do when I hear them talking in that strange-sounding tongue, that it provides your Irish with far greater opportunity for indirection and circumlocution than does plain old English.

Linearity is not an Irish hang-up—and it's less a hang-up once you cross the bridge at Athlone.

The closer we came to Galway City, the more agitated my wife became, as did Fiona, who had never been there.

"Isn't it glorious, Dermot Michael! Isn't it the most beautiful place in all the world! Wasn't it nice of God to turn on the sun for me as soon as we got out here! I can hardly wait to see the bay!"

Good-dog Fiona barked enthusiastically at the prospect!

"I've been thinking, Nuala Anne. . . ."

"Have you now?"

"You don't have to sound so skeptical. I do it on occasion. . . ."

"When you're not resting your eyes."

"Right. . . . Anyway, I've been thinking we should buy a house over here. . . ."

She went, as the proverb puts it, bananas. She laughed; she cried; she shouted; she kissed me and then laughed and cried all over again.

"Dermot! You're a wonderful man altogether! I'll pay for it out of me royalties. Won't it be wonderful! Southport Avenue and Galway Bay!"

Nuala still believed that we were not able to afford things—just as did all my own family. It was fine with her that I didn't have a job. But, when she quit her job at Arthur Andersen to devote all her time to singing, she felt that we had lost all steady employment and were living on the cusp of financial disaster. Since she was an accountant, she appreciated theoretically that I had put the money I had made (by mistake) in my years on the Mercantile Exchange into various investment portfolios, all of which were riding up with the various markets. She also realized that the royalties from my novel were in tax-free municipals. But her west of Ireland caution made her suspicious of all such speculation, even though her accounting instincts told her that the stock market was (presently) the place to be.

However, she refused to check the market reports to find out how we were doing. Indeed, when by accident she saw on the telly what the DJ and NASDAQ were doing she screamed in alarm: they were too high altogether! She was not interested in my arguments about the "New Economy." What goes up, Dermot Michael, must come down.

I pointed out that this was literally untrue, but that made no difference.

"We'll buy it together," I said soothingly.

She then weighed all the pros and cons of where the house should be. The issue remained unresolved when we turned through Oranmore and caught sight of the bay. She made the driver stop the car, jumped out on the side of the road, and sang "Galway Bay" at the top of her voice.

Fiona barked her approval.

"Isn't it grand, Dermot Michael? Isn't it the most brilliant blue in all the world?"

She hugged me fiercely. Therefore, it was inappropriate for me to respond that the blue at Amalfi was much more brilliant. What did I know anyway?

Except when to keep my big mouth shut.

We drove through the city, which seemed even more prosperous and busy than it had a year and a half before. It was filled with young people, many of them students at the National University of Ireland, Galway (as UCG was now called), but others tourists from all over Europe. The city had surely not been that prosperous since it was the port for trade with Spain back in the fifteenth century.

"I wouldn't want our house to be too far from this beautiful city," I said.

"Maybe up on Lough Corrib, close to the golf course."

She was still obsessed about beating me at golf. That, I swore to myself, she'd never do.

We drove through the city, which its boosters call the Venice of Ireland because of the nine channels that the Corrib River creates as it dashes towards the bay. Then we turned left through the resort community of Salt Hill with its lovely old nineteenth-century hotels and its ugly new ones. We passed the golf course where, my wife informed me, she would beat me the next day.

I laughed, much to her annoyance.

"I will, Dermot Michael; I really will."

"How much of a handicap am I going to have to give you?"

She snorted in disdain. Nuala Anne does not need handicaps.

A few miles west of Salt Hill the scenery changed. On the left Galway Bay was still Galway Bay, but on the right we left behind the greenery and entered the stark, desolate, and unearthly beauty of Connemara or, more properly, Iar Conaught—West Connaught. (The name Connemara is reserved by the purists for the western half of the peninsula.) We were now in the Gaeltacht, the Irish-speaking region. My good wife had shed her exuberance. She was now quiet, pensive, serious. In recognition of this change, Fiona rested her huge head on Nuala's knee.

According to a book I'd read on the Irish rural landscape, Connemara had three distinct districts: the mountains—like the Twelve Bens, which loomed in the distance on our right as we drove along the bay—the bogs, and coastlines (on Galway Bay and the south and Lough Corrib on the north). Along the shores, dairy farming, some fishing, and kelp gathering on the strands were ways to stay alive. In the other regions potato farming had flourished on the sides of the mountains, far up where the English did not want the land until the famine. The two vast estates, the D'Arcys', at the far end around the town of Clifden, and the Martyns' (Hazel Lavery's ancestors), had been wiped

out by the famine, too, because there were no crops
and no income even for the landlords. The D'Arcys
and the Martyns had stolen the land from the
O'Flahertys, who had owned it before Cromwell—and
kept the poor burgers of Galway City in terror. Herself—Grace O'Malley—was the wife of an O'Flaherty.

Nuala's family had survived the politics and the wars
and the famines and the plagues for a thousand years
and more in their little hut. Now they could get on Aer
Lingus and fly to America for their daughter's wedding. Somehow they had finally won.

"Will we like the new house, Dermot Michael?" she
asked softly.

Well, at least she had spoken to me in English.

"Woman, we will. Whatever it looks like, your ma and
da live there, so naturally we'll like it."

"The old place was so picturesque."

"And so uncomfortable!"

" 'Twas that indeed."

The ur-Nuala was now in the car with me, the proto-
Nuala, the shy and quiet girl from Carraroe—shy and
quiet and with a wicked Camogie stick in her hand.

We passed through the town of Spiddle, the unoffi-
cial capital of the Gaeltacht, the place where the summer contests, from poetry to sailing, took place.

"Was it here you crewed in the Galway hooker
races?"

"Ah, no. It was out beyond in Roundstone."

"And you lost?"

"We did. We weren't very good at it."

"Just like golf."

"I'm very good at golf. If I could hit it as far as you
do, wouldn't I be better?"

"Woman, you would. But you can't. And you won't."

She laughed softly. In the Gaeltacht, Nuala Anne was

quiet about everything. As I remembered, she even walked softly instead of bounding.

Under the clear blue sky and the bright sunlight, the countryside was lovely, desolate but utterly distinctive, like the landscape of another world—or perhaps one on the far reaches of this world. The next parish, as the Irish like to say, is on Long Island. Yet we were only twenty minutes' drive away from Galway City, twenty-five minutes from Galway Airport with flights to Dublin and Manchester and London. The occasional new bungalow or villa warned us that the modern world was not so far away.

We took a right turn to the north and followed an inlet of the bay.

" 'Tis your ma's homeland, Dermot Michael."

" 'Tis."

Nuala had a special relationship with my grandmother, though she had never met her. Not in this world, anyway.[1]

We drove through the small town of Costelloe, which is on the land bridge leading out to Carraroe.

"This is where your man lived after he sank the boat," my wife said as she pointed at a large building that bore the sign: "Costelloe Fishing Lodge."

"Which man and what boat?" I asked, knowing that the closer she was to home, the more obscure she would be.

"*Titanic,* of course," she said in a tone of voice that implied I was an absolute idiot for not knowing what boat. "J. Bruce Ismay, the managing director of the White Star Line and himself telling the captain to break the record crossing the Atlantic so they couldn't turn fast enough to avoid the iceberg. They said all

[1]*Irish Gold*

them ghosts haunted the eejit for the rest of his life. Poor man."

She shivered as if the ghosts might still lurk in the bogs and rocks that were all around us. We were only thirty miles from Galway and on another planet.

"We're almost home," she said as we bumped carefully along the narrow road.

"We are," I agreed, figuring there was little point in arguing about whose home.

Nuala grabbed my hand, seeking reassurance for her return home. I'm always glad to drive back to River Forest, but the town is not a religion with me.

Carraroe (the Red-Colored Quarter in Irish) is a fist, shoved out into Galway Bay, for all practical purposes an island surrounded on all sides by the bay save for the narrow strip of land connecting it to the rest of Ireland. Moreover, it is dotted with lakes. The village is a network of roads and lanes—lined by whitewashed stone fences—with water on both sides. The cottages and bungalows were washed with pink and blue and white and green, bright spots of color against the rich blue of the sky and the sea.

We passed the small industrial park where computer parts were made and where Annie worked part-time because, like her daughter, she didn't trust the American stock markets.

"Aren't those statues grand altogether?" Nuala Anne said as we passed the Open Air Sculpture Park where the work in metal sculpture of Edward Delaney is exhibited.

"Grand," I agreed, though I thought they didn't fit in with the setting, but once again this was hardly the time to argue.

When the sun is shining, it might just be the prettiest place in the world. But most of the time, the sun doesn't shine. Then it's the next best thing to living under the sea.

"If there really is global warming," Nuala said pensively, "all this will be covered with water, won't it, Dermot?"

"Maybe not. Five thousand years ago it was two degrees Centigrade warmer and they farmed all year round in the west of Ireland."

"That was up beyond in Mayo, and themselves on the top of a big cliff. Ah, they'll not see our kind again, will they?"

"You're talking like you're an Aran Islander."

"A character in a John Millington Synge play," she said with a soft laugh. "Ah, well, we live while we can. . . . Next turn, Dermot."

The new McGrail home was a pretty light blue, very much in keeping with the setting. A tour bus, doors open, stood expectantly.

"Isn't it grand, Dermot Michael? I knew it would be brilliant. . . . Now, mind, watch your language. We don't want to shock me ma and me da."

"I'm not the one who talks like I'm from the north side of Dublin."

"The tourists are here. I should help with the tea. Do you mind, Dermot?"

"Why would I mind?

She dashed around to the back of the house, Fiona in hot pursuit. Just before she turned the corner, she remembered where she was and slowed to a graceful and deliberate walk, the hoyden turned Gaeltacht matron. Fiona, surprised at the change, skidded to a stop.

I grinned and helped the driver bring our considerable luggage into the house. It was a small bungalow but three times larger than the old stone cottage. It contained a parlor, a dining area, a kitchen with cabinets and all the new equipment, and three small bedrooms. Even two "conveniences," which was "excessive" by Irish standards, especially since you were only a few years away from outdoor privies. Still, it's what the Germans wanted and you built a home these days with the thought that someday a German would buy it.

The home was tastefully decorated, save for the old prints of the Sacred Heart and St. Teresa of Lisieux, which had been brought from the former house, family icons. A cabinet contained pictures of the children and grandchildren, including one of a radiant Nuala Anne on her wedding day, standing next to a clumsy lug who had no business messing up the photo. Next to the cabinet was a Camogie stick, club as I called it. No way did I want that back on Southport Avenue.

In the corner stood a television, a VCR, and a CD player, all gifts that I had managed to insinuate into the house with the argument that they were from myself and herself. That way herself need not worry about each gift I bought.

I didn't have to look to know that the disk was *Nuala Anne Goes to Church* and the VCR tape was of the RTE show from the Point.

There was, needless to say, a Brigid cross made of reeds over the door.

"You won't be needing the car again today, sir?" the driver asked.

"No, Sergeant," I said, guessing at his rank. "We're fine. We'll use the McGrails' car to go to church tomorrow and to the golf club."

"As long as you're out here, all we have to do is keep an eye on the bridge up beyond."

"I think we're pretty safe in this part of the world."

"I don't know about that, sir. The west isn't always as peaceful as it looks."

I knew the crime rates. It was as peaceful as it looked, indeed the most peaceful place in Europe.

These days, anyway. Thanks to Kevin O'Higgins.

I thanked the sergeant for his protection.

"Not at all, sir. 'Tis an honor to take care of that one."

Not a mention of her oafish husband. Ah, well, we live while we can.

I heard singing outside. German singing. I walked out the back door, just to make sure that no one was hassling my wife, not that I could do anything other than bring along her Camogie stick.

The Germans were young and harmless. Mind you, they all stared at herself, in her faded jeans and white Chicago Yacht Club sweatshirt. I didn't mind their staring, though I thought some of them did it a little longer than was necessary.

Fiona pranced from table to table, accepting the enthusiastic admiration of our guests.

"*Ja, ja,* nice doggy."

The McGrails had expanded their garden. Now it covered a patch of land between the bungalow and the cottage, the latter now with a new thatch roof (and conveniences inside, I knew, for the tourists). The dense garden, the new tables and chairs, and the lake beyond the cottage made a picturesque setting for tourists looking for quaint Irish scenes.

Well, they were welcome to it.

Annie came over and kissed me, and himself shook my hand.

"Jesus and Mary be with this house and all who live in it," I said in the only Irish I knew.

They giggled at my accent and replied in English that they wished that Jesus and Mary and Patrick be with those who come into the house.

I stole three scones from Annie's tray, smeared them with heavy cream and raspberry jam, and poured meself a cup of tea.

Myself.

I did not permit them to pollute my tea with milk.

The Germans tried to sing "Galway Bay" and made a mess of it.

"Youse do it all wrong," Nuala informed them, relinquishing for the moment her quiet Gaeltacht lass persona.

"*Ja,* you sing it then!"

"Well, I must might. . . . Dermot love, would you ever bring me harp?"

The Germans noticed me for the first time.

"Woman, I would."

So I brought the harp and so she taught them how to sing "Galway Bay" and the "Kerry Dance" and, God save us all, "When Irish Eyes Are Smiling."

And then she explained who Colm of Iona was and sang "Sail the Soul."

"The lass is a terrible show-off altogether," I said to her father.

"Sure, we could hire her here if she ever needs a job."

It was time for the Germans to leave, which they did with much handshaking.

"*Ja, ja,*" a young woman said to me, "she sings very well. She should record, *nein?*"

"She does," I said, reaching into my shoulder bag and producing a disk.

I gave a dozen or so away, which is why I had brought the bag out with me.

The Germans were deeply impressed.

As they damn well ought to have been.

No way we were going out for supper. Annie was preparing a "good, solid Irish supper for you."

Nuala insisted, despite her mother's protests, that she would stay in the house and help with dinner. I should take poor little darlin' Fiona for a run on the road. I darted into our bedroom and donned shorts, a T-shirt, and running shoes. At the last minute I grabbed my shillelagh. It would do no harm to carry it.

Fiona must have thought she'd died and gone to heaven. She rushed ahead of me down the road, barked at the cattle and the mild-mannered Galway ponies, wagged her tail at the elderly men and women, accepted petting from delighted children, jumped over fences, and chased away a couple of dubious sheep-dogs who tried to block her romp.

The local folk all nodded politely. They knew who I was, but, shy people that they were, they did not intrude on my privacy. I was too busy keeping up with the good-dog Fiona. She discovered a strand, the Coral Strand I would learn later, so called because of its color in sunlight, more shale then sand, vaulted a stone fence, and plunged into Galway Bay. The cold water didn't bother her in the slightest.

The sky was blue above us and it was still warm, but mists were forming out on the bay. The Aran Islands were barely visible, dark shapes in the lighter shapes of mists.

Fiona galloped out of the water, rushed up to me, and shook the water off her fur, drenching me.

"Bad dog," I complained.

To prove what she thought of my reproof, she shook herself again. Then she picked up a stick, brought it to me, and laid it expectantly at my feet. I ignored it. She barked, her feelings hurt. I picked up the stick and tossed it down the beach. She retrieved it, brought it back to me, and wrestled with me for possession. We played the game several times. I finally tossed it in the water. Unhesitatingly, she raced after it.

Then suddenly she wheeled and rushed back onto the strand, barking furiously.

I looked around to see what had roused her ire. A small blue car had stopped alongside the fence over which Fiona had vaulted. Two men, tough and unkempt characters in their late twenties, were picking their way towards us on the shale, one with his arm in a sling. He carried a knife, his companion a cosh.

Our friends from the Pembroke Road bridge.

"Nice to see you again," I said, grabbing my shillelagh. "Maybe I can break a few skulls this time."

Fiona growled dangerously. I advanced towards the two men and waved my war club at them. They hesitated, glanced anxiously at the wolfhound, and then ran back to their car, jumped into it, and pulled away down the dirt road.

This time I didn't chase them.

"Come on, girl," I ordered my sidekick. "We have to get back to Nuala."

We sprinted down the road in the direction, I thought, of the McGrail bungalow. But the network of lanes, fences, and water confused me completely. Unfortunately, they confused the wolfhound, too. Fiona checked her mad dash, looked around in confusion, sniffed the air, and barked in protest.

The two of us waited a few moments and then ran in the opposite direction. The mists drifted in from the Arans and towards us. We stopped again.

"We're lost, girl," I told her, desperation in my voice. "We've got to find Nuala before they do."

She started to run again, right into the mist. I hoped she knew where we were going, because I certainly didn't.

A big car loomed up in front of us. I shouted; the wolfhound howled. The car, which had been moving slowly because of the mist, halted abruptly.

It was a Benz. Our Benz.

"Two of them are here on the island!" I shouted at

our cop as he rolled down the window. "We've got to get back to the house before it's too late."

I actually said that. And I'm supposed to be an accomplished novelist with a special gift for dialogue.

The man threw open the door; we both bounded in, soaked to the skin and breathing heavily. He started the car and spoke into his transceiver at the same moment.

"Blue car," I gasped. "Must have got here before us."

We turned a corner, emerged from the mists, and there, radiantly blue, was the McGrail bungalow.

I hugged Fiona. "We've both made fools of ourselves, girl," I said. She snuggled close to me.

How much, I wondered, does this huge and intelligent beast understand? If she could speak to me, would she have said, "You blundered, amadon; I knew exactly where the house was."

"We'll be looking for them, sir," the copper said. "And we'll keep a watch around the house all night. Our relief will be along later."

"You could use a bite of dinner?"

"Oh, yes, we could, sir. Ms. McGrail brought us tea and scones earlier."

Naturally.

Fiona and I went into the house and were reprimanded for running around in the fog and getting ourselves all wet.

"It was all her fault," I pleaded.

— 24 —

THIS TIME didn't me ma and I talk in Irish while we were preparing the meal and me da outside folding the tables and chairs after them poor dear tourists had left. I know You're an Irish speaker, so I don't have to translate for You, like I'd have to for me poor dear Dermot. You also know what a terrible indirect language Irish is. Yet wasn't me ma more direct this time than when we talked about it in English? And didn't she start the conversation herself?

"Don't they say that there's passionate hunger inside of every woman, no matter how prim and proper she might pretend to be?"

"Haven't I heard that said, too?"

"Them that knows more about it than I do tell me that until a woman is able to satisfy that hunger, the marriage won't be everything that it should be?"

"Don't you know that yourself?"

Wasn't that an awful thing to say, and meself in a mood to be difficult?

"Well," she says with a toss of her head, "I'm certainly not one of them prim and proper women, am I?"

"I never said you were."

" 'Tis wrong, they say, for a woman to think that it's up to her husband."

Hint, hint.

"Why would it ever be up to him, poor dear man?"

" 'Tis true."

Silence.

"Don't the prim and proper women spend their whole marriage waiting for their husband to be a magician?"

"And some of themselves pretending all along that everything is fine?"

Wasn't that candid of me now? Am I really a prim and proper woman?

"Well, isn't there a bit of the prim and proper woman in all of us? Aren't we afraid of what will happen if we abandon ourselves completely? Sure there's nothing wrong with that, is there?"

"Och, there is not."

She did say "abandon." She really did. That's the key word, isn't it now? To give yourself is one thing; to abandon yourself is something else again. I guess there is a lot of the prim and proper woman in me.

"But aren't we only half a woman until we overcome that fear?"

Wow, as me poor Dermot would say.

Meself half a woman? And pretending all the time that I'm a full woman. And getting away with it because I'm such a focking faker.

It has to stop. Help me, please.

IT WAS the kind of typical Irish dinner Ma used to make—roast beef (well done), carrots, beans, mashed potatoes with pot liquor on them, and a big dish of chocolate ice cream.

No wine. Ma didn't believe in it, and the elder McGrails were not yet into the French and American affectation of wine with dinner. However, we all had a small sip of Connemara, the local whiskey, which would burn the throat out of anyone who wasn't Irish.

We praised their new house. They blushed and smiled.

"I don't miss the old place one minute," Annie assured us.

"It's difficult altogether," her husband agreed, "to grasp the change, if you take me meaning. It's almost like we're living in a television program—a warm, dry, comfortable house. Annie and me wanted this life for our children. We never expected it for ourselves."

"Aren't we afraid every morning when we wake up that it will all have been taken away from us overnight?"

"Shush, now, Ma," Nuala insisted. "No one's going to take it away from us."

Her parents were skeptical, just as so many Americans had been skeptical after the Second World War, expecting as they did that the Great Depression would come back. It never did, not yet anyway.

There was not even a slight smell of turf in the house, though a stack of it stood near the fireplace. The electric heating apparently was enough. It was strange to be in a house in rural Ireland that was not permeated by your authentic west of Ireland smell— turf blended with cattle manure.

Nuala, now wearing a simple gray dress, had brought dinner plates out to the drivers, two of them this time, waiting on the road, and a large bone to the famished Fiona.

"Will those poor men be out there all night?" Annie wondered.

"Ah, no," her daughter reassured her. "There'll be another team."

No further questions were asked. They knew as well as we did that the men were Gardai.

After dinner we adjourned to the garden, where a bottle of Baileys was produced along with water tumblers to drink it—no cordial glasses in this part of the world. No ice either.

Fiona, who had been having a great time with her bone, rushed over to join us, delighted that we had the good sense to come outdoors where she was. A full moon shone over our heads, though it was still dusk in Ireland even late in the evening. The moon was not shining over the Claddagh or, from our perspective, over Galway Bay. However it was shining on the small lake behind the McGrails' house. Nuala and her mother had thrown sweaters over their shoulders. I reflected again on how similar they were in face and figure, if not in contentiousness.

"Them eejits again?" Nuala had asked me when I had come out of the shower earlier.

She didn't miss much, did she?

"And one of them with a broken arm."

"They were coming after you?"

"One had a knife and the other a cosh. They're amateur thugs. They saw Fiona and my shillelagh and decided against a fight."

She removed the towel from my hands and completely the drying process, much to my delight.

"Sure you're a gorgeous man, Dermot Michael," she had said admiringly.

Under those circumstances I had almost told her how frantically the wolfhound and I had rushed back to protect her and her parents. Then I had realized that my panic was foolish. They would have been quite capable of taking care of themselves. Nuala with a garbage can (dust bin here) cover in her hand was as dangerous as I was with an Irish war club.

So I had kept my mouth shut.

"The Gardai will stay around?" she had asked.

"They will."

"What do they want, Dermot?"

"It's hard to tell. They're not very good at being thugs, and they're taking terrible chances."

"Someone is paying them a lot of money."

Out in the garden after supper, she hummed "Galway Bay" again and we all joined in softly, so as not to wake the Baby Jesus I presumed. I kept my mouth shut also about the fact that from where we were we could not see Galway Bay. Instead I sipped from my tumbler of Baileys.

Fiona curled up at my feet and went to sleep.

"It's easy to see whose dog she is," Annie McGrail said with a laugh.

This, I realized, would soon become the conventional wisdom.

We sat in companionable silence for many moments.

In Ireland love is often communicated by total silence.

"You're going down beyond below to Limerick," said Gerry McGrail. It sounded like a simple observation, but it was in this part of the world a question intended to begin a conversation.

I never have figured out why the Irish combine three prepositions as adverbs when they're talking direction.

"Aren't we now?" I said, an Irish response that caused by wife to giggle.

"And you'll be staying at that castle over across beyond the Shannon?"

"We will," Nuala replied, cutting off my embarrassing effort to sound like a native.

Silence. Someone sighed.

I waited.

"It's an interesting place altogether, isn't it now?"

"A bit of history there," I said, either now in the groove or at least not embarrassing my wife.

"Aye, there is that. . . . Mind you, it's a fine hotel, they say."

More silence.

"Back in Catholic hands, I hear."

" 'Tis not right for us to judge what happened so long ago," Annie warned. "Still it's nice when the wheel turns, isn't it now?"

We all sighed.

"They were a brave young couple, weren't they?" Gerry continued. "Himself with your Victoria Cross and herself fighting off both the Irregulars and the Tans."

"All so long ago," Nuala said, very softly.

Her father sighed. "No story in Ireland ever loses anything through repetition, but don't they say that she was hiding some of the lads when the Tans came back."

"Came back?"

"They'd been there before."

Silence.

"The Kerry men had come before and tried to burn the Big House down, and an English officer living there. The Tans drove them off. Then the Tans came back again later."

It could not have been much later, because the Tans (who killed 238 people during their time in Ireland) had run amok for only a year.

More silence. If Gerry smoked he would have been puffing on his pipe. I filled Nuala's tumbler with more Baileys.

"Some strange things happened that night. Me own da who fought in the Free State Army because he didn't much like your Cork men who were running the Irregulars told me once that there were a lot of tales told about that night."

"Were there?"

"Aye, there were. The woman was killed somehow and the house burned down. Most of the Kerry men escaped and served with the Irregulars. Me da said that most of them were shot by the Free Staters when they captured them. He wasn't there when it happened, but he says that the orders came down from higher up. They were killing a lot of folks in those days."

"Is the castle haunted?" I asked.

Annie replied in the very words her daughter had used on our ride out, "Och, isn't every castle in Ireland haunted."

"The owners don't advertise that, do they now?" Gerry said. " 'Tis all about their golf course."

"Where I'm going to beat your man," Nuala insisted. I ignored her.

"Anything about the officer who commanded the Tans?"

Yet more silence.

"Me da never said anything about him. Funny thing, there's never been any talk about him."

It was in England that Henry Hugh Tudor was a bad name, not in Ireland. Odd.

"Those things happened so long ago," Nuala said, speaking even more softly this time. "Seventy years and more."

"In Ireland, child, that's only yesterday."

Yet more silence.

"Did your father ever encounter any trouble for serving in the Free State Army?" I asked.

"Don't we in the Gaeltacht look on such things a little differently?"

"We remember as long as anyone else, maybe longer," Annie added. "But aren't we easy on forgiveness?"

"Your children, too?" I asked.

Everyone laughed.

I poured myself a little bit more Baileys.

Gerry brought to an end our conversation about Castle Garry.

"Didn't they all say that she was a very brave woman? Maybe she wanted to die to be with her husband again? Me da told me once that they said Mass for her in the Catholic church, just as they did for himself when he was killed."

Gerry rose from his chair and took a book off an end table. He opened to a page in which there was a bookmark and with considerable flourish sat back in his chair.

"May I read you a bit about Carraroe, Dermot Michael?"

"Sure," Annie McGrail said with a Nuala-like snort, "is there much chance of him saying no and yourself already to begin?"

"When your man was young and was writing that play

about the islands, he toured the west of Ireland and wrote down what life was like in them days."

"Synge," Nuala Anne said, fearing that the allusion was too obscure for me.

"Didn't I know a young woman once who told an audience that she'd lost the only playboy of the Western world?"

"And didn't she get a dozen roses for the first time in her life?"

And didn't tears of happiness flood her eyes at the memory.

"And didn't she forget to say thank you?"

"And wasn't she scared altogether?"[1]

Gerry waited patiently till we had finished our pas de deux and then began his story.

"He called it Between the Bays of Carraroe. It was the world in which our grandparents courted.

" 'In rural Ireland very few parishes only are increasing in population, and those that are doing so are usually in districts of the greatest poverty. One of the most curious instances of this tendency is to be found in the parish of Carraroe, which is said to be, on the whole, the poorest parish in the country, although many worse cases of individual destitution can be found elsewhere. The most characteristic part of this district lies on a long promontory between Cashla Bay and Greatman's Bay. On both coastlines one sees a good many small quays, with, perhaps, two hookers moored to them, and on the roads one passes an occasional flat space covered with small green fields of oats—with whole families on their knees weeding among them—or patches of potatoes; but for the rest one sees little but an endless series of low stony hills, with veins of grass. Here and there, however, one comes in sight of

[1] *Irish Gold*

a fresh-water lake, with an island or two, covered with seagulls, and many cottages round the shore; some of them standing almost on the brink of the water, others a little higher up, fitted in among the rocks, and one or two standing out on the top of a ridge against the blue of the sky or of the Twelve Bens of Connaught.

" 'At the edge of one of these lakes, near a school of lace or knitting—one of those that have been established by the Congested Districts Board—we met a man driving a mare and foal that had scrambled out of their enclosure, although the mare had her two off-legs chained together. As soon as he had got them back into one of the fields and built up the wall with loose stones, he came over to a stone beside us and began to talk about horses and the dying out of the ponies of Connemara. "You will hardly get any real Connemara ponies now at all," he said, "and the kind of horses they send down to us to improve the breed are no use, for the horses we breed from them will not thrive or get their health on the little patches where we have to put them. This last while most of the people in this parish are giving up horses altogether. Those that have them sell their foals when they are about six months old for four pounds, or five maybe; but the better part of the people are working with an ass only, that can carry a few things on a straddle over her back."

" ' "If you've no horses," I said, "how do you get to Galway if you want to go to a fair or to market?"

" ' "We go by the sea," he said, "in one of the hookers you've likely seen at the little quays while walking down by the road. You can sail to Galway if the wind is fair in four hours or less maybe; and the people here are all used to the sea, for no one can live in this place but by cutting turf in the mountains and sailing out to sell it in Clare or Aran, for you see yourselves there's no good in the land, that has little in it but bare rocks and stones. Two years ago there came a wet summer, and the people were worse okay then than they are now maybe, with their bad potatoes and all; for they couldn't cut or dry a load of turf to sell across the bay, and there was many a woman hadn't a dry sod itself to put under her pot, and she shivering with cold and hunger."

" ' "You're getting an old man," I said, "and do you remember if the place was as bad as it is now when you were a young man growing up?"

" ' "It wasn't as bad, or a half as bad," he said, "for there were fewer people in it and more land to each, and the land itself was better at the time, for now it is drying up or something, and not giving its fruits and increase as it did."

" 'I asked him if they bought manures.

" ' "We get a hundredweight for eight shillings now and again, but I think there's little good in it, for it's only a poor kind they send out to the like of us. Then there was another thing they had in the old times," he continued, "and that was the making of poteen [illicit whiskey], for it was a great trade at that time, and you'd see the Gardai down on their knees blowing the fire with their own breath to make a drink for themselves, and then going off with the butt of an old barrel, and that was one seizure, and an old bag with a handful of malt, and that was another seizure, and would satisfy the law; but now they must have the worm and the still and a prisoner, and there is little of it made in the country. At that time a man would get ten shillings for a gallon, and it was a good trade for poor people."

" 'As we were talking a woman passed driving two young pigs, and we began to speak of them.

" ' "We buy the young pigs and rear them up," he said, "but this year they are scarce and dear. And indeed what good are they in bad years, for how can we go feeding a pig when we haven't enough, maybe, for ourselves? In good years, when you have potatoes and plenty, you can rear up two or three pigs and make a good bit on them; but other times, maybe, a poor man will give a pound for a young pig that won't thrive after, and then his pound will be gone, and he'll have no money for his rent."

" 'The old man himself was cheerful and seemingly fairly well-to-do; but in the end he seemed to be getting dejected as he spoke of one difficulty after another, so I asked him, to change the subject, if there was much dancing in the country. "No," he said, "this while back you'll never see a piper coming this way at all, though in the old times it's many a piper would be moving around through those houses for a whole quarter together, playing his pipes and drinking poteen and the people dancing round him; but now there is no dancing or singing in this place at all, and most of the young people is growing up and going to America."

" 'I pointed to the lace school near us, and asked him how the girls got on with the lace, and if they earned much money. "I've heard tell," he said, "that in the four schools round about this place there is near six hundred pounds paid out in wages every year, and that is a good sum; but there isn't a young girl going to them that isn't saving up, and saving up till she'll have enough gathered to take her to America, and then away she will go, and why wouldn't she?"

" 'Often the worst moments in the lives of these people are caused by the still frequent outbreaks of typhus fever, and before we parted I asked him if there was much fever in the particular district where we were.

" ' "Just here," he said, "there isn't much of it at all, but there are places round about where you'll sometimes hear of a score and more stretched out waiting for their death; but I suppose it is the will of God. Then there is a sickness they call consumption that some will die of; but I suppose there is no place where people aren't getting their death one way or other, and the most in this place are enjoying good health, glory be to God! For it is a healthy place and there is a clean air blowing."

" 'Then, with a few of the usual blessings, he got up and left us, and we walked on through more of similar or still poorer country. It is remarkable that from Spiddal onward—that is, in the whole of the most poverty-stricken district in Ireland—no one begs, even in a roundabout way. It is the fashion, with many of the officials who are connected with relief works and such things, to compare the people of this district rather unfavorably with the people of the poor districts of Donegal; but in this respect at least Donegal is not the more admirable.' "

Gerry closed the book solemnly.

He sighed loudly. So did the rest of us. We waited in silence. He cleared his throat. "It was only a little better when herself and I were growing up. Not so much hunger and a lot less consumption, but until 1960 it was still pretty grim. It seems like only yesterday and yet centuries ago. We wouldn't be Irish if we didn't think we might lose it tomorrow."

"You won't," I said firmly.

They all sighed again.

Later in our bedroom, with the lights out and the moon peeking beneath the drapes, Nuala took my hand.

"I'm sorry, Dermot Michael."

We had kind of implicitly agreed that it would be awkward making love in her parents' house, especially since the walls were not all that thick. I wondered if her parents were equally shy.

How often did people their age who were still attractive physically and patently in love do sex?

Often enough, I decided, whatever that may mean.

So we were lying in bed, Nuala in a long T-shirt and I in my shorts.

"You should be, woman," I said, "and meself the soul of patience ... but would you ever mind telling me what you're sorry for?"

"For excluding you from our conversation back in Ballinasloe. I was so excited to be near the Gaeltacht again that I forgot meself."

I had forgotten completely, but I knew enough not to say that.

"Didn't I enjoy watching you have so much fun?"

"You really are sounding like any Irishman, Dermot Michael Coyne. We have to get you back to Yankland soon or you'll go native. You'll say something every five minutes like 'me da.' "

"Mr. Coyne, he dead."

She snickered. "I'm also terrible sorry for acting the way I did at Jury's."

Aha. Which time at Jury's? Better not to ask. She probably had been so bad that she would be insulted if I didn't remember.

It isn't easy being married.

So I didn't say anything.

At all, at all.

"You did the right thing by reading your man from Glentrasna."

John O'Donohue.

"Well, Nuala, you were all worn out."

"And you made fun of me, too, and wasn't that wonderful?"

Just so long as you don't do it too often.

"You were pretty funny," I said, crawling out on a very long and tenuous limb.

She laughed. "Wasn't I a terrible onchuck!"

An onchuck is kind of a woman amadon. Kind of.

"I'll never do that again, Dermot Michael. Never."

"Never is a hell of a long time," I said, quoting Harry Truman.

"Well, not till next month anyway!"

"Good!"

"I don't know why Herself wants me to do all these things, but what a terrible disgrace of an Irish woman I would be if I didn't do them because I was afraid."

"Fear will never stop you, Nuala Anne McGrail," I said, drawing her close.

"Not as long as you are around, Dermot Michael Coyne."

YOU SHOULD FUCK HER NOW. The Adversary suddenly appeared in bed with us. *NONE OF THIS SHITE ABOUT BEING SHY IN HER PARENTS' HOUSE.*

"A lot you know about women," I told him.

He went away then and left us alone. We both slept calmly and peacefully in the knowledge that our love, however imperfect and inexperienced it was, would be as durable as the love between her parents.

The next morning we went to Mass at the local parish church. The liturgy and the sermon were both in Irish. Me wife . . . damn it, MY wife . . . sang some Latin hymns, which they all seemed to know. As a concession to the Yank in the church—and perhaps to the Guards—the final blessing was in English.

"Well, now," said the elderly but lively priest, "don't we have another blessing from your man up beyond above in Glentrasna, which is good for all of us to hear. Doesn't he call it 'A Blessing of Solitude':

" 'May you recognize in your life the presence, power, and light of your soul.

" 'May you realize that you are never alone, that your soul in its brightness and belonging connects you intimately with the rhythm of the universe.

" 'May you have respect for your own individuality and difference.

" 'May you realize that the shape of your soul is unique, that you have a special destiny here, that behind the facade of your life there is something beautiful, good, and eternal happening.

" 'May you learn to see yourself with the same delight, pride, and expectation with which God sees you in every moment.

" 'In the name of the Father, and the Son, and the Holy Spirit. Amen.' "

"See," said my wife, nudging me in the ribs before I could do the same to her.

Later on the golf course, she was not a happy camper.

" 'Tis not fair at all, at all," she said grimly, after I had driven a three-hundred-yard green.

"I'm stronger," I said mildly, spoiling, however, for a fight.

"That's not fair either, but, sure, you never practice and you still hit the ball that far."

"Doesn't my father say that if I practiced more I'd win the championship at Oak Park every year?"

I had already won it once, but I don't particularly like competition, unlike my wife, who lives off it.

"At Long Beach, too," she added, still grim as she teed up her golf ball. "I can beat you with me irons and me putter."

"Woman, you can, not a doubt about it, at least the short irons. However, golf is not just about irons. It's about woods."

"That's what's not fair."

Her drive was perfectly presentable for a woman, 175 yards and straight as an arrow.

"Nice shot," I remarked.

"Gobshite," she sneered.

Strength and some skill got me on the green; luck put me close enough to the pin so I sank the putt for an eagle. A glowering Nuala Anne had to be content with a par.

"What did you think of your man's story last night?" she said as we went to the next tee, not even congratulating me on me eagle. My eagle.

My man, in this instance, was her father.

"Well," I said, teeing up my ball, "he certainly confirmed that there is a mystery down there at Castle-garry."

"Aye," she said. "It was so long ago. What has it to do with us?"

"Isn't that my question most of the time?"

I swung my seven iron. The hole was a tricky par 3 with a good-sized Galway lake at its edge. My shot arched high in the air and dropped on the green, an easy two-putt away from a par.

"We have to go down there," she agreed as she prepared for her five-iron blast. "Only, I wish I could go home tomorrow."

"Home?"

"Southport Avenue. Where else?"

Her shot landed about ten feet from the cup, closer than mine, but just a little too long.

"What do you think happened at Castle Garry in 1922?"

"They killed her, only I don't know who they are or what she wants us to clear up. Maybe they didn't kill her. Maybe she wanted to die."

Right.

As we walked on to the green, I heard her sob.

"Nuala! What's wrong?"

"I'm such a terrible little gobshite of a wife!"

I put my arm around her. She was trembling with sobs.

"You'd better putt," she said through her tears. "We don't want to hold up them focking amadons behind us."

Not being very competitive, I was ready to settle for a par even though there was a good chance she'd sink her ten footer. So I inched my golf ball up to about a foot and a half away.

"Och, Dermot," she said through her tears, "you should have gone for it."

She went for it of course. And missed by an inch.

"Two pars," I said meekly.

She was still weeping when we arrived at the next tee.

I embraced her again.

"Woman, you're not a little gobshite of a wife."

That set off another round of sobbing.

"What makes you think you are?" I persisted, though I was wary that my question might be too direct for the woman and the time and the place.

"I didn't congratulate you on your eagle! And it such a focking brilliant shot!"

"Just a little strength and a little luck."

"Strength," she murmured, "to get it there, skill to put it so close to the cup."

"Pure luck."

And it was.

"And meself such a focking competitive woman, always wanting to win."

"I like competitive women," I said, truthfully enough. "Then I don't have to be competitive. I just have to glide along on my brute strength and my luck."

She stopped weeping and began to laugh. "You're such a dear, sweet, wonderful man, Dermot Michael Coyne!"

" 'Tis true," I said with a mock sigh.

She was so badly shaken by her sobbing jag that she

had to dab at her eyes with a tissue all the way to the clubhouse. However, she competed as fiercely on the three remaining holes as she had before her burst of guilt. Nonetheless, she did compliment me on my drives.

"Focking brilliant!"

"Thank you."

"I even half mean it!"

We swam in the pool, though the mists, this time thick and grim, had drifted back from the bay and covered the countryside. The fog had chased away the other swimmers. The pool was chilly, not as chilly as Galway Bay, as transferred to me by the ineffable Fiona.

" 'Tis too cold for you Yanks and too warm for you Irish people," my wife informed me.

"It notably warmed up when you dived in," I said through chattering teeth.

She was wearing a blue bikini that was modest by the standards she usually adhered to at Grand Beach.

"Gobshite," she said, splashing me.

"When do you show me the place where you and your mother skinny-dip?"

Though she had often insisted that there was such a place, I wasn't sure that it really existed.

"Never!" she said, trying to shove me under the water. " 'Tis a private place altogether. Besides, you'd never swim in Galway Bay, not at all, at all."

" 'Tis true," I said, wrestling with her.

We both dragged each other under the water. She was one tough and strong woman.

"Not quite strong enough," I taunted her—and swam away as fast as I could.

We climbed out of the pool, shivering and gasping for breath.

" 'Twas great fun," she announced.

"Frigid."

"Refreshing."

While I waited for her in the lobby of the clubhouse, I picked up the *Sunday Tribune*—Dublin, not Chicago.

We seemed to have made the news again.

Father Placid Clarke had told their arts correspondent that the concert had just barely broken even. "The expenses of bringing over an America singer are enormous," he complained. "They're not very generous people you know. I feel badly let down by their selfishness."

However, a certain Michael Patrick Dennis Dunn, the well-known Dublin barrister and spokesman for Nuala Anne McGrail had replied, "Father Placid is singularly ungracious. My client and her husband have paid all their traveling and living expenses themselves, including their taxi ride in from the airport. They have not accepted a single shilling from Irish International Aid. His statement is close to defamatory. If it is true that the concert earned very little money, despite the huge crowd which filled the Point Theater, a formal investigation by the fraud section of the Gardai of the I.I.A. finances might be appropriate. The least Father Placid Clarke could do is present the public with a detailed accounting."

Father Placid Clarke had bluntly refused to do that. It remained to be seen what further action Mr. Dunn would take.

Though I didn't know that we had a spokesman in Dublin, I saw the workings of the fine Irish hand of my big sister, Cynthia Marie Elizabeth Anne Hurley, Counselor at Law. Poor Father Placid, he had run into a very large freight train.

The other news about us, though only indirectly, was a profile on Maeve Doyle, "the greatest Irish folk singer of our time."

Maeve Bounces Back!

The theme of the article following this headline was that Ms. Doyle was recovering from a sharp decline in her popularity.

"Of course," the singer observed, "if a person insists on the highest professional standards, there will come a time when those who are moved by the shallow fashions of the moment will lose interest. One expects that to happen. My husband and I were candidly surprised that such an interlude was so long in coming. We are now satisfied that it has passed and that the real Irish people, those who know their own musical heritage and value fine music are rallying to our support."

Her husband, who was also her manager, was a large, slightly dazed looking fellow with thick black hair, according to the picture which accompanied the article. He was described only as a "prominent musicologist who specializes in traditional Irish music."

Ms. Boyle went on at some length about her academic and vocal training, her daily exercises to keep in practice, and the "absolute necessity" of maintaining the highest standards when singing folk music.

The reporter, who perhaps had a bit of mischief in her, observed that the folk who had originally sung the music might not have understood that necessity.

"We owe it to their memory," Ms. Boyle replied, "to keep alive their songs in the most perfect way possible. It is unfortunate that some of the younger and more inexperienced singers do not appreciate that they could easily destroy a fragile tradition."

She had sweetly passive-aggressive words to say about several singers of whom I had never heard and of the woman who had invited us to Glenstal. She also dismissed Sinéad O'Connor and Dolores O'Riordan (of the Cranberries) as barbarians. Her only comment on my wife was that "she ought better to stay in America where she belongs."

Probably nothing defamatory in that, though it ignored Nuala Anne's Gaeltacht roots. The reporter noted dryly that Irish was not Ms. Doyle's first language, though she sang it very well, according to many Irish-speaking music critics.

Aha.

We had made some wonderful friends in Dublin.

"A phone call for you, Mr. McGrail," a polite young man with flaming red hair said to me.

Mr. McGrail was it now?

"Yeah?"

Silence.

"Who's calling?"

More silence.

"We want our money!" a hoarse voice shouted into my ear. "We want it soon, you focking gobshite, or we'll cut off her tits and your balls."

The phone clicked off.

I hung up calmly and walked out to the car.

"Inspector Murphy," I said to the copper (having learned his name and rank from my wife), "I just had another call from your friends in the 'Real' IRA. They threatened dire harm to my wife and myself."

"Focking bastards," he said. "Excuse me, sir. . . . I'll call the Commissioner."

"You do that."

We drove back to Carraroe, picked up Gerry and Annie, and drove back for dinner at a restaurant on the bay side of the road. It specialized in extraordinary Norman cooking, the man of the house being a Gaeltacht native and his wife a cook from Normandy. We complimented.them on their cuisine. They asked Nuala to sing "Galway Bay" for them, though the mists were so thick that one could not even see the bay, which was only a few yards away.

— 26 —

CASTLEGARRY DID not look in the least sinister. Outlined against the setting sun, which had turned the Shannon Estuary orange and gold, it was a typical late-eighteenth- or early-nineteenth-century Georgian manor house, not as big or as ornate as those that survived near Dublin and hardly a place for peers of the realm. The prospectus said it could accommodate eight couples in comfort, plus one honeymoon suite. Crowded comfort, most likely.

She had reserved the honeymoon suite for us. Naturally.

"It doesn't look haunted," I said to my wife.

"It isn't the real house," she replied. "That was burned to the ground."

"A few walls might have survived," I suggested.

" 'Tis true," she sighed. "That's enough to preserve whatever haunts might be here."

One approached Castlegarry on the traditional tree-lined road and then turned at the end of the trees to see the house itself—neat, clean, and welcoming. Trim lawns all around it, a freshly raked gravel drive in front of the door, tall but orderly shrubbery, large formal gardens radiant in the sunshine on either side of the house. Someone had spent a lot of money to create an image of a "Big House" that was fit for Hollywood. Well-heeled American tourists would bring home snapshots to demonstrate that they had spent time in a "real" manor house. Their relatives would not dare comment that it looked kind of small, compared to Ashford Castle.

"Your man there in the doorway spent a lot of money on it," Nuala commented.

Fiona, sensing that the car was slowing down, stood up, arched her back, and licked my hand.

The man in the doorway fit the picture of the owner of a manor house, tall, a bit stout, iron gray hair, a rubicund face, and a bright smile. He was flanked by two servants in uniform, a butler perhaps and a maid.

"Upstairs, downstairs," I whispered to herself.

"What's that?" she asked, patting the good-dog Fiona's large head.

"Series, on the telly, about Edwardian England."

"Och, I wasn't alive then, Dermot Michael. Sure, it was never as neat and clean as it is now, not in Ireland, was it now?"

"And it never had eighteen holes tucked away behind that avenue."

Paddy MacGarry opened the car door for us and helped us out of the car.

"Mr. Coyne, Ms. McGrail, you're most welcome to Castlegarry . . . you, too, girl. . . . Ah, you've found a stick, have you now? Would you ever go chase it for me?"

Fiona dashed madly after the stick, forgetting her new friends for an even newer friend.

"Welcome to you, Inspector," he said to the Garda. "We've made all the arrangements for you and your colleagues. We're delighted to have you with us."

Hotel owners are supposed to be genial. Was this

fellow a little too genial? A bit of a gombeen man perhaps?

"Peace be to this house and all who live in it," Nuala said piously, in Irish of course, as we went in the door.

He replied in Irish that was fluent but not as fluent as hers, "And I hope this will be only the first of many visits to Castlegarry. It's been in my family for almost two hundred years. Its predecessors have been on this land for almost half a millennium, ah, but that's another story, isn't it now. . . . Come in and look at our great room, as we call it."

"You've done a remarkable job of restoration, Mr. MacGarry," I said, glancing around the room, which was both a historical museum and a comfortable place to sit before the turf fire.

"Thank you, sir . . . and Paddy, if you don't mind."

"Dermot," I said tersely. Then nodding to herself, "Marie Fionnuala Anne."

"Nuala," said herself as she nudged me.

"The place almost burned to the ground during the Troubles back in the twenties, only two walls standing. Stood idle for a long time till we persuaded a syndicate in Dublin to back us in its restoration. It's been a very successful project, let me tell you."

Nuala nudged me again. I glanced at the wall next to the entrance to the room. On the wall hung a full-length life-size portrait of a beautiful blond woman in a long white dress with a blue sash around her slender waist. She was trying to look serious and responsible, but mischief leaped from her brown eyes and her full lips.

"Gussie Downs," I said, almost reverently.

"That's right, Dermot. She was the last of the direct line. A wonderful woman, by all accounts. Her husband"—he gestured to a wedding photo on an end table—"was killed in the war."

The young couple, solemn and aloof as was the style in wedding pictures in those days, looked like children. They were, I thought, about the same age at the time of their marriage as Nuala and I.

"Victoria Cross," I said. "Ninth Scottish Division."

Paddy raised an eyebrow, "You've done your research, Dermot."

"Storyteller," I said, realizing that an idea for my next novel had been fermenting in the basement of my brain. Gussie and Arthur would not be forgotten.

"They're buried out below beyond on the banks of the river. She died in the fire."

"Tans?"

"Maybe," he said with a sigh. "Or maybe the Irregulars. . . . It was all a long time ago."

"They became the Irregulars only after the treaty," I said.

"She didn't start the fire," Nuala added softly.

MacGarry showed us to our room, the honeymoon suite, on the second floor. It overlooked a garden of spring flowers and the Shannon Estuary, thirty feet down a cliff. The tide was at ebb. Muddy flats, turned copper in the light of the fading sun, reached out into the dark blue river. Much of the rain that fell on this soggy green isle rushed out to sea from the mouth of the Shannon, only to be picked up by weather fronts rushing over the Gulf Stream and dumped once again on Ireland. River run . . .

Nuala Anne, in a kind of trance, stared out the window.

"They're down there," she said, pointing to the right of the house.

There were two gravestones only a stone's throw behind the garden.

Paddy MacGarry seemed puzzled. He had expected a young woman singer and a blond ape. Instead the woman walked in a kind of mystic daze and the ape knew a lot of history, maybe too much history.

If we cared for a bite to eat, they'd saved some supper for us. Would a half hour be too soon?

It certainly would not.

They'd provide a bite for the wolfhound, too. She would spend the night in a kennel they happened to have. During the day she could roam the grounds or ride with us over to Glenstal, which was a grand place altogether. Wonderful men, the monks, let me tell you.

The bedroom of the honeymoon suite was not as small as I had expected. It was supposed to look like a typical Victorian bedroom, complete with a canopy over the bed, though the bed was substantially less than queen size. There was a screen behind which the woman could dress and undress, a fireplace, a small desk with an inkwell, a lantern with a lightbulb in it, and several deep chairs with thick cushions. Naturally, there was a modern bathroom with a tub and shower, central heating, and a discreetly protected electric heater, just in case the Yank tourist wanted to be toasty warm while pretending that he had stepped back in time a hundred and fifty years.

In the much smaller parlor, we would have a couple of comfortable chairs, a larger desk, a fireplace with turf piled in front of it, a fifteen-inch color TV, and life-size paintings of Augusta and Arthur on either wall, she in evening dress, he in the formal red coat of an English army officer. He was wearing the Victoria Cross. Both paintings were posthumous, though not at all bad.

"We should go down there and pray after supper," Nuala, still gazing out of the window, murmured.

"Is the place haunted?" I asked

"Not by evil anyway."

"Come look at the paintings in the parlor."

She glanced at them briefly. "They're all right, Dermot. She'd like them both."

Would she now?

Downstairs we were greeted by Antonia MacGarry, a tall, slender, and handsome woman who was clearly in charge of the house. She was from Dublin but spoke with the near-English accent that some of the upper-middle-class Dublinites affected. She was wearing a long black dress with a string of pearls. Real ones.

"We didn't know when to expect you," she said with a pleasant smile. "We knew you didn't plan to be here for supper. But we didn't want you to go to bed hungry your first night at Castlegarry. So we've heated up a few leftovers."

Vegetable soup, Beef Wellington, mashed potatoes, carrots, peas, cabbage, red wine, and apple crunch with heavy cream. Nuala ate sparingly, her mind elsewhere. I had two helpings of everything.

Paddy joined us. I had not made up my mind about him, but I was impressed that he had not claimed to be in the direct line of the MacGarrys.

"There are easier ways to run a profitable hotel," he told us with his relaxed grin, "but none which are quite as challenging or quite as much fun. There's a lot of history in this place, as you know, Dermot. We have a small clientele, but more than two-thirds of our guests are repeaters. They love the warmth and the color and the relaxed atmosphere of the place."

"And the golf course," his wife added.

"Do you play golf, Dermot?" he asked me, his small eyes glittering.

"A little bit," I admitted. "So does herself."

"I hope we can have a round then while you're here."

"I'm sure we can."

He would want, poor man, to bet on it. Since he

didn't look much like a retired Irish golf champion, I didn't think I'd lose much.

But, mind you, I'm not the competitive type—not until I run into someone who wants to compete with me. Or, even worse, someone who thinks I'm a pushover.

Why do people always think I'm a pushover?

The castle and the land immediately around it were all that were left of the MacGarry holdings. When all the debts were paid and all the farms turned over to the farmers, Paddy's father, a pharmacist up above in Clare, as the only surviving kin inherited the strip along the Shannon. He tried to sell it, but no one was interested. Paddy himself had gone to the hotel management school they used to have at Maynooth before it became a fancy university. He'd managed hotels down in Waterford and then in Dublin. He met Tonia at a dance in one of them. On their honeymoon they came out to Limerick. She saw the ruins of the castle and had the wonderful idea of restoring it as a hotel.

"Sure, Paddy, you're just the man to do it."

He hadn't been much interested in the direct line of McGarrys. Rich, stuck-up Protestants, his grandmother had said. But, he confessed, he fell in love with the history and the idea.

Tonia's father persuaded some of his friends to have a go at restoring the place as an exclusive hotel. They had sunk a lot of capital into it and had made very little money on their investment for several years.

"Now, however, thanks to you Americans, they are very pleased indeed with their return, let me tell you."

He did not, however, know all that much of the history of the McGarrys. They were warriors, descended from Normans, who fought other Irish lords before the English came, then fought the English, then became Protestants and fought for the English wherever the

English fought. They died in places like Saratoga, Austerlitz, Lucknow, Balaclava, Kabul, Khartoum, Isandhlwana, Natal. Lady Augusta's father had died in the Boer War, leading a troop of cavalry at the relief of Ladysmith. Their graves were over in the Church of Ireland Chapel. They mostly died young, as did poor Lady Augusta's husband. They were as generous with their tenants as they were with their lives and were well loved by the people in Garrytown. In truth they were neither English nor Irish but a mix of both. They stayed out of local politics but discreetly supported Parnell during the Land League and Home Rule debates. They were Protestants theoretically but were always great friends with the local priests and even the bishops of Limerick.

"There seem to have been rumors," Tonia continued, "that after Lord Downs' death, Lady Augusta became a Catholic. The parish priest said mass for her in his church. Every Catholic in Garrytown came. It is even said today that he also blessed her grave."

"Both the graves were neglected and overgrown when we came back here," Paddy continued. "We fixed them up. We owed that to two very brave young people."

"Your father knew nothing about Lady Augusta's death?" I asked.

"If he did, he wasn't talking about it." Paddy shrugged his shoulders. "I think he might not have wanted to know too much about it."

"Pour some heavy cream on your apple crunch, Dermot Michael," herself instructed me. "It would be wrong to waste it." She sounded just like Ma.

"We are not historians," Tonia explained. "We are interested in history, of course. Who in Ireland isn't? But we don't want to disturb the dead, if you take my meaning."

Indeed I did. If you poked around too much, you might find something that would sour the clients of your nice little gold mine of a hotel.

"Her ancestors seemed to involve themselves in losing battles, didn't they?" I asked. "Strain of recklessness in the family?"

Paddy laughed. "Not in our branch. We've all been disgustingly conservative. However, if you were in the English army in the eighteenth and nineteenth century, there were a lot of military disasters available."

"The English lost every battle but the last one," Tonia said.

"Still," I pushed the point, "they seemed to have led the charge."

"As far back as you go in our history," Paddy admitted, "there was always a young McGarry leading a charge somewhere."

We went into the great room for our coffee and liquor. Naturally, herself and I opted for Baileys. We were not offered an option about drinking it on the rocks. Some of the other guests had drifted into the room for their nightcaps. My wife arranged herself near the harp and plucked on its strings absently.

Actually, it was not absent plucking at all. She was waiting for and indeed expecting an invitation to sing.

"Would you ever be so kind to favor us with a song, Ms. McGrail?" Paddy MacGarry asked.

"Well, I wouldn't want to bore you now," she said with totally false reluctance.

"She thought you'd never ask," says I.

She sang American songs—"The Streets of Laredo," "Shenandoah," "Dance, Boatman," and "Irish Eyes." Our fellow guests joined in loudly in celebration of the eyes of the Irish.

She did not do "Molly Malone," for which God forgive her.

When we went back to our room she decreed that we must don our running clothes, collect the darlin' girl, who needed the exercise after being cooped up in the car all day, and run a few miles. That meant five or six.

Our first stop was at the graves. The gravestones were simple—"Lord Arthur Downs V.C., 1884–1918," "Lady Antonia McGarry Downs 1888–1922." A carefully tended garden embraced both resting places. Nuala and I knelt to pray. Fiona, sensing the solemnity of the situation, sat on her haunches and watched us.

After several minutes of intense prayer, my wife stood up, brushed the dirt off her knees, and sighed.

"No empty graves?"

"Not at all, at all."

"Are they at peace?"

"He is."

"Tomorrow when we come back from Glenstal, I think we'll talk to the parish priest."

"He'll know a lot," she agreed. "Come on, darlin' girl; we all need to run."

So we ran under the moon, which washed the Shannon silver and created eerie shadows all around us. We visited the various "monuments" that remained from earlier castles—a wall of a medieval tower, an old monastic graveyard with a few tombstones slanting in opposite directions, a pile of stones that, according to the leaflet in our room, was all that was left of the chapel of the great monastery of St. Conan, the vine-covered Church of Ireland church, also dedicated to St. Conan, where Augusta's brave and reckless ancestors were buried.

"You Irish Catholics," I said to my panting wife, "are remarkably tolerant of these fellows. They were part of the oppression after all."

"Sure, aren't they Irish like everyone else?"

That, I thought, was a typical argument on this strange island where the principle of contradiction was considered to be irrelevant.

Then we delivered the good dog to her kennel and returned to our room. I jumped into the shower. A surprisingly amorous Nuala Anne joined me. For a moment I thought we were close to something special, and then somehow, even though we made gentle and tender love, that something special slipped away.

YOU BLEW IT AGAIN, ASSHOLE, the Adversary informed me. *CAN'T YOU TELL THAT THE WOMAN WANTS SOMETHING MORE?*

"But what?" I answered, knowing that he had a point.

IF YOU'RE TOO DUMB TO FIGURE IT OUT, WHY SHOULD I TELL YOU?

Since the Adversary was actually part of me, there was no reason to expect that he would know any more than I did.

Could one be tender and fierce at the same time?

Maybe, but I didn't know how.

27

"A WOMAN," me ma says to me in Irish, when we're leaving this morning, "has to be generous with her man."

" 'Tis true," I say, thinking I'm plenty generous.

"And doesn't that mean more than just making love when he wants to?"

"It does," I say, not knowing exactly what it means at all, at all.

So I think about it all the way down here. Dermot, poor dear man, is interested in what they're saying on the radio about Father Placid and the investigation of IIA's finances. The money from the concert has been frozen, which means he can't spend it and neither can anyone else.

Next time I do something for charity, I'll check into it a lot more carefully. And meself an accountant at that!

Still, I'm wondering what generosity means.

I thought I was very generous tonight, drying him with me towel and asking him to dry me. 'Tis great fun altogether. We drove each other out of our minds, and the moonlight coming in off the Shannon. But whatever is supposed to happen when a man and a woman abandon themselves didn't quite happen. I think we were close. But somewhere we weren't close enough.

Should I blame him or meself?

That's a silly question. I'm ashamed of meself for asking. We both need to get the hang of it.

And we will, damn it.

Sorry. We will with Your help.

Which I expect, and the sooner the better.

This isn't exactly her room. Nor is this the bed where she and her husband made love for the first time. But it had to be in about the same space. I suppose it took them awhile to get the hang of it, too. Maybe even longer, because they knew a lot less in those days than we do today. Still, too much knowledge can be a problem, can't it now?

Well, I promise You one thing: we'll work it out before we leave here!

And, Augusta Downs, I know you're lurking around here someplace. I know you brought us here to do something for you. I half-think you also are going to reward us for being here. Well, you know what I want.

Give me the courage I need. I'm going out of my mind with desire, and I don't quite know what it is that I desire so much.

28

WE STOPPED at the parish house in Garrytown on our way to Glenstal. Father Mike MacNamee, the P.P. (Parish Priest, the rank we would call Pastor in the U.S.), was a lively little man in his midseventies. He wished us a joyful welcome to Garrytown, threw a stick for Fiona, brought us into the house, offered us a pot of tea unless we wanted something stronger (we did not, Father, but thank you), congratulated herself on her wonderful performance on the telly, and assured us that we were part of a critical religious revolution in Ireland.

Garrytown was little more than a hamlet through which a National Secondary Road, N-69, passed on its way to Loghill, Foynes, and eventually Limerick. A group of old stucco houses that whitewash, colored trim, and flowers made picturesque, it hugged the road in appealing pretense that it was the way Ireland used to be. But the healthy people, the TV antennae, and the cars belied that claim, if anyone cared about that. It was a pretty little town with attractive stores, two pubs (the Limerickman and the Harp and Shamrock), and a small, neat church of the sort built at the end of the last century when the Church in the west of Ireland had finally struggled out of the famine disaster and begun to prosper from the redistribution of land.

Compared to similar little towns along the north side of Galway Bay, however, it not only was snug and prosperous but had been so for a long time. Moreover, like the castle it was far enough out on the estuary to absorb the Gulf Stream warmth, which created a thin veneer of subtropical climate. Garrytown, like some places on Dingle, Kenmare, and Bantry Bays, enjoyed a few cautious palm trees.

In his cozy library, lined with modern theology books, he poured our tea (not polluted by milk), served us scones, which "I hope aren't too hard now" (they were not), and finally asked what he could do for us.

"We want to know the whole truth about Lady Augusta McGarry Downs," Nuala Anne said flatly, adopting a very direct and very American approach, perhaps because she sensed that this was the best way to deal with this attractive little man.

She was wearing a summer suit, black with gold buttons, and the whole accompanying professional accountant regalia—panty hose, heels, makeup, hair in a tight bun. You have to establish with those Benedictines, and themselves all so smart, that you are a responsible, mature adult and not merely a silly little girl who sings on the telly.

"Do you now?"

"We do," she insisted. "We know she didn't start the fire. We know about Major General Sir Henry Hugh Tudor, we know about the death of Kevin O'Higgins, and we think it's time the whole truth be told about her."

Even from someone who could play fast and furious games with the truth when she was of a mind to, this was a series of assertions that took my breath away.

"Do you now?"

"We do."

"And you'd be thinking that I know something about all these matters?"

"We do."

"And suppose that I do now," he said with an affable little smile. "Why would I be telling you what I know?"

"Because it is time. Because Lady Augusta wants the truth to be told. Because she didn't start the fire."

"You're sure she didn't start the fire, are you?"

"I am."

"How would you know that? No one knows how the fire started."

"I do."

Father MacNamee sipped his tea, petted Fiona's head, glanced at me, and then asked, "You'd be one of the dark ones, would you?"

"Sometimes," Nuala Anne admitted.

"There're still a few of your kind around, mostly older. 'Tis said there were more in the old days. I'm not sure whether that's true."

"Maybe today the dark ones ignore the signs."

"Aye," he said, nodding his head. "Maybe they do. . . . Your ma one of them?"

"Of course not. Me aunt. You know that's the way of it."

Maybe he did, but I didn't.

"Aye, I do that. . . . Funny thing, when I saw you on the telly the other night and saw how close you were to the music and its meaning, I half-suspected that you knew a lot of things about the music that no one else knew. . . . Tell me, does it bother you much to see things and know things?"

"No, Father, it does not," she said calmly. "I have this good man to take care of me. He's used to it now. So isn't it fine if I can do a little good with it?"

"Where is this good man?" I said, pretending to search for him.

Both the priest and my wife laughed, a little too readily, I thought.

"You're sure about the fire?"

"Haven't I said so?"

"It makes sense," he said, frowning in deep thought. "The McGarrys were all crazy, wonderful but crazy. She was the most sensible one in generations, but she was a little crazy, too. . . . I always liked to think that she was not that crazy."

"She was brilliant," Nuala asserted, "wasn't she now? I'll give you that she might have started the fire if she'd thought it necessary. But, as much as she missed her husband, she did not want to die."

"Hm . . . ," said the priest. "Now suppose I can find out something more to tell you about her, what would you do with it?"

"It might not matter if anyone else knows the truth, Father. We have to know it. It's time that someone knows it. On the other hand, it might matter that the whole truth be told. My husband writes wonderful novels. He's thinking about one on her right now. He won't write it if she wouldn't want it written."

How the hell did she know that I was thinking about a novel?

Oh, well, it was part of the package, wasn't it?

"Some people do know," he said. "I suppose you'd say not enough?"

"I would."

"Aye, I thought you would. . . . Now tell me, how do you get along with the folks up beyond above in the castle?"

"They're very warm and gracious hosts," I said, since patently my wife did not think that the question pertained to her rubrics, "and very skillful. It's a fine hotel."

"And himself?"

I hesitated, suspecting that I was taking a test. "A good man, hardworking, creative, knows a little more than he lets on. Probably inherited a touch of the gombeen man from his father, the chemist up beyond above in Ennis, but herself keeps him in line."

The priest threw back his head and laughed like a diminutive Santa Claus.

"Now, Nuala Anne, which one of youse is the real dark one?"

"Me man," Nuala said, beaming proudly, "is not at all fey, Father. He's just very, very smart."

I blushed. She'd never said that before.

"And," she went on, her chin tilted defiantly in the air, "he understands people and that's why he writes novels. He knows me better than I know meself. He knows me so well that sometimes he scares me."

Do I now?

This was my day to shine.

"I suppose your man wants you to play golf with him, Dermot?"

"It's been mentioned."

"You've played golf before?"

"A little."

Nuala snorted. "Me man just says that because he's humble and knows how to out hustle a hustler. His handicap, Your Reverence, is two, and that's when he's not being competitive."

"Between two and three," I said to set the record straight.

"Good enough for him!" The little priest pounded the coffee table and then poured us all another cup of tea. He also passed a piece of scone to a grateful Fiona.

"Well, Dermot," he went on, "you'll teach your man a lesson he needs."

"Anyone who plays a man on his own course," I said, sounding like a golf course Solomon, "ought to know his own limitations. Fair play to him if he takes me."

"Not a chance!" me wife proclaimed exuberantly.

"I wasn't really changing the subject, Nuala," the little priest said with a self-effacing smile. "I know better than that. I think your man up beyond above in the castle knows more than he lets on."

"But not very much," I observed. "He's afraid to know too much for fear his charming legend of lovers from long ago might be spoiled. It could be disastrous for business."

"Aye, I think so, too. . . . Well, I'll have to ponder all of this for a day or two. Maybe ask around a bit. . . . I hope you won't mind waiting. You'll be down beyond below in Glenstal singing with all me good Benedictine friends for a couple of days, won't you?"

"We will."

"Now I hope this won't offend you too much, but I have to ask. Would you ever have a priest in America who knows you well enough to . . . well, act as a reference?"

"What about your man here?"

Nuala stood up, stepped over the bulk of Fiona, and removed a book from the little priest's shelf. *The Achievement of David Tracy.*

"You know your man?" the priest said, impressed.

"Isn't me husband's brother his C.C.?"

"Is he now!"

"And himself telling a story at our wedding?"

"And yourselves having friends in the hierarchy?"

"A few," I said, not thinking it worthwhile to mention our friend Eddy Hayes,[1] the former Bishop of Galway, or my uncle, the Bishop Emeritus of Alton, Illinois, to say nothing of Nuala Anne's good friend Cardinal Sean.

[1] *Irish Gold*

"Isn't that grand? Well, I won't have to make any calls, will I now? Sure, could you stop back the day after tomorrow?"

We could.

We left the parish house with his blessings and best wishes for our session with the Benedictines.

"Your man will call the little bishop anyway," Nuala informed me. "Good on him for doing it."

"I didn't know that I scared you because I know so much about you, Nuala Anne McGrail."

"Och, Dermot, you do. I don't have many masks left to me that you don't see through. Pretty soon you'll take them all 'way and I won't be able to hide at all, at all."

"Then what will happen?"

"I wish I knew."

"What do you think will happen?"

Silence.

Fiona bounced into our car and curled up on the seat. We followed her.

"Any news, Inspector Murphy?"

"It looks like the IIA books are a terrible mess altogether. Father Placid apparently was taken in by some good Catholic laymen, the kind of fat, plausible crooks who took a lot of his money to 'invest' for him. Make a big killing quickly. Only the schemes didn't work. He'd intended to use the receipts of the concert to cover his losses. He has, by the way, left the country."

"Oh," Nuala said.

"Any reason to think that his good Catholic laity are after us?"

"The Commissioner isn't sure. There's layer upon layer in the scandal. Drug cartels involved."

"Great."

"Commissioner says not to worry."

"Great."

He closed the window between the back and front of the Benz. Nuala had expressed an intention to practice her Gregorian chant.

"To return to my question, Nuala Anne McGrail?"

"Maybe you'll stop loving me."

"Do you think that likely?"

Silence.

Then, "I don't know. You're a good man. Too good. I'm a shite of a wife. I'd try the patience of a saint."

"I'll leave you?"

"No, but maybe you should."

"Am I permitted to worry about that instead of you?"

"Maybe you know all there is to know already."

"Maybe I do."

"I'd better practice me chant."

So she practiced her chant and I pondered the difference between the self-confident young woman who had tackled Father MacNamee with such skill and the worried country girl who was afraid I'd stop loving her.

SHE'S FAKING SEXUAL PLEASURE, the Adversary informed me. SHE WANTS TO MAKE YOU THINK YOU'RE A GREAT LOVER. SHE DOESN'T DISLIKE IT, BUT SHE'S NOT GETTING MUCH OUT OF IT. NOW SHE FEELS GUILTY.

"Nonsense. How dare you think such things?"

I DARE BECAUSE I'M PART OF YOU. YOU'VE SUSPECTED IT FOR A LONG TIME AND COVERED IT UP BECAUSE YOU DON'T KNOW WHAT TO DO ABOUT IT.

Nuala Anne playing the sexually satisfied wife role?

How would she know what it is?

For that matter, how would I know?

What do I do?

The mists that had been lurking just off the coast of Ireland during our time in the west had changed to rain clouds and then rain—drizzle (a soft day)—when we left Castlegarry and then a downpour as we neared

Limerick. The estuary was the color of a tarnishing silver plate.

My wife stopped singing long enough to comment as we drove into Limerick town, "Doesn't it rain too much altogether in this focking country?"

Limerick looked like Gary, Indiana, as we drove through; no, better, it looked like Whiting, Indiana, without the oil refineries. The windshield wiper on our car scraped back and forth resolutely, giving us an occasional glimpse of the road ahead. Good-dog Fiona struggled up to her haunches next to me and stared out the window, apparently fascinated by the rain.

Nuala kept on at her chant practice. I closed my eyes and imagined I was in the chapel of a medieval cloistered convent and a haunting voice was singing behind the opaque chancel screen. My lost love.

Except I hadn't lost Nuala. Not yet. Not ever.

And certainly not to a convent.

I had just about persuaded myself that the Adversary was dead wrong about her when she paused in her practice.

"Are you asleep, Dermot Michael, and yourself with the big bitch's head in your lap?"

"Woman, I am not. I am imagining meself in a medieval cloister, listening to a nun singing behind a chancel screen."

I opened my eyes. Fiona licked my hand to indicate she wanted to be petted.

"Good girl," I murmured to her. She closed her eyes.

"I wanted to say again what I was after saying in the parish house. You're the smartest person I know."

"Smarter even then George the Priest?"

"The poor man knows a lot, but he's not as smart about people as you are."

"Smarter than your friend the little bishop?"

"Sometimes he's a little slow."

"I'm pretty good at hitting golf balls, too!"

"Och, you're also impossible!"

"I thank you for all the compliments."

She frowned, hesitated, and then blurted out, "When I'm with you I feel like I'm completely naked all the time. You know everything about me."

What do you say to that?

"Nothing hidden?"

"Not a thing." She bowed her head miserably.

"And I still seem to love you?"

She nodded, her eyes averted.

"Even more?"

She looked up at me, her eyes filled with tears. "Even more," she agreed in a whisper.

Then she went back to her chant. I continued to pet Fiona and imagine that the good wolfhound was my companion during my wanderings through medieval France when they were building Gothic cathedrals and earlier, a Celtic Catholic version of Henry Adams maybe.

I returned to the question of marital sex. What were the odds that an inexperienced young woman like my wife would achieve full sexual satisfaction during the first week of our marriage?

Practically zero.

Then why would she appear to have done so? Because she had read the books about what it was supposed to be like and was a good actress?

Why should she want to fake it?

Because Nuala Anne had to be good at everything and immediately, whether it be Camogie or sexual romping.

Also, she wanted to please me in the worst way.

Oh, yeah, I was the smart one. I knew all about people, especially about her, right?

I should have expected that would happen. How could I have been so dumb?

HAVEN'T I BEEN TELLING YOU THAT ALL ALONG?

"Beat it."

I was the experienced male lover, wasn't I?

Yeah, right!

YOU DIDN'T WANT TO FACE THE POSSIBILITY THAT SHE WAS PRETENDING. YOU DON'T HAVE THE SLIGHTEST IDEA WHAT TO DO ABOUT IT EVEN NOW, DO YOU?

My conversation with the Adversary was interrupted by the inspector's announcement that we had entered county Tip and were at Moroe, the small town outside the abbey.

We turned down a side road and into a hilly park with the usual tree-lined drive. Glenstal was a twentieth-century foundation in an old country home, larger and more elaborate than Castlegarry. However, it already looked like a medieval abbey with its cluster of gray stone buildings constructed around a quadrilateral courtyard into which we drove.

Two monks and an attractive woman in her thirties waited for us. Inspector Murphy opened the door for us again, even though he knew I disapproved of a cop of his rank playing servant.

Fiona, as was now her practice, bounded out ahead of us and headed straight for the monk who I assumed had to be the abbot.

The cop winked at me as I followed herself out of the car. "Sure, don't we have to keep up the act now?"

Our hosts and hostess must have wondered what crazy people they had invited to participate in their recording. We arrived in a Mercedes limo, followed by a trailing car and preceded by a maniacally friendly wolfhound. One of us was a gorgeous young woman dressed in black like she was ready for a papal audience and the other a big gorilla-type character in a Notre Dame sweatshirt and jeans.

Being Irish, however, they were charming and cordial. The abbot threw a stick for Fiona, apparently the price of admission, and then wrestled with her when she brought it back. The other monk and the woman admired her, petted her, informed her that she was a very good dog.

Which Fiona knew anyway but liked to hear again.

The abbot said it was fine to let her run in the fields and bark at the cattle and the sheep.

Abbot Fabian and Brother Killian showed us into a small parlor; Maureen, the woman in charge of the recording and herself the principal singer, told me wife several times how grateful they all were that she had come to sing some Marian motets.

"Och, and meself never singing chant before," Nuala said, opting for her shy country lass image.

We were served tea and scones, the latter very fresh, while the abbot told us about the monastery.

"We earn our living here by running a boys' school, a first-rate one, we like to think. We also try to be an ecumenical and liturgical center and have a special interest in relations with the Russian Orthodox Church. We have a collection of icons that we'd like to show you. Our recordings have been quite successful. They help us to pay some of the bills for the conferences we convene, and they say something about the new and the old in Irish religious music."

"We were really excited that you agreed to stop by," Maureen said again. "After we saw you on the telly the other night, we knew that you understood religious music and Irish music better than any of us did, so we're doubly grateful for your visit."

"You'd almost think she was Irish, wouldn't you now?" says I.

"Me ma," Nuala said shyly, "says I have a Yank brogue."

More laughter.

"Wasn't it terrible that they let that awful woman say such horrible things about your wife?" Maureen said with a shake of her pretty curls. "Everyone knows she's a bitter failure, but they still let her sound off against the rest of us!"

Obviously she meant Maeve Doyle.

"Failure, is it?" I said, slipping into the local pattern of speech again.

"An awful failure. Doesn't her husband, who is her business manager, think he's a marketing genius? And didn't he produce her latest disk? And wasn't it a disaster? And herself becoming so precious in her style that she puts people to sleep."

No punches pulled there.

"Poor woman," said our shy lass from Carraroe.

"You're right, dear," Maureen agreed. "I'm sure she's heartbroken. But she's good enough to make a great comeback if she'd leave off complaining about the rest of us, and the Irish people not liking moaners."

Well, they did a lot of moaning for a people who didn't like moaners. It was all right to moan, so long as you did it with a certain style.

"And hasn't the poor woman had an awful problem with her credit card?"

"Oh?"

"Isn't she one of them that can't stop buying as long as she has the card in her purse? Didn't she run up an awful bill?"

"Poor woman," Nuala said again.

We finished off the tea and scones. I was disappointed that there was no apple crunch with heavy cream.

We were then conducted into another and much larger room where a cluster of monks waited for us. I felt like Brother Cadfael coming home after solving a mystery. As one man they stood. My wife stopped, taken aback by this sign of respect. She hesitated shyly again and then began to sing.

"Salva Regina!"

The monks promptly joined in the hymn to the Mother of Jesus with which compline—their night prayers—usually ended:

> " *'Salve Regina, mater misericordiae:*
> *Vita, ducedo, et spes nostra, salve*
> *Ad te clamamus, exsules filii Evae.*
> *Ad te suspiramus, gementes et flentes,*
> *in hac lacrimarum valle.*
>
> " *'Eja ergo, Advocata nostra,*
> *illos tuos misericordes oculos ad nos converter*
> *Et Jesum, benedictum fructum ventris tui,*
> *nobis post hoc exilium ostende.*
> *O clemens, O pia, O dulcis Virgo Maria.' "*

(Hail Holy Queen, mother of mercy:
Our life, our sweetness, and our hope.
To you we cry, banished children of Eve.
To you we send our sighs, mourning and weeping,
in this valley of tears.

Turn then, O most gracious advocate,
your eyes of mercy towards us.
And after this exile show us
the blessed fruit of your womb, Jesus
O clement, O merciful, O sweet Virgin Mary.)

Nuala did not try to project her soprano voice over the monks. Rather, she blended in with them, providing another and richer color without violating their monastic tones.

Time stood still for a moment when they were finished.

Then the monks burst into applause.

"That's one we won't have to practice," Maureen said with a sigh. "I'm sure we can do that again over at the university tomorrow."

My wife blushed modestly and shook hands with each of the monks who came up to be introduced. Not a chance she would forget a single name.

The Eucharist was next and lunch would follow. We were ushered into a chapel. It was plain, as Benedictine chapels are supposed to be, but no one would have confused it with a Quaker meetinghouse. The upper walls were painted tastefully in rich and dark colors— simplicity and brilliance combined. The liturgy itself was also simple, brisk, and restrained. Father Benedict would doubtless have been pleased.

The Dominicans had taught me in high school; the Holy Cross Fathers and the Jesuits were in evidence if only rarely actually in the classrooms at Notre Dame and Marquette. All three orders had despaired of my "laziness." I had never encountered the Benedictines before, but I was impressed with their wit and warmth and hospitality.

"God," George the Priest had told me once, "respects all orders equally. But God is, in fact, a diocesan priest."

It had seemed reasonable to me.

AS THE Mass progressed, an ominous pounding assailed the roof and the walls of the chapel—wind and rain. I wondered how poor dear Fiona was faring. Then I told myself that she was, after all, a hound dog and could take care of herself no matter what the weather.

I prayed fervently for wisdom in my relationship with my priceless wife—who, next to me, was softly singing along with the monks.

And she once thought that she had to be an accountant. Perhaps she still did.

I noticed that Inspector Murphy went up to Communion with us, as did a woman who had been in the chase car, obviously a woman cop.

After Mass, he stopped me in the vestibule of the chapel.

"More news from the boss, Mr. Coyne. It seems that Father Placid or one of his gombeen advisers took out an insurance policy on the concert. If it didn't take place, they made a lot of money. Moreover, their contract with the Point required only a small fee if they canceled the concert. They would have had enough money left from the insurance to cover all their bad investments."

"Yeah!"

"It is not absolutely clear that Father Placid knew about this arrangement."

"If they had to cancel it, they would have had to return the money, wouldn't they?"

"Certainly, to whoever asked for it. But I'm sure they figured that many Irish people would not mind the money going to the poor overseas. Don't we have a long memory in this country when it comes to famines?"

"So, if there's no concert, they pay off their debts and earn some money for their organization, too?"

"That's what the boss thinks."

"Why not just cancel? Cite 'artistic differences' with me wife?"

My wife, damn it all!

"Wouldn't the insurance company have been a bit suspicious?"

"Wouldn't the kidnapping have made them suspicious, too?"

"We're not dealing, Mr. Coyne, with master criminals, are we now?"

"Dermot," I said for perhaps the fifth time.

Outside, the squall had passed through and was now rushing towards London and Warsaw and points east. A sharp gash of blue cut the sky as low clouds scudded past us, as if trying to catch up with the rain. Waiting for us outside the chapel was one very wet and very unhappy wolfhound. I grabbed her just before she jumped on Nuala and destroyed altogether, as the locals would have said, her black suit.

"Did you think we were going to desert you, darlin' girl?" I asked as I struggled to keep Fiona off my wife. "No, Fiona!" I said firmly.

Having been given her instructions, she relaxed and slobbered all over me.

We were led back to the room where we had scones

and tea for our lunch. Fiona accepted several large bones and settled down just outside the door.

"That was a very lovely liturgy, Father Abbot," Nuala said diffidently. "Prayer slipping up to Heaven to God and catching him unawares."

"Her," I said.

She gave me one of her "Shush, Dermot" looks.

"Both male and female," Brother Killian said briskly, "and neither male nor female. So, sure, can't God be imagined either way?"

"Isn't that interesting?" Nuala said respectfully—as if she hadn't heard the same thing in almost the same words from the little bishop.

"I hope I didn't offend you, Dermot, with my remarks about Maeve Doyle's manager?" Maureen said uneasily.

Under the circumstances, herself was not likely to deny that I was her manager. Obviously, however, I was supposed to.

"I'm not herself's manager, Maureen. She manages herself. By profession she's an accountant. So she manages the two of us."

The persona she was wearing forced Nuala Anne to ride to my rescue. "Sure, isn't me husband a very successful commodity trader as well as a best-selling author? Isn't it easier for me to keep the books because I've had a couple of courses in bookkeeping and he hasn't?"

Yeah, sure, and we'd worked this arrangement out in careful conversation, hadn't we?

In fact, she had simply taken over the bank statements when they came into the house.

We then went on a tour of the school, inspected the plans for a conference and residence center (for scholars in residence), and visited the dazzling Russian icon museum in a basement room converted into a cavelike structure, almost a catacomb. The icons were so beautiful that my wife wept softly.

With the return of good weather, faithless Fiona had deserted us and was doubtless out chasing cows and sheep and perhaps other dogs—or perhaps pursuing local children from whom she would demand attention and affection.

Then we returned to the chapel to practice the motets Nuala would sing. All four were brief hymns to the Mother of Jesus, normally sung by the monks at the end of the day. What a young woman's voice was doing in the cloister might be open to question. However, as Maureen pointed out to us, Ireland at one time had monasteries of men and women, though in separate enclosures. Hadn't St. Brigid herself presided over one such?

That certainly made it legitimate, did it not?

"They weren't Benedictine monasteries," the abbot cautioned us. "Benedict was an Italian. If he knew about the Irish practice—and there's no reason to think he did—he certainly would not have approved. Our idea, however, is to show that chant is a much more flexible musical rhetoric than most people, including many priests, think it is. One can combine male and female voices without doing it any violence. Indeed, when congregations sang chant—and some of them did, though we don't know how many—men and women obviously sang together."

"Nuala Anne seems to understand," Maureen added, "exactly how to do it. She does not try to overwhelm the male chorus, as many sopranos would . . . not that she couldn't do it if she wanted to."

"Och," my wife replied, "wouldn't that be a terrible thing to do?"

Still the pious, innocent Galway lass.

I had whispered to her during our tour the information from our cop.

"Maybe," she had replied skeptically.

"The chant," said the abbot, "is called Gregorian after Pope Gregory the Great, who reigned from 590 to 640 and was a Benedictine of a sort. He had been Prefect of Rome, Lord Mayor, I suppose, then went off to a monastery but was soon called back into the service of the papacy. Justinian had reconquered North Africa and part of Italy in his campaign to restore the old empire. Gregory became the Pope's Ambassador to the Emperor in Constantinople. His charm, intelligence, and piety made him a success, and it was not surprising that he became Pope, though he himself much preferred the contemplative life."

"It would be like Rich Daley becoming Cardinal Archbishop," I said.

"Perhaps," the abbot said, not quite understanding the metaphor. "He certainly supported church music, though there is no reason which we know why his name became identified with the plain song we now call Gregorian. He lived in a time of chaos. Germanic barbarians dominated what was left of the Western German Empire—Angles and Saxons in England; Goths and Franks in Germany, France, and Spain; Vandals in North Africa; Lombards in Italy. Most likely these invaders were only a veneer over earlier and perhaps Celtic populations. However, there was not much left of Roman political authority. The Church was gradually stepping into the vacuum because no one else was available. The tribes fought among themselves and with the Emperor. Plague swept the world, particularly Italy. The rural populations were drastically reduced. Famine was endemic. The Lombards periodically raided what was left of Rome. The Imperial legation from Constantinople withdrew to Ravenna, which replaced Rome as the civil capital of the Western Empire. Gregory, a member of an old Roman family, one of the last, sat there calmly among the disease and death and confusion and tried to act as leader of the Catholic world. He was the last one for half a millennium who could do so and the last one ever to preside over a theoretically united Christian Church."

"Such chaos," I commented, "is hard to imagine today."

"It was hard for Gregory to accept, too. The old lines of communication were breaking down. It took a long time for the letters he diligently wrote to reach the bishops among the Franks and the Angles to whom he was trying to write. He soldiered on, however, half-suspecting that the monasteries would be the Church for hundreds of years. Incidentally, he had a fight with our Columbanus, who demanded that the Pope enforce our dating of Easter, which Columbanus believed was the only correct one. Gregory seemed to have agreed, but he said he could not change a custom of long standing. Eventually the Romans imposed their standard on us."

"Can we change it back now?" Nuala asked, the shy Galway lass becoming the Irish nationalist.

"I don't think so," the abbot said, smiling—and realizing for the first time how many different masks lurked in my wife. "The most important thing to remember about Gregory is not the music, though that's part of it. He was what we would call a pluralist. He believed that there was room in the Church for diversity. He reversed the policy of his predecessor Innocent I, who three hundred years before said that everything had to be like the way it was in Rome."

"He wouldn't be elected Pope today," I said.

"I don't think so either," the abbot said with a shrug. "Gregory told Augustine of Canterbury to take over the wooden houses of worship of the Angles and turn them into Christian churches. He advised Augustine to adapt every custom that was not opposed to Christianity. The missionaries to the Anglo-Saxons even took over the name of the feast of their goddess of spring and the dawn, whose name was Eoster, for the celebration of Our Lord's Resurrection, complete with the bunnies and lilies and eggs which were Eoster's symbols of fertility and new life. That was Catholicism at its most open and most generous. We've not always been that way, much to our shame."

"And that's what we're trying to do in Ireland today," Maureen added. "We're rediscovering the Celt in each of us and marrying it to modern post–Vatican Council Catholicism."

"As your man said, Here Comes Everyone."

"Couldn't you imagine that Gregory and Columbanus and Augustine are here in the abbey with us today?" Nuala remarked, her eyes wide and solemn.

I almost looked around to see if the three sainted monks had entered the chapel.

"Columbanus," said Brother Killian, "would be furious that we were celebrating Easter on the wrong date. Not all the Irish have been pluralists.

"Gregory," Brother Killian added, concluding our little lesson in things Gregorian, "was either the last of the Roman popes or the first of the medieval popes, depending on your point of view. Soon the Pope would be the Bishop of a ruined city, cut off from Africa by Islam and from Byzantium by increasingly acrimonious theological and political conflicts. All he had left were the Germanic tribes in northern and western Europe."

"And Ireland," I added.

The four real Irish laughed.

"Sure, there's always been Ireland, hasn't there now?" the abbot agreed. "But on its own terms."

Nuala insisted that she needed fifteen minutes of practice with Maureen before the monks joined us. Alone.

The abbot, Brother Killian, and I wandered outside.

"Dairy country," the abbot said, gesturing at the rolling fields. "West Tip and Limerick have always been dairy country, Kerry too. The famine didn't hit as hard here as up by Connacht, where they lived off the potatoes planted high up in the hills or on the edge of bogs in land that the English didn't want."

"During the Troubles everyone burned down the creameries, the Black and Tans and then the Irregulars," Brother Killian continued. "You destroy the centers to where the dairy farmers bring their milk, you destroy the economy of much of Munster."

"Killian is a native of Limerick," the abbot explained. "His father owns a creamery—a very modern one, I might add."

"The Irregulars were very active out here, I understand," I said, hunting for folk tales about the Troubles.

"Indeed they were," Killian replied. "Unlike your men down below in Cork, they had fought against the Tans, too. Bloody times out here in those days."

"Revolutionary violence," the abbot said with a sigh, "is less common among the really poor—your folks up in Galway and Mayo—than among those who have something to fight for and want more. The Kerry men were the most prosperous and the most bloody."

"They really killed Kevin O'Higgins, then?"

The two men stopped to look at me in surprise.

"That's not what DeVere White says, is it?" Brother Killian said cautiously.

"Another version," I persisted, "says that it was not planned at all. A kind of accident, like the death of the Big Fella. Three Kerry men with guns happened to pass him in their car and seized the opportunity of the moment."

The abbot nodded. "That's what we have always been told out here. The last of the four Whelan brothers."

Fiona had joined our threesome, panting heavily.

"Too much running around, is it now?" I asked her. Then to the two monks, "The Whelan brothers?"

"Tommy, the last one. Jimmy, Danny, Stevie, and Tommy. They were terrible, reckless and cruel men. They burned creameries and homes, ambushed Gardai and soldiers, robbed banks, shot their enemies in the back. They fought the English and fought the Free State, fought anyone they could find to fight, mostly because they loved the robbing and the burning and the killing. Respectable parents, too."

"Anarchy does that to people," I said. "Or maybe more likely brings it out."

"If you believe the stories—and in Ireland stories improve with time—the Free Staters," Brother Killian explained, "caught the Whelan gang after they had ambushed one of their columns and killed several of their men. At that time late in our Civil War, O'Higgins had persuaded the cabinet to give the army authorization to execute such men. So the Free Staters shot them all and left them for dead."

"The irony of it," the abbot said as we arrived back at the door of the chapel, "is that they say Tommy was powerfully affected by O'Higgins's forgiveness. He reformed completely. He became a member of the Dáil in Dev's party and advocated the same tough policy against the IRA in the late nineteen-thirties. His grandson is a junior minister in the ruling party's cabinet today."

Bingo!

"Stay, Fiona," I ordered as the three humans entered the chapel.

She didn't look happy about the command but curled up at the door and went promptly to sleep. So there, too!

Nuala was ready to sing. The monks' *schola cantorum* had assembled.

"The first motet," my wife announced, "is the final monastic hymn of the day during Lent. It's called *'Ave, Regina Coelorum,'* 'Hail, Queen of Heaven.' It anticipates the joy of Easter."

She sang the first line, and then the monks joined in. As before, her voice blended easily with theirs.

> " *'Ave, Regina coelorum,*
> *Ave, Domina Angelorum,*
> *Salve, radix, salve, porta,*
> *Ex qua mundo lux est orta.*
> *Gaude, Virgo gloriosa,*
> *Super omnes speciosa,*
> *Vale, o valde decora,*
> *Et pro nobis Christum exora.'* "

> (Hail, Queen of Heaven,
> Hail, Mistress of the Angels,
> Hail, root, hail, portal,
> From which the world's light has risen.
> Rejoice, Virgin glorious,
> Above all others most beautiful,
> Farewell, O most gracious,
> And for us to Christ entreat.)

"The next hymn," Nuala explained with cool confidence, "is the 'Easter Good Night' song. Mary represents the mother love of God. She suggests that in the center of everything is love like that a mother feels for her newborn child. In this song she is told to rejoice because her son is not dead. Life is always stronger than death."

" *'Regina coeli laetare, alleluia!*
Quia quem meruisti portare, alleluia,
Resurrexit, sicut dixit, alleluia!
Ora pro nobis Deum, alleluia!' "

(Queen of Heaven, rejoice, alleluia!
For he whom you were worthy to carry, alleluia,
Has risen, as He said, alleluia!
Pray for us to God, alleluia!)

"If you live on the ocean like I did when I was a child and you learn to fear the terrible storms that batter your house and threaten the lives of your friends who are fishermen, you know what it's like when you look out and see a star. It says that the storm is over. Those who are still out on the bay can follow it safely to shore. In this next hymn we hail Mary as the star of the stormy sea of our life."

Nuala was, I thought, not without some prejudice, getting better and better.

" *'Ave, Maris stella,*
Dei Mater alma,
Atque semper Virgo,
felix caeli porta.

" *'Sumens illud ave*
Gabrielis ore,
Funda nos in pace,
Mutans Evae nomen.

" 'Solve vincia reis,
Profer lumen caecis,
Mala nostra pelle,
Bona cuncta posce.' "

(Hail, Star of the Sea,
Loving Mother of God,
And Virgin immortal,
blissful Heaven's portal!

Receiving that "Ave"
From Gabriel's mouth,
Establish us in peace,
Reversing "Eva's" name.

Break the chains of sinners,
Bring light to the blind,
Our evils do drive away,
All good things do ask for.)

"I don't know about you," I said to her as we drove back to Garrytown, "but I found that a very moving religious experience."

"It exhausted me altogether," she sighed, curling up in a knot next to the already-sleeping Fiona.

Since both my females were asleep, I turned my attention to sorting out the various mysteries that were rattling around inside my head—ruling out any consideration of the mystery of Nuala Anne.

— 30 —

I SAT down at the tiny desk in our Victorian master bedroom, laid out a sheet of Castle-garry stationery, opened my Bic pen (spurning the inkwell and the old-fashioned quill that accompanied it), and began to outline what we knew and what we didn't know. When she woke up, she'd glance at my schema and nod politely. That was not the way she solved mysteries.

She had thrown off her clothes and jumped into bed as soon as we entered our room. I had hung them up carefully. I donned my running clothes, found Fiona, who was wide awake again, and ran along the Shannon under the thick gray sky. I tried not to think of the mysteries. I'd clear my head with exercise and then approach them logically and rationally, with a fresh mind.

The rain beat down upon us during the last quarter-hour. Fiona loved it. So did I. Nothing like a run in the rain to clear your mind of all distractions.

I returned a now thoroughly exhausted Fiona to her kennel and dashed into the house.

Paddy MacGarry had been waiting for me. "Doing a little running in the rain, is it now?"

"There's nothing like it at all, at all."

"I hope you don't mind, Dermot. The Anglican Archdeacon of Limerick usually has supper with us once a week. He's a grand fellow and Vicar of the little chapel down below. He knows a lot of the history of this place. Father Mike comes along sometimes, but he has a meeting tonight."

"I'll be happy to meet him."

"And, mind, the weather is supposed to clear off tonight. Tomorrow morning will be grand for golf."

"I'll be looking forward to it."

Nuala had decreed that I could miss the practice at the university the next morning and "teach your man a little lesson on the links."

Nuala was still in deep sleep. An explosion in the next room would not wake her. So I took a shower, dressed for supper (dark blue sports coat, light blue slacks), and began to outline our mysteries.

1) *Who killed Kevin O'Higgins?*

Most likely a man named Tom Whelan who had seized the accidental opportunity to avenge the killing of his three brothers at the end of the Irish Civil War.

2) *How was that connected with the mystery out here at Castle Garry?*

In all likelihood the bloody Whelans were involved in the battles here in 1921 and 1922.

3) *Why didn't Gene Keenan tell us more about O'Higgins's death?*

Because he feared the public outcry if it were revealed that the grandfather of a cabinet minister had killed the founder of the Gardai.

4) *Who is trying to do harm to Nuala and myself?*

Either Father Placid and his cronies, who wanted to collect insurance money to cover their financial losses; or Maeve Doyle and her husband, who hate Nuala; or some fringe IRA crowd. I figured it would be Father Placid. Fear and greed were stronger than envy.

5) *What had happened here between Hugh Tudor and Augusta Downs?*

We do not know, not yet. Perhaps Father Mike MacNamee will be able to tell us.

I looked over the list. It was far from persuasive. If the death of O'Higgins was so tenuously related to what had happened at Castle Garry, why was it linked to Nuala's experience of the fire out here? Obviously her fey perceptions did not have to fit human logic, yet still the connection seemed thin.

I could understand Keenan's fear, but wasn't it a little foolish to fear that a killing seventy years old could cause a parliamentary crisis? Maybe not in Ireland.

Couldn't the Father Placid crowd have found excuses to cancel the concert without kidnapping Nuala?

What could General Tudor have done here that would have made him a disgrace in England?

I rolled up the paper and threw it in the wastebasket.

Rain continued to beat against the window. Thunder rolled overhead; lightning crackled above the whitecaps on the Shannon. Should I try to wake my wife up?

"Nuala Anne," I said cautiously, "it's 6:00."

She opened her eyes and glared. "Too early in the morning."

"In the afternoon. Drinks are at 6:30, supper at 7:00."

"Brigid, Patrick, and Columcille, man, why didn't you wake me up!"

She vaulted out of bed, covered herself with her robe, and dashed for the bathroom.

"Because I feared for my life!" I shouted after her.

I thought about her lovely naked body I had seen all too briefly while she ran for the bathroom. She had been drying me off after showers lately. Would not turnabout be fair play?

When the shower stopped running, I went into the bathroom.

"Dermot," she said uneasily, "what do you want?"

She was wet and delicious. I took the towel out of her hands.

"Fair is fair," I said.

She gulped uneasily and turned her gaze away from me.

" 'Tis true," she said.

I dried her slowly and carefully. She accepted my ministrations passively, her head tilted back, a touch of a smile on her face.

"I think I might hire you to do this often," she said as she twisted to my touch.

A firestorm was building up inside me. Now was the time. NOW!

"We'll be late for supper," she said timidly.

I lost my nerve. And my fire.

"You're right; we will."

ASSHOLE.

"We'll finish later," I said uncertainly.

"We will," she said, also uncertainly.

I SAID ASSHOLE.

"I heard."

The Archdeacon of Limerick, a certain Clyde Smith-Rider, was a trim bald man in his late thirties with vast red eyebrows, a clerical dog collar, and a very sexy blond wife, Vicki. He talked a lot; she talked very little but watched him with total adoration.

Nuala seemed to like the woman, so she had to be all right.

We kept our mouths shut while the guests quizzed the archdeacon about the history of the castle.

"The McGarrys' propensity to die young," he said in a clipped Oxford drawl, "is historic. The first Norman lord after routing the Gaelic Irish near Limerick died a year later, of natural causes. He wasn't thirty. Three of them were killed at the siege of Limerick, leading an attempt at a Catholic counterattack. One died at the battle of Saratoga in America, leading a charge against General Gates. Another tried to lead a break out at Yorktown, despite Lord Cornwallis's orders. Cornwallis knew the English were beaten. The McGarrys never accepted defeat. There is an old folk story that the Irish chief O'Brien O'Donohue put a curse on the first McGarry with his dying breath."

"Cornwallis fought here, too, did he not?"

"Oh, yes, Mr. . . ."

"Coyne."

"Neither dark nor a foreigner, it would seem. . . . Yes, he fought here and in India, too. He was a sound man. If the various governments had listened to him, they would have had none of the troubles they later had both here and in America. The last two hundred years of Irish history would have been very different."

"I see . . . I'm not dark, but I am a foreigner."

"Hardly a foreigner, with Mayo antecedents and a Galway wife."

Clever guy.

I knew about Lord Cornwallis and Ireland, but I wanted to learn whether the Archdeacon did. Alone of the English leaders of his time, Cornwallis recommended freedom for Ireland.

A brief hint of a smile from my wife in her gold-and-black slip dress suggested that she knew I was looking for a fight and a half, as they would say in Ireland, and approved.

Who the hell cared if we were late for dinner? I thought as I admired her breasts.

"But would you say that Lord and Lady Downs were reckless?" I continued, tearing my eyes away from her.

"Lord Downs was not a McGarry, so he shouldn't have been a target of the alleged curse. He was a brave man, surely. Very brave, but hardly reckless. As for Lady Augusta, the facts around her death are shrouded in mystery. I think my good friend Father Mike knows a lot more than he's saying on the subject. But that's Father Mike."

"Actually, me husband's grandparents on his mother's side were from Galway, too. Probably his ancestors were Viking pirates who washed up on the Connemara shores like a lot of other folk."

The Archdeacon smiled at her benignly. He and his wife must have been the only people in the country who had not seen Nuala perform on the telly.

"Why would her death be shrouded in mystery?" I asked. "It was in the twentieth century, was it not?"

He sighed, not like a real Irishman sighs, but still it was a valiant attempt. "It was different out here in those days. People were still able to hide their secrets."

"What about Major General Sir Hugh Tudor?"

Smith-Rider frowned. "I can't say I've heard his name, Mr. Coyne."

"Och, you can call him Dermot, Your Rivirence; everyone else does."

I decided that I would continue to stare at her breasts. She was my wife, was she not?

A WIFE YOU LET DOWN JUST AN HOUR AGO.

"Shut up. I'll take care of that soon."

WHEN?

"Soon."

"He was the General Commanding of the Auxiliaries and the Cadets during the War of Irish Independence. He apparently was involved in some of the fighting out here."

"The Black and Tans . . . strange, I've never heard of him."

"He was also the O.C. of the Ninth Scottish Division. Lord Downs was his Chief of Staff when he won the V.C. His father and his father-in-law were both deacons at Exeter."

"Really!"

"A great friend of Churchill."

"Which is probably why he was General Commanding here. Churchill thought that the Tans were a great idea. Did Tudor command in Palestine?"

"He did and then he resigned, allegedly when the IRA killed his aide by mistake."

"In Palestine? Hardly likely!"

"He died in exile and disgrace in Newfoundland."

"Why disgraced?"

"I'm not sure."

"Fascinating. I'll see what I can find out, if you're interested."

"Very."

"I have some friends who are chaplains in the British Army. They may know. Stop by the vicarage tomorrow if you can."

"After golf," Nuala advised.

"After golf."

"You'd better be careful of your man," Archdeacon Clyde warned me. "He has quite a reputation as a golfer."

"That will make it interesting."

"Just a friendly little game," Paddy MacGarry said, rubbing his hands together.

His wife frowned in disapproval.

"Could I ask you a question you might think rude, Archdeacon?"

"I'm sure it won't be rude, Dermot."

"Do you think that the Catholics in this country have been astonishingly tolerant of the Church of Ireland?"

"The Irish," he said with a bright smile, "are the most tolerant people in the world. In most other countries we would have been packed up and shipped home, even if we didn't have a home. . . . My family has been here for four generations. We're Irish and nothing else. . . . They have no reason to be gracious to us, yet they always are. When we started repair work on our cathedral in Limerick—which was the Catholic cathedral before the Reformation—didn't the local Catholic bishop weigh in with the first thousand-pound contribution? It's astonishing. They don't get nearly enough credit for it."

"The Irish rarely get credit," I replied.

Everyone around the table laughed, even my wife, whose eyes glowed with approval.

If I had let her down, apparently she had forgiven me.

We ran again with Fiona in the patchy moonlight. The rain had stopped, but the trees still dripped. Exhausted when we returned to our room, we collapsed into bed and into sleep almost instantly. No time, no thought of lovemaking.

The Adversary left me alone, perhaps to indicate that he had given up on me.

—31—

FOCK THE focking dinner!
Pardon me terrible language.
We were almost there, though I'm not sure where or what there is.
And I lost me nerve and mentioned dinner.
And then he lost his nerve.
And the fire inside me went out.
And I guess the fire inside him went out, too.
I'm frustrated. I want whatever it is that women are sup-posed to get out of sex, even if them as me ma calls the prim and proper don't get it.
The next time I'll keep me focking mouth shut.
I promise.
He should be furious at me, but he's not. Is that good or bad?
Probably good.

— 32 —

PADDY MACGARRY watched my first drive with wide eyes. The first hole on his beautiful golf course was a 350-yard par 4, with a water trap that seemed as big as Galway Bay at 200 yards.

"Most aim short," he warned me as I teed up.

"I imagine they do."

The course was also a local country club. Two members had joined us, a local lawyer and his son, a student at Limerick University. I assumed that the lawyer was to share in the fleecing of Dermot Michael Coyne.

"You'll beat the shite out of them all," herself had said as she kissed me before she climbed into the car, along with Fiona. The latter seemed to be in some doubt as to whom she should accompany. I shoved her in after Nuala.

"Woman, I will."

I felt cool, relaxed, and at the top of my game. I took no practice swings. I simply hit the ball a mighty thump.

It was not one of my better drives. Instead of 300 yards it went only 260, 270. However, it cleared the lake with ease.

"Holy shite," said the kid from the university.

"A little short, I said modestly.

"Nice shot," Paddy said, gasping for breath.

He was so unnerved that he hit his first drive into the lake.

I didn't understand the betting protocol. There were all kinds of side bets and special matches. But it didn't matter. I was going to win everything.

Like I say, I'm not a very competitive fellow.

"Would it be out of place, Dermot," the lawyer asked me with a quick smile, "to ask what your handicap is?"

"I usually play at Oak Park Country Club in my family's neighborhood, though sometimes at Long Beach, where we spend part of the summer. The two places seem to agree that I merit about a three. I think that's a little too low."

"Holy shite," said the kid from the university.

Despite my inadequate drive, I put my iron shot up on the green, twenty feet from the pin. I waited patiently for the rest of the foursome to catch up with me. Then, pushing my luck, I aimed my putt for the hole, just as herself would. It dropped in with a loud clunk.

Birdie on the first hole.

I'll give Paddy MacGarry full credit. He was a good sport.

"I'd say they were excessively generous with that handicap."

We had a grand time. I ended up one over par, which was not bad, considering that I had not played the course before. My wife would be pleased with me. However, she would add that if I had worked on my iron shots and my putts I would have done much better.

And I would say that it would not be fair to be better at the short shots than she was.

I also ended up eight-hundred pounds richer.

"I'll split this between Father Clyde and Father Mike," I said.

They hailed my generosity.

"When a guest beats me," Paddy said with good grace, "I tell him that I'll get mine back next year. I hope you come back next year, maybe for our tournament, but I know I'll never beat you."

"My irons were hot today," I said with utterly fake modesty. "Nuala usually beats me in the short game."

"I don't think I want to play her either."

"It might be risky. She's a fearsome competitor."

I showered, changed into slacks and a knit sport shirt, and walked down to the vicarage. The Archdeacon's wife, in a sleeveless summer dress, let me in with a shy smile. A sexy woman, I decided, who doesn't know she's sexy. I wonder if my wife knows she's sexy. Probably not.

"That's a very pretty dress," I said.

"Thank you," she said, blushing furiously.

It would have helped if I could remember her name.

"Dermot," the Archdeacon said, rising from the chair in his study where he had been working over bookkeeping sheets, "you must think I'm the dumbest man in Ireland. I fear I didn't catch your wife's name. I heard the concert on the radio, driving up from Cork, but I did not see it. My wife said I was a terrible eejit."

"That's what women say."

"She made a tape for me that now I'm going to have to listen to. I hope you'll explain to Nuala Anne."

"I'll tell her, but she's not the kind that needs or wants celebrity treatment. . . . Incidentally, Father, here's half the winnings from the golf course. The other half goes to Father Mike."

"A nice ecumenical split, Dermot," he said, taking

the bills. "We'll put it in the cathedral repair fund . . . four-hundred pounds!"

"I had a lucky day!"

"What did you hit?"

"One over par. My wife will criticize me for not working on my iron shots."

"Your wife is a breathtaking young woman, Dermot."

"So is yours, Father."

A strange phrase for an American Irish Catholic to speak, but, what the hell, according to George the Priest, St. Peter was married.

"Thank you. I tell her that often. Sometimes she believes me, but not often."

" 'Tis the way of it," I agreed.

"I have a peculiar perspective on Ireland," the Archdeacon said thoughtfully. "Though we have been here for four generations, I am still something of an outsider, by ancestry, religion, and education. That gives a point of view which is somewhat interesting, if not altogether without biases of its own, if you take my meaning?"

I nodded. I wasn't quite sure that I did, but I was prepared to wait him out.

"I watch football, of course, but I'm afraid that I don't think that the fate of Ireland depends on the success or failure of our soccer team—or any of our athletic ventures, as far as that goes. I don't think Ireland has to prove anything to anyone or ever did."

"We may not share the same perspectives, but I agree."

"So I am skeptical of our interludes of manic enthusiasm and disconsolate self-rejection."

His wife poked her head in the door. "Did your man feed you lunch out on the links?"

"Woman, he did not," I admitted, admiring again her radiant sexuality.

"When Dermot was through with him, Vicki, I don't think poor Paddy could afford it."

"Good enough for him! . . . So, Dermot"—she smiled gently—"you could eat some sandwiches and pastries along with your tea and scones?"

"I won't resist the suggestion . . . if you'll join us."

"Yes, Vicki, by all means. Dermot has not come for spiritual counseling. Sure, can't he get that down below from Father Mike. . . . He has, my dear, just given us four-hundred Irish pounds of his gambling prize for the restoration of the cathedral. I would think that's worth a sip of sherry in the garden, wouldn't you?"

He followed his wife out of the room and returned with a very old bottle of sherry. He opened it and then led the way out the doors into a shaded and lush garden, thick with humidity.

"The woman, as you may imagine, Dermot, is a constant distraction," he said, filling two of the three glasses he had brought out and placed on an old wooden table.

Triumph on the links, an attractive woman who admired me, a sunny day in a humid garden, and sherry under a palm tree . . . och, Dermot, be careful.

"To finish me point, Dermot Coyne"—he raised the crystal sherry glass in a toast—"I think that 'modern Ireland' is, as you Americans would say, for real. I believe in the Celtic Tiger. I also believe that this is a golden age for Irish literature, music, and art. I finally believe that we may also be entering a golden age of Irish spirituality, despite the problems both our churches experience here. What is surging up from the theologians and the musicians and the ordinary people like your astonishing wife is grace, grace superabundant, grace overwhelming. It is an exciting time to be Irish."

"And to be a priest?"

"Indeed." He filled my glass again. "Did you think of being a priest, Dermot Coyne?"

"Not for long. My older brother is the priest in the family. I'm the sennachie, I guess."

I had never claimed that title before. Shows what a glass of sherry and a humid day in Ireland will do to me.

"An even older vocation. . . . Ah, my dear, it looks stunning."

He was referring to the array of sandwiches, scones, and cakes, but he meant his wife.

I devoured the tea sandwiches (from which, as is customary in these islands, the crusts had been cut) like I thought I would not see food for several more days. Clyde filled Vicki's glass, and she poured my tea, accepting with a puzzled frown my wave-off of the inevitable milk.

"To conclude my little homily, which poor Vicki has heard far too many times, from the sixth to the ninth century the Western world looked to Ireland for spirituality. Allowing for all the proper qualifications and caveats, I think that we are entering into a similar era."

"I agree completely," I said. "It's an exciting time to be Irish and to be Irish-American."

"Your wife," Vicki said simply, "is such a lovely young woman."

"Funny thing, I've noticed that, too."

We all laughed and continued to destroy the sherry bottle. Their children, I learned, were in school in England and would soon be coming home for the long vacation.

"Now as to your man Major General Sir Henry Hugh Tudor, O.B.E., I talked to my friend who is the chaplain at Sandhurst, the Royal Military Academy, this morning. He called back in an hour or so. It seems that at certain of the upper levels of what's left of the officer corps Tudor is still, if not a legend exactly, a story, a cautionary tale."

"Oh?

"He was a brilliant field officer. He might well have ended up as Chief of the Imperial General Staff. He did not want to go to Ireland, but his friend Churchill persuaded him, a terrible mistake. He knew regular warfare; he knew nothing about guerrilla war. He made a mess of it, but anyone would have done that. His men killed 238 people, by British standards on this island not all that many. However, the English people were fed up with war and fed up with Ireland. They wanted it all to go away. He fired General Crozier, one of his subordinates, for not being tough enough. Crozier went home to England and labeled him 'Bloody Tudor' in the English press, with the damning allusion to Bloody Mary, if you take my meaning. The image stuck, even though he won a libel judgment. He served in Palestine; there was an attempt on his life, blamed improbably on the IRA. The army was fed up with him and suggested that he retire. He more or less disappeared from sight."

I had heard most of this story before. "How a cautionary tale?"

Vicki filled our sherry glasses again.

"His was a classic case of a field commander who should have stayed away from political battles," the archdeacon continued, "especially in Ireland. He should have turned his friend Winston down cold. 'Stay away from Ireland,' they warn the young men at Sandhurst, 'or you'll go the way of poor old Hugh Tudor.' "

"And his name is hardly known here."

"He kept it out of the Irish papers. Besides, there were many other English general officers to hate. Field Marshal Sir Henry Wilson for one . . . He was the Chief of the Imperial General Staff. He approved the killings of Catholics in the North. Collins ordered his assassination."

I had heard that story. "But not Tudor's?"

"No . . . and not General McCready, who was in charge of all military operations. Like Cornwallis he had the good sense to want to get the English out of this country. It was too late for anything else, but no one in the English government realized that. So they stayed in part of Ireland and made a bad situation worse."

"The Tudor story doesn't make much sense, does it? Why go into exile for more than forty years because of libelous charges?"

"There is a darker side to the story, one that makes me shiver."

"Indeed?"

"You must understand that from the point of view of the young men at Sandhurst, and their instructors, too, as far as that goes, these events happened long ago. Tudor, Michael Collins, the lot of them, are no more real human beings then Wellington or Napoléon. They are stories of men who died long ago. . . ."

"Tudor died in 1965."

"Really? He must have been quite old."

"Ninety-five."

He paused in his story.

"What is the darker side of the story, Clyde dear?" his wife asked.

"It's all very obscure. Hints that he became involved in a love affair while he was here."

"He would not have been the first, would he?"

"He apparently ordered her execution when she wouldn't submit to him. Even if there was never any proof of that, the story would stick to him."

"Lady Augusta?" Vicki asked in horror.

"My man at Sandhurst knew none of the details."

"Isn't there a story in the village," Vicki asked, "that she is not the one buried up there on the edge of the Shannon?"

"I've heard it," her husband agreed. "I've always dismissed it as nonsense. . . . It doesn't fit with this story. . . . Have you heard that, Dermot?"

"It's completely new to me," I said, thinking that my wife had a bad habit of becoming involved with empty graves.[1] "I've heard her name linked with General Tudor's, however."

"What will you do if you find out the truth, whatever that may be?"

"In general I believe that one should let the dead bury their dead, like Jesus said—unless someone's reputation needs to be rehabilitated. Or perhaps it means the same thing, some restless spirit needs peace."

My host and hostess nodded solemnly.

"Your wife is fey, of course," Vicki said.

"A little bit."

"Just like you play a little golf."

We all laughed uneasily.

"I've always felt that Father Mike knows more about the tragedy of Augusta Downs than he lets on. But Mike seems to know more about everything than he lets on. Could it be nothing more than a canny old parish priest playing a little game?"

"Perhaps."

I ambled back up to the castle with a woozy head and unsteady legs. I knew from the way the vicarage couple extended their arms around each other as they waved good-bye to me that they would make love as soon as I was out of sight.

Well, more power to them. That's what humid, sub-

[1] *Irish Whiskey*

tropical summer afternoons were for on the very edge of the Celtic fringe.

I napped, showered, dressed in tan slacks and sport shirt (an ensemble, like all my clothes, selected for me by herself), collected my shillelagh, and wandered down to the door of the castle to await the return of my wife. What was taking so long?

I waited fifteen minutes, a half hour, an hour. I went back into the hotel and dialed Glenstal. I hung up before anyone answered the phone because I remembered that the rehearsal today was at the University of Limerick.

Finally, when I was almost ready to call the Guards, the Mercedes turned the corner from the lane of trees and pulled up to the door, the chase car following it faithfully.

The door opened; Fiona popped out and ran up to me. She stood on her hind legs and licked my face, as if she had feared she would never see me again.

"Good doggy." Nuala Anne eased her temporary rival aside. "Dermot Michael," she whispered, "them eejits are in the Limerickman. I was afraid to tell Inspector Murphy because he would have thought me round the bend altogether."

Her uniform today was black jeans and a black blouse with a gold Celtic cross.

"What eejits?" I said stupidly. "Who's the Limerickman?"

"The people from the bridge are in the pub. Tell Inspector Murphy, Dermot, before they get away again."

— 33 —

"SOME INFORMATION received, Inspector Murphy. Our friends from the Grand Canal are having a pint over at the pub in Garrytown, the Limerickman, I think it's called."

"You're sure?"

"Nope. But it's worth a look."

"That at least. . . ."

He ran over to the chase car. A young constable (male) dressed like a scruffy hippie came back with him. Nuala, Fiona, and I piled into the backseat.

"I'm not sure you should be coming along," the Inspector objected.

"You'll need some identification."

"Maybe."

He started the car and spoke into his transceiver as we sped down the lane and out to the main road.

"My name is Stevie," said the young cop in the front seat. "I look like I should be sitting all day in a pub."

"With only one pint, tough," said my wife, winning a grin from Stevie.

"A few drops every hour or so."

We parked a hundred yards away from the Limerickman.

"We have backup coming down from Limerick," the

Inspector informed us. "If they're still in there, I'd just as soon wait till we have everyone in place. Stevie, you go in and have a look."

Nuala whispered in my ear, "Maeve Doyle might well be in there, too. And her husband."

Stevie jumped out of the car, gave us a jaunty wave, then slouched down the narrow street like he had nothing to do and nary a care or worry in the world.

"Good actor," Nuala Anne said tersely.

"Takes one to know one."

She giggled.

Fiona sensed that we were with cops again. She sat up on her haunches and panted tensely, eager to do her police duty. I took her collar in my hand.

We waited twenty minutes, then a half hour. Stevie strolled out of the pub and in our direction.

"You'll be happy to know, Mr. Coyne, that your man's arm is still broken. The information received is correct. Isn't Ms. Doyle in there, swilling down the pints with the best of them?"

"Do they look like they're going to be in there awhile longer?"

"I don't think so, Chief. They look like they're on the last pint."

"Damn! What's taking them eejits from Limerick so long! Climb in, Stevie."

He spoke into his mike and started the car. We inched down the street till we were only a few yards away from the door of the Limerickman. A white-painted table and two chairs stood outside the door. I wondered how hot it had to be in Ireland before you drank your daily pint outside. The chase car followed us and then stopped maybe thirty yards behind.

Fiona slobbered happily. She knew the drill.

"I'm ordering you two to stay in the car," Inspector

Murphy said briskly. "You've already proven you're better than these amadons."

"Yes, sir," Nuala said fervently. "Me man and me never look for a fight if we can find someone else who will do it for us."

"If they come out, we will apprehend them at once. This time they don't get away."

Thanks to Kevin O'Higgins they weren't carrying guns. What if the alleged perpetrators, as American cops would call them, were armed?

We waited. Then we waited some more. Irish mists were slowly rolling in from the estuary.

What were they up to? Were they planning to have another go at us tonight?

"I thought it might be Father Placid's friends," I said to Nuala Anne.

"Oh, no," she said, "it couldn't be them."

That settled that. Watson had been wrong again.

The door of the pub opened. Maeve Doyle swayed out, followed by the dark giant who was her husband. Then the two thugs, one with his arm in a sling. Not very smart of them to show up here. But then they were not a very smart bunch.

Our two Guards moved quickly out of the car.

"It is my duty," the Inspector said solemnly, "to place you all under arrest on the charge of disturbing the peace and criminal assault. I advise you to come along quietly."

"Fock quietly," said the thug without the broken arm as he pulled a knife and advanced on the Inspector. "Get out of me way, Garda, or I'll stick this in your heart."

I kicked open the door of the car and released Fiona's collar. "Go get him, girl!"

With a howl of outrage and a single mighty bound, she hit the thug and knocked him off his feet. He dropped his knife as he fell. She fastened her teeth on his throat. He was too frightened to scream.

Maeve's husband also pulled a knife. They had come prepared for serious cutting business.

The cops were unarmed, but I wasn't.

I had never used a shillelagh in a fight before. It turned out to be a very useful weapon.

I hit the dark giant's arm with it. He dropped the knife.

"I'll strangle you!" he shouted at me.

"Not with a broken leg you won't!"

I hit his leg and he crumpled to the ground. Maeve was suddenly all over me, kicking, punching, screaming, cursing.

Then she, too, was on the ground. My wife stood over her, brandishing the pub's white chair.

"Won't you ruin your voice, sweetie, shouting like that?"

I collected the two knives and handed them to Stevie.

Then the reserves from the chase car arrived and took the whole sorry bunch of them into custody. Nuala had to persuade Fiona to release the man with the knife.

"Good doggy, good, good doggy. Now let him go so our friends can take him off to the lunatic asylum where he belongs."

The publican, in his white apron, and a couple of patrons stumbled out.

"Here, what's going on?"

"Gardai!" I said nonchalantly. "Taking criminals into custody."

Maeve Doyle was back on her feet now, sobbing hysterically as a woman Guard cuffed her.

"Poor woman," Nuala said, carefully returning the

chair to its proper place. "Dermot Michael, we don't need that shillelagh anymore."

"I like the feel of it."

My victim lay on the ground, moaning softly. I was pretty sure that I had not hit him hard enough to break his leg.

Then, sirens roaring, the Guards from Limerick arrived. Major Reno coming too late to the Little Bighorn. Except that the outcome was a little different, due mainly to Fiona and me shillelagh.

My shillelagh.

"I thought I told you two to stay in the car," Inspector Murphy complained, not too seriously.

"Weren't we just giving Kevin O'Higgins a hand?" Nuala said innocently.

Just as she had done at the Point, Fiona was prancing around nervously, wanting praise and reassurance.

"Good dog," I said, bending over to hug her. "Grand dog, super dog, brilliant dog!"

She licked my face in gratitude.

"Inspector," the woman Guard said, "this woman has a scalpel in her purse."

"Intended for my face, no doubt," Nuala observed grimly.

The criminals were herded into a squad car, moaning and screaming and protesting. Maeve's husband, Pete "Pig" Doyle as he was called, was loaded into an ambulance.

"The Commissioner wants to talk to talk to you, Dermot," Inspector Murphy said, handing me the phone.

"Dermot Michael Coyne," I announced serenely.

"You're out of your focking mind!" Gene Keenan exploded.

"You gave us the wolfhound and me the shillelagh. Didn't we have to use it now when it looked like some of your people were about to be hurt?"

"And herself with a bar stool?"

"Just a little outdoor chair . . . You know what these west of Ireland women are like, Gene, when they become angry."

"Focking Grace O'Malley! . . . She was the one who knew that they were in the pub?"

"Certainly."

"Just knew it?"

"Isn't that the way the dark ones work. . . . Incidentally, you can tell your friend the junior minister that we won't tell the story about his grandfather."

"I figured you'd figure that out. He doesn't mind. He thinks it's a wonderful story about the power of forgiveness."

"Does he now?"

"And we picked up those phony Real IRA types who were making the phone calls. A bunch of young punks from out in Tallaght. Drugs mostly. They saw an opportunity and went for it."

"And Father Placid?"

"He turned up in New York and apologized to everyone. Very contrite. Promised that all the money taken from the fund would be paid back eventually. He's there begging his American supporters for help, and himself blaming it all on herself because she's American."

"Will you extradite him?"

"We'll sure try. We don't hold with clerical immunity anymore. Incidentally, all the money from the concert is safe. It will take a couple of months, but it will go to the poor in Central Africa."

"Grand!"

"So that clears it all up, doesn't it?"

"Not quite."

"Oh? What else are you two up to?"

"We want to find out why Lady Augusta Downs was

not buried in that grave next to her husband."

Next to me, Nuala, who had been listening to the conversation, looked startled. Then her face set into a deep frown.

"You'll never find that out."

"Never say never, Gene. It's a hell of a long time."

I hung up.

"Himself," Inspector Murphy informed us, "said that you should keep the car till tomorrow, when we'll get another driver up. Would you ever mind driving it back to the castle?"

"I think we can manage that," Nuala replied, in her role as family spokesperson.

When the Guards and all their cars had departed, Nuala turned to the astonished publican and said, "Can we have two pints of the best for me and me man and a large bowl of water for me panting friend?"

He sat us on the two outdoor chairs with great ceremony under a rather stunted palm tree and with even greater ceremony served us with two of the best. He also enthusiastically petted Fiona as he served her dish of water. She slobbered over him before she turned to her drink.

"First of all," I said to my bride, "how was the rehearsal?"

She shrugged indifferently. "It was all right, I suppose. They all keep saying that I'm brilliant, but me da always said that you should never trust these Munster folk when they praise you."

"You'll do the actual recording tomorrow at the university?"

"That's what they say. First thing in the morning. Isn't it true that they can make the sound more like you're in a chapel than when you're really in a chapel?"

"You'll be happy when it's over?"

"Won't I ever? . . . Don't they want me to sing two more hymns?"

"Chant?"

"No. Schubert's 'Ave Maria' and a Palestrina 'Regina Coeli.' They're bringing over the Limerick Symphony to back me or maybe to drown me out if I'm too terrible."

"They had a lot of nerve asking you to do that!"

"Sure, Dermot, they're such nice people. What difference do two more songs make, especially since they're both lovely?"

She wasn't sure she could sing either of them well enough to be recorded, but she was sure that she wanted to try.

That's my Nuala Anne.

SHE'D BE THAT WAY IN BED IF YOU GAVE HER HALF A CHANCE.

"Leave us alone."

"The 'Regina Coeli' is a wonderful polyphonic melody from the sixteenth century. I'm going to sing the soprano, and the fiddles do the rest."

"Sounds tricky."

" 'Tis, but 'tis kind of fun, too. Right now I'm terrible tired . . . and, Dermot, I haven't been doing my voice exercises. Won't Madam be very angry with me when we go home?"

"I don't think so."

Madam was the retired opera singer who, in the rabbit warren called the Fine Arts Building on Michigan Avenue, played the role of Nuala's voice coach. She was a stern taskmaster, but she adored Nuala.

"How did you know it was Maeve and her mob that were chasing us?"

"Who else would it have been?" She waved her hand impatiently, as if the matter had never been in doubt. "Don't your man and his crowd have enough trouble now as it is without chasing after us? They're amadons and gombeen men, but they're not crazy. Maeve and her man are crazy with envy, and their thugs wanted to get even with you, and themselves thinking the Gardai would never find them."

I did not observe that the Guards had found them only after Nuala told them where to look.

"Why the TV when they tried to kidnap you?"

"I'm sure one of them will tell your man in Dublin everything, but I suppose they wanted to warn American singers to stay away."

"Off-the-wall mad!"

"But dangerous just the same. They probably would have held me till after the concert and beaten me up a little, though they certainly liked knives, didn't they?"

I shivered. And felt a little less guilty about my work with the shillelagh.

"As for the eejits from Tallaght, they were pretty clearly phonies. If they were really affiliated with the lads, they would have kidnapped me and then asked for the money. And the lads wouldn't have fouled up the kidnapping either. I wouldn't be surprised if someone in the Real IRA tipped off your man about them."

She waved her hand again and sipped a tad more of her Guinness.

Amazing, Holmes.

Elementary, Watson.

"And you beat your man today on the links," she went on, "did you now?"

"Naturally. I won eight-hundred pounds, half of which I gave to the Archdeacon, and the other half I'll give to Father MacNamee tomorrow afternoon when we see him."

"Good enough for him," she beamed as she sipped very carefully on her pint of Guinness. "You saw Clyde and Vicki, did you now?"

"Saw them and ate lunch with them and killed a bottle of excellent dry sherry with them."

"And ogled her boobs?"

"Only because you weren't there."

She snorted scornfully. "Still," she said, "I don't mind so long as you look at me more than you look at her. Her boobs are really pretty. She's entitled to admiration."

"That's generous of you."

She waved her hand for the third time. "Realistic!"

Then, serious again, she asked, "Did Clyde say that Lady Downs might not have been buried there beside the Shannon?"

"Vicki did, as I remember it. . . . He had talked to the chaplain at the Royal Military Academy at Sandhurst. Most of the story we already know. General Crozier returning to London and labeling him 'Bloody Tudor.' However, it appears that there were also rumors of his ordering the execution of a woman with whom he was romantically linked."

"And, in those days, if she were a Protestant it would have bothered the IRA a lot less than it would bother the English . . . especially if she was the wife of a war hero."

"And, Nuala, a war hero who had been his chief of staff and won the Victoria Cross."

She nodded sadly and took another very small sip of her pint. "We still don't know what really happened, do we?"

"We don't. Maybe Father MacNamee can tell us tomorrow afternoon."

"And Vicki said she might not have died in the fire?"

"She said that there are tales told around here that she wasn't in the grave, vague and imprecise tales. You know the kind, a wink, a nod of the head, an obscure phrase or two?"

"Do I ever!"

"Do you, er, sense that those stories might be true?"

She shut her eyes as if she was striving to sense something, anything.

"I know that she's dead now, but that's no help. She'd be over a hundred years old. . . ."

The publican came out and asked if we'd like a bit more. "Wasn't it grand altogether the way you apprehended them criminals . . . especially your darlin' dog here?"

Fiona, who had calmed down and was now preparing to snooze, absorbed a head scratching with great pleasure.

Nuala spoke to him in Irish, apparently asking a question.

He started in surprise, hesitated, and then answered very guardedly.

Nuala persisted.

He relaxed and answered at some length.

"I'll be driving back, so I won't need another pint, but sure, isn't me husband dehydrated altogether?"

As he went back into the pub, she touched my hand with her fingers. "Shush, Dermot; he's going to tell us something more after he thinks about it while he's drawing your drink."

He returned and placed the pint in front of me.

"Sure, don't you draw it perfectly?" I said. "The foam could not be better at all, at all."

He smiled, his jolly publican smile, and spoke in Irish again. Then he went back into the pub.

"What was that about?"

"I went into me Galway Irish to let him know that I wasn't some tourist from Dublin. I asked him when Lady Downs was really buried up there at the castle. He said that she was killed by the Tans in 1921. I said that we knew that wasn't true and that wasn't it time the whole truth be told. He went through the whole story of what a brave woman she was and how she had saved the lives of a lot of the lads by setting fire to the house. I told him that we knew she didn't set the fire. He went in to think about that."

"And then?"

"He came out and said that he didn't really know anything and didn't want to be quoted, but, when he was a lad about ten years old, back around 1968, wasn't there talk of strange goings-on up at the ruins of the castle. And didn't some of the old women say that wasn't it Lady Augusta herself coming back to be buried with her husband?"

Wow!

"She would have been in her late seventies then . . . after General Tudor's death. . . . Do you believe your man, Nuala Anne?"

She thought about it. "I believe he's truthfully telling us about the stories. Does he believe it really happened? In this part of Ireland, that's a foolish question, Dermot Michael. We half-believe any good story . . ."

"But full-believe none of them?"

"As I've been telling you lately, Dermot love, you're getting to know me kind all too well."

"Most of the people in Garrytown must know the story?"

"I'm sure they do . . . and your man up beyond above has never heard a word of it. He's an outsider and, worse, a Clare man. Maybe his grandchildren will hear the legend someday, if they still own the castle."

"Father Mike knows it?"

"Och, has anything at all happened in this town for the last thirty-five years that himself doesn't know?"

"Wouldn't he have been here when she was buried if the story is true?"

"And won't I begin our conversation tomorrow by

saying to him that we know he presided over her interment one dark and stormy night?"

We went back, showered, and dressed for drinks and supper, and listened as Paddy MacGarry celebrated my achievements on the golf course.

"You finally ran into a railway train, did you now, Paddy?" his wife said with some amusement.

"One of your 747 jets," he replied sheepishly.

He was a good sport all right. It was, however, also good business to admit that you didn't win all your matches on the links.

Nuala sung her four Marian motets after supper, a cappella, and Schubert's "*Ave*" with the help of the house harp. Everyone praised her enthusiastically. She blushed modestly, still the shy country lass from Connemara.

Later we made love. It was sweet and pleasurable, as it always was. But there was no fire speaking to fire.

"Tomorrow night," I promised the Adversary before he had a chance to express an opinion.

"WOULD YOU ever mind doing it just one more time?"

My wife, in faded jeans and her Marquette sweatshirt, was edgy. She did not like the demands that each motet be sung five or six times, "until it's perfect, love."

She glared at the sound director.

"All right," she said tersely.

Sexual frustration, I informed myself, not wanting to give the Adversary a chance to say the same thing. This afternoon when we are back at the castle I'm going to do it. I don't know how or what, but I'm going to do it and be done with it. I can't let this go on. The woman is not made of stone.

She had recorded the four Gregorian antiphons and the Schubert *"Ave Maria."* However, the polyphonic *"Regina Coeli,"* in which she sang against the strings of the Limerick Symphony, was a bit more difficult. As far as my tin ear could tell, she had done it perfectly the last time.

I glanced at the abbot, who was watching me keenly.

"It would be worth my life to intervene now," I said, "but I thought it was perfect the last time."

"I'm admiring your patience, Dermot Michael," he said with a smile.

"I suppose these guys have a job to do."

"They don't seem to realize that they're teetering on the edge of a volcano."

"Ready, Nuala Anne?" the director asked.

"Last time," she said firmly.

"Absolutely," the director said, perhaps realizing that, good or bad, it was indeed the last time.

"Someone just drew the line," Father Abbot whispered.

When she was singing the Gregorian antiphons, she kept her light and larklike soprano voice under strict restraints. But the polyphonic motet gave her a chance to play.

She carried the whole orchestra, the monks who were listening, and all of us in the control room along with her. We were at the Resurrection celebrating with the mother of Jesus his return from the dead.

The last notes died in the air. There was a long pause of awe and expectation, then cheers. Nuala blushed and bowed, and fell into my arms.

Her body was tight with need. In our embrace there was challenge and demand. Maybe the embraces had been that way before and I had simply not noticed. Now, however, the fierceness of her hunger was too obvious to ignore. I'd better do something about it and soon.

Mere lovemaking would not be enough. It had to be something spectacular.

Could I be spectacular in bed?

Well, apparently I never had been.

I didn't like to be under pressure to perform. That's why I had given up competitive sports.

On the other hand, when the chips were down . . .

"You were focking brill, Nuala Anne," I said, holding her close and responding to demand with demand of my own.

"I can't believe I sang like that," she said. "Madam won't believe it either."

The wife of the president of the university, who had been present for the recording, invited us to supper out at their home in Newport the next evening. The abbot would be there and Maureen and her husband and a few other people, including a bishop and the Archdeacon and his wife. Not, however, the Archbishop of Cashel (in whose domain the abbey was theoretically located). I gathered that he was not a whole ton of fun.

If he had come and acted archepiscopal, Nuala would doubtless have spent much of the evening quoting her good friend "Cardinal Sean." She might even do that for a plain old bishop, whom everyone called Willie.

"Can we ever stay over another day, Dermot Michael?" she asked me, as though my vote mattered.

"Even a couple of days," I said. "We both need a rest. Grand Beach can wait."

Two days of intense and reckless lovemaking, I promised myself.

WHO ARE YOU KIDDING?

After drinks and a buffet to celebrate Nuala's triumph, we toured the spanking new and impressive university, collected Fiona, and found our driver (one of Mike Casey's men), whom we asked to take us to the parish house in Garrytown. And we hoped to the solution to our last mystery.

I PUT the envelope on Father MacNamee's desk.

"A small contribution from your man up in the castle."

He looked up from the tea he was pouring and smiled.

"Beat him, did you now?"

"As everyone between Limerick and Killarney knows by now."

He made no attempt to open the envelope, doubtless because he already knew what was in it.

"You met me colleague, Very Reverend Father Smith-Rider, have you now?

"I have."

"Beautiful wife, isn't she?"

"A woman like that clutters up a vicarage, doesn't she?" I replied.

"She would that," he said with a wink. "Still, few of us would object. And they may be closer to the old way than we are."

Nuala Anne must have felt that there had been enough clerical chitchat. She dropped her bomb.

"You were present when Lady Augusta was finally buried up there thirty years ago, weren't you, Father MacNamee?"

If he was surprised, he didn't show it. "Sure, wasn't I the parish priest? Didn't I have to be there?"

"She had been in a convent, hadn't she?"

"Where else would she be if she wasn't buried up there in 1921?"

"Carmelite? The same one in which Kevin O'Higgins's daughter is today?"

"What other one would it be?"

He was smiling genially through her litany of questions. Nonetheless, he seemed impressed.

I sure was.

"She saved the lives of those Kerry men, didn't she? The Whelan boys whose execution O'Higgins later ordered?"

"Not to say executed exactly," he said. "There was a standing order in the Free State Army to shoot such people on sight."

"All except Tommy, and himself having a conversion experience?"

"And his grandson a junior minister in the government today, Foreign Office I believe. . . . Isn't it all strange, Dermot Michael?"

"And kind of glorious, too," I replied. "And very, very Irish."

"Och, it is that. . . . Well, now, Nuala Anne, there isn't much more for me to say, and yourself knowing the whole story."

"The truth is in the details, Father, as me man always says."

I'd never said anything like that in all my life. I did not, however, disagree with the sentiment.

"Well, let's see where we can begin? I suppose it is with the old fella who was my predecessor here, Canon McGinn. He'd been here fifty years, first as the Catholic curate, then as the parish priest. That means he was here before the Great War. Became a great friend of Lord and Lady Downs. Played Irish football with him on the pitch. His predecessor, old Canon Muldoon, was also a great friend of theirs, a man way before his time, the old canon. Was friends with the Anglican Vicar, long before anyone approved of your ecumenical dialogue, if you take me meaning."

"He said the Mass here in the church when Lord Downs was killed?"

"He did and nary a word of protest from our man in Limerick. He knew better than to take on the old canon. Well, me canon, Canon McGinn that is, always thought that Lord Downs had become a Catholic in the trenches. That's probably true, you know."

"Of course," Nuala said impatiently, as if she didn't need to be told such self-evident things.

"Anyway, me canon was dying when I came down here to be administrator. He told me all the stories about the McGarrys and what wonderful people they were and themselves being Protestant and that it was time we put aside all that Reformation nonsense and say we were one church. I was fresh out of Maynooth then, and I thought the canon was a heretic but a wonderful heretic.

"So finally as he lay in that room there dying, doesn't he call me in and says he has a secret to tell me. 'Lady Downs didn't die in the fire and isn't buried up there next to her husband. She's still very much alive, he says. . . . Now, lad, don't ask too many questions because the answers are none of your business. She had grand reasons for what she did. The old canon and I did it for her, and I'd do it all over again if I had to.'

"Well, I'm brimming over with questions, but it's none of my business, like he said. 'I visit her a couple of times a year in the Discalced Carmelite convent, where they call her Mother Augusta. . . .' That's what he said. She was the Superior there, young woman, did you know that?"

"I did not, Father. But it doesn't surprise me."

" 'I want you to go up and see her a couple of times a year, just like I did,' the canon says to me. 'She likes to know what's happening in Garrytown, poor woman. And in my desk are the instructions for her burial when she dies. They know about it in the cloister, and they are committed to honoring her wishes.' "

"And you visited her regularly?"

"I did that. She was a wonderful woman, the happiest woman I've ever met. I think that's important to remember, Nuala and Dermot. She found happiness in the cloister, not the same kind of happiness as when her man was alive but happiness just the same.... When she knew she was dying didn't she send for me to make sure the arrangements were still on. They were of course. It was no problem at all, at all, to bury her up there late one night, though how you knew it was stormy I can't figure out."

Good guess, I thought. With my wife in one of these detective moods of hers it's hard to tell how much she knows through her *Homo antecessor* (or whatever) genes and how much is quick guesswork—if there's a difference between the two.

"She told you why she disappeared?" Nuala persisted.

"I didn't ask. When you're with a woman like that, you don't ask. She gave occasional retreat conferences outside the cloister; her last one was for priests, if you can imagine. It was in the days immediately after the Council when we all had such great hopes . . . until the amadons in Rome ended them. She even went to Rome for a meeting of the order and had a lot of influence on it. Wasn't she the most impressive woman I've ever met, saving yourself, Nuala Anne?"

It was a sincere compliment. Nuala nodded politely. "We'll see what I'm like in fifty years, Father Mike."

"But she did write a document for you, didn't she?" I interjected.

Nuala started in surprise, causing the snoozing Fiona to look up sharply. "Go back to sleep, darlin'; me man was brilliant again."

"Och," said the smiling leprechaun priest, "aren't I surrounded by dark ones?"

"Did she know that General Tudor died in 1965, three years before she did?" I asked.

"If she did, she didn't say. I didn't know it meself. She cared for him or at least felt sorry for him. She had ways of finding things out, and herself in the cloister."

"She probably found out where he was and wrote him, forgiving him," Nuala said thoughtfully.

"It would be very like her. . . . She was not a mournful person. She had absolute confidence that the castle would be restored. She carried grief over her husband's death to the grave. But she had long since given up mourning. She prayed to him every day."

He paused and shook his head.

"The last time I saw her before she died, she gave me the document I'm going to show you . . . give to you. 'Father Mike,' she says, 'you know that I didn't enter Carmel to expiate my sins, don't you?' And don't I say, 'Mother Augusta, I never thought you did.' And she says that the old canon tells her that what happened between her and General Tudor that night was, under the circumstances, not a serious sin. . . . I told you that the old canon was way ahead of his time, didn't I?"

"He was that," Nuala agreed, now patiently waiting out the old man's story, since he had promised to give us—well, to give her—Mother Augusta's final testament.

" 'My whole story is in this, Father Mike,' she says. 'This and the little book I did about me husband that you have in your rectory. Just as I am certain that Castle Garry will be restored someday, I am also certain that sometime people will come along who want to know my story. For a long time I felt, well, too bad for them. It's none of their business. But I realize now that it's wrong to think that way. My story is just a little bit of them terrible times, but it also shows how grace works. I'll be with Arthur soon, and he'll want to know why I didn't put it all down, and himself loving history. Moreover, I think Himself will be a little upset with me, because it's a story of His grace. So here it is. Give it to anyone who wants to know what really happened out here if you think you can trust them. You read it, too, because I want you to know the whole story when you sneak me into the grave where you'll bury me forty decades too late.'

"And then doesn't she laugh? She was a great one for laughing, Mother Augusta was."

— 36 —

I don't know who you are, you who will read my story. I am uneasy about telling it to someone I've never met, someone who might not even be alive today. We Irish always want to see the expression on someone's face when we tell a story, so we can win them over as we talk. Well, it can't be helped. I hope you will be tolerant of my weakness and my failings and forgive me. Perhaps you would have behaved very differently if you were in my circumstances. Perhaps not. I ask you to be tolerant of the world in which I grew up, just as you would want those born after you to respect your time and your culture, even if it were not their own.

I hope that my biography of my husband will tell the first part of my story. My heart was breaking when I wrote that little book. But I had to do it. I had to record what a wonderful man he was and how deeply I missed him. I was a very young woman then and perhaps too sentimental. I feel that I hardly know the author of the book, but I admire her restraint.

While I was writing it, I was thinking seriously of what to do with the rest of my life. I did not want to become a recluse living in a gloomy old manor house in which everything was frozen in the spring of 1918. I realized I could marry again. I was not sure I wanted to do that. It would be difficult, I knew, in my social class to find another man like my Arthur. I would always be making comparisons. Moreover, while I enjoyed the pleasures of the marriage bed with Arthur, enjoyed them intensely, there had always lurked in the background a, what shall I call it, a hint of another love, another kind of love. It was like that with Arthur, only deeper and richer and more demanding. As long as we were together it was not an option. The lover who lurked, just around the corner, was content to leave me alone. He did not, definitely did not, want to take me away from my husband. He left me alone when Arthur was in the trenches, too. Nor did he intrude in my life when I was paralyzed with grief. But he did let me know he was waiting.

I went to Canon Muldoon about it. "Can I become a contemplative nun?" I asked him. "Is that what God wants of me?"

He was not surprised at all. Nothing surprised the canon. "What do you think, Gussie?" he says to me. I think he's calling me, inviting me, very gently, very tenderly, but very persistently. "You don't want to marry again," says the canon. "I wouldn't mind," I says, "though it would be hard to get used to another man. But this other lover is very persistent. Is it God?" I asked.

"Who else would it be?" he says, and that was the right answer, wasn't it now?

Then he says that it's possible for someone to be involved with both a human lover and a divine lover. Men and women have done it. I told him that I was sure some had, but I didn't think that was possible for me or what this persistent lover wanted of me.

Then I asked him how I could enter Mount Carmel, and myself not even Catholic. The canon said that would be no problem at all, at all.

Then it was 1921 and the "Troubles" came to Ireland. I was not afraid. We had always been close to our tenants, and Garrytown was hardly a revolutionary hamlet. But anarchy has no memory. One stormy night a band of the Irish Volunteers, most of them from down below in Kerry, appeared in front of our house. They were badly drunk. They beat some of the servants and set fire to the outbuildings. They were removing furniture and paintings from the house. I went out to chase them away. They laughed at me and cursed me and then tied me to a tree and threw mud at me. I was soaking wet from the rain, which had started again and which was putting out the fires. I thought they would kill me. I was terrified, of course, but I was ready to die. I would join Arthur sooner rather than later.

Then a British Army patrol showed up and surrounded them. A British officer cut me down from the tree. He said he was General Tudor from the Ninth Scottish Division and that Arthur had been his chief of staff.

He carried me into the house, and we made love. I was frightened and lonely and hungry. I cannot say I was raped, but if I were in full command of myself, I would have said no to him. It might not have done any good.

He was a wonderful lover. I think I could have fallen in love with him and married him, if I had not found out later that he had a wife and children in England.

As we were lying in each other's arms after love, I heard rifle shots outside. I paid no attention. When he left the next morning and I went outside to try to salvage what I could from the raid, the servants told me that the Brits were Black and Tans and had shot all the men whom they had captured.

You can imagine my desperation. I believed that the English government had no business ruling Ireland. Our family had supported Home Rule for fifty years. We should not have been a target. Now I understood that every landlord in the west of Ireland was a fair target. Moreover, I had committed a sin, fornication surely and probably adultery, too. Our own Vicar had gone to Dublin with his family, for which I no longer blamed him. So I went to the canon, who assured me that under the circumstances it wasn't a serious sin. The canon, as you say, Father Mike, was way ahead of his time. Maybe even a little bit ahead of the present time. I am sure now, however, that I was not fully responsible and have long since forgiven myself, as I'm sure God has forgiven me.

I did not enter Mount Carmel because of that incident. I was not seeking a place to do penance for a sin which, at worst, was not my fault. But the incident made it clear to me that I would have to decide soon.

I said I would leave the castle as soon as the Troubles were over. We were all fools then. We thought the Troubles would be over in a few months. We were sure that the British Army would leave Ireland as General McCready wanted them to and that Home Rule would finally take effect.

We didn't realize that the Troubles would go on for years and never really end, not even today.

General Tudor came back several times. He was always respectful and always persistent. I told him that I would not commit adultery again. He said that he and his wife were close to divorce. He would divorce her and marry me.

Did he mean it?

I didn't know then and I don't know now. Perhaps he didn't know himself. Officers coming home from the war in those times found it difficult to adjust to family life. Perhaps he and his wife were really estranged. He was lonely, as I was, and overwhelmed by the carnage of the war and the violence in Ireland, which he did not, could not, understand.

I told him that I was grateful that he had saved my life, but that I did not believe in divorce.

Suppose, I used to ask myself in those days, that he was not married. Would I marry a man who had shot down captives in cold blood, a man who was the O.C. of the Black and Tans? Not very likely, but there was no point in bringing up that point, since adultery was my main argument against any romance between us.

He never tried to push himself on me. He probably thought that he was a perfect officer and gentleman and had never violated me. I had not resisted, had I?

Was I tempted?

I was a young woman of flesh and blood, alone in the world, and frightened. Certainly I was tempted, especially since the Church of Ireland tolerated divorce. I suppose there was enough Catholicism left from my ancestors that made me resist that path.

Yes, I was tempted, severely tempted.

Fortunately for me, I did not really believe that he would break up his family for me. Rather, I suspected that once the war was over he'd go back to England and his family and forget about me.

There was also this other love, lurking patiently all the time.

Then, just before the truce and the withdrawal of the Auxiliaries and the Cadets, the IRA came again to Garrytown, again up from Kerry, again dangerous wild men. This time, however, they were on the run from the Tans. They were all very young. The leaders were four brothers named Whelan, nice respectful young men, despite their later reputations. They took over the house as a kind of sanctuary, feeling that the Tans would not attack an English, as they saw it, manor house.

I didn't try to tell them that I believed in their cause, that I was Irish, that my husband had died a Catholic, and that I was almost a Catholic. I didn't think then it would have made a difference. Later when I accompanied Kevin O'Higgins's daughter, who is one of our nuns, to the annual Mass they have and again met Tom Whelan, now a totally changed man, he told me that it would have made a difference, but they were not going to harm us anyway.

Tom is a remarkable man. He will go to his grave sorrowing for what he did that Sunday morning and grateful for Kevin's forgiveness and for what it made possible in his life.

Then the lorries appeared with the Cadets.

I was at a loss as to what I should do. I really was on neither side. I knew the men in my house were very dangerous men and would do more harm. If Ireland's cause was my cause—and it

was—then their way of fighting for the cause was
not my way. On the other hand, the Tans were no
better. I didn't want another massacre on my land.
I went outside to forbid them entrance to my
house, as daft an idea that a still-romantic young
woman could possibly have.

They shouted obscenities at me. Hugh Tudor
stood there in his puttees and his Sam Browne belt
and glared at me coldly.

"You'd better decide pretty quickly whether
you're English or Irish," he said in an icy voice.

"I'm Irish," I said flatly. "And English, too. As
you very well know, General Tudor, my husband,
who is buried behind that house, earned the Victoria Cross. As both an Irish and English gentle-
woman, I forbid you to enter my house."

I turned on my heel and strode back towards
the door of Castle Garry. As it turned out I saved
the lives of my servants and of the IRA men. I had
delayed just long enough for them to escape from
the back doors of Castle Garry before the shooting started.

When the shooting started, I had not yet
reached the house. I think they were trying to kill
me. Did Hugh Tudor give the order to fire? I must
say candidly that if he did, I did not hear it.

I fell to the ground, trying to escape the bullets,
I suppose. Something hit my head and I lost consciousness.

Later, as dawn was breaking up the night, I
awoke and saw that our lovely house was a mass
of rubble with only two walls standing. I had a
large lump on my head and a bad headache. Otherwise I was all right. I found it hard to believe
that the house was gone. All traces of our family

history and of my love with Arthur had been obliterated in a crazy burst of gunfire.

For a moment I felt hate. Then I realized that my lover had sent an unmistakable message. I hurried down to the Catholic parish house, awakened the canon, and told him I wanted to leave for Mount Carmel immediately. I was admitted the next day, a penniless postulant with only the clothes on her back.

The canon had a way of managing things. He arranged for the sale of some of the property which was left and provided me with a dowry for the convent. He told me that the IRA men had escaped, as had my servants. He had arranged with the undertaker, the only other person who has ever known the truth, to bury a wooden casket in the grave next to Arthur. He promised me that when I died he would see that I was really buried there.

" 'Tis better," he said, "if you disappear altogether."

It was. Much later, when Ireland was free, I could have claimed some compensation for my property. But I did not need or want the property. Lady Downs was dead. There was no reason to bring her back to life.

I heard nothing about General Tudor. I prayed for him of course. But I did not want to know what had happened to him. Tom Whelan told me four years ago at the Mass in Booterstown that Tudor was still alive. He had been living in exile in Newfoundland for thirty-five years. Kind of like he's doing penance, Tom says.

For the men and women the Tans killed? I wondered. For killing me?

I wrote him a short note, assuring him of my

prayers. I received an equally short note back. He thanked me for my prayers and asked me to continue them because he needed them. He said that he had become quite good friends with an Irish priest who lived near him. That was all.

My new lover has not deceived me. Like all love affairs ours has had it ups and downs, mostly because I am a selfish and weak human. But He always has been with me and will be with me when the time comes in the very near future for me to go down into the valley of death.

He will walk with me, and Arthur will be waiting at the end of the valley.

So, my young friends—I must think of you as very young—there is my story. As I read it over, I find it banal. Perhaps you will, too. In any event, I have been loved twice in my life, both times by wonderful lovers who in some fashion are the same lover. I have lived and died a happy woman.

Nuala piled together the sheets of the manuscript, written in a clear and forceful hand, and gave them back to Father MacNamee. In exchange he gave her a manila envelope.

" 'Tis a photocopy," he said. "Do I understand you have her memoir of Lord Downs?"

"And her poetry, which she never mentions."

"Maybe she wrote more in the convent. You'd have to ask them about it."

"Did they know the whole story?"

"The Prioress who admitted her did. I presume that the subsequent ones must have or the burial arrangement would not have survived. They never, never regretted it."

"I'm sure not."

"She had no way of knowing whether Tudor thought he had killed her?" I asked.

"I don't know, Dermot. I don't know. Who can say what he thought or what he cared? Maybe he would have fled to Newfoundland anyway. He must remain a mystery."

I looked at Nuala. "End of the road?"

"End of the road, Dermot Michael. I am reluctant to take this with us, yet I know she wants us to have it."

We shook hands with the P.P., who still hadn't opened the envelope, and left the rectory, Fiona trailing after us.

" 'Tis a relief to get that off my mind," Father MacNamee said with a sigh. "A great relief altogether."

"Well, Nuala?"

"Do you want to tell the story, Dermot Michael?"

"I do."

"Then Gussie will be happy to have it told at last."

We walked slowly back to the castle under the thick clouds that hovered over us.

"Well," I said, "we'll have two more days here with nothing to do."

"More golf?"

"Maybe a little bit, but mostly lovemaking."

She looked at me anxiously, knowing that we had come to our turning point.

"Two whole days, Dermot Michael?"

"Two whole days."

She gulped but did not protest.

"That might prove interesting. . . . Do you mind if I take me shower first?"

"Not at all."

— 37 —

"DERMOT MICHAEL, whatever are you doing!"

"We have three hours before supper."

She was quite dry after her shower. I continued to rub her with the towel, insistently, passionately.

"I know that. . . . Och, Dermot, you're scaring me!"

"We can't use dinner as an excuse to stop."

"I don't want to stop!"

I loosened her hair so it fell on her naked shoulders and breasts. She gulped and stiffened.

I ran a finger across her breasts, brisk, imperious, possessive. She moaned. Her mouth hung open. I ran my finger back, more slowly.

"Dermot! . . . ," she exclaimed, her shoulders sagging.

She was pale, hesitant, frightened, but, no, she didn't want to stop. Maybe we were already half there.

My fingers worked their quick designs on her belly and then her loins. I had visited those wonderful scenes before but never in a context like this. Then they returned to her breasts, this time much more slowly

She threw back her head and cried out wordlessly.

"There's a terrible fire inside of me, Nuala Anne."

"Inside of me, too, Dermot Michael," she gasped. "But I'm afraid."

"So am I, but we're not going to quit now."

There is, I reflect now, few joys in life greater than to face a beautiful naked woman who desperately wants you to challenge her to the depths of her sexuality.

Was I up to it?

Damn right I was.

But my heart was beating rapidly and my throat was dry. I musn't blow this opportunity.

"Och, no, Dermot, don't ever stop. . . ."

"I won't."

"Aren't you playing me poor body like it was a violin?" She was smiling now and her eyes were round and glowing.

"A rare and priceless violin."

"A Stradivarius?" she asked.

"What other kind?"

Suddenly we both were convulsed with laughter. Whatever the inhibitions were that had stood in the way between us, they vanished.

Then I understood for the first time that sexual ecstasy is comic. We both started to laugh as we challenged each other and drove one another further and further away from the restrained sanity and the decorous propriety of ordinary life.

We were two pillars of fire dancing around each other, crossing back and forth, enveloping each other, possessing each other and being possessed by each other, soaring together to the skies. It was a scenario as old as humankind but new and fresh and young.

We both cried out, screamed, and laughed. It was on wings of laughter that we flew to the heavens. Then with final cries and final laughter we plunged back to earth, astonished, spent, exhausted but happier than we'd ever been in all our lives.

"Now that was nice, wasn't it, Dermot Michael?" said my sweat-soaked wife as we huddled, breathing heavily, in each other's arms.

"Woman, you'll do till a better comes along."

"It took us long enough to get here."

"Not long at all, I think."

"You're right, Dermot love," she sighed. "Not long at all."

We hadn't done it perfectly. We were new and inexperienced. But we'd done it. And we'd get better. We had not disposed completely of all our fears and hesitations, but we had routed them.

YOU SHOULD FUCK HER AGAIN, the Adversary insisted, JUST TO LET HER KNOW YOU CAN.

"I don't need to do that."

YOU'D STILL HAVE TIME BEFORE SUPPER. THEN YOU COULD DO IT AGAIN TONIGHT.

"That wouldn't be fair to her. I don't want to use her."

ASSHOLE.

I fell asleep and then felt a woman on top of me, her demanding breasts pressed against my chest. What choice did I have but to respond?

—38—

I DIDN'T realize it was so much fun. Sure, didn't me ma just about say that? But I thought it was terrible hard work. And it wasn't at all, at all! It was terrible scary at first, and then when I kind of gave up hiding and abandoned meself it was just like an airplane taking off, no effort at all, at all. I just sort of soared into the sky and rode the clouds.

Me man is a grand man altogether, and I thank You for him. I almost said that he doesn't deserve me. But he thinks he does . . . and I wouldn't say this to anyone else but You. . . . I'm beginning to think I'm not all that bad a wife at all, at all!

Nuala Anne great in bed!

Who would ever have thought it!

I want to squeal with joy!

And we'll get better at it, too. Like himself says, it won't be that good all the time, but it will always be good and sometimes even better!

I almost died of pleasure!

I used to say that I believe You existed, but I didn't think You gave a good shite about us, meaning me. I never really meant that, but I'm sorry for saying it. I've always known You loved, but I could never understand why. So you send Dermot Michael as Your representative. Now I know You love me for the same reason he does.

I'm afraid to say it, but I will anyhow.

You love me because I'm lovable.

There, I've said it and I'm glad. I hope You're glad, too.

Every time I think about all the things we did to each other I shiver with delight!

Mother Augusta, I know that somehow you are here with us. Not out in that grave but here in the house that was yours. You love us. You wanted us to come here. You want us to tell your story. It looks like I will have two lovers at the same time. Help me to give both of them whatever they want from me.

I'll call me ma in the morning. I won't say anything, but she'll know from the tone of me voice.

Thank You again.

We played with each other like two little puppies. Wasn't it grand fun! Brilliant!

I'm not a prim and proper wife at all!

I'm a grand and glorious wife!

Nuala Anne good in bed! I still can't believe it.

But I do believe it.

Will we be able to do it again?

What if we can't?

That's silly.

I tell You what, if You don't mind I'll wake the poor man up and we'll do it all again. You don't have to go away. I don't mind You watching.

You'll watch anyway.

Dear God, the fire is burning in me again! Worse than ever!

Well, I'll just pull the sheet off him and roll over on him like this and then go mad.

I love You.

— EPILOGUE —

ON THE anniversary of Kevin O'Higgins's death, my wife and I entered the Catholic church in Booterstown. A plainclothes cop moved to stop us at the door and then backed off when he saw that we were accompanied by the Deputy Commissioner and his wife.

There were perhaps sixty people present for the Mass, only a sprinkling in the large church. They all seemed to be respectable members of the upper-middle class, no one looking remotely like a revolutionary. They wore ordinary summer clothes, as we did, light dresses, summer suits. Like us they entered the church quietly, though hardly with a mournful air. An elderly Carmelite nun knelt in the front row, Kevin's youngest daughter.

The priest who presided over the Eucharist wore white vestments. I accepted on the authoritative testimony of my parents the fact that at one time the Catholic funeral services had required black vestments and somber Latin. How could one have so completely missed the point of our faith?

The music was from Father Liam Lawton's Mass for Celtic Saints. Nuala sang softly next to me. If anyone heard her or recognized her they gave no sign of it.

Perhaps the rules were that you never recognized people at this memorial.

The middle-aged priest read the Gospel in which Jesus teaches the "Our Father."

"The key phrase," he said, setting the Gospel book aside, "in this prayer is 'forgive us our sins as we forgive those who sin against us.' This is the fundamental truth Jesus came to teach us. This is the core of our faith. This is the most important truth we Catholics have to offer the rest of the world today as always, even though we have often not lived it ourselves. Note carefully, my friends, that there is no question here of earning God's pardon. We do not plead that He forgive us *because* we have forgiven others. You do not bargain with God, not even for forgiveness. Quite the contrary, God's pardon is an implacable given. In this prayer we rather promise God that we will forgive because we have been forgiven—we will manifest His forgiveness in our forgiveness of others. This is what Catholicism means.

"We are here today because one man said, 'The killing has to stop; I forgive you.' These words had an astonishing redemptive power for his family, for those who killed him, and for their families, and, if I may say so, also for Ireland. Someone, who knows about this annual Eucharist, remarked to me recently that only in Ireland could something like this occur. I don't know whether that is true. I do know that if Irish Catholicism means anything at all, something like this should most certainly happen in Ireland.

"The killing has not yet stopped on this island, but there is much less of it than there used to be. We seem finally on the verge of the peace for which so many men died seventy-five years ago. We already have our freedom. We also seem to have prosperity. What Kevin dreamed about has come true, perhaps not quite the way he planned, but it still seems to have happened.

"If we wish to sustain this remarkable phenomenon that has been called modern Ireland, we must not forget the importance of forgiveness in our age-old tradition. If we do forget it, much of what we have achieved in the last three-quarters of a century could be lost again. So we pray today that forgiveness will complete and perfect the healing process that Ireland and the whole world need."

Nuala leaned over and whispered in my ear, "That's why we had to do all these things, Dermot love, to learn about forgiveness."

I nodded.

You don't argue with your mystics. Especially when she's your wife.

Afterward there was a buffet in the parish hall. The people chatted amiably with one another, talking about their lives since the last Eucharist, a year ago. I finished off several sandwiches and pastries because Ma had always said it was a sin to waste food.

Gene Keenan introduced us to Tom Whelan, the Junior Minister in the Foreign Office, a bright-looking young man, accompanied by a bright-looking young wife, who, it turned out, was a lawyer.

"She wants to be president of Ireland someday," he told us. "You have to be a woman and a lawyer to be elected these days."

"Well, I'll never name you prime minister," she said in reply.

"Gene has been telling me of the astonishing detective work you two have been doing since you've been here in Ireland this time . . . and herself performing so brilliantly at the Point the other night."

"We have been rewarded," I said, "with the best wolfhound in all of Ireland."

"So I understand. . . . Is she Irish-speaking?"

Nuala Anne said something in Irish.

"As her first language? Well, that's all to the good. . . . Let me be honest with you: It's time that the whole story be told. It was so long ago. So much tragedy and heartache. But so much generosity and faith."

I thought briefly of Archdeacon Clyde's comment that men and women who lived long ago become historical figures and cease to be human beings. They rather become icons, legends from whom we can learn, but not flesh-and-blood people like us who can suffer as we do and have. Was not all this goodwill just a little shallow?

Then I thought of the Carmelite nun with whom we had shaken hands, and herself, as my wife would have said—and probably would say—so radiantly lovely.

No, this scene of goodwill was not shallow at all.

"If you want to tell the story, Dermot, you certainly have my permission. Lady Augusta is surely the most astonishing character of them all."

"What do you think about that other and very different astonishing woman, my fellow Chicagoan, Lady Hazel Lavery?"

He frowned pensively. "She was a remarkable woman, magical, one might say. Certainly lonely and haunted. She lost both her father and her first husband very early in life. Sir John Lavery perhaps replaced her father. The many lovers she claimed never adequately replaced Ned Trudeau, who died in her arms a few months after their marriage."

"And herself pregnant."

"Precisely. . . . She had a vivid imagination. Historians I've talked to tell me that she had many fewer lovers than she claimed. Her pretense to be virtually Michael Collins's widow was certainly fantasy."

"And Kevin?"

"You know, Dermot, I kind of doubt it. It doesn't fit what we know of his stern, upright character. Doubtless he was enamored of her; most men that knew her were. He wrote her some silly letters. Sleep with her? It seems most unlikely. Moreover, she was skillful at editing the letters, cutting parts out, and showing different ones to different friends. I don't doubt that she persuaded herself that they were lovers, just like she persuaded herself that Winston Churchill was her lover. I do doubt, however, that in either case she bedded them."

"Maybe," I said.

Later I asked Nuala Anne what she thought.

"We wouldn't be all that far from wrong if we said that your man probably had the right of it."

Before we left Ireland we receive a manila envelope with a Garda Siochana letterhead. Inside there was a photograph of an elderly nun. There was no mistaking the hint of mischief that glowed in her eyes or tugged at her mouth.

Later, soon after our return to America and before our first trip to Grand Beach, Nuala and I went to 415 Ninth Avenue, between Cleveland and Larrabee Streets, where Hazel was born. St. Michael's Church loomed in the background. The building had long since been torn down and replaced by new town houses. Our next stop was the house on Astor Street where she grew up. There we prayed that this restless, haunted, and beautiful woman had at last found peace.

One morning in late September, as our first wedding anniversary drew near, I was awakened from deep sleep in our home on Southport by someone persistently nudging my thigh.

"Nuala? . . ."

The nudging continued. It was followed by a bark.

"Fiona? . . . What's the matter, girl?"

I was pushed out of bed.

Someone was being very sick in the bathroom.

Fiona barked insistently and nudged me towards the bathroom.

"All right, all right!"

Nuala, a robe around her shoulders, was kneeling on the floor and vomiting into the toilet.

"Nuala!"

Fiona barked again, a demand that I stop whatever was troubling her beloved mistress.

"What's wrong!"

"It's that focking bitch!"

"What focking bitch?"

"Your focking daughter!"

"My daughter?"

"That focking little Mary Anne."

I knelt next to her and put my arm around her protectively. "You mean little Nell Dermot?"

"I'm going to have to fight with her for the rest of my life," she wailed. "This is only the beginning!"

She retched again.

"Course, we'll bond by fighting."

"Bond against her father?"

"Who else?"

"Whom else."

She fell into my arms, laughing and crying. The crying, however, was joyous. Fiona settled down, content with her early morning's work.

"Oh, Dermot Michael! I've never been so happy!"

I did not even think of questioning whether our child would be a girl.

—NOTE—

ONCE, WHEN I was in the land of my ancestors, I heard a story about the annual Mass for the family of Kevin O'Higgins and the families of his killers. I do not know whether the story is true, but it seemed very Irish to me and typical of the complex and fascinating culture of the country. This story is about how that Mass, should it exist, might have come to be.

There are, as I note in the book, different stories about who killed O'Higgins on his way to Sunday Mass in July of 1927. It would appear, however, that like the death of his hero Michael Collins, the assassination of O'Higgins was a chance event. It is astonishing that no one has written a scholarly biography of him. More than anyone else he created peace and stability in the emergent Irish State. My explanation of who killed him and why is fictional, but there is no doubt that he died because of his vigorous efforts to end the violence and the terrorism at the end of the Irish Civil War.

There is no Castlegarry or Garrytown on the bank of the Shannon Estuary. All the people and events that occur in that place are fictional. Major General Sir Henry Hugh Tudor, however, did command the Black and Tans during the Troubles. He did withdraw in disgrace to Newfoundland, where he lived in exile till

1965. I am grateful to Superintendent James J. Lynch, Ret., of the Canadian Railroad Police for telling me the story of Tudor's forty years of exile in Newfoundland. My attempt to explain his disgrace is a work of my own imagination. He will, I suspect, forever be a mystery.

The material about Connemara is based on the wonderful book *Atlas of the Irish Rural Landscape*, by F. H. A. Aalen, Kevin Whelan, and Matthew Stout.

I am grateful to President and Mrs. Edward Walsh of the University of Limerick (which is a lovely city when it's not raining) for inviting me many times to that wonderful part of Ireland and for introducing me to the CD *Faith of Our Fathers*, which gave me the idea for *Nuala Anne Goes to Church*.

I am, finally, grateful to the monks of Glenstal Abbey for their constant hospitality. Though Abbot Fabian and Brother Killian are creatures of my imagination, the abbey in reality is at least as wonderful as I describe it.

I'm not certain where Nuala Anne acquired all her insights into Irish mysticism. Maybe she was born with spiritual mists floating around in her lovely head. But patently, as her friend the little bishop would say, she also has read Father John O'Donohue's wonderful spiritual essay *Anam Cara: A Book of Celtic Wisdom*.

AG
First Sunday in Advent, 1997

TOR BOOKS